THREE RECKLESS WORDS

A GRUMPY SUNSHINE ROMANCE

NICOLE SNOW

Content copyright © Nicole Snow. All rights reserved.
Published in the United States of America.
First published in February, 2025.

Disclaimer: The following book is a work of fiction. Any resemblance characters in this story may have to real people is only coincidental.

Please respect this author's hard work! No section of this book may be reproduced or copied without permission. Exception for brief quotations used in reviews or promotions. This book is licensed for your personal enjoyment only. Thanks!

Cover Design – CoverLuv. Photo by Michelle Lancaster @lanefotograf.

Proofread by Sisters Get Lit.erary Author Services.

Website: Nicolesnowbooks.com

ABOUT THE BOOK

Is there any coming back after you blow your own wedding to pieces?

I braced for the fallout when I left my emotionally unavailable groom.

I expected the tears, the family wrath, the drama galore.

I found the perfect little cabin to hide out and heal.

But I never planned for *him.*

Archer Rory makes my bridal breakdown look tame.

A gruff single dad with a genius son.

A billionaire control freak who only speaks common sense.

Also, the man who's now my landlord, my boss, and my protector.

Whew.

I think we were doomed the instant I agreed to help him with some *very* special bees.

Maybe it's the big daddy vibes he breathes or the way Mr. Heartless secretly cares.

I'm sure the hottest minute of my life when his lips stormed mine has nothing to do with it.

Oh, but every day we're drifting closer to those three reckless words.

And once they're out, will it be heaven or heartbreak?

1: OUCH! THAT STINGS (WINNIE)

When I was little, I was always told my wedding would be the best day of my life.

In my humble opinion, that's a *lot* of hype for one day where everything must go right, and any error could spell disaster.

What if the groom gets hammered the night before in one last blowout of bachelor glory and can't stand up the next day?

What if a bridesmaid twists her ankle?

God, what if there's *rain*?

Or, what if the blushing bride hits her breaking point, gets cold feet, and goes flying from the venue like a fox on the run?

Yeah. That last catastrophe speaks to me.

That's why I'm ripping down the highway in a car with streamers cascading from the back and JUST MARRIED soaped on the windows in white letters so thick I can barely see out the back windshield.

That's why I'm trapped in shoes that pinch my feet and a corset that crushes my ribs.

That's why I'm still wearing this prison dress.

Welcome to my life.

It sucks.

My hands hurt from clenching the steering wheel for dear life, and the A/C fights a losing battle against the sweat dripping down my face in the July heat. If I'm not careful, I'll blow the thing out on its max setting if I don't die from heat exhaustion first.

At this point, the only thing I'm craving is freedom from this godforsaken dress.

I would sell my *soul* to get out of this thing.

It's tight, it's uncomfortable, and it's a savage reminder of the life I've just blown to pieces.

Also, the man I abandoned, basically at the altar.

Basically.

Oh, God.

I mean, it wasn't technically *at the altar* in front of a big crowd with their mouths hanging open. I'm not that borked in the head.

I never made it down the aisle. I didn't stop and stare at my fiancé like a deer trapped in the headlights. No one was knocked down in my great escape.

Small blessings.

Still, too bad I made it to the part where I was zipped up in this hell-dress and there was no chance of persuading anyone to take it off again before I scrammed.

Especially when every passing face I saw before I ditched was twisted in a *What the hell do you think you're doing, little missy?* kind of way.

I wonder what Holden would—

Nope. Don't think about him.

He's probably livid. I just humiliated him in front of his entire social circle, but I doubt he's wounded.

My fiancé—ex-fiancé?—cares just as much about me as I care about him.

You do the math.

It's not a big number, barely in the low double digits on a scale of meh to soulmates.

I turn off the highway, taking a little road skirting a forest. Then I'm forced to slow down for a series of bends that make me glad this Chevy has decent suspension.

Otherwise, I'd probably be careening over the hill to my fiery doom, making this even more of a bloody red-letter day.

I don't even get a chance to appreciate what being a race car driver feels like. This dress squeezes me with the force of every turn until I'm sure I'm about to crack a rib.

Then I see it.

The sign for the cabin, black with silver letters that spell out Solitude.

"Thank God," I mutter.

The wood front with soaring windows looks new and shiny and modern, just like the pictures on their website. When I turn, the ample glass reflects my headlights back at me.

That's glamping for you, I guess. All the bells and whistles of a pretty modern home with just enough trees around to let rich people think they're communing with nature or whatever.

Right now, I don't give a crap, just as long as the place has a cozy bed and a shower.

Oh, and scissors. I'll use the jaws of life to pry this dress off if I have to.

I might also hunt down whoever decided to make wedding dresses a team effort.

They're the only kind of dress you wear that's not self-sufficient. They're not *supposed* to be.

They invite icky crowds to help you put them on, and then they expect your long-suffering husband to fiddle with buttons or awkward zips or laces to eventually peel the sweaty, smelly thing off.

It's so not hot. Not sexy.

And it's inconvenient as hell when you're alone.

The tires crunch as I pull up outside the cabin and switch off the engine.

Blissful silence falls over everything.

It's been a long-ass drive from Springfield, but I'm here.

Finally.

Just half an hour or so outside Kansas City. Saved by the first place I found beyond the city limits that had a vacancy on short notice.

My snort sounds slightly snotty as I struggle out of the car, my phone in one hand and my enormous getaway bag that was resting on the passenger seat in the other. I swiped the cutting cake too and threw it in the back.

Smart move. If it's too late for any decent food, at least I can eat my feelings in sugar.

The place is even nicer up close with its black walls with wooden accents hugging those ginormous windows.

Makes sense it would look like a mini palace, considering how much it cost for three days. I've never stayed at a luxury rental solo before.

The front looks inviting enough, despite the modern look. Decent porch, cute little fence, solar lights, and I think there's a garden out back.

Tomorrow, I'll investigate, after I've put a bandage on my life.

I pull up the email with the code and totter awkwardly to the front door.

Whoever said corsets were a must was *lying* through their teeth. I'm about three seconds away from passing out.

They'll find me in a day or two and the coroner will have to list 'wedding dress' as my cause of death.

Is that better than 'Holden' himself?

Ugh, won't that be lovely?

As I make my slow, painful way to the front door, I spot tall white boxes through the windows that give me a glimpse of the gardens behind the cabin.

I can feel my eyes light up.

Boxes for bees?

I stop and stare for a solid minute, grateful there's no one around to wonder about the weirdo chick in the wedding dress getting her eyes stuck to the ether.

But bees.

Here, of all freaking places, there are *bees*.

For the first time today, I crack a smile. Not a small one either, but one of those messy heartfelt crazy grins that makes my lungs hitch with joy.

So, yeah. Tomorrow I'll *definitely* check out the garden, first thing. Or maybe if there's still enough sunlight when I extract myself from the evil dress, I'll—

My heel snaps and my ankle twists sideways.

My smile breaks like falling glass.

I practically face-plant on the path.

Holy hell, today is *so* not my day.

In fact, the bees are the only thing stopping today from becoming the worst day in history—and yes, that's a big fat exaggeration and Mom would tell me I'm being dramatic, but bite me.

Today has sucked baboon ass.

I can be a little dramatic. I deserve it.

So I climb the wooden steps, swearing my way to the front door and punching in the code on the little concealed number panel, praying it'll work.

I *need* this to work.

If it doesn't, I'm probably just going to curl up on the porch in a lump of misery.

Then the door clicks and flashes a green light.

There's a brief second where I can't believe my luck before I'm scampering inside and flicking on the lights.

It's spacious and cute with a large open-plan kitchen. The interior matches the outside, shiny and fancy and new.

But I'm not here for the luxury gas stove or the pretty stone marble island or the leather sofas that could eat me alive.

I'm here for one thing and one thing only.

Scissors. Or a knife.

Though, given my track record with sharp objects and a sense of my own mortality, scissors are a far better option today.

I don't want to slice open an artery and turn myself into a crime scene. I just want to get this *damn dress off.*

Four drawers later and a lot of banging around, I find exactly what I need. Meat scissors.

Amazingly sharp and never used by the look of them.

With my phone running low on power, I leave it on the counter, ignoring the five hundred messages and panicked calls that bombarded me all the way here. Then I drag my bag into the luxe bathroom.

I try to avoid my own reflection as I slide the scissors down my bodice and snip away.

The noise feels cathartic, in a way, like shedding an unwanted skin.

Chop, chop, chop.

I keep going, methodically slicing through lace and silk, shredding the torture instrument wound around my chest like a snake.

Finally, it's off, piling in ribbons of white fabric by my feet.

Now I'm just standing in the fancy lingerie my mom bought for my wedding night—which is weird, by the way—and I'm only t-minus three seconds from crying. It has absolutely nothing to do with how stupid and useless I think garter belts are.

Sighing, I rip the lingerie away and twist the shower on. Steamy water blasts out instantly, filling the room with a soothing heat.

Just in time.

My chest heaves as I step under the spray, and for the first time, I let my feelings bleed.

Ugly sobbing.

Honking.

Blubbering like a baby.

Look, it's not that I'm sad about trashing my sham of an engagement.

The whole thing was a joke from the beginning, and I'm glad to be rid of it. Plus, my ring finger feels lighter without that hulking diamond on it. *Win.*

It's not even the way I shamed myself forever in front of everyone I know. If I ever live this down, I'll know for sure there's a benevolent God.

No, the thing that's demolishing my heart right now is the fact that I've just lost my *life*.

The whole package.

If I'd just had the courage to say no, to walk away sooner, I wouldn't be here, ugly crying in a strange place that's beyond my budget.

I wouldn't be a runaway with no one left to turn to.

I wouldn't be *alone*.

Sighing roughly, I close my eyes and tip my face up to the hot spray, pinching my lips together. At least the water feels good, washing away the sweat and panic, obscuring so many bad memories with its sensory overload.

One itty-bitty step toward un-fucking my life, maybe.

Not that I'm about to erase this mess with one nice shower.

Eventually, I know I'll have to face the music, but that's a tomorrow problem.

Tonight, I just want to forget.

To feel like a human being again, and not a sweaty heartbroken slob with a corset in ruins.

I take my sweet time in the shower. There's this high-end body wash that smells like fresh vanilla and citrus, courtesy of the host.

I still use the shampoo and conditioner I brought. I've got special stuff to handle the curls, because no matter how fancy the products are here, they won't know how to tame my hair.

Let's be honest, *I* barely know what my hair needs. It's a constant trial and error, because the second one product gives me smooth, sleek curls, my hair decides it's ready to rewrite the rules.

And God, this morning, Mom insisted on doing my hair for me.

I think it was meant to be some sweet mother-daughter bonding thing on the worst day of my life. All she did was make my hair frizzy and stick a veil over it like that would solve all my problems.

This time, it's not raw grief that makes my chest heave like a wolverine chewing through my vital organs.

It's anger.

It's knowing this entire crapfest could've been avoided if my family hadn't believed I'd be better off with Holden Corban, the golden boy. The man who only wanted me so I could be a trophy wife accessory on his arm.

He didn't court me.

He *wore* me like one of his gaudy gold watches.

I don't hate Holden for being what he is, but that's not to say I like him.

I don't think he likes me, either.

He pretended to care just enough because it's what everyone around him expects from an arranged marriage. Also, the optics were great for his career.

I'm sure they're looking pretty heinous right now.

I only step out of the shower once my fingers resemble red, wrinkled sausages and start toweling myself down, calmly and ritualistically.

Dry off, rub product through my hair, wrap it up, get dressed.

My clothes smell like me. They look like me, too.

Big white tee with a picture of Seattle on the front. Never been, but who cares when you're buying discount t-shirts to sleep in? Add a pair of pajama shorts, and I feel like a new woman.

Even though I'm planning to sleep like the dead, I spray on thick perfume, hoping to keep the sensory distraction going.

My perfume, this time.

Not Mom's designer stuff or the perfume Auntie Sarah ponied up for my wedding day so I could smell *sophisticated*.

I almost died choking.

No, this smells like me, and it helps me relax.

I've got this place to myself for three whole days. I'm determined to spend every second decompressing from life.

I'm on the verge of another broken smile when my ears start ringing.

A noise outside?

So much for relaxing.

My heart starts thudding.

What *was* that, anyway?

It sounded like a bang, a little like someone knocking something heavy over.

I'm suddenly horribly aware that I'm in the middle of nowhere. Alone and isolated with my misery.

Of course, I left my phone on the counter like a magnificent idiot.

It's probably dead from losing power, too. I didn't stop to dig out my charger and plug it in.

Great work, Winnie. Safety 101 and you fail.

I chew my lip, mulling over my options. With my rancid luck, it'll be a rabid racoon, which I can fight off and then enjoy a blistering round of painful shots.

But at least I *can* fight it off.

What if it's a prowler?

I swear I can feel the blood draining from my face.

Oh, boy. Here we go.

Between knife-wielding bandits and wild animals foaming at the mouth, I'll take the furry doom for sure. If it's human and he means to do me harm, I doubt I'll get a crack at a miserable ER visit.

Stop it. Pull yourself together.

You're not this scared of a stupid racoon pawing around.

I am, in fact, very afraid of a stupid plague racoon, but hiding in the bathroom won't solve anything. If I could just call animal control...

My phone is on the counter. Hopefully it still has a little battery life.

I just need to creep out and get it.

Balling up my spare towel like a club, I pad to the door and turn the handle slowly, carefully opening it.

Nothing out there but darkness and the LED wall light in the hall.

Okay. This is fine.

If it's a dumb racoon, I have my weapon of choice—well, not choice, but I've got a weapon. If it's an intruder—

I guess I've still got a weapon.

"Hello?" I call loudly, stepping into the hall.

It's past sunset now with the moonlight dappling in through the windows, bathing the living room in this ghostly light.

There's no movement. Nothing to suggest there's anything nefarious waiting for me out there.

Heart in my throat, I take a few more steps, waiting for the inevitable axe murderer to leap out of nowhere and finish me off in one brutal swing.

But when Mr. Murdery doesn't materialize, I hurry to the kitchen counter and snatch my phone. It's still alive, thank God.

Barely. Looks like one of those annoying updates just ran, leaving it to boot up extra slow.

The screen lights up my face.

Sweet Jesus.

Come on, come on.

Why today?

Another noise makes me jump, something rattling.

"Hello?" I yell again, brandishing my towel club. "Who's there? Anyone? If you're a racoon, I'm all out of snacks!"

Silence.

Could it be some appliance thunking as it kicks on? The air-conditioning or plumbing?

Maybe I imagined the noise and I'm just letting paranoia cross my wires. Maybe—

No, I hear it now.

Laughter.

Blaring like a loud movie, followed by an explosion that bursts color over my eyelids.

Screaming, I leap back until my hip bangs the island, stuffing the towel in my mouth to stay quiet.

Yep.

Someone's here to blow me up.

I thought axes and knives were bad enough, but no, it's some intruder freak armed with *explosives*.

Did Holden send them? Some kinda weird assassins hellbent on wiping me out because I had the audacity to flee from his clutches right before his coronation?

No, that can't be right.

He doesn't even know I'm *here*.

Despite myself, I see faces splattered with blood and creepy crooked smiles painted on oversized masks. Like every good horror movie, maybe they're brandishing a gun or two.

I'm so ready for a total nightmare.

What I'm not expecting is two young boys to push the sliding back door open and come running inside, their hair mussed and eyes bewildered.

I finally remember to stop screaming.

A teenage girl follows them, stopping with her hands on her hips when she sees me.

Unlike the boys, who freeze up and trade worried glances, she seems irritated and rolls her heavily outlined eyes.

"Shit, Colt," she says. "I thought you said this place was free for the weekend?"

I blink, sizing them up slowly.

The boys are lanky like they've just hit their early teenage growth spurt, all thin arms they haven't grown into yet. The girl, she's aiming for a more mature look with the heavy makeup, but she can't quite pull it off.

If I had to guess, they might be thirteen or fourteen.

"That just fucking figures," one of the boys says. Colt, I

presume. He looks like a sweet kid, and despite the language, his eyes are round and worried behind his black framed glasses as he looks at me. "Um... I'm really sorry, ma'am. We must—this is the wrong place. Obviously. There's another cabin down the road, and I guess we just got confused? Right, Bree?"

He shoots the girl a desperate look.

"Yeah, confused. Whatever." The girl shrugs.

I'm calling crap.

This road looks like the end of nowhere. We're practically sitting in the woods. And they're so young—high schoolers, maybe not even that.

Summoning my courage, I march over to the sliding door they came through and slam it hard enough to make the glass quiver.

Outside, the solar lights illuminate a grocery bag on the deck with what looks like a fireworks stash.

Normally, I'd say live and let live, kids do dumb stuff all the time, but this is so not the night.

The kid looks at me again, swallowing thickly before he says, "Lady, are we cool? Can you just—"

"Sit down," I snap, wheeling back around to face them.

The two boys shuffle their feet, but the girl just stares at me, putting on her best grown-up bitch face.

Tough luck, missy.

I'm not fazed by any attitude tonight.

"We're sorry we disturbed you. Like seriously," the boy tries again.

I glower until he stops talking.

"I don't care about you disturbing me. I care about the fireworks out back. That's what the noise was, right?" I shake my head, barely able to believe their stupidity. "Have you guys not noticed it's summer? It hasn't rained for a few weeks and we're at the edge of a forest?"

"Have you noticed it's like, none of your biz?" The girl folds her arms, sulking.

"Princess, why aren't you sitting?" I wait for her to stop rolling her eyes. "Unlike you kids, I rented this place out for the night, so I know I had to give my details online. I had to prove I'm over eighteen."

Colt swallows as he sits, almost like his legs give out from under him. Good. "I—"

"I'm not here for excuses, kiddo. You want to screw around and play stupid? Fine and dandy. But there's *no way* I'm letting you guys do it here with fireworks on dry grass. Have you ever heard of wildfires? Do you want to start one?"

Oh God, I sound like my dad. When did I learn to lecture?

When did I become so boring and uptight?

"What are you gonna do? Call the cops?" the girl challenges. She hasn't sat, but her face seems paler now, and I get the first hint of fear in her eyes.

I think I have a plan.

First, I lock the door and head past them to the welcome basket on the kitchen island—which I didn't notice much when I first came in. But there, lo and behold, is a help line typed neatly on a card.

Let's be real, the police are probably stretched thin out here and have better things to do with their time. And considering these guys are babies who look like they're about to piss themselves, I don't think it's worth scaring their souls out and potentially slapping them with a juvie record.

Kids are idiots.

It's an age-old fact.

When I was their age, I was the same way. Now that I'm coming down from the shock of the rabid racoon slash prowler being three clueless teens, I'm slightly less tempted to cuss them into next week.

This is precisely the sort of crap I might've pulled if I'd ever had the freedom to do it.

"No police. You're welcome," I tell them coldly, fingering the info card and the number printed across it. "But I do want your names so I can tell the rental company, Higher Ends, and they can get in touch with your parents."

From the devastation on the kids' faces—especially Colt's—that might be the worst threat I could make.

Awesome.

II: BAD BEE-HAVIOR (ARCHER)

This kid will be the death of me.

Fatherhood, that's something I signed up for wholeheartedly a long damn time ago, back when I was a different person. My priorities were different then, fumbling around after startup ideas in loud bars after work.

The second we found out we were having Colton, though, I was all in.

I have been ever since.

I knew playtime was over. I needed to man the fuck up and be the kind of dad who has his shit together to give his son the best crack at life possible, and I've been busting ass to make that happen.

I'm still keeping that promise, I think, even if it's won me a lot of grief and a few grey hairs.

Long hours at the company, building up a money machine and a legacy that will unlock his dreams? Check.

The best education money can buy in the Kansas City metro? Check.

Parent-teacher meetings, homework help, extra classes, taking trips out to feed his curiosities? Fucking check.

When he was really little, every time I wasn't at the office, I was with him.

Free time? I forgot the meaning of the word.

Back then, I remember thinking it might get easier one day. When he was older, more mature, maybe I could finally have a break. He'd grow into himself by his teens and be more independent. More responsible. Less clueless, especially with how smart he is.

Ha.

Turns out, I'm the guy with clueless stamped on his forehead.

And it's the *one night* this week when I thought I'd get a quiet evening at home to crack open a thick porter and spend the evening scouting Higher Ends' next acquisition in the crowded luxury rental space we've muscled our way into.

Then life happened.

My boy reminds me you don't get to sleep on being dad.

I grit my teeth as I narrow my eyes at the road.

I'm not pissed that he showed up at our newest property and set off a few fireworks, though I'll still ground him for a week just for that.

The worst part is, Colton fucking lied to me.

He said he was hanging out at his friend's house to work on a chemistry project tonight.

It was believable when he's become part mad scientist, already doing college work well beyond his grade level in math and science.

Fireworks aren't chemistry.

And fuck, I'd really gotten into figuring out where we can expand this glamping line—its success has triggered a whole new direction for our company if we want to invest more. I've mapped out some new land we could build on, thinking about our branding, and I was about to crack open my beer when the assistant called.

A reported break-in at our premier cabin, Solitude.

And the intruder is my own son.

Quiet evening, obliterated.

All I could do was be happy I hadn't started drinking because now I've got to personally haul ass up there and handle this myself. No way can I hand something like this off to an employee.

My own flesh and blood did this, and then he bullshitted me right to my face.

If the boy wants fireworks, he's about to get them.

My nostrils flare as I squeeze the wheel, wanting to get this whole episode over and done.

The sooner I can chew him out, the faster I might figure out where the hell this whole escapade went wrong. Every father expects a little teenage rebellion, sure, but you never expect *how* your half-grown kid decides to kick you in the nads.

He used to be a good kid, too. Quiet, serious Boy Scout type. Hardworking as well.

Well liked with his books and anime and wood carving. Colt spends whole weekends planning his next project for science fairs and watching animated strong men yell at each other in badly dubbed English.

Now, I've got him breaking and entering at my star properties.

What the hell happens in a year or two when he's older? When he can finally drive, and then when the day comes to turn him loose for college?

Inwardly, I groan, stomping the gas.

I finally hit the turn for Solitude and pull up next to a newer looking vehicle parked there. A Trailblazer. Smaller than some of the other models, but still a decent-sized SUV.

I guess the occupants hear me arrive. Before I've reached the front door, it swings open, and a woman wearing a baggy tee and plaid pajama bottoms steps out on the porch.

It takes less than a second to notice she's stunning.

She can't be that old, probably in her mid-twenties.

Long curly auburn hair that looks a little damp in the porch light.

Sparkling green eyes made to shame emeralds.

Full plush lips for whispering secrets.

Legs, hips, and just enough softness around her waist to threaten a man with a good time—or else break his heart to hell and back.

For a second, I almost stop moving, staggering forward like this dumb beast caked in cement.

Any other night, I could gawk at this woman for hours.

Maybe we'd lock eyes and she'd smile with those heart-shaped lips like the start of every bad hookup. Maybe I'd give in to my baser instincts I normally keep chained up.

Tonight is not that night.

Her jaw looks tight, her eyes are restless, and she's right on the edge of unloading pure venom into the gold star jackass who got her into this mess.

Technically, that jackass is me.

And now I have to deal with the fact that my bored-ass son probably scared her out of her skin.

"Hello, I'm Winnie," she says as I approach, her voice clipped.

"Archer," I say, trying to force a smile that doesn't fit my face.

Christ, I want this over already.

The fact that she's looking at me with the same caution I have leveled on her just makes this worse. So is the fact that it's less anger than fear on her face, I realize.

They must've rattled her so bad she cried, judging by the puffy marks under her eyes.

"I'm sorry about all this," I rush out. "This isn't remotely in line with our brand, and it's certainly not what you should ever expect from a stay at our properties."

"It's... it's life, I guess. I'm the forgive and forget type. Do you want to see him?" She steps back to let me inside as I nod.

My eyes lock on Colt immediately, sitting at the island with his friends. He looks up like the guilty little imp he is as I stride over.

"Explain what the *hell* you think you were doing. Right now," I snap.

Then I notice the cake.

The fucking *wedding cake.*

It's there, smack in the middle of the table, complete with royal icing and pink and purple flowers and a miniature bride and groom discarded off to one side. For some unholy reason, all three kids have a plate heaped with large half-eaten slices.

I have to rub my eyes.

Colt might be stupid, but there's no denying his luck.

Only my son crashes a honeymoon and winds up eating wedding cake. What a life he has.

Correction, *had.*

Seeing this, his ass is grounded until Christmas, and that's almost six months away. Hell, maybe I'll put him under house arrest until he's eighteen, because what the ever-loving fuck is going on?

He gives me a pained smile and pushes his plate toward me. "Uh, Dad? You want some?"

Kill. Me. Now.

I open my mouth, trying to find the right words, while the woman—Winnie, she said—sidles around behind the kids. She puts a hand gently on Colt and Evans' shoulders like she's protecting them.

From what? Me?

I don't like where this is going.

Look, I've never been known for my bottomless patience when someone pushes my buttons, and tonight my diplomacy well is pretty damn dry.

"Don't be too mad at them," she says softly. "They screwed up big-time, yeah, but doesn't everyone when they're young?"

I realize I'm scowling, staring through her, so I try to moderate my expression.

She's a customer, you dolt. Don't make this worse. If she's willing to let it ride with a stern warning, be grateful. Get them home and then you can deal with Colt.

Preferably, without a review or a lawyer up your ass.

"I gave them the cake," she continues.

I draw a deep breath, then another, shaky confusion slashing through my anger.

"Why would you—can I ask why?"

"Oh, well… I laid into them when I first found out. I was upset, but I felt bad. Plus, I figured it would keep them out of more trouble." She eyes the cake sadly. "It's not like I can eat the whole thing alone, anyhow."

Alone?

I don't follow.

Whenever her new groom emerges from wherever he's hiding, she won't have to eat the whole thing herself, I'm sure. Also, she didn't need to reward my boy and his co-conspirators for being absolute hellraisers.

"Thanks, Winnie," Colt says, grinning up at her. She returns the smile, though I notice the expression doesn't quite reach her eyes.

"He tells me you're his dad?" she says, looking at me again. "And that you'll take Briana and Evans home?"

"I will," I growl, giving Evans and Briana, Colt's almost-crush, a glare. "And I'll certainly be telling their parents what happened here."

"*Dad!* Not cool." Colt stabs his cake with his fork.

"I'll tell you what's cool as soon as we get to the car, young man," I warn him, and he falls silent again, still tearing at his cake like he wants to murder it.

"Oh, it's fine. I told them off plenty." Winnie leans against the counter now, her slim arms folded. Through the open door to the bathroom, I see a pile of white that looks like a wedding dress. "They're just kids. No need to ruin their life."

"Kids who broke into private property, a space you paid for with a reasonable expectation of safety and peace." I pinch the bridge of my nose, rubbing between my eyes. I so didn't need this shit show tonight, even if she's being weirdly accommodating. "We've taken up enough of your time, Miss Winnie. We'll be out of your hair in a flash. You can be sure I'll be crediting you with a free stay for your trouble."

"Oh. Um."

"Is that a problem?"

"No, not at all." She hesitates. "I kinda wondered if I could get an extension on my stay? Like, what are your weekly rates? I'll pay for the rest of it beyond what I booked, of course."

I look at her like she's insane.

She must be.

What person would ask to continue a honeymoon here after this disaster? Then again, with the wedding cake out and her dress on the floor, it could be a casual situation where they plan to spend the week in bed.

"You want to know the weekly rates," I say, checking to make sure I heard her right.

"Yeah, I mean..." Her teeth pull at her bottom lip, sucking like it's a comfort. I watch her for too long before I realize what I'm doing.

Fuck.

It's too late and too awkward for this kind of crap.

"I can afford it if that's what you're thinking?"

"No. I'm just surprised you'd like to stay longer, after everything."

"The kids? I'm sure it's a fluke. A one-time thing." She glances over at them with what could almost be fondness.

Colt has finished greedily devouring his cake. He's looking at me with suspicion, or maybe hoping Winnie can plead his case before he's sentenced to the doghouse.

Cool it, boy. It's coming.

"I mean, sure, they scared me at first," Winnie says with a laugh, "but I like this place a lot. I just got here but I can tell it's really calming. I can't wait to see it in the daylight. It also has bees!"

Bees?

For the third time tonight, I'm shocked almost speechless.

I honestly forgot we had a few bee boxes at the end of the garden.

I didn't think it would be a draw for most people. I mostly let it ride because my landscaper suggested it, an add-on that punched his happy environmental buttons.

But Winnie lights up like a Christmas tree.

Not just a quick smile. More like something switched on inside her.

It's rare to see a brightness like that. Her eyes glimmer, her smile glows, and I swear her entire body rises, poised on her tiptoes, giving the illusion she's about to go airborne.

Weird? Hell yes.

Of all the things in the world to get excited over, this woman picks bees. But if it saves her from suing me and somehow convinces her to pay us *more* money, fine.

I've never understood customer psychology.

"Yes. Yes, there are bees," I say after a second, when it's

clear she's expecting a response. I clear my throat. "I'll look into the weekly costs and make sure we have no booking conflicts on the calendar, and then I'll get back to you or your husband, Winnie."

Boom.

The spark in her eyes instantly snuffs out.

Her heels sink back to the ground.

Her shoulders tense and she grips the countertop, hard enough to turn her knuckles white.

"No husband. Just me," she says quietly.

Shit.

I am baffled.

I glance at the wedding topper. Definitely a bride and groom, right? Or maybe that groom is a more manly bride? Is she...

"My bad," I say quickly, shaking my head. "Your wife, then. Your partner. Significant other?"

Yeah, I'm flailing.

"Nope. Nada. None of the above." Her throat ticks as she swallows, shaking her head roughly. "There's no one else. It's just me."

Oh.

"I see," I say flatly.

Just her, with a pretty little wedding cake on the table and a wedding dress on the floor. I've *heard* of these people who marry themselves, but I never thought I'd meet one.

Goddamn, what sort of crazy does Solitude attract?

We just opened this place not long ago.

But she sends me a pleading look, and even though an urge to play detective eats at me, I let it go.

I still have Colt and his minions to sort out.

I turn back to my son, who shrinks in his chair.

"So," I say, tapping my fingers against my bicep as I look

at the way the kids trade panicked glances. "Who wants to tell me what you guys were doing here?"

"We really *were* at Evans'," Colt says. The other two nod furiously. "We were doing science, Dad. I was helping them with that summer project for extra credit."

"Right." I let silence fall as I wait for the rest of it.

"Even Bree," he says. The girl takes another bite of cake, smacking her lips like this is no big deal. But her shoulders and neck show tension.

Her dad's a hardass construction manager and a former Marine. He's going to be mad as fuck that she's out here causing trouble, and I don't blame him.

So am I.

"It was my fault, Mr. Rory," Evans confesses, hanging his head. There's a smear of icing on his plate still, and he looks at it sadly. "My brother, Jack, he offered to drive us out here. We figured it would be sort of fun to light off a few."

I study each kid slowly.

"So Jack chauffeured you guys all this way to dick around with my guests?"

Shamefaced, Colt slides a company key card over.

"We... we thought it would be empty," he mumbles. "I checked the schedule yesterday at your office when we stopped by. There was no one booked."

"Oh, my." Winnie's cheeks flare red. "Yes, it was a very last-minute booking. I'm sorry."

"No. You do *not* apologize for my boy and his friends when they could've burned this place down and you along with it," I snarl and immediately regret it.

Damn.

See, this is why Patton is the client-facing brother in the rare cases where we need to deal with our base personally. I don't have the bedside manner for it.

"Sorry," I mutter.

To my surprise, the flicker of a smile crosses Winnie's face again. "It's been a long day for me, too. I totally get it."

Colt looks at her with dawning respect. Guess it's been a long-ass time since somebody has taken to me snapping at them so well.

"Yeah, sure," I say. "Long day. Not helped by fools with contraband fireworks." I hold back on calling them little assholes, even if that's what they are. I'm not looking forward to telling their parents what I caught them doing.

I switch my attention to the brown bag by the wall.

Not that I need anyone to tell me what's in it. More fireworks, I'm sure.

Enough to destroy this place, the surrounding woods, and get me investigated for arson and insurance fraud.

Colt and Evans, taking their usual shit a step too far, and probably trying to impress Briana along the way.

I'm lucky I'm not stuck in a police station with burly cops and firefighters growling questions in my face.

"Let me guess," I say, "Jack bought you the fireworks too? Anything else you'd like to add?"

"Dad, we... we weren't firing them off next to the house. We set up in the gardens. It was stupid, yeah, but we used common sense."

Common sense?

I'm never a violent man with my boy.

But I'm closer than I've ever been to smacking him across the face.

"They really weren't. Not that it makes it okay. It's super dry out there." Winnie positions herself between me and the kids like she thinks she needs to shield them or something.

Annoying.

I look at her, waiting for more.

"I think they only set off a couple before I noticed. Basically just a big dumb Roman candle and a little bottle rocket."

"Leave this to me. I know how to handle my kids when they're doing their damnedest to ruin my property," I say coldly. This time, she does flinch back. "You just focus on having a nice stay, Miss…"

"No Miss. Just Winnie."

"Fine, Winnie. We've ruined your night enough and these guys need to get home. Thanks for your trust, and you enjoy your stay now." I dig around in my pocket and fetch a business card, leaving it on the island for her. "If you need anything else, here's my personal number."

"The only thing I need is a little peace and quiet for once," she says under her breath, so quiet I almost don't catch it.

Yeah, no shit. Isn't that on everyone's list? It's how I wanted my evening to end before I had to drive out here.

"We'll get out of your hair." I wave to Colt and the others, who slide off the seats.

"Thanks for being cool, Winnie," Evans says, giving her a fist bump, which she returns with a brief grin.

"Steer clear of the fireworks, guys," she tells them. "It's a slippery slope. Listen to your dad."

"Gotcha."

Colt waves goodbye, and even Briana, who's never smiled in my direction once, flashes her a smile.

"Hey, wait," Winnie says, just as I'm at the door, finally escaping. I have to bite back a sigh as I stop and the kids head out into the night. I unlock the car for them and the lights on my SUV flash. "You'll be in touch, right? About the extended stay?"

"About the bees, you mean?" I'm not sure why I bother saying that.

Maybe because this night desperately needs some comic relief.

"Yes, the bees." She puts her hands on her hips. Even though she must be ten years younger than me, she gives me the same kind of look my mom throws around when she thinks I'm being difficult. "Is that a problem?"

"Not at all, ma'am."

She blows out a long breath and leans against the doorway. "Just let me know if I can stay, okay? It's really important and I'd love to know ASAP."

That much, I can do.

What I can't do is indulge the insane urge to ask what the hell is really going on with her.

I don't like dealing in mysteries.

As soon as anything suspicious shows up, I like to get to the bottom of it. That's always been my thing, and I sure as hell don't want to stop now.

But her life—her uniquely Winnie weirdness—that's none of my business.

Important to remember before I start pawing at some beautiful woman's background when she clearly wants to keep it secret. Doesn't matter if I can't forget how she froze up when I mentioned a husband.

And the wedding dress, which looks like it's been ripped to pieces when I glance at it again.

What happened here?

What was supposed to happen before she was interrupted?

She doesn't seem crazy enough for seances and magic, and she's too shy and soft-spoken to be a theater kid.

"I told you, Winnie, I'll let you know the minute I've checked the schedule." I fight to keep the impatience from my voice. The sooner I get out of here, the better. "I'll be in touch tomorrow. We have your details in the system."

"Oh, my details?" She swallows, like she hadn't expected me to say that.

"Yeah. You filled out your name, email address, and phone number on the online form." I wonder why she squirms uncomfortably. Why is she acting like she doesn't want me to know anything about her?

That nonsensical dress haunts my brain again.

Surely, it isn't something criminal? But I'm at a loss, trying to imagine what.

Smuggling drugs for some shady group with a stopover at a luxury property seems like a weird way to do it.

"Yeah," she says, her voice a breath. "That's all private, though, right?"

"Our privacy policy was outlined on the website, yes." I definitely don't have time for whatever paranoia she's suffering. "We only keep your data as long as you're here. I promise we don't sell it to any third parties. As soon as you're out of here, the system automatically deletes it, unless you sign up for our rewards and offers. I won't have your number any longer."

"Oh." Her eyes widen. "*Oh.* I wasn't worried about—I didn't think you were…" She trails off. Even in the dim light from the kitchen, I see her blush. "Sorry. I didn't mean to make it sound like I'm—"

"It's fine."

Yet she looks like she wants to say more, rocking forward on her heels before slumping backward. "Sorry again. I just really need this stay."

With the bees, apparently.

No husband, just bees.

Bizarre, but not my problem.

None of this is, and I have no intention of adding her to my plate when I have real discipline to dole out to Colt and his crew.

"We'll talk soon," I promise.

She gives me a shy little half wave, my cue to go.

Fucking finally.

The kids are waiting in the car, talking nervously among

themselves. Their lips stop moving the second they see me coming.

Colt, he's up front with me, and the other two are strapped in the back.

Without hesitation, I start the engine and back out of the driveway, feeling three pairs of eyes drilling into my head.

"We're super-duper sorry, Dad. Honest," Colt says, twisting his fingers on his lap.

"...are you really gonna tell my mom?" Evans asks in a small voice.

"You bet your ass I will. And your father, Briana. It's not personal, it's just what I do."

She scowls like I just told her to wipe off her makeup, but I don't give a shit.

That's what dads are for—to be the stonehearted voice of reason teenagers won't appreciate until they're ten years older.

Truth be told, I think I'll be pissed for a while too, whatever Winnie wants be damned.

If there's no spouse, then she probably doesn't have kids.

She doesn't get what it's like.

Sure, she might be trying to play it cool, but she called this in. I have no doubt she was freaked in the moment, whatever she thinks now.

And with fireworks popping off next to miles of woods in a midsummer drought, these jokers could've ignited an inferno that would've needed the National Guard called in to put it out.

Besides, it doesn't make sense that she's trying to play it off like nothing happened. She's the one who made the big deal about it in the first place.

Not to mention the cake, the dress, the nagging mystery of what she's up to.

Something's going on back there, no question.

As I drive through the darkness in stony silence, my gut screams that tomorrow won't be the last time I talk to Winnie.

I should keep an eye on her.

Just in case.

III: NO QUEEN BEE (WINNIE)

*C*hocolate, the purest way to a woman's heart.

As a nice bonus, it's a great pain reliever, too.

I'm talking magic cure-all for being dumped, losing out on your dream job, and yes, even when you flee your own wedding and the raging dumpster fire of insane consequences.

The highest rated bakery in Kansas City is The Sugar Bowl, and by God, it's good. In the day I've been here, after throwing out the remainder of the wedding cake I never want to see again, I've eaten my own weight in sugar.

On their website, they offer these fun local packages you can get delivered.

When I saw 'breakup box,' I didn't hesitate.

Because let's face it, I've definitely broken up, and not just with *a man.*

I've broken up with everything: my past, my present, any future I ever imagined.

RIP to the girl I used to be.

The fact that I tried to go along with the wedding at all is proof she was too stupid to live.

Old Winnie, she was optimistic to a fault. She kept thinking maybe, just maybe, this *could* be the right move because so many other people wanted it.

If only she'd stopped to consider the hard truth.

It wasn't right because *I* didn't want it.

Stupid?

Yes. Fabulously so.

But I guess that's what you get when you're raised to make your family proud above all else. And by proud, I mean letting your father marry you off like a prized asset meant to be leveraged.

Gross.

But now I'm free.

And I've decided a healthy part of this freedom means devouring three huge chocolate eclairs in one sitting while I work on relinquishing any and all fucks related to pleasing my dad.

The damage is done. There's no way he'll be proud of me again.

So, I might as well enjoy the sugar high and the sunshine.

The summer sun certainly warms my back as I wander along the well-tended paths through the garden.

My fingers are already smudged with dirt, but that's what I get for not finding gloves.

There's something peaceful about plucking weeds to pass the time, though. There aren't that many when this place has perfect maintenance, but still.

There are also so many flowers—the bee-friendly kind like lavender—and I kneel down on the path, clearing space around them.

Lazy bees at work drift by, humming gently around me like this sweet lullaby.

I really hope I get that extended stay. If I can't freeze this moment forever, I'd like to stretch it out a few more days, at least.

Just me and the bees and this sunbathed garden.

Nothing more, nothing less, and no freaking worries.

Maybe someday I can find a more permanent place like this. I'll stay for the week, the month, a whole year or two.

I'll slowly become the crazy bee lady I've always wanted to be and live my best life.

No more Dad. No more Holden. No more nasty weddings. No more Springfield.

The thought doesn't make my throat tighten with anxiety anymore.

I guess that's the power of bees, because if I was cooped up in some hotel room somewhere else, looking out at the city skyline, there's no way I *wouldn't* be sobbing into my wine and pizza.

It's way too peaceful here for shedding tears.

Sighing, I crouch down to pull out another weed and sit back, looking at my handiwork. A bee lands on the flower I just cleared space around, and I smile.

"Hi, buddy."

Its little antenna waves as it hunts for pollen, collecting it on its legs like a dusting of gold. Nature is so beautiful it hurts sometimes.

At least by helping, I'm giving them more space to do their vital work, making this garden bloom and turning their effort into delicious honey.

I'm also giving myself a Winnie-specific therapy session no money could buy from any shrink.

I'm so engrossed in my work I don't notice the rustle of footsteps behind me.

But I do hear a throat clearing.

Swearing, I stand and turn, all in one movement that

would be smooth if I didn't spin face-to-face with the grumpy owner dude from yesterday.

He's a damn giant.

The way he towers over me alone is enough to make me unsteady.

I take two steps back, giving up on being smooth.

Honestly, that's also because I forgot just how *good-looking* this bear of a man is.

It feels illegal for anyone to be this attractive with his short dark hair, piercing blue eyes, and God, that jawline.

Yes, he's older. Late thirties, maybe.

Huge big daddy vibes as the kids would say.

The tiny lines flaring out from the corners of his eyes prove it when he frowns. Probably his permanent expression.

I don't think I've seen him smile. Not that he had good reason to look happy last night, but he has a face that doesn't seem like it remembers how.

Even when he's standing in front of me in this slice of Missouri Eden, he looks like he just walked in after Goldilocks ate his porridge.

Scowly or not, he's hotter than sin.

"Um, hi." I tuck my hands behind my back just in case he hasn't noticed the mud under my fingernails. Hopefully he hasn't also noticed the fact that I wiped my face with those hands and probably have dirt smeared on my face.

"Hello," he says curtly, still frowning. "Were you… weeding?"

Oh, good. He noticed.

"Not too much, your garden doesn't need it. You keep this place up very well. I was just passing the time."

"I see." He pauses like he's trying to remember why he's here. "I'm Archer Rory, by the way."

"Yes, I remember the name from your card…"

Archer, huh? Like the muscly men with bows and arrows in ancient times.

His name fits the old-timey vibes he gives off.

And the fact that the gaping age gap between us means he was probably born in the Viking age.

A silly image flashes in my head of him shirtless, streaked with blue paint, swinging an axe around over his head. I clap a hand over my mouth and bite back a giggle.

No, this modern man in his sharp suit and perfectly trimmed beard is about as far from wild warrior as you can get.

Pull yourself together.

"I'm Winnie, but I think you already knew that?" I drop the hand I extended automatically because I remember I've got mud on my fingers.

"I remember," he says. "You introduced yourself last night. I have all your details."

"Oh, right. Sorry, sometimes I space out." Talk about awkward.

"I'm sorry for disturbing you like this. I tried the door but you weren't answering."

"I was out here."

"Weeding, yes. I have a landscaper and lawn crew for that. They come every week."

"Well, many hands make light work and all." I pin on the world's cringiest smile.

We stand in uncomfortable silence, unsure what to say.

I debate if I should invite him in or see what he has to say first.

Eventually, I decide that if I invite him in, it feels like I'm encouraging him to stay, and no matter *how* hot he is, I'd like to get back to my peace and quiet soon.

I'm not in the mood for hot, growly interlopers today.

"So, you must be here for that schedule thing," I say,

looking out across the garden rather than at him. "Have you figured it out? If this place is free so I can stay another week?" I wait a beat and when he doesn't immediately reply, I add, "I won't lie, I was expecting you to just call."

"Your phone is off," he says blandly.

Oh, crap.

I wince. Good point.

I forgot I put it in airplane mode after I scarfed down those eclairs to block the steady stream of nonstop messages from people ready to have me committed for going full runaway bride.

"Yes, my bad. I forgot I had it off. Anyway, do you have news?"

"Yes and no." He tilts his head slightly as he looks at me, like trying to piece my mysteries together into a picture that makes sense. "Truthfully, I didn't just drop by because you want to stay longer. I had a man call my office this morning looking for you."

A man? What man? Who would—

Oh, no.

No, no, no, this is bad.

Holden or my dad. It has to be.

They're both equally awful.

"Carroll Emberly," Archer continues. "I figure he's your father."

I close my eyes, turning numb to the tips of my toes.

Partly in defeat, but also because I don't want to see the way Archer keeps looking at me. Especially the distrust in his eyes, like he's convinced I'm some sort of danger.

Look out, here comes Winnie, queen of all screwups and burned bridges! Watch out, or she'll set you on fire, too.

"*Is* he your father?" he presses.

"Yes." I give up and open my eyes again.

"He seemed concerned. He wanted to know where you were. It sounded rather urgent."

Well, obviously.

Dad makes everything sound urgent. Pretty easy when you're used to snapping your fingers and people go running like obedient dogs.

He'll want me to come home as soon as possible with my heart in my hands.

As far as he's concerned, I've just made the biggest mistake of my life.

That's why my phone is off.

I don't have to face the train wreck yet if I don't hear the violent crash.

Dad calling, demanding my return in that high-and-mighty way he has.

Mom, too, pleading with me to grow up and beg Holden to take me back. Does she ever do anything besides echo my father?

Dad's the big dominant personality. Mom is a willow blown around in a storm. Beautiful, graceful, but ultimately forever bent to his will.

God, maybe Holden himself tried calling, still trying to persuade me to come back instead of giving up on a 'good partnership.'

What he really means is a profitable one, and Dad strongly endorses his view.

Sighing slowly, I fold my arms and look at Archer, who's still waiting for a reply. I'm sure he wants me to spill the truth so he knows he isn't dealing with a total wacko.

Tough luck, big guy.

"Did you tell him where I am?" I ask quietly.

He frowns like he's annoyed by the question. "No. It's not our company policy to give customer details to anyone else without a damn good reason. This doesn't qualify as a medical emergency or an official missing person case. Not yet anyway."

"Thank God." I heave out another sigh. "I mean, cool. If he calls back, don't tell him where I am. Pretty please?"

"Winnie."

Holy hell.

This man should *not* be able to say my name like an entire thunderstorm condensed into one word.

"Yes, Archer?"

"Be straight with me. What's really going on with you?"

At least he's asking me directly this time. "It's fine. Nothing for you to worry about."

"Are you in some kind of trouble with your family?"

"Trouble? What?" I wrinkle my nose, laughing painfully. "I mean, it depends how you define trouble, I guess, but—"

But he's absolutely right and he knows it.

His face hardens. I raise my hands defensively.

"Not legal trouble. Nothing like that. I haven't broken any laws. Feel free to do a background check if you want."

"Then what kind of trouble are we talking? I deserve to know if I've got your dad calling my office, damn near demanding we give up your location."

Awkward silence.

It's starting to feel familiar.

"Look, I hate to do this, Archer," I say. Really, I don't, when the alternative is worse. "But this is none of your freaking business, okay? It's personal. I'll worry about my trouble, and you worry about yours, making money hand over fist with these fancy cabins or whatever else you do."

His scowl says he totally doesn't believe a word I say.

Ouch.

"Dude, if my dad keeps calling, just block him. Is that so hard? He's a big important guy, kinda used to getting his own way. He won't like it but he can't do much more than complain."

Understatement of the century.

As I read Archer's face, I regret my words.

Is he a younger clone of my father? He's big and successful and important enough to own these beautiful places. Then again, I doubt he's ever been elected to state office, which *might* keep his ego in check a little.

Trust me, I know. Nothing turns people into raging entitled monsters like a whiff of political power.

Archer shifts, folding his arms and holding my gaze like he's expecting me to back down. But I'm no stranger to intimidation and I've hit my limit.

This big gruff evil eye business isn't changing my mind.

"Fine," he snarls at last, his voice grating with annoyance. This must be costing him—but I don't care as long as he gives me some peace. "As I said, it's corporate policy to respect your privacy as long as you're not breaking the law."

"*Just* company policy?" I raise an eyebrow.

I swear his teeth snap together so hard he might've cracked a molar.

"And mine, personally," he growls. "I don't get off on prying. Normally, I'd be too busy to give one shit about your secrets, lady."

Ouch again.

"Sounds good. Personal integrity matters," I force out.

"Yeah, we agree. That's why, if you won't tell me what's going on, I'm afraid I can't guarantee you a longer stay than what you've booked."

"What? You just said you cared about my privacy!" My heart tries to leap out of my chest.

"I'm afraid it's a bit personal. Higher Ends has had its share of troubles the last couple years. Real, criminal issues that would probably make yours look like a cakewalk," he says, and he makes it sound so *reasonable* that I want to scream. "This property has a lot of interest as one of our newest and best offerings. I'd be a fool to risk that on a handshake agreement."

I step back. The dread burning in the pit of my stomach flares into anger at this corporate beast who thinks he's too good for my money.

"Excuse me?"

"I know this is disappointing, however—"

"First of all, hold the bullshit," I snap.

He steps back like he's not used to someone speaking over him.

Actually, given the way he reacted last night when he picked up the kids, I don't think he's used to people making his life difficult.

And is he using the same voice on me he used with the kids?

Well, sorry, Mr. Archer Man.

I don't believe in being talked down to like I'm one of your son's teenage friends.

"This might be a popular place, but does that mean you're going to be charging other people more than you're charging me?"

"No." His eyebrows descend over his eyes.

"So, it's first come, first serve, and I'm here first. Why isn't that good enough?"

"That's not what I said—"

"That's *exactly* what you said." I don't know why this hits so hard, but it does. My chest hurts. "You don't want to rent this place longer because it's gotten a lot of interest. You want to replace me with someone who won't cause you any weird phone calls."

His jaw clenches as he stares at me. I wait for him to deny it or say *something* to redeem himself, but he just says, "I don't want to invite more trouble into my company, Winnie. It wouldn't be fair to my brothers, my business partners. They've suffered enough, right along with me."

I hate that he sounds like he actually cares for them.

Sigh.

"I *told* you... my trouble isn't the legal kind."

"And I told you I had your father on the phone demanding to know, in no uncertain terms, where the hell you are." Archer looks just as exasperated as I am now, his huge barrel chest rising and falling and his eyes like blue flint. "I'm trying to protect my company, Winnie. This isn't anything against you, it's simply—"

A bee lands on his shoulder, and he raises a hand to smack it away.

My jaw drops.

I did not just see that.

I'm not thinking when I throw myself forward, grabbing his giant wrist with my small hand, shielding the bee with my other hand.

The little bug flies off.

Archer looks at me like he's fully convinced I'm insane.

We're way too close. I can see details I never expected, like the tiny flecks of green in his eyes and lines around his mouth that *might* mean he can smile.

But he's really, really not smiling now.

"What the hell was that?" he demands, an edge to his voice.

"Do you have *any* clue how much bees are struggling right now?" My voice is high, but I can't control it. "And you... you were about to kill it without thinking."

"Do I—what?" He blinks in shock.

"People keep destroying their habitats. We're killing them with diseases and chemicals. You thought you were just swatting a pesky bug, but every drone is vital. Without bees to pollinate our flowers, we'll be the ones starving someday. And no honey, oh my God," I continue, my voice wavering. "That's becoming as rare as gold. I don't think you get how delicate bees are, how *important*—"

Archer frees himself from my hold, swearing under his breath.

Then, to my utter embarrassment, I burst into tears.

Not little tears, either.

Big, snotty dumb ones that have been building in my chest all day.

Before, I held them back while I was enjoying the sunshine and the bees. But this stupid fight, this intrusion with Archer, reminds me why real life is too much right now.

I stumble backward, almost falling, and cover my face with my hands.

Congratulations, I guess. He just proved I'm no queen bee.

I hate crying.

And I hate crying even more when this human wall walks forward and takes my wrists. I think he's about to shake me to restore some control.

Only, his fingers are surprisingly gentle as he tugs my hands away from my face, hiding the pathetic mess I've become.

When I dare to look, there's something almost *tender* in his eyes. An empathy I don't expect.

No way. I have to be misreading things in my own scrambled brain.

This is Archer, Mr. Heartless Incarnate. King of Silent Threats and Barked Orders.

Jesus, Winnie, stop crying.

"Hey." His voice crackles like a warm fire. Not fair. "Winnie, shit. I'm sorry about the bee."

I want to tell him to let go, to walk away and leave me

with my crazy self, but instead I choke on another sob. It's so disgustingly wet I make a noise that's half mewling cat and part parrot.

Yep. I'm about to die from mortification.

If the ground could open up and swallow me right now, that would be cool. I think I could start over in India or China on the other side of the world.

Wherever Dad has no reach.

But the ground doesn't open, of course.

And when Archer releases one hand, I don't even fight to free the other. There's something comforting about the way his huge fingers envelop my skinny wrist.

"We'll work something out," he tells me. "Whatever the hell I think, it's not a hard rule. I could be convinced."

There's something so weirdly reassuring about his promise, this steely-eyed stranger bending rules for me in my darkest hour.

All I can do is nod as he leads me back to the cabin.

IV: ALL BEES-NESS (ARCHER)

I should have fucking known this would happen.

First Dexter, with Haute and Junie and that whole fake fiancée mess. Then Patton and Salem with his surprise son and an unthinkable betrayal that brought them together.

Two marriages.

Two ridiculous, dangerous situations that could've torpedoed the company and a whole lot more.

Now, it's my turn at the drama wheel.

All over a damn woman.

Thankfully, I'm immune to falling in love.

Been there, done that. Mistakes made and lessons learned.

That's what happens every time, though, whether we like it or not. Maybe it's some weird curse on the men in the Rory family.

After witnessing my brothers' chaos, I always figured trouble might find me again someday.

Still, I never expected it to come from a woman this young and troubled.

Not from this annoyingly strange, beautiful, wounded, bee-obsessed weirdo who's currently wiping her face and trying to gather her thoughts. At least she's using tissues now instead of my sleeve.

I can't decide if she's an easy paycheck or somebody who'll lose it and light this place on fire. Total wild card.

She brushes her mass of coppery, curly hair back from her face, sniffling loud enough to wake the dead.

Yeah, I think the ugly tears are behind her now.

"S-sorry about that." She hiccups and threads her fingers through her hair. It looks silky, even tangled up, and for a second I wonder what it would feel like in my hands.

Then I wrench my thoughts back to the present.

We've established she's pure chaos.

There's no predicting what she'll do next.

If I was all cold logic, I'd take her to a psych place and get her some help right now.

Still, I can't help feeling bad for her. I also hate that I wonder if she's truly crazy.

There's a big black trash bag near the front door. I'm almost positive it contains her wedding dress. Who just tosses a dress like that?

And the ice-cold message my assistant passed on to me from her father definitely confirms something's up, even if she doesn't want to tell me the details. Fine, I won't press her, but I need a hint, goddammit.

Her father could be worried, knowing she's prone to a mental crisis.

On the other hand, what if he's the one causing her grief?

A controlling, crazy tyrant dad who wants her back so he can lock her up and keep abusing her.

I know what a fucked up place this world can be.

Still, I need *something*.

Reassurance this won't blow up in my face if I help her

with an extended stay against my better judgment. It shocks me that I want to help her.

Probably because she's so broken, so desperate, so unpredictable.

People with stable minds don't break down and swing at strangers over fucking bees.

Then again, it wasn't really about the bees, was it?

It's whatever's haunting her—whatever trauma chased her here.

No matter what I do, I'm not throwing her back to the wolves and having that on my conscience.

So I nudge the tissue box closer, just in case she needs more, and rest my forearm on the breakfast bar.

"I meant to thank you for putting up with my son and his friends. You handled the shit they pulled with pure class. Also, I'm sure he'll be grateful you've given him the only sugar he's getting for the next month in non-fruit form."

"Grounded, then?" She smiles.

"You bet. Their dumbass stunt could've gotten him put under house arrest for real, not just cooped up without horror movies or games."

She gives me a lopsided smile.

"Yeah, I told them. I think I channeled my inner mom to be honest. I've never been the lecturing type before, but it just came out. I felt a little crappy about it. That's why I gave them the cake."

"You shouldn't feel bad."

"I called Briana 'princess' and told her to sit the hell down." Her eyes turn glassy at the memory. I notice they're a sea-glass green, shiny and bright with just enough woe glittering to draw a man to his doom.

The redness around her eyes really brings out their color, I'm sorry to say.

"You handled it better than me. If I'd found them shooting

off rockets on my lawn." The way my fist tightens says everything.

She shrugs. "I was mad at first. Then I realized they were just kids and we all do stupid stuff when we're young. Especially when we're talking boys trying to impress girls."

I snort, drumming my fingers on the table because she's right.

Dex and I pulled some crazy shit back in the day. Patton had to work to keep up when he got older. It used to drive Mom insane.

But we're not here to talk about my past or even Colt.

I just wanted to get her mind unpanicked, make her feel comfortable enough to talk about whatever it is that made her melt down.

"I guess you've got questions," she says in a quiet, hurt voice that's somehow worse than the tears.

"You know I do."

"Right. Yeah. Because of the crying and bee freakout..." She levels a cool stare on me. "Bees are important, though. You shouldn't kill them."

"Noted," I clip.

"But fine—*fine*—so maybe there's something else going on with me."

I don't mean to look at the garbage bag again, but I can't help it.

Winnie notices and her shoulders sag.

"It was supposed to be my honeymoon," she whispers. I keep silent, just watching her as she lets the words sink in. The hurt lining her eyes and mouth make her look older, though she can't be more than mid-twenties.

"Here?" I ask when she doesn't add anything.

"Oh, no. Not here. Although this place would make an amazing honeymoon suite if you wanted to market it as one.

We were actually going to Italy. Florence, then on to Venice and Rome."

"Romantic choice."

"Yes, well…" She sighs again. "Long story short, the whole thing collapsed at the last minute. I was having doubts and decided I couldn't do it, so I left." Her words hang in the air for a second like she wishes she could snatch them back. "And I don't think my family will ever forgive me. I basically stranded him at the altar, or close enough."

Fuck, that's harsh.

I tap a finger against the coffee table as I think. The dress in that bag suggests she was wearing it when she arrived, which underscores how 'last minute' she means.

And she was the one who left him.

Maybe she's still in love with her fiancé or there's some other scandal there, but that's not my problem.

Mine is the fire-breathing father who called, demanding his daughter's whereabouts. I wonder how he thought to call us if this wasn't a honeymoon destination.

Did he hit up every decent rental option in the state?

Winnie laces her fingers together and leans back in her seat, facing me with surprising directness, considering how she just cried all over my suit jacket.

"I'm hiding out, in case it wasn't obvious," she says, her voice clear.

"I gathered that," I say dryly.

"Oh, right."

"And your dad wants to know where you are."

She winces. "Can we just leave him out of this for a bit? I want to talk about me. Or at least, the option of me staying longer."

Whatever.

I told her I could be convinced, but she's going to have to sell it—and hard. Make me believe I'm not fucking up royally by letting an unstable, heartbroken stranger crash in our star property.

My brothers can confirm I'm not the softhearted one.

I don't hand out favors left and right.

If you want a softie, try Patton.

Or even Dexter now that he's married. Juniper turned him into one more of those marshmallows she puts in her Rocky Road cupcakes.

Me, I've never had much reason to let emotions threaten my business.

Even if seeing her cry like this with all her unfiltered hurt gives me the weirdest ache in my chest, along with this annoying urge to help her feel better.

But I already opened my mouth.

I told her we might work something out, and I meant it.

"Convince me," I say point-blank. "Why should I let you stay?"

"Because I'd pay you?" She raises her brows.

"A reason that makes it worth the potential shit your father will fling my way when I'm covering for you, I mean."

"You're worried about that?" She waves a dismissive hand. "All you have to do is use *that* voice. You know, the dad voice you've used before. Just tell him you can't give away client details, and voilà, case closed. He's a legal wonk, he'll totally understand."

Like hell.

In my experience, people as persistent as her old man rarely fuck off just because you tell them to.

There's something about the way she props her chin up on her hands as she looks at me, waiting for me to agree. It makes me curious what she'll say next.

"Okay, let's table that for now," I say carefully. "Tell me, why do you want to stay here?"

Her lips curl into a smile that dimples one cheek, an

uneven look matching the chaotic hair and teasing light in her eyes. "Do you always play grand inquisitor with all your guests?"

"Only the ones who spell trouble."

"You're afraid of me? Seriously?" She huffs loudly. "What? Are you afraid I might cry you to death?" Her expression tightens a fraction and she adds, "I really am sorry about that, by the way."

"Don't apologize. There's no need."

"That's up for debate, but fine. The fact is, I can definitely afford to go somewhere else if I wanted, but… I don't. It's comfy here. It's away from the city, it's pretty, and did I mention the bees?"

God help me, I almost smile.

Almost.

"Another two weeks here and I'll have my life figured out," she finishes. "I just need time. I swear, I won't break anything."

I can't fucking help it, I raise an eyebrow.

She takes her lip and bites down, hard enough to turn the skin white.

"Fine," she says. "I might not have everything figured out, but it'll be a start. We can work from there."

We? She says it so confidently, like in two weeks we'll be best friends, hashing out how she'll reclaim her life or some such shit.

Like she expects me to be involved.

I lean back in my seat next to her, grateful that she's stopped doing that lip biting thing. The woman is too cute for her own good.

"Also," she says in a wheedling voice, like she's revealing the hidden Ace up her sleeve, "if you give me some peace and quiet, I've got connections that could boost your company's profile."

Bold claim.

Strangely, she says it with confidence, which is unusual for bullshit artists unless they're *really* good at bluffing. For all I know, she might be.

I know next to nothing about this woman except for the fact that she came spinning in here in a wedding dress and she's obsessed with bees.

Still, it's an interesting claim. I'd be lying if I said it didn't pique my interest.

"What connections?"

"I was a senate staffer for a while." Her tone says she isn't proud of it. "I left on good terms, mostly. I got to know the whole beltway crowd in DC while I was there, and those people are always traveling."

"Senate staffer?" I blink in disbelief.

Her? Miss Bee Crazy worked for a US Senator?

"Don't ask and I'll tell you no lies." She holds up a single finger. It's perfectly manicured, though she's gnawed at the skin around it. "Just trust me. These people, they would *die* for glamping places like this when they hit the road, even for work. I have no doubt they'd take my recommendation seriously."

Damn her.

It's like she's tapped into what we're really looking for. Higher Ends wants to expand beyond our Midwestern foothold, recent trouble with doing that in Minnesota aside. We're always looking for places with affluent clientele and reasonable investment opportunities.

If she's telling the truth, she has the demographic part down.

It's like this aura around her.

Her special kind of crazy must be contagious.

Nothing to do with the fact that she might have a good reason for her madness and she just needs a break.

I don't do breaks.

I don't do soft.

I just do business.

"Okay," I growl, pushing up from my seat. "You can stay for another two weeks at the agreed rate. I'll inform my staff not to accept any calls from your father and your details will remain private, per company policy. Unless—" I hold up a finger. "Unless you give me a good reason to change my mind. Don't do it."

"Your policy is mine!" she says cheerfully.

I don't smile, though the corner of my mouth twitches.

"Don't push your luck, Winnie."

She sobers up immediately, lifting her hair off the nape of her neck. I spy a constellation of small freckles there and look away.

"I'm only gonna push one time for this, but… can I get a closer look at the bees?" she asks.

"Are you allergic?"

"Would I ask to look at bees if I were, silly?" She sounds offended.

I snort. "Woman, I think I've got to check, seeing as they're my bees on my land and the last thing I need right now is a lawsuit after you wind up getting stung thirty times. For now, leave the boxes alone."

"*Fine*, Mr. Buzzkill." She slides off her seat and twists around to face me just as I'm preparing to leave, elbows propped on the counter, watching me with hooded eyes. "For the record, I'm not allergic, and yes I know what I'm doing with bees. If I get stung, I won't sue you."

I almost crack a smile again. What the hell has she done to me?

"I'll need that in writing."

"…was that a joke?"

"Do I look like a comedian?" Fucking never. Except when

chaotic redheads push back when I least expect it, maybe. "You can do whatever else you'd like while you're here. Whatever floats your boat, if you waive all liability and you keep a safe distance."

It's obscene how much her face lights up at the thought. Her eyes turn from emerald to peridot, dancing at the thought of her damn bees.

I'll never understand it.

"Thank you! Thank you so much," she gushes as I head for the door. "Sorry for sucking up so much of your time. I know you've got a kid and probably a wife at home to get back to and oh, it's the weekend, too..." Her voice trails off.

I give her the coldest smile.

Let's not make this personal, even if it already is. Better to keep her at a distance.

"Colt keeps me busy," I say.

Then I walk out and leave her in peace, hoping like hell I don't regret this.

* * *

I DON'T HAVE a spare minute until evening, when I can finally sit down in the living room with my laptop and a glass of cold brew.

I have Winnie's full name from her booking details, so I punch it into Google.

The first result is a brief tabloid article trumpeting the "Emberly-Corban Power Wedding Meltdown!"

Brutally interesting.

I scan the piece for info, and fuck, there it is.

When she mentioned powerful connections, she neglected to tell me her father oversees justice in the whole goddamned state.

I thought I recognized his name, and now I know why.

The man who called the office hounding us for his daughter's whereabouts is none other than Carroll Jackson Emberly III, the Attorney General of Missouri.

My eyes scan the article, quickly reading.

The engagement was announced late last year by Missouri Attorney General Carroll Emberly and Senator Klein Corban, the father of the groom.

A DC senator.

Bingo again.

When she said she'd spent some time as a staffer, I didn't know she was working for her own future father-in-law.

Technically, father-in-nothing now.

The more I read, the more this feels like some bizarre medieval arranged marriage. Aside from her name, there's no mention of Winnie until the end.

Some photographer took a grainy image of her hunched behind the wheel of her car, wedding dress on and angry determination in her eyes.

It doesn't take long to find that picture everywhere on social media.

I'm amazed there's no attempt to squelch it to save the family some embarrassment. I'm no stranger to rich political types with their heads lodged up their asses. The only thing they hate more than losing money is having their drama splashed out in public.

The article was posted half an hour ago. No doubt Mr. Attorney General will try to have it pulled, but it may be too late, judging by the views and shares stacking up.

The spectacle draws laughs and predictably shitty comments from locals like a lightning rod.

Damn.

Out of morbid interest, I look for Winnie herself on social media. Her accounts are private, but her profile picture shows a laughing redhead holding flowers.

I don't bother blowing up the image to see, but I can almost guarantee there's a small fluffy bee on one of them.

I snort loudly.

She may be bonkers, but she's still a smoke show, and I'm not normally blue balling over textbook crazy redhead types.

There's something different about her face here. Not just a filter or the fact a professional clearly took the photo.

There's something real and gentle and beguiling about her, like this photo captured a rare moment where she really was happy. She's not faking a smile because she's trying to persuade some stuffy jerkoff to let her rent his star property a little while longer.

My lip curls as I sip my beer.

Do not feel guilty, you asshole.

You have every right to be careful.

Before I get to wonder what a real genuine Winnie smile looks in person too long, Colt comes in. I shut the laptop before he sees I'm gawking at the girl he almost lit on fire.

"Hey, Dad." His voice only drags a little. He's covered in dust and cobwebs from cleaning the garage.

"Hey, kiddo. Don't sit down yet," I say as he heads over to slump down beside me. "Go shower first. Did you get it all done?"

"Yep, I even cleaned the ATVs. Wiped the old dirt off them and everything."

Ah, hell.

I may breathe fire that would make a dragon jealous, but it's impossible to stay mad at him for long.

Even when he did something as remarkably stupid as dicking around with fireworks on a million-dollar rental property. Maybe he's only doing his chores to get back on my good side, but at least he's *doing* them, and without complaining, too.

"All right." I nod. "You're telling me you're done for the evening?"

A quick smile crosses his face, and for a second, he looks like a younger face I used to see in the mirror.

"Better be. I'm beat."

"Homework done?" It's not exactly homework, but it's the summer math stuff he signed up for to prep for organic chemistry this fall.

So far, the accelerated summer class looks like another breeze for my mad scientist son.

If only his common sense was as sharp as the rest of his brains.

"Yeah, it was easy. I thought Calc was gonna be harder." He hesitates as I shake my head.

"Boy, don't brag, or I'm putting you to work in accounting next year."

He chuckles like he always does at my deadpan delivery, slowly tugging at the sleeve of his shirt to pull up a cobweb stuck there.

"Since I'm done with everything, can I go to Uncle Pat's tonight? He said it'd be cool to have a sitter for Arlo."

My eyes narrow like a hawk.

"Did you miss the part where you're grounded? Until further notice?" I fold my arms. "You're barely through day one."

"Yeah, but that was for *fun* stuff, I thought? This is Uncle Pat and Arlo. Aunt Lemmy's cool with it too, obviously."

There's no way I'll refuse him and he knows it, especially knowing how good he is with little Arlo. I still can't believe my idiot younger brother skipped the whole infant part and wound up with an instant first grader.

I don't want Colt thinking this shit will be easy, though.

"And Uncle Pat asked you today?"

"Yeah." Colt holds up his phone to show me the text. "See, Dad?"

Fucking Patton, bypassing me like the insubordinate prick he is. I know Colt loves being treated like an adult, but last night proved he's far from it.

"I see." I lean back in my chair and watch him. "Go shower and I'll think about it. No promises."

It's the best I can do.

He speedwalks away, almost at a skip, and I sink back down on the sofa.

No one ever tells you how difficult being a single dad is when it comes to handing out discipline.

Or, hell, being any kind of dad, I guess.

The surprise family aged Pat about ten years, almost overnight.

It also made him talk relentlessly about Arlo. Some days I'm not sure he remembers what making money is.

He flips back and forth from moaning over how worried he is every time the kid gets a cold to singing Salem's praises. He's so in love with his wife it makes my stomach churn.

Only Dex triggers a worse gag reflex with Junie.

Of course, Patton's only getting started with fatherhood. He's in the easy stage.

Later on, you have to balance your son becoming a man and navigating the world with making choices you wouldn't agree with. That makes dealing with an unexpected stomach bug he passes on to you or a nine o'clock rush to the drugstore for supplies to finish some project he *just remembered* easy as pie.

How to be a parent, how to be approachable, that's what they never tell you. I'm still wrestling with how to be a human shepherd.

How do I make sure Colt turns into the best young man he can possibly be?

I spend more time on that than anything.

And I know it's me, myself, and I making the decisions.

Just because that's normal doesn't mean it's fucking easy. Sometimes when I'm idling after a few drinks, I wonder what it would've been like with a woman in the mix, a proper mother to share the responsibility.

Then I remember Rina cut herself out of our lives.

I remember why I was happy as hell to say good riddance.

Snarling, I drag a hand over my face, stretching my skin.

I love who Colton is now.

I love the bright, innocent kid who still grins at me after he's solved some math problem that looks like Coptic Greek.

Yet I also get this dread, this evil sense he's slipping away, off to the no man's land of adolescence where wolves prowl, waiting to chew up the smartest, kindest kids.

He's making decisions like sneaking away to fucking Solitude to play with literal fire, instead of helping his buddy Evans with chemistry like he was supposed to.

What do I do with that when there's no playbook?

I have to write new rules on the fly.

"Dad? Can I go now?" Colt swings in front of me, freshly showered and changed into a pair of jeans and a *Breaking Bad* shirt that sticks to his wet body. His hair sticks up in spikes.

"On one condition." I hold up a finger. "You promise to check in, and you do it religiously. If you step one foot outside Uncle Pat's place, or I find out you had Evans or whoever over, you'll be grounded until you're old enough to drive. I'm not playing, you hear?"

"Okay, okay! Jeez." He rolls his eyes, but I'm still waiting. "Yes, Dad. Got it. Read you loud and clear."

"Good. C'mon then, little man." I haul myself up off the sofa, but as I'm about to leave to drive him over, I check my phone and see I've missed a call.

From Rina.

Fucking Rina.

My ex-wife. Colt's joke of a mother. A ghost I've barely thought about in years.

She usually never gets in touch outside Christmas except during her vacations, one of the few times her guilt starts eating her bad enough to give a shit about Colt.

"Hey, Dad?" Colt hovers by the door, looking like he's going to fall through it as he glances back at me. "You coming or…?"

"On my way." I swipe the missed call notification away and follow him to the garage.

I do my best to banish Rina from my mind, but she keeps creeping back in.

What the hell could she want?

I can deal with her later.

This week seems determined to massacre my hopes for peace and quiet.

Between my ex-wife and Winnie, the drama wheel feels like a steamroller, ready to grind me under.

V: BEE HAPPY (WINNIE)

Once, I ripped off a nail.

We're talking my entire nail, gone just like that, all thanks to catching my finger in a door.

It hurt like Hades, the worst pain I've ever experienced. I went to the hospital, only for them to tell me there was nothing they could do except hand out antibiotics to keep it from getting infected.

Eventually, a new nail grew back.

For a while, it was just this ugly bruised nail bed that throbbed every time I moved my hand.

I vowed I'd never do something so stupid again, and so far, I haven't.

But right now, I swear to God, I would rather rip off *every single one* of my fingernails than take my phone out of airplane mode.

I gnaw at a hangnail as bad habit takes over, staring at the stupid black screen, considering my options. Which are basically zilch, not after Dad forced my hand by calling Archer's company, demanding answers.

I grit my teeth, swallowing thickly as I stare at my reflection.

Okay, let's do this.

I tap the icon to resume service and let ten thousand notifications appear, pinging like a choir.

My knees waver and I sit down abruptly, thankful for the stool behind me. That could've been messy.

Winnie Emberly, daughter of the Attorney General, found dead from having split her head open on the floor after panicking over her phone.

Though maybe sudden death would be better.

This is physically, emotionally, and spiritually painful.

As my phone reconnects and the messages fly in like bullets, I genuinely consider tossing it into the nearby woods and tuning out the world again.

Maybe I'll find some pliers.

Pay my penance that way.

Give the universe its pound of flesh if that's the cost of a little freedom.

Instead of looking at the texts and nonstop app messages my phone keeps launching at my face, I pull up Instagram. Yes, it has plenty of its notifications flooding in, too, threatening to drown me.

Gobs of people have tagged me, laughing about the oh-so-hilarious fact I fled my own wedding and left my young, handsome groom stranded like a very rich beached seal.

Yes, it's all true.

But when you consider the fact that I never wanted to get married, and that on the morning of the big day, Holden messaged me about dropping my tiara—the only part of the wedding I liked—you can hardly blame me.

I rest my forehead on my arms, hunched over, as if making myself smaller might encourage the universe to stop flinging crap my way.

The tiara was beautiful.

My grandmother gave it to me and it was this gorgeous silver thing, elegant and lovely with a large gleaming bee in the center. Not obnoxious, just pure class, but Holden decided he didn't want any bees in his wedding.

Let that sink in.

His wedding.

Not ours.

Never mind the fact that the tiara was the only thing about the stupid wedding that actually mattered to me.

Ironically, it wound up being the shot to the face I needed to remember he never cared about me in the slightest.

This was an arranged marriage, and nothing more. Definitely not the wacky rom-com kind with a happy waiting at the end.

Ugh.

My eyes pinch shut, but I can feel the tears coming.

Bad memories rush back, burning my mind.

The way Mom tried to stop me, practically clinging to me as I headed for the door, even if she didn't know where I was going.

That first hit of sweet relief when I was free, followed by the chest-crushing panic that still hasn't stopped choking me.

I'd stopped at a gas station on the outskirts of Springfield to book this place, last-minute, and drove the rest of the way like crazy.

How Dad even found me is a mystery.

No one knew where I was going, considering I came up with Kansas City as my destination on the fly. Not even Lyssie, my bestie.

He shouldn't have been able to find me so quickly. I don't care if his lofty connections could outshine a bloodhound in tracking.

I lift my head and see my face the way it looked the morning of my wedding.

All artificially primed and pruned, every stray hair on my body obliterated, my eyebrows and lashes and lips more overdone than an Egyptian mummy mask.

My nose tingles when I touch it, still sore from removing every blackhead it'll ever have.

My cheekbones feel like they've moved to a different zip code.

I think the whirlwind treatments from those stylists Mom brought in ruined me.

I still don't look completely normal.

When I see my face, I don't see Winnie.

I see a porcelain doll, everything they wanted me to be.

Oh, Mom was delighted, though.

She touched my back so softly that morning and crooned in my ear, *Winnie, you look radiant! You're going to make him so happy. But can't you smile a little?*

No, Mom.

Hell no.

You'd have a better chance of getting a girl to grin when she's on death row.

Shaking my head, I look at the black bag holding the torn remains of my dress. I still haven't dragged it outside to the trash where it belongs.

Guilt is weirdly powerful.

That gawdy thing cost over ten thousand dollars—yes, my stomach churns just thinking about it—and maybe I shouldn't have cut it up like a paper snowflake. If it was intact, I could've donated it, at least.

But aside from it being the most uncomfortable dress I've ever worn, it really was a prison suit in white.

Desperate times.

Desperate measures for erasing a cruel symbol of what

they almost forced me to do, and I can't feel too bad about tearing through the beautiful silk. Why not when I just cut the rest of my life to ribbons?

And because I must hate myself and I want to rub salt into a fresh wound, I read through some of the Twitter posts about my 'big day disaster.'

DCToiletScrubber: The look on the senator's face with his noodle of a son stranded at the altar #WeddingFail #EmberlyPatilla

Lilmeatballgirl84: OMG. OMG still cannot believe she left him on their WEDDING DAY??? Is she on drugs? #WeddingFail

Tungstentastesgoodsometimes: Holy f_king wedding fail. Winnie Emberly does NOT know good dick. I would DIE for a ride on that stallion.

The last inane post just had to include a photo of Holden with his million-dollar grin, looking all handsome in a navy suit, his dark-blond hair combed back.

His sharp face beams its 'I'm better than you' energy at the camera.

His favorite expression I've seen a thousand times.

Several people comment with fire gifs and a large dog drooling.

At least the hashtags haven't hit the main trending lists. *Yet.*

I mean, it's not like Dad or Senator Corban are A-list celebrities.

Sure, Dad was elected to his second term and he acts like everyone in Missouri knows who he is, but that's not actually the case. He can walk down the street without being mobbed. You ask the average person about Carroll Emberly, and they'll give you a puzzled look unless they're a huge election dork or a high-powered lawyer.

But this wedding was his thing. His baby.

Dad and Holden's father cooked up the arrangement because they smelled opportunity if their political dynasties could merge. Never mind what works best for the kids getting married, because we apparently live in the seventeenth century.

Holden, though, he has a little more of a cult following. Mostly on Instagram, where he draws women who worship the young and rich and sickeningly spoiled like frogs on a pond.

One night, he spent half the evening in his DMs, just laughing.

I couldn't decide if I was more icked out by his rudeness, mocking his fans, or scared he'd hooked up with a few of them.

My skin crawls just thinking about it now.

Another red flag I ignored.

And the idea that I had the *nerve* to detonate my life and dodge a screaming bullet feels surreal.

This can't be me.

This can't be the girl who was called into Dad's office last year when he suggested an engagement and *agreed* with a nervous smile and not a single word of protest.

Although, to be fair, this situation feels more like a direct hit than a near miss.

Maybe the bullet wasn't Holden after all—it was running away and becoming estranged from the entire world I used to know.

Figures.

Honestly, I feel bad about my big promises to Archer, everything I said about recommending his cabins to people in high places.

I mean, I was desperate. I would've promised him the moon just to keep my pretty hideout place for a few more days.

There's something about this place that makes me feel

like I belong in a stupid, entirely irrational way. An oasis in the steaming crater carved from my life.

But after what I pulled, I'll be lucky if anyone in the old DC crowd ever says more than two words to me. And those two words will probably be *"the fuck?"*

Which would be justified, I suppose. In their world, it isn't about pissing off people personally.

It's about pissing off the wrong people with the right connections. Once you've angered the petty cannibal gods of American royalty, you become radioactive to anyone who fears their wrath.

My old friends and coworkers would never understand conscience. Or turning down the perfect paper marriage for the silly dream of having a husband someday I might actually want.

Honestly, they don't think about marriage much at all when they're so focused on money and careers. In DC, you either move up fast or get buried. Random hookups in hotels with people who are *probably* clean are as romantic as it gets.

Because, you know, that's less of a career risk than marrying the wrong person.

But if they did think about marriage, the kind of political marriage I could've had with Holden probably feels like a dream come true.

Disgusted, I push my phone away, ignoring all the DMs from friends to news outlets wanting interviews.

I've seen what a loveless marriage looks like. Maybe Mom loved Dad back when they were young, but he's been so laser-focused on his career that everything else was pushed to the sidelines.

And maybe he loved her once in an abstract sense, but he's forgotten now. She's just there to smile at the cameras like a pretty prop made to support him. I was there, too, playing the perfect daughter.

Until now.

Guess that's what happens when you push the line until something snaps.

You shove a girl too far, and she'll blow her wedding to smithereens and run off to a glam little cottage with bees and no big scary obligations around to ruin her fairy tale.

Speaking of bees...

I hop off my seat, leaving my phone, and head outside to check on them.

The sun feels like a warm bath on my skin. The sweet scent of the flowers hangs so thick in the air I inhale happily, feeling the misery leaving my soul.

It's liberating, being able to turn my back on my phone and my responsibilities and my old rotten life.

Here, life feels good.

As long as it lasts, I'm going to make the most of paradise.

* * *

MAKING the most of paradise today involves investigating the bees at the very edge of the garden. There are more than I thought, six sets of boxes total, all parked pretty close together. But there's one more set a little closer to the forest, I notice.

Langstroth boxes, they're called. A classic hive for the traditional beekeeper and my personal favorite.

There's something important to me about the bees feeling protected and not needing to rebuild too much every time their honey gets harvested.

Of course, this is also the most efficient method for doing that. Not necessarily the best for the bees, but I've always been a honey lover, and we only harvest a little.

I wonder if Archer would mind if I had a closer look?

I haven't seen any beekeepers around, which feels like an

oversight. Bees are perfectly capable of looking after themselves, but this is a manmade nest. Whoever set it up should be making the rounds near daily to keep the bees safe and comfortable.

Luckily, I'm here now, and I can do the job just fine. I *want* to do it.

I take my time studying the environment, pondering my next move.

The bees are happy on their own without human interference, doing normal bee things. It's crazy relaxing just being around them.

But I want to do more than watch them from a distance. I want to investigate the honey and make sure the hives are healthy.

So I walk forward, every movement measured and calm.

Bees aren't like wasps. Sure, they'll defend their nest if they think it's in danger, but as long as I don't look like a threat, they won't attack.

A few curious scouts land on me as I approach. I smile as they rest for a second before flying off. People have this terrible fear of bugs with stingers, but most bees aren't naturally aggressive.

Bees are predictable.

Definitely easier to deal with than people, only lashing out when it's life or death.

If only the world could figure it out, then maybe they'd lay off the insecticides and poisons and give bees a little more space to coexist.

I don't care how crunchy and naïve that sounds, it's totally true.

And when I think about it for too long, my throat tightens until I push the thought aside.

These are pretty bees.

Slim brownish gold honeybees with gently striped bodies, happy by all appearances.

I reach the first box and look it over critically. The wood looks like it's been treated, which is good. There are plenty of holes for the bees to exit and reenter the box.

Moving slowly, I remove the lid from the shorter box to check out the extra honey stored inside. More bees buzz up around me, but I don't freak out.

One even lands on my nose for a second and then flutters away.

"That's right, guys. I'm a friend," I murmur, gently pulling the lid off and setting it on the ground.

Loud buzzing fills my ears, but that's not what grabs my attention. There's something purple between the panels.

It can't be.

I hold my breath, icy calm so I don't agitate them.

I've done this plenty of times before without the full suit, but that doesn't mean I'm impervious to getting stung if I slip up, if I move too fast or shake too much.

I lift the first of the ten frames carefully. Small bees cling to the honeycomb and more swarm around me to investigate as soon as they're disturbed.

I almost drop the frame right there because my eyes weren't lying.

It's flipping purple.

Look, I know honey can get colorful, but there's no mistaking this. I stare down in disbelief, drinking in this bright, royal-violet gold, rare and delicious.

"Sorry, honeys," I whisper as I swipe the tiniest dab on my index finger and slide the frame back into place.

Once it's secure and the bees are safe, I close my eyes in bliss and try it.

Holy nectar.

Okay, forget The Sugar Bowl. That place might have

some of the best sweets I've ever devoured—but it has nothing on this honey.

It's a shot of pure sugar to the soul.

Rich. Magnificently sweet. Faintly floral like wine.

I've never tasted anything like it.

"Easy, easy. Don't freak out," I tell myself like the bee crazy spaz I am.

Trembling, I back away from the hive slowly until there's plenty of space between me and the bees.

Then I squeal.

I start dancing on the spot.

This is *insane*!

A surprise miracle that feels like it was planted here just for me to find.

I throw my fist up and whoop, listening to the way my voice echoes back from the forest.

So maybe I have issues.

But I also need to investigate. If this is what I think it is—

No. No, I need to check first. Don't get too excited.

I can't go popping off, making big claims without hard *facts*. If there's anything Dad taught me, it's that.

I don't even bother getting my phone before I go vaulting over the fence at the edge of the garden and head straight to the woods, looking for—well, I don't know what. Something out of the ordinary.

Something the bees have been using to craft this magic honey.

I rush forward, holding my hands out to the dappled sunlight making its way through the trees. The whole runaway bride thing feels like a bad dream now.

Who cares what's happening back home—this is why I'm here.

Bees. Honey. Something *important* that doesn't mean pleasing everybody else.

Go ahead and call it stupid, but I haven't been this thrilled in ages.

But these aren't technically my bees. I have no earthly right to get this attached.

For all I know, I might be breaking some rule in the fine print that will have Mr. Gruff Stuff throwing me out tomorrow.

Still, less than an hour later, I'm dirty and smiling deliriously as I stagger back inside the house.

First things first—water.

I guzzle down a full glass to rehydrate after being in the hot sun and then start on one more. I'm pretty sure I've burned myself despite the sunscreen I slathered on this morning, but there's no helping that.

I don't even care.

I'm bouncing on the balls of my feet when I grab my phone, swiping past all the notifications—how can they just keep coming?—and find Archer's number.

I can't sit on this, consequences be damned.

This man has a right to know he's sitting on bee-made *gold*.

VI: TOTALLY BEE-GUILED
(ARCHER)

I should've known it would be impossible for me to get a little quiet.

Working in the home office doesn't mean I don't have distractions. It just means whoever wants to hound me does it through my phone.

First Dexter, who doesn't even bother with a greeting when I pick up.

"I have an idea," he says.

"Hello to you too."

He makes an impatient sound. "Yes, hi. Anyway, I was thinking... The Cardinal has been one of our most successful ventures, right?"

"Yeah."

The Cardinal is Patton's baby, mostly. There's no denying the hotel that really isn't a hotel has outperformed our loftiest expectations with minimal problems. Better than anything I thought Pat would ever do, even if he had some major help from his now-wife.

Don't get me wrong, he's a good businessman.

He has good instincts. But Salem's management took a

serious investment with long-term potential and spun it into one of our best moneymakers ever in record time.

"Of course," I tell him. "What's your point?"

"Why did we stop at one?"

That's what I thought he might say. I press my phone closer to my ear. "Because buildings like that are unicorns and they require monster capital."

"We have the money."

"Still a gamble," I growl back, although he might have a point. "Did you have a where in mind?"

"Saint Louis."

Still in Missouri, then. It's a logical step—the second biggest city in the state, and it would be like a stepping stone for future expansions. We could even spin off the same Cardinal branding, considering how much attention that property keeps getting in travel blogs and video reviews.

"And what brought this on?" I ask.

"I was thinking about Junie's bakery expansion. My brain just went there," he admits slowly. "We could time ours to match and bring the best of Kansas City east."

"She's thinking of opening a bakery in St. Louis?"

"I mean, it makes sense. It's a big place, plenty of opportunities. Plus, I've checked, and I think there could be a gap in the market for another luxury high-rise with our model."

Hmph.

If there's one thing I trust Dexter to do, it's research. Especially after the whole Haute affair that almost sunk us, he's insanely diligent, even if he doesn't burn himself out working like he used to.

"It's your lucky day. I'll consider it."

"Good. Patton already agreed," he says smugly.

"Big fat fucking surprise you went to him first," I growl, trying not to roll my eyes. "He'll still be bragging about The Cardinal in a retirement home someday."

Dexter chuckles. "Careful, man, your jealousy is showing."

"Fuck off, Dex."

His voice is perfectly calm as he laughs. "Just wanted to plant the seed. We want to move fast, so can we expedite your second-guessing?"

"I told you I'll think about it. Call a meeting in a few days, after I've had time to look into it, and you can pitch it properly with numbers."

"Thanks, Arch. I'll have my homework in on time like always." He snorts. There's a muffled sound in the background. "Anyway, I'll let you get back to your brooding. Don't be too hard on Colt for the fireworks. I heard about it from Mom."

"My son, my problem," I snarl.

I place the phone on the table, screen up, and turn on speaker so I can check through the messages that start buzzing in. Weirdly, they're all from Miss Sugarbee.

"Junie just called you, didn't she?" I ask, remembering that muffled sound. He has a bad way of setting his phone up where you can tell if someone else calls.

"Maybe."

"Go back to your domestic bliss, fucker."

"Sure thing, prick."

I grin as I end the call.

It's not the worst idea, expanding our star success, just as long as we lay the groundwork right. I send a note to our assistant to dig up basics on the St. Louis market and then turn my attention to those weird-ass texts.

Winnie: Archer you won't believe this but you have THE BEST BEES

Winnie: Literal bee golf

Winnie: mold

Winnie: *gold ARGH

Winnie: *The honey is purple and believe me when I say that's sooo rare. PURPLE HONEY*

What the fuck?

Of course, she includes a bee emoji after every message.

All I know about bees is that they hurt like hell when they sting you.

I'm starting to regret the day my landscaper talked me into setting up those bee boxes.

Frankly, I'm not sure I'd believe her if it wasn't for the photos she attached, which show a rack of honeycomb and the most purple honey I've ever seen in my life.

It looks more like paint, something you'd use to dress up a pumpkin on Halloween or smear on a canvas while you're watching Bob Ross.

I ignore the rest of her garbled incoming texts, which keep raving about this bee-given miracle and how I need to come over *this instant*.

I'm wincing when I call her.

"Archer! Hi. You got my messages?" She picks up immediately.

"Yes," I say cautiously. "I got them, all right."

"Isn't this amazing?" She practically squeals. No, scratch that—she *does* squeal, though she has the grace to move her phone away from her mouth when it happens so she doesn't blow out my eardrum. I put her on speaker and lean back in my chair. "I've seriously never seen anything like it. I've only heard of this kind of thing before."

"What, do you moonlight as a beekeeper on top of your senate staffer job?" I wouldn't be shocked if it's true.

"I'm no professional, no, but my grandparents gave me a good start. I know what I'm doing around bees. You have to believe me when I say this is unicorn honey. Like total freak of nature stuff. Honey so purple it almost glows? Do you know what that means?"

"No. But I have a feeling you'll enlighten me."

"Yes! People will pay *through the nose* for this honey, Archer. You don't even know what medicinal qualities it might have, and it's pretty yummy, too. So sweet you could dribble it on ice cream."

What a weird image. My gut churns, unsure whether it sounds appetizing or absolutely revolting.

I close my eyes and pinch the bridge of my nose.

This isn't bad news, no, but the fact it's this girl and these fucking bees again has me worried. Earlier today, her dad left another frosty voicemail. This time on my personal cell, which he must have blackmailed out of someone or pulled serious strings to get.

He damn near demanded a call back to confirm she's renting my cabin.

"You need to come over and see it," she says. "I know this sounds bonkers over the phone, but just come and I'll show you. It'll make more sense in person, I promise."

Sure.

It'll make the same sense as hearing about this batshit honey does now, except instead of a photo, it'll probably involve her dancing around like a manic pixie while I get stung in the face ten times.

"I mean, assuming you're not too busy," she adds, almost like an afterthought.

"Fine," I say, if only to humor her. "I'll come, but no pulling apart bee boxes and pissing them off."

"Yay! I'm so pumped. See ya soon."

That makes one of us.

I end the call before her puppy energy changes my mind and push the phone back across the desk with a sigh.

Christ, what am I getting myself into?

Colt walks in as I'm still processing how best to deal with

this level of crazy, and when I pick up my phone, he gets a good look at the screen and stops cold.

"Dad, why are you looking at potassium permanganate?"

"Potassium perma-what now?" I stare at him.

"It's an oxidizing agent. They use it a lot in hospitals for sanitation. It's bright purple like that."

Have I mentioned how much my little mad scientist scares me sometimes?

"No, Colt, this is honey. Apparently."

"Honey—what? Does honey get purple?"

"Supposedly, yes. I'm going to find out in person." I pinch the bridge of my nose again. Odds are good I'll regret this tomorrow, but I've already committed. "I'm headed out there now to take a look. Do you want to come and get some fresh air?"

"Hell yeah!" He punches the air. "Uh, sorry."

If he's this excited to leave the house for purple honey, I guess being grounded is getting to him.

Good. That's the entire point.

It also means there's an extra pressure in my chest as we head out together, back to the place where all our latest troubles started.

* * *

When we get to Solitude, Winnie's waiting for us.

She throws the door open the second we pull up in the driveway.

"You brought Colt along? Nice!" she says, her eyes shining as she sees him. "Come on in, guys."

"Hey, Winnie," he says almost shyly.

"It's good to see you again. Your dad treating you okay?"

"Could be better." Colt grins up at me.

"His dad is right here," I say dryly.

Her smile is infectious as hell, I'll give her that, bright-green eyes dancing as she leans closer to Colt.

"Blink twice if you need help," she whispers, loud enough for me to hear.

Colt laughs.

I press my lips together so my amusement doesn't show.

Gone is the broken, lost bird from before. In her place, there's this fairy creature whose energy is palpable.

She beckons us to follow, her fingers fluttering, and Colt takes a seat by the island, just like before.

I lean against the counter, not wanting to get too comfortable.

"So," I say. "Purple honey, huh?"

"I did some investigating before I called you. You saw the pictures, right?"

"Yes, I saw the pictures."

"Right, well, that says it all." She beams at me. "I checked out the woods around your property to see if I could find anything obvious that might explain it. There's a rare crop of kudzu and black locust trees about half a mile in."

"That's what's causing it?" I ask, unsure I'm following her.

"Yes! Probably, I mean. It's unusual this far north—the purple color—and I've never seen this exact shade before. I can't find a good match looking online." Unable to keep still, she starts pacing. "It's crazy, though. I never thought I'd find anything like this here."

I glance at Colt, but he's just propped his head up on one hand, watching her movements. If she's not careful, she'll burn a hole through the wood flooring.

"Do you have more land?" she asks suddenly.

"What?"

"More acreage? Do you own any of the forest?"

I fold my arms. "What does it matter to you?"

Although my property line extends generously into the woods, I'm not just leasing it out to bee-obsessed wackos.

"You could expand the hives and sell this stuff like crazy." She stops pacing and stops in front of me, staring up, all big green eyes and fierce dreams.

I have to take a step back. I've never seen this much passion before.

"I'm not surrounding this place with bees, Winnie. They're upscale rentals, and most folks in our demographic like their getaways bug free."

"Okay, okay. That's fair." Striding off again, she rubs her temples like she's trying to think, to find just the right words to convince me to join her next crazy scheme.

Instead, I scope out the place.

The black trash bag is still crumpled on the floor where she left it. I wonder if she's having second thoughts or if she needs some help getting rid of it.

Leaving everything behind on your wedding day must be damn hard. If her tears the other day were any indication, she's definitely struggling. At least, she *was* before the enchanted honey showed up.

Fucking bees.

Of everything that might have pulled her out of that slump, I never expected it to be bees and their weird purple goo.

But this is a place made for rest and relaxation. Surrounding the property with busy hives doesn't exactly give those vibes. I've already had to add a clear disclaimer to the bottom of the property about the bee presence just in case anybody with a serious allergy ever tries to rent it.

Something I don't think she read before she showed up.

Hell, judging by how she behaves, she didn't bother reading through the website fully—she checked if it was available and booked it on the fly.

"Are you going to collect it?" Colt asks Winnie.

She turns to him. "Hmm?"

"The honey. Do you have a way to harvest it? If—" He glances at me now, his eyebrows pulled together. Somehow, the boy manages to look so old and young at the same time. "If Dad's okay with it, I mean."

Beautiful timing.

Winnie also looks at me. I'm pretty sure I feel the hit like a hornet jammed in my ear.

Goddamn, this woman can speak whole volumes with her eyes alone.

"If it's done safely and carefully, I won't object," I say.

"You can do it if you like," she tells Colt. "It's perfectly safe."

"I meant you, Sugarbee," I growl. "I wasn't inviting my son."

She blinks at me. Her emerald eyes dim, flashing me a dirty look.

I fold my arms. "They're bees. They're dangerous when they get riled up."

"Not unless you're allergic and you go swinging at their nests. They're not Africanized killer bees."

"They can still do damage."

"Only if provoked." Her smile drips sweetness, beguiling my son, who's only just discovered puberty and pretty girls. "I'll show you guys, okay? Just follow my lead. Or if you want, you can stand back and watch while I do it."

"Do you have beekeeping equipment?" I ask, my arms still folded. It feels like a me-vs-them situation, but if Colt didn't look at her with those harvest moon eyes, we wouldn't be in this situation.

She nods. "Yes, actually. I found some in a shed by the garden. Someone must come by to check on them, huh?"

I shrug.

I guess they do.

Truthfully, I haven't involved myself in the day-to-day beekeeping crap. That's why I have a maintenance crew.

"Winnie, do you know what you're doing?" I demand.

"Yes. Trust me. I checked and you have an extractor." At my blank look, she sighs. "It separates the honey without damaging the comb. That way, the bees don't need to rebuild after we mess with anything."

"I see." Barely, but that's not the point. "I don't feel fully comfortable with this."

Am I being unreasonable?

She might be mad about bees, but I don't know enough about her to trust my son and this strange woman around a whole active colony, all armed with stingers and bad attitudes.

Colt was stung a few times as a kid, so I know he's not allergic. Still, I've heard stories of people who become allergic after being stung too many times, or just as life happens.

No way do I want to risk any nasty surprises.

"I get the hesitation," Winnie says brightly, shrugging like it's no big deal. "No need to worry, I'll do it myself. You guys can keep your distance."

"Yeah!"

With Colt's enthusiasm, there's nothing else to do but follow her outside into the balmy evening sun. There's a reason we called this place 'Solitude' and it lives up to its reputation.

As promised, there's a shed tucked into the corner of the garden. She disappears inside before reemerging in a white suit complete with hood. There's black mesh around her face and she's wearing bulky gloves. She gives us a big thumbs-up.

"This is the super," she explains, tapping the top of the

first bee box she comes to. "Any excess honey the bees make goes in here."

"Why there?" Colt asks.

"Most hives make extra honey, but we don't want to grab too much. Did you know the average worker drone only lives for six weeks and makes about a twelfth of a teaspoon of honey in his entire life?" She tilts her head toward us but it's impossible to see her expression behind the hood.

I'm sure she's giddy.

Colt nods, awestruck.

My lips curl with irritation.

Just to check that she's not talking out of her ass, I pull out my phone and do a quick search.

Dammit, she's right.

Of course, she is.

I decide not to stroke her ego by telling her and shove my phone back in my pocket, folding my arms as I watch her.

Beside me, Colt stares like he's watching the greatest show on Earth.

"It's so cool how she isn't scared," he whispers.

I don't know Winnie, but I know her well enough to say, "Cool or absolutely bonkers. Time will tell."

"Dad, she's just passionate. You could learn a thing or two. But what if she gets stung?"

"Why don't you ask her?" I bite off.

Colt cups his hands over his mouth as she removes the first frame, which is so thick with gold bees it's impossible to see anything underneath.

"Hey, Winnie!" he calls. "What happens if you get stung?"

"I'm not allergic, so nothing to worry about." She shakes the frame, dislodging most of the bees back in the box. "I don't mind. It hurts a little, but it's not so bad, really. There are way worse things."

Like a clown who leaves you so heartbroken you run hundreds of miles to find bees as a distraction?

I wonder.

There are so many little flying bugs surrounding her now. I can barely see what she's doing, but she's moving slowly, carefully. She doesn't seem to mind the way they crawl all over her.

Just watching it makes my skin itch.

It's not a quick process, either.

After she's dislodged the bees with lots of patience, coaxing, and promises—yes, she reminds them constantly she's their best damn friend—Winnie puts the frame in a clear bag.

Repeat for another nine frames caked with honey, and finally, she's on her way back.

A few bees still cling to her stubbornly.

Not necessarily to attack, I think, though I wouldn't put that past them. More like raw curiosity, I guess.

That makes two of us.

The bugs must be as baffled as I am over this bright, sexy woman invading their space.

"My bad. I wore the wrong perfume today," she explains once she's next to us again.

"Wrong perfume?" I know as soon as I've asked it's a dangerous question.

I caught a whiff of it when she invited us in, and even in that big white space suit, she smells wonderful. Floral and succulent with a hint of cinnamon-like heat underneath for just the right sizzle.

Damnably enticing.

Damnably annoying that she has to remind me.

"It attracts the bees. Certain scents do," she says matter-of-factly. "No big deal except I don't need a load of them following me around."

Colt ducks back as a bee flies in front of my face. I have to grit my teeth to step back gracefully and not swat it out of midair.

I'm not scared of them, no, but who likes bugs hovering around their face?

Only, as I look at Winnie wearing the widest smile I've seen, I have my answer.

"Off you go, guys. Head back home," she coos to the bees clinging to her. "Okay, perfect. Let's go. The extractor is in the shed and I've already set it up. We can finish up there."

Colt holds the door open for her and we head inside, shutting out the rest of the bees. With all three of us in here, the space feels cramped.

I'm surprised to see she wasn't kidding about setting things up. It looks like a miniature lab in here with a small foldout card table and equipment I've never seen.

I lean against the wall, my arms folded. This industrial-grade honey harvesting was *not* what I had in mind when I came over.

She eyes me like she knows I'm scolding her behind my withering gaze, but all she says is, "Wow, three's company in here for sure. Can I get a little space, guys? I just need to get out of this gear."

I nod pointedly at the wall crammed up behind me, and she rolls her eyes, tugging off the helmet and shaking out her hair.

"Okay, I get it. Just think small."

Think small? Who the hell does she think she is?

But before I can say anything, I get another whiff of her smell, this time from her hair. I close my mouth before anything stupid comes out.

"So next we need to uncap the honey to collect it," she says, standing next to a metal trough. Beside it, there's a gleaming chrome drum with one half of its lid open. "Do you want to try this, Colt? Careful, it's hot."

"Sure!" He takes the knife Winnie gives him and slices down the frames on both sides, which peels the honey off surprisingly neatly. He's intently focused on keeping his hand steady, biting the inside of his cheek.

That's the boy I'm used to, a workhorse with a genuine interest in solving problems, always fascinated by the world around him and willing to learn more.

Not the little shit who sneaks out behind my back to dick around with fireworks.

This Colton Rory will always make me proud.

Winnie shoots me a glance like she knows what I'm thinking—hell, maybe it's written on my face—but she accepts the frames as Colt finishes them, putting them neatly in the extractor.

"Okay! Now we extract the honey. Easy-peasy." She makes sure everything's in place and closes the lid. Almost immediately, the machine whirs, and she nods with approval. "This is a nice newer model."

"Sure," I agree.

I guess my crew must've thought of grabbing some honey for themselves. I didn't even know this stuff was in here.

"Now we just need a jar. Anything like that around?"

"Yeah! I bet we can find something in the kitchen." Colt grins at her.

Winnie sends another quick look at my folded arms. The smile that flashes across her face is small and knowing.

"Let's wrap this up. Better to get your dad out of here before he bursts a blood vessel or something from all this fun."

This time, Colt laughs with glee. It's almost worth being the butt of her dumb jokes to see that expression on his face again.

On the way back to the house, Winnie showers us with

mention your father's the goddamned Attorney General sooner?"

"Oh, um… crap." She winces.

"*Crap* is right."

"I know. I know, you're right to be concerned."

"The Attorney General of Missouri, Winnie. Not just some random business jerkoff."

"I *know*." She wilts, hiding behind her hair before brushing it back from her face. She opens one eye to peek at me. "Will you still keep my secret?"

No woman has the right to be this alluring when she's a walking curse.

"Did I say I wouldn't? I'll keep it, yes, but so far he hasn't given up."

"He called you again? Oh, God."

"A voicemail. To my personal number this time. Who knows where he got that."

She sighs heavily and collapses on the sofa, her head lolling back. From this angle, I can see the way her hair cascades down her neck onto the cushions.

God, this woman.

What the hell is she doing to me, making me think of hair cascading at all?

"You're right," she whispers, looking at me from basically upside down. There's no hint of her earlier joy or the teasing glint in her eyes now. "I haven't been thinking this through. Don't worry, Archer. I'm going to face the music soon, I promise."

"When?" I tap a finger against my bicep, trying to fight back my skepticism.

"My dad can be awful and pushy, but he's not *that* insane. It's a family matter. He won't drag you into court or something."

"A family matter," I echo coldly. "And what? You'll just snap your fingers and fix it?"

With a groan, she heaves herself up and walks over to me.

There's something hollow in her eyes now, like the shimmering happiness before has dried up into a desert. I hate to see it.

Vulnerability, that's what this is.

Every time she mentions her old man, it's like she loses another spark of life.

She stops in front of me and we lock eyes.

"Look, I know you don't trust me. I wouldn't trust me either under the circumstances," she whispers. Her little nails trail up her arms, tracing white lines across her skin. "And I get it, I really do. But this is—this is about the bees." She waves a hand toward the gardens. "This place is everything I need right now, and I think the bees might need me, too."

Fuck.

Here comes the guilt trip, speeding toward me like a train loaded with dynamite, and the worst part is *I get it.*

I really do.

She needs to feel like she has a purpose, some higher calling, something that needs her just as much as she needs it. Hell, I've been there plenty of times.

Colt and the business give me easy closure there.

I don't think about it often, but when my old man died when I was young, I had the same crisis. The whole family spiraled. Three young men who had to grow up mighty fast while Mom confronted her demons at the bottom of a wine bottle.

It's why I joined the army. I needed to feel like I was doing something worthwhile, helping make the world safer and stable when I needed order the most in my life.

And fuck, as I stare down at her, the way she tugs at the

knot holding her blouse together, I know exactly what I'm about to say.

"How long do you need?"

"A month tops. The money's no issue, I promise—"

"I'll clear the schedule for this property. You can have your month here with the bees."

Her mouth drops and her eyes widen. I'm half convinced she's about to hit the floor until she does something worse.

She hugs me.

Not just a little hug, no, not like the ones I get from Junie and Salem when my sisters-in-law come over. Polite little hugs done more from friendly habit.

This is different.

A second later, I'm buried in lush, sweet-smelling woman, rapidly losing every damn bit of my mind.

She's soft and she's warm and her arms are around my neck. Her ear feels cold against my cheek and her hair falls all over my face.

Yes, she smells fucking incredible up close.

Not just the perfume from earlier, but—the *honey?*

Shit.

Before I can even think, I wrap my arms around her tight.

Her hair feels like spun silk. There's no helping the way I caress it, stroking the curls, threading them through my fingers while I breathe her in greedily.

She softens, sinking into me, her breath so hot against my neck.

Fuck me, I hold on tighter.

"Thank you. Thank you, Archer!" Her voice cracks. "This means so much to me, you don't even know."

True.

Right now, I only know one thing—it's been too long since I've had a woman in my arms when this little troublemaker feels this good.

She's a total stranger. A *client.*

I've made a business arrangement with her, and now she's—

She's burying her face in my neck like I've just saved her life. Clinging to me like I've rescued her from drowning or burning alive.

But I haven't, I just agreed to take her money like any other paying guest.

I promised her shelter from the storm in the most miserly, selfish way possible.

Every instinct I have howls at me to keep her where she is, but the thought that I haven't done anything to deserve her gratitude feels shit enough that I ease her back, my hands on her waist.

Her eyelashes are damp as she looks up at me, curiosity sparking in her eyes. It reminds me of the night sky captured in emerald. Her lips part on another breath too much like a low moan, and dammit, I'm still holding her waist.

She's so deliriously soft in my hands, so close.

If I just lean down and claim her bottom lip with my teeth, I'll see how she sounds when she—

The door opens and Colt bounds back in.

"You guys, it's so purple! Like a blueberry smoothie but brighter," he says, like he can't quite believe it, not seeming to notice the fact that I was about two seconds away from breaking every rule about professional relationships.

But he notices a second later and stops mid-step, staring at us like he has to rub his eyes to believe them.

"Shit," I mutter.

I let Winnie go and she stumbles back, rubbing her nose with the back of her hand. Her cheeks are redder than a fire truck.

Though her eyes are still bright with fresh tears, there's

no mistaking it when she looks at Colt. She's still wearing the same confused, happy smile she had before.

The smile I stupidly painted on her face like the grabby, horny old goat I am.

"Sure is, Colt," she says. "If you like, you can take some home, but you'll have to strain it yourself. You can do that through a piece of muslin or a cheesecloth, though. It's easy enough. We can also check the extractor for a little sample."

"Grandma would love it. Right, Dad?" He looks at me for permission.

Anything made with love or artsy passion is Mom's religion.

"She would," I say slowly.

"Great. I'll go check the jar," she says. "There won't be much in there yet, but it'll give you guys a taste, and you can always come back for more."

Fuck no.

The last thing I need is to come back with her here alone. This visit proves I can't be unaccompanied with this woman.

"We'll wait by the car." I hate how damn awkward I sound.

Colt gives me a weird glance that almost wrinkles his nose, but he doesn't say anything as Winnie heads to the shed and I lead him outside.

I have just enough time to get behind the wheel and let Colt climb in the passenger seat before Winnie returns with a mason jar quarter-filled with the most purple honey I've ever seen.

"I know," she says with a sunny smile, giving it the kind of look most people reserve for money or kittens. "Doesn't it look like a dream? You'll have to strain it for good measure—don't eat it as is or you'll get a lot of chewy bits."

"Right." I take the jar from her. "I'll follow up with you about the rental contract soon. Watch your email."

"Thanks."

I start the vehicle, handing the jar to Colt and pulling out onto the road. We ride in silence for a few minutes as he examines the honey, turning it over in the evening light.

The stuff really glows like it's backlit, an edible fantasy prop bizarrely made real.

"Dad, can I ask you something?" he says suddenly. "Are you, like... into Bee Lady?"

"What?" It comes out like a gunshot.

"You just... you're letting her stay. But I can tell you don't really want her to. I overheard you talking to Mrs. Potter at the office, about the trouble Winnie's dad could cause. You hate surprises."

Stupid me. That's what I get for discussing the latest call with our receptionist while I poured coffee in the kitchen.

I should've known the boy eavesdrops like an attentive fox, always listening, even when he looks like he's glued to his phone.

"She's a paying guest, Colt. A few weeks of covered bookings are worth putting up with a little crap," I say calmly.

"Dad, it's okay. You would've told most other people like her to move on by now. Maybe you should, too. Just move on. If you like her, I say go for it."

"I don't *like* her." My voice grates like a rusted engine when I lie this hard. I clear my throat, hot as hell under the collar. "You're reading too much into this, boy. I'm only letting her stay because she's paying. It's business."

"Yeah, but she's *weird*." He laughs. "Weird in a good way, I mean. But still. You don't do weird. Or is this like an opposites attract sort of thing? The girls at school love those books."

"It's an I-will-kick-your-ass if you don't drop it." My face feels molten. "Money's money, Colt. End of story."

Scowling, he goes silent, but I can feel his eyes on me when he's not looking at his phone.

It takes all my willpower not to carry on, building a better lie in my defense.

Whatever, though.

Better to take my own advice and drop it.

Drop her.

Stop thinking about how *good* she felt when I touched her, aching to slide my hands down to her ass.

If only it was that easy.

If only Winnie Emberly didn't give me the worst sweet tooth for something far forbidden than neon-purple honey.

VII: DON'T BEE FOOLISH
(WINNIE)

I give myself two full days of rest.

Two days of absolutely nothing but harvesting honey, geeking out with my online bee people on Reddit and TikTok, and stopping to enjoy life.

Relaxing. Eating well. Sleeping well, even. Turns out, being away from my controlling family and an ex who never loved me works wonders for my mental health.

Who knew?

But now it's time to face the music, just like I promised Archer. Um, never mind the fact that we had a flipping moment.

If Colt hadn't walked in on us, I'm sure his big gruff face would've kissed me—and I wouldn't have objected one bit. I would've loved to feel his beard against my skin when I was already climbing him like a tree.

But the teenager showing up was honestly for the best.

Still, it's not fair leaving Archer to fend off Dad alone.

I know my father, and he's a human dog with a bone. He won't let up once he has someone in his sights, meaning I'll have to persuade him I'm both okay and not coming back.

It's just that…

I chew a nail as I stare at my phone. I've kept it in airplane mode, mostly, only turning it back on for brief stretches when I can stand the message barrage or I want to get online.

Being without it has been kinda liberating. The phone feels like a tether to my old life, and with it off, I can pretend the past doesn't exist.

If only.

With a heavy heart and fingers that absolutely do not shake—because that would be ridiculous—I switch modes and wait for the notifications to come screaming in.

My phone buzzes like a manic vibrator for a good three minutes.

I drum my fingers as I wait.

Finally.

I find my dad's contact and call him.

"Winnie?" he answers instantly, breathing heavily. "Is that you?"

"Hi, Dad. Who else were you expecting?"

Silence.

It spreads down the line like a flash freeze. He just has this weird aura where he doesn't need to say a single word to stop your heart. I guess that comes with being Attorney General, the power to intimidate.

But I'm so sick of it I'm not scared today.

"Winnie," he says, a warning in his voice. "What the hell did you think you were playing at?"

Closing my eyes, I sigh so heavily I'm sure he can feel it in his bones on the other end of the line.

"Isn't it obvious, Dad? Like really?"

"Hardly."

"I couldn't go through with it. The wedding, marrying Holden, living that life… no thanks."

"Winnie—"

"I know. I know I should've made my mind up much sooner, and trust me, I wish I had"—it's not like I wanted to be a pushover for so long—"and yes, I'm *sorry* for putting everybody on the spot and wasting a lot of money. But I couldn't marry a man who didn't love me. I couldn't settle for being his arm candy."

"Goddamn you, stop being so childish," he snarls. "Do you know I nearly launched a statewide manhunt after you left? I was on the phone daily with state troopers. I thought you were mentally unwell, that you'd snapped. For all I know, maybe you have."

"*Dad!* That's not fair. My mind's never been clearer."

"We had a plan, Wynne. Then you burned it and left to chase these—these ridiculous juvenile fantasies."

My spine stiffens.

That's classic Dad, all right, dismissing everyone else's needs as immature perversions because they don't align with his. Has he ever *tried* to relate once?

"I'm not chasing fantasies," I say through gritted teeth. "You're not being fair. I want you to listen."

"Then what *are* you doing? We had everything mapped out, and if it comes down to being happy, Holden would have given you a wonderful life. He would have provided for you, everything you ever needed."

Everything but love, he means.

Without love, I can't do it.

I can't marry a man I have no feelings for.

"I never felt anything for him, Dad. We barely know each other."

"Nonsense! You've been attending charity events and campaign mixers together since you were sixteen. You always sat beside Holden. I made sure of it."

"You tried pairing us off, you mean. That doesn't mean I

knew him, much less liked him." I'm pacing now, frantic energy firing through my veins. "So what if we attended a few stuffy speeches? We barely talked, and when we did, it was always about surface stuff. I know his political ambitions. I know he hates gravy. I know he met three former presidents."

"Now listen—"

"But that doesn't mean anything. I know shit like that about celebrities, people I've never met."

"Watch your language," he says, danger thrumming in his voice.

Oh right, I'd forgotten.

Perfect ladylike daughters of the illustrious Carroll Emberly don't *swear*.

They don't curse or wear short skirts or drink more than two glasses of wine at big glam dinners.

The many times Holden or Dad discreetly stole my second glass of wine from my hand because it wasn't *appropriate*, I swear.

The memory alone leaves me vibrating with rage.

I'm so over it. I can't stop the words spilling out now.

"Holden never once opened up to me," I say. "I don't know anything but the basics about his childhood and growing up as a senator's son. I don't know his fears, his dreams—not his ambitions, but his *dreams*—or his weaknesses."

Dad sighs, pure derision cutting through the phone like a razor.

"Don't do this to me again, Winnie." His voice is heavy and exhausted.

Maybe so, but I'm not stopping.

"I know he's allergic to cats. I know he doesn't like shrimp, but I don't know what he would do if he found a hurt squirrel in his backyard. I don't know what he's like when he's cooking, or even if he *can* cook because we've only eaten at restaurants."

"And? I don't know what that has to do with—"

"I don't know what he looks like first thing in the morning before he's washed his hair. I don't know what he looks like when he laughs—I mean really laughs." Honestly, I'm not sure that man can laugh. I think he's missing the humor gene. "We've been together since..." I stop, thinking back.

Since Dad pushed me into Senator Corban's office as an intern right after college and that stupid Geopolitics degree I never wanted.

Since they organized it and I just went along with it for a couple years because I longed for Dad's approval, and if dating Holden—or pretend dating him—was what it took, I was prepared to do it.

I was ready to put my personal life on the line for someone else's career. Pathetic.

"It's always business with Holden," I say. "He dated me because he had to, because it was the logical step before we could get engaged, and he always put in the bare minimum."

Dad makes a noise of irritation. "Marriage isn't about romance, Wynne. How long do you think that lasts, anyway? A good marriage needs a strong foundation, based on practicality and mutual benefit."

Any questions I had about whether my parents ever loved each other are answered in one fell swoop. My heart pinches.

"Holden behaved like he was *entitled* to me, Dad." I know I sound angry. It's all coming out now, every last scoop of hurt he served up over the years.

"Your union was a hope of ours for a long time."

"That doesn't mean he could come and go as he pleased. It doesn't mean he doesn't have to *try*. Is it so hard to buy me flowers or take me out to a nice orchard with bees? I don't need expensive presents. I just want him to *want* to be with me."

"What are you saying? Of course he wants to be with you." Dad's voice is reasonable now. "I wish you could hear yourself. You're not thinking clearly."

"No, Dad. I'm thinking perfectly clear for the first time in my life. Ever since you told me he was going to propose and you just expected me to say yes."

Why did I say yes?

Why did I go along with any of it when it made me so heartsick?

"He's a forgiving young man," Dad says. "I know this mess has been horribly embarrassing for him as well, but I know he'll be able to move past it if you come back. Just think about it, Winnie. Merging our families means all the resources and opportunities you could ever want for yourself and your future children—"

Children?

Children?

I laugh hysterically, cutting him off.

"Kids? With him? You've *got* to be kidding." There's no way I could have so much as a puppy with that man—literally, too, seeing as Holden is allergic to, like, anything with fur.

How I went this long thinking I could survive with Prince Anti-Charming feels mind-boggling. Totally insane.

"I'm not doing it," I say loudly, in case he hasn't gotten the message. "Marrying Holden—no way. I can't. I won't."

"So what now? You're throwing your whole life away to run off to Kansas City and do what, exactly?"

I swallow thickly.

That's a valid question, but at least for the next month, my life is sorted. "I have… things."

"Things," he spits back. "I see."

"I do! I found a place that needs a beekeeper—"

"Are you serious?" He barks out a brutal laugh that chills my spine before his voice turns glacial. "You're an adult and you can make your own decisions. I can't stop that. However, that doesn't mean we'll stand by and support you while you trash your entire life. Especially when you throw away every opportunity we've ever given you."

"Dad—"

"No, Wynne. Your feelings may matter to you, but they won't change my mind. I also won't have you relying on us to bankroll your mistakes," he says, his voice hard. "Consider your trust gone."

My stomach drops through the floor.

Holy shit.

Holy shit!

The trust is what I've relied on to pay for everything. It's *mine*, and it has been mine since my eighteenth birthday. I haven't been expecting to live off of it forever without working, no, but it was a steady backup. A reliable money cushion.

Having a trust fund is a special privilege I'm very well aware of, yes, so I want to make the most of it, to use it to pursue something that matters.

But now if it's gone—

At least I still have my grandparents' trust. It's not as big, but it'll give me a month here. I can use that time to figure out my plans.

Get a new job somewhere. Start fresh.

"To be clear, that includes your grandmother's trust, too," Dad says. "Until you come back home, you're not getting another cent from us."

"Dad." My voice cracks with panic.

Here come the hot, furious tears.

"Did you think I'd fund your reckless daydreams indefinitely? If you want to do this, you'll do it alone."

Tears sting my eyes.

I'm not relying on my dad to bail me out.

I'm relying on *my* money. It's always been mine, to do whatever I choose.

"You can't," I whisper.

"Can't I?" He softens his tone, placating me. "Come home, and you won't have to worry about this anymore."

"So what, this is blackmail, then? A threat?"

"This is reality, Wynne. Welcome." He's back to being the hard, icy man I remember from my childhood. "I only hope you wizen up soon. Come to your senses before I contact any lawyers."

Before I can say anything, he hangs up.

I stare at my phone blankly.

Lawyers? Is he going to sic his lawyers on me because I don't want an arranged marriage?

Shit.

I shouldn't have spent so much on that stupid last-minute bachelorette party in the Keys with my best friend Lyssie. It was miserable, anyway.

I was sick with anxiety from marrying the wrong man the entire time.

I couldn't enjoy it.

Without the trust money, I have enough for maybe another week or two, if I'm frugal. Then I'm completely homeless.

I drop my head in my hands.

This is awful. Complete disaster.

I have literally nowhere else to go that doesn't involve crawling back to Springfield and winding up at Dad's mercy. Even if I crash with Lyssie, he'll find me.

It's tempting to cry, but after two days of feeling at peace, I don't want to ruin it by bawling my eyes out again.

No matter how short-lived it is now, this place is happy.

When I leave—and I will almost certainly have to leave—I can cry then. I'll spill my tears in a crappy hotel room, if I'm lucky, and a cardboard box if I'm not.

No way am I going back home.

Dad can blackmail me all he likes.

I can get a job as a waitress or something.

I can figure *something* out. I just need time.

I glance at the kitchen and all the sleek new equipment I haven't used yet.

The worst part isn't figuring out what to do from here.

It's having to tell Archer everything before I make any big decisions.

I hate it, but it's only fair.

* * *

THE INTERCOM next to the large gates buzz me in and I pull up outside the front of his house, which looks like it was dropped right out of some modern architecture magazine.

It's all white stone and the two wings flank me on either side. Large windows with black modern frames keep it from looking too old-fashioned.

Hot damn.

I figured he did well for himself, but this is better than I expected. This is actual multimillionaire status, if not billionaire with a *B*.

Not flashy politician money, no, but the kind of wealth from guys like Dad's donors, the people who buy their puppets in government.

Even Dad's historic home looks like a modest bungalow compared to this. Archer Rory's anti-humble home is big enough to rival the richest DC hacks and lobbyists living in Fairfax and Arlington.

How much did this house cost to buy? To build? Five or ten million, at least. And in Kansas City, which hasn't caught up to the pricing insanity of the coasts, that buys you a *lot* of house.

I'm trying to breathe.

Then again, it makes sense he'd have a mansion. It's a family, right?

The Rorys. Of course, they're swimming in money.

Suddenly, the cheesecake in my hands feels like the world's worst peace offering. It basically screams 'I'm broke, save me.'

I mean, yes, technically that's what *I'm* screaming, but now that I'm here, this whole thing feels like a mistake. A sitcom setup for a funny humiliation.

I rap on the large black door before I can change my mind, though, and for good luck press the doorbell linked to the camera that's wired in.

I'm expecting a butler to answer, wondering who this peasant is intruding on his master's turf.

But there's nothing from the screen.

In the time it takes for someone to come to the door—probably because they had to trek across the Atlantic to get here—I've rethought every life decision and concluded they're all wrong.

This is probably the most wrong yet.

But maybe no one heard the doorbell? They might not be home.

Maybe I should leave while I can and pretend this never happened, before I embarrass myself and—

Then that huge black door groans open.

"Hey, Winnie. I thought it might be you." Colt stands on the other side. The lazy surprise on his face becomes a welcoming grin. "You here to see Dad?"

"If he's around, yes. Um, I looked you guys up. I brought

cheesecake." I hold up the glass container with my pathetic offering.

"Cool!" His face lights up, which eases this torture a tad. I still wish I'd brought something else, or at least remembered a gold serving dish under it. "He's in his office. I'll let him know you're here."

As I step inside the mansion—literal *mansion*—following his lead, I'm greeted with soaring walls, gorgeous high-ceilings brimming with natural light, and a wooden floor that leads me into a wide, open concept kitchen with a huge dining room attached.

Colt scampers off, and I take my time looking around.

I wonder how you ever get used to a house like this. Do you ever learn to stop feeling small?

I thought the kitchen at my cabin was impressive, but this is like four times bigger, with dark marble counters, a large island, and a rounded old-world arch leading into the dining room, which is flanked by bookshelves along the walls that reach to the ceiling.

So many books.

It's like a mini library, except for one wall by the window overlooking an insanely large garden and pool. There's nowhere to sit except the huge dining room table, all stunning and glossy wood, large enough to seat... a lot of people.

There are also red paintings of cardinals hanging on the walls. They all look like the same artist's work, the birds striking different poses in new landscapes and seasons.

I'm sensing a theme.

"Gorgeous," I murmur, reaching out to touch the modern frame. The signature in the painting's corner is large and loopy, with a *D* and a *R* intertwined, but I can't quite make out the name.

"Winnie."

I whip around to face the voice behind me, clamping a hand over my mouth.

"Oh—hi. You... you startled me."

"Clearly." Archer folds his arms as he looks at me, more bear than man.

It's insane how hard he rocks the daddy look. Like you'd *know* he's a dad just by looking at him, stoic and intense and maddeningly hot.

He's just wearing trousers and a button-down shirt today, no jacket to be seen. And holy hell, it shows off his shoulders, two massive hills honed by pushing boulders. What does this man *eat*?

"What are you doing here?" he demands.

Right. Back to business.

I clear my throat, nodding at the painting I was admiring. "They're so pretty. I was just wondering where they came from."

"Oh, that." His arms loosen slightly. "They're my mother's. She's been painting for years."

"Cardinals, huh? Is she big into birds? They're really pretty."

"They've become a family symbol of sorts." His mouth opens like he wants to say more but thinks better of it. "Colt says you brought cake."

"Oh, yeah!" I gesture at the container on the table, which looks laughably tiny in this cavernous room. "It's not much, but I figured I should bring you a peace offering."

"What peace offering? Didn't know we were at war." After raking his eyes over my body, he picks up the cake and cracks the lid open to sniff. "Smells good," he says, and I swear there's a trace of surprise in his voice. "What is it?"

"Cheesecake. Honey and lemon. I whipped it up with some of the honey from the hives."

"I see the purple. Impressive, knowing that's not dye." He

puts the cake back down and turns his attention to me, which I could do without because now I'm ready to throw myself on his mercy and my courage is sputtering. My cheeks are red, mere seconds from combusting. "So why are you here?"

"Well." Deep breath. "I thought begging might work better in person than over the phone."

"Begging?" His frown hasn't left his face, which makes me feel worse.

I'm in his space, making him feel weirded out, and it's so large and elegant and oh my God this is humiliating.

"I spoke to my dad earlier today..." I draw in a long breath and exhale, focusing on not letting it shake on its way out. You know, just in case I'm tempted to fall apart. I wrap my arms around my shoulders, hoping I can hold myself together. "He's kind of a control freak. Maybe you guessed that. He likes to keep a tight lid on money that's rightfully mine."

"I see," he says slowly.

"And right now, the lid just kinda stuck—it's locked. Permanently. Like throw away the key." This time, I can't stop my voice from shaking.

My eyes sting.

I blink harshly, another black mark on the long list of embarrassing things I've done in front of this man.

But he's so close to me now.

I don't even know when he got this close, but I can see every detail of his blue-and-white striped shirt, so tight against his biceps it looks like it's painted on.

His sharp scent washes over me. No man has any right to smell this good, like mint and citrus and fresh laundry thrown together in this unholy union.

God, it would be so easy to lean forward.

To rest my forehead on his chest, safe and secure in his wall of heated human stone.

"I can't afford the cabin anymore," I blurt out. I have to say something before I lose my courage and start honking ugly sobs. "I thought I could, honestly, but he's pissed that I'm not coming home and—" The lack of oxygen makes my head spin, and I take a breath. "And the point is, I don't get access to my money again unless I go home. He's holding everything except my bank account hostage."

Archer's mouth is a hard, flat line.

Big surprise.

I'd be pissed too if this weird bee girl showed up with a runaway bride sob story to complicate my life. I've already cost him his patience, his time, his sanity—and now I'm asking for his financial well-being, too.

I don't let myself stare at his face for too long.

"I see," he says again, this strangely gentle tone that says maybe he really does understand.

"I'm so sorry, Archer. I never meant for any of this to happen. The last thing I wanted was to make myself your problem." My whole body is shaking now. *Get it together, Winnie.* "I know this is dumb and you must be furious. I know—"

"Winnie, stop. Just look at me and breathe," he rumbles.

He's even closer now.

I can feel his wonderful body heat, this invisible aura comforting me, stroking me like a kitten right down to my bones.

He's so tall. I have to look up to meet his gaze and those ice-blue eyes that aren't so icy after all.

In fact, they're more like a wide, welcoming sky.

I blink so fast it hurts.

Sad, scalding tears fall down my face.

The shame just keeps piling up. This is the third time I've cried in front of him.

"Breathe," he says again.

I hadn't thought this bear of a man could sound so gentle. He runs a hand up my arm to my shoulders and the gesture is so reassuring, I have to fight to keep my eyes up. If I'm not careful, I'm going to melt right into him.

"I'm really sorry to come here like this, crying all over you. To even *ask* for something I don't deserve."

"Enough. Stop apologizing." The corner of his mouth twitches like he wants to smile, but he holds back, his eyes speaking with warmth and seriousness. "It's going to be okay. Whatever else happens, I need you to know that."

"Easy for you to say," I whisper.

"We'll work something out. It's a premier property and this involves the company, so I'll have to talk to my brothers, but they're not unreasonable. No one's throwing you out on the street, Winnie."

I frown, trying to hash out what he's telling me.

"You mean you're... not kicking me out?" My knees feel like they'll crumble under me.

"Nah." The other side of his mouth twitches and he loses his grimness. "You've just tapped into a honey gold mine on our property, right? Why the fuck would I fire my top bee expert?"

Holy hell.

Only Archer flipping Rory could leave my heart in shambles with a single question.

I sniff back the ugliness, wiping under my eyes. "That's crazy generous, but I'm no expert. I don't have a degree in entomology or anything. I just love bees."

"False modesty. You're a bee nerd and you ought to be proud of it."

"No, really, I…" I finally figure out what he's doing. "Oh. Well, I mean, I guess I'm not *not* an expert."

"There we go." Just like that, he slides an arm around my shoulders and tucks me against him.

I look up to find his eyes fixed on my face. Such warmth, such fire, it curls my toes and sends heat flooding my veins.

Twisting to get a better look at him, I balance myself with a hand on his arm. It feels way too natural, too easy, too close to a real attraction.

If we're not careful, this could get very weird. Especially if I can't make myself care whether or not it's right and—

"Dad! Hey, Dad!" Colt comes pounding through the kitchen to where we're standing.

Archer springs back, releasing me like I just burned him. His cheeks are heated and mine are definitely torched.

Why do they always say karma's a bitch?

Because I think déjà vu might be worse.

Colt stops and looks between us, but his eyes are wide with whatever news he's brought, demanding his dad's attention.

"Um, just thought I'd let you know Mom's here," he says urgently.

Oh.

Oh.

Oh, flaming crap. The *wife*.

How could I forget?

Just thinking a man like this would be alone with a kid, that's the height of insanity.

About as crazy as almost kissing a married man and then blubbering all over him.

Archer takes another step away from me and clears his throat as I stare numbly at the cake, feeling like I've had a bucket of cold water tossed in my face.

Archer has a wife. Colt's mom.

Of course, of course.

And while he was comforting me, all soft and sexy and tender, I let my idiot brain fly off into fantasyland, where men built like oak trees and richer than sin magically fall in love with girls who have nothing but honey to their names.

I willingly forgot there must be a woman in his life.

It all makes perfect sense, though.

But for some reason I don't dare focus on, the thought of a wife stings. It's becoming a huge effort to breathe for a different reason now.

Congratulations, Winnie Emberly.

You just won the Too Stupid To Live award.

VIII: BEE IN YOUR EAR (ARCHER)

*S*onofafuck.
Shit.
Rina? Rina here, right now?

Her timing couldn't be worse.

Colt keeps looking at me, waiting for some answer, but the wires in my brain are too crossed to process this bullshit.

One second, I had Winnie in my arms, crying and begging for a favor and feeling too damn good. The next, my ex-wife shows up to hammer my coffin shut.

This day is cursed.

"Dad?" Colt asks when I don't move.

"You guys are busy, that's cool. I should be going," Winnie says abruptly, taking another step away. "Enjoy the cake! We can talk later about anything else. I have your number, Archer."

"Wait, hold up." I massage my temples. "Colt, stay here. I need to speak with your mother for a minute. Winnie—"

"No, it's fine. I'm sorry for taking up your time," she says, still retreating away from me.

She looks like a frightened deer, ready to flee, tucking her auburn hair behind her ear and not meeting my eyes.

That's also my fault.

I shouldn't have tried to comfort her. But when she said her tyrant father cut her off from her inheritance, it set off a bomb under my ribs.

Watching her desperation, seeing her cry—or at least, trying valiantly not to break—just made it worse.

What choice did I have?

Her dad is a royal piece of shit, Attorney General or not.

I had to step in, to give this vulnerable young woman some breathing space. The only thing she truly asked me for.

I saw the whole universe looking at me through her, asking for a favor, and I answered.

Now, since no good deed goes unpunished, I've got Rina on my doorstep, waiting to fuck with my head.

There's nothing else I can bark at Winnie to make her stay, especially with Colt standing there, so I stride through the house to where Rina waits outside the front door.

It's been several years since I last saw her face-to-face. One glimpse reminds me time is passing.

She looks healthier than the last time I saw her, her cheeks less gaunt and some wiry muscle running along her thin arms.

She still looks like a walking paint splatter. Bright-red pants and a dark-blue and white shirt that's a couple sizes too big. There's a scarf over her chestnut hair and oddly colored contacts in her eyes. Indigo-violet.

The kids would call this look Boho, I think. To me, it's just modern hippie shit.

For Colt's sake, I'm glad she looks like she's in a better place, even if I'd love to snap my fingers and make her instantly vanish.

Sighing, I fold my arms and lean against the doorframe,

praying Winnie doesn't choose this moment to run out of the house. If she just gives me a few seconds, I'll have Rina out of here.

"What do you want?" I demand.

"Hello to you, too, Arch. You're as pleasant as ever, I see." There are even more tattoos up Rina's arm than I remember, all mystical-looking faces and symbols. I notice them as she rubs a hand up it. "Can we stop the glaring? Can't a girl drop in and see her son?"

"You mean the son you walked out on a long time ago? That son?" Barely two sentences and I'm already fuming. I don't give her time to respond. "Drop-ins aren't welcome here. We live a busy life."

Drop-ins also aren't typical for her. At all.

Usually, she just takes Colt on her time off for vacations or the odd holiday every year or two, and that's that.

She'd make a better aunt than a mother, the cheery, distant kind you only hang out with once a year before they disappear into the ether again.

I've been fine with this pattern because it's predictable.

The last thing Colt needs at this stage in his life is a loose fucking cannon of a mother hanging around, becoming a bad influence. He's at the age where he needs good people who really care about him. Stability. Order.

Undaunted, Rina purses her lips as she looks at me. The hole where her lip piercing used to be seems larger than ever.

"Who's this?" She smiles wide enough to eat her face.

Her gaze flicks past me. I bite back a groan.

Of fucking course.

Of course, Winnie chooses this exact second to head out.

"Oh," Rina says, stepping back to let Winnie pass. "Sorry, Archer. I didn't realize I was interrupting time with your girlfriend."

My girl—

What the fuck?

"Sorry, sorry!" Winnie hisses as she breezes past. "I really should be going. Archer, thanks again, and let me know what you think of the cheesecake."

Disaster.

Rina tilts her head like the smuggest creature alive as she looks up at me, a thin smile playing at the corner of her mouth. "Interesting. Colt never mentioned her."

"No need. She's just—a friend. Also, since when does my private life concern you?"

My skin burns behind my beard.

Shit, why is this a thousand times more embarrassing than it has to be? Even if Winnie *was* my girlfriend, what does it matter?

Rina and I were done a decade ago.

She's been out of my life for ages. She doesn't get to have an opinion on what I do anymore, much less a say.

Doesn't change the fact that this is goddamned miserable.

There's a knowing look in her eyes. If I'm not careful, she'll call me out for blushing like a kid at prom.

"Well, can I come in?" She doesn't really ask, brushing past me like she owns the place.

Enough of this shit.

Snarling, I grab her arm. I'm about to push her the hell out of my house when Colt appears at the end of the foyer.

He just stands there, watching us intently.

For a second, he's not thirteen, he's five again.

And here I am, manhandling his mother's arm like she's a prowler barging in to raid the house.

"Dad?" he asks, his voice small. "Is everything okay?"

Rina lights up in a way I didn't know she could.

Everything about her is brighter, airier—her eyes under those stupid contacts, her smile, the way she holds out her free arm to him.

"Oh, Colt! Baby!" she croons, beckoning him closer. "I came to see you, honey."

Colt glances at me and after a second, I release her arm with a sigh that grates my throat.

Rina flings herself forward with her arms outstretched, waiting as he walks toward us. When he's close enough, she folds him up in the world's most awkward hug.

He's almost taller than she is now, and he keeps looking at me over her shoulder for reassurance.

Yeah, this is weird, and not just because two of the three people standing here wish the other one never existed.

Rina's always been an absentee mother. If it wasn't for the fact that Colt deserves to have some kind of mom in his life, I would have cut her ass out years ago.

Her very presence rings alarm bells. She's either decided to be more active in his life or she wants something.

Probably more cash to fund her wanderlust and endless art projects. It wouldn't be the first time. It's not alimony ordered by a court, more like *fuck off* money I send every few years as ex-wife repellent.

But Colt, he's smiling at her now as she pulls back and pats his cheek affectionately.

"Holy crap, Colton, you've gotten so big," she gushes, tears in her eyes. "When did that happen?"

When you weren't around to see it. Obviously.

"I'm thirteen, Mom," Colt says.

"I know *that*, baby. It's just, well… it's like you're a new person every time I see you. I have to relearn how to hug you, that's all." Her smile fades, turning wistful now. I've never seen her like this. "Are you holding up okay?"

"I'm fine."

Holding up? As if I'm not the reason he's happy and healthy and mostly keeping out of trouble?

"Of course you are! You look great. Your dad looking

after you okay? Helping you with schoolwork?" The audacity of her question makes me bristle, and she shoots me a quick, nervous glance before adding, "I'm sure he does."

"Why are you *here*, Rina?" I bite off again. We've moved past the glaring stage to proper death stare. The front door is still hanging open and I'm happy for it to stay that way. The sooner she leaves, the better. "What's going on with you?"

"Nothing's 'going on,' Archer. I told you, I came to see Colt." She wraps a protective arm around his shoulders, flashing me a pouty look.

What the hell ever.

If she wants to have this talk in front of our son, I can play ball.

I push past her to the great room. The white sofas are all gathered around the glass table and large doors that slide open to the patio. It's the first time she's been here since the place was remodeled, and her eyes are wide.

"Shit, Arch." She laughs as she looks around. "Do you ever slow down and take a break from showing off?"

"I have good taste and watch your language." I sit on the sofa, folding my legs.

"*Dad*. It's not like I haven't heard it before. You swear all the time." Colt stops trailing Rina like a puppy and sits beside me.

"Doesn't mean you need to hear it from your mom." I know I'm being a flaming hypocritic here. I've slipped up and sworn in front of Colt often enough, but the fact that she's here doing it uninvited pisses me off.

Rina touches a hand to her dark brunette hair, cut short now. It's stylish, though lost in the dangling orange earrings that look like miniature dreamcatchers.

She's always been a mix of things, a human tornado in the worst way.

Aside from being half the reason Colt exists, she's the biggest mistake of my life.

She's someone I figured out I don't need around after enough grief. Especially now, when I'm dealing with whatever mess Winnie and her family are about to bring crashing down on my head.

"This is so formal," Rina says after a moment. She taps her fingers against the white leather. She's nervous, being here after so long, I realize.

That figures, seeing as she's ghosted for so long.

What I really want to do is chew her up and spit her out like bad bread. Not to mention give her the hell she deserves for checking out of Colt's life before I send her packing.

Preferably without a check or whatever she's angling for now, but if it speeds this shit up, I'll bribe her.

Only, with Colt sitting beside me, I remember we're his parents. Rina's his mother forever, no matter how much I regret our relationship.

"Okay," I say, spreading my hands across my knees. "Are you really back in town for Colt, Ri?" The nickname falls off my lips accidentally.

I curse myself. Fucking bad habits.

After so long, you'd think they'd slough off like dead skin.

She blinks, maybe at the nickname, but recovers quickly. "Yes, I am. You don't sound convinced."

"Not the point," I mutter, shaking my head. I inhale slowly. Here goes. "If you're looking to spend time with your son, we can figure something out. As long as Colt agrees."

Her eyes flick to Colton, who squirms uncomfortably.

"Course I want to, Mom," he says. "That's cool with you, right, Dad?"

"Sure, sure. I just need to know it in advance, and it needs to be planned. Can't have anything disrupting your schoolwork." I aim a sharp look at Rina. "Colt has a busy summer. Another accelerated class for college prep."

"That's my little genius," Rina says quickly. She smiles, hands working on her lap, subtly stroking her fingers in this nervous tic she's always had. "We can pull something together ahead of time. Most of my weekends are free."

Colt smiles shyly.

I take a deep breath. This is what being a divorced parent really means. Letting your boy spend time with his deadbeat mom because it makes him happy.

"What are you up to now, hon? More chemistry?" Rina blinks happily.

"It's just summer school, Mom," he offers. "For math."

"A calculus course through a local university," I tell her. "If he completes the class with a C or better, he gets college credit. It's Colt, so he'll get it."

As long as he isn't distracted with any stupid goddamned drama you've towed here, I don't add, though I'm thinking about it.

"Oh, hey, that's awesome." Rina gives me a startled look. I force a smile to reassure her it's a good thing. "Nice one, kiddo! Guess you inherited your dad's brains for numbers."

I hate the way she sounds so surprised.

If she bothered reading one damn report card I email her every few months, she'd know exactly how gifted he is.

Colt glances at me mischievously. "Grandma says I'm smarter than Dad was."

"That's because I was part troublemaker. You're not doing that," I growl, ruffling his hair. "There was a time when my folks thought I'd never graduate."

"Wasn't Uncle Pat worse?"

"Uncle Pat was the youngest, so he had to make a choice between being the hardest working—which Uncle Dex had in the bag—or being the brat." And obviously, he chose the easier route.

Until he wound up with an instant wife and kid, along with the scare of his life, I would've said he was destined to continue being a little punk forever.

It's weird to think how we all wound up here.

Especially because when we were kids, we couldn't stand each other. Now we're co-owners of a company. Successful, as Rina pointed out.

She gives a small, unsure smile.

"Just let me know when you're free, okay? We'll figure it out."

"Sure." I stand, signaling this meeting is over, and thankfully she gets the hint. I guess I gave her enough of what she came for. She doesn't argue as I lead her back to the front door and out.

I'm still bracing to be hit with a money request the second we're alone.

"See ya soon, Colt," she says brightly, giving him another hug. This one seems less awkward, but it still looks like neither of them know what to do with each other.

Colt is all lanky arms and legs she isn't used to, so she pats his back with hesitant hands.

"See you soon, Mom."

"Archer. Arch." She swallows as she looks at me. "Thank you."

I give her a curt nod, escorting her out, biting my tongue the whole way.

I don't breathe again until she heads back to her Jeep, gets in it, and pulls away.

Goddamn.

This nightmare could've been a lot worse, all things considered.

I exhale slowly, trying to pull all expression from my face —mostly suspicion and frustration. It feels too easy.

Rina coming back like this must mean something's up, and nothing good.

"Mom seems different," Colt says as we both watch her drive away. The automatic gates close behind her.

"I guess."

"Do you think she's okay?"

"She's fine, Colt. She came here for you, right?" I clap him on the back before heading back inside.

Never mind different.

For Rina, this was totally out of character, and that's what gnaws at me.

I don't know what's coming, but it feels like another bucketload of chaos.

* * *

It turns out I don't need to call a meeting to discuss Winnie's situation.

Dexter is ready to fire full throttle with his starry-eyed St. Louis expansion plan. After Rina leaves and I get my head screwed back on, I head into the Higher Ends office.

We chose the Cardinal Conference Room at our headquarters in Lee's Summit. With the traffic and everything else that's happened today, I'm almost five minutes late.

My brothers beat me there, seated with their laptops open, ready to laugh at me. Dex already has the projector on when I walk in.

"You're late. Is today the apocalypse?" Patton leans back as I shut the door behind me, tilting the chair off its wheels.

"Sit properly before you break your neck, dickhead."

"You're never late."

Dex taps his pen against the large table. "He's not wrong. What happened? Traffic?"

"I would've settled for a fender bender," I say, grabbing

the closest chair. "You really want to know, Rina dropped by."

"Oh, shit." Dex drops his pen. "Rina as in... *Rina-Rina?*"

"Rina as in my ex-wife from Satan's Express Rina, yes." I eye the screen, which shows a picture of a high-rise in what I'm guessing is St. Louis.

"Whoa." Pat lets his chair hit the ground, leveling himself out. "Don't think you're getting away without talking about this, Bro. Rina? What the fuck?"

"Mom mentioned she was back in town," Dexter says. It's so unexpected, I stare at him. He wrinkles his nose. "Rina visited her yesterday, I guess. I heard about it this morning."

"Mom?" My throat goes dry.

That suspicion I had earlier tastes like burning bile.

"Guess she wants something," Patton says. "What did she ask you?"

"She wants more time with Colt."

Dexter frowns. "No money? She's not dying, is she?"

I snort, though the idea crossed my mind. Next time I talk to her, I need to do some fishing. See if I can find out if she's come down with a terminal illness or some shit.

"You guys need to talk, even if you're on shitty terms," Pat announces. "This book I read says it's all about communication. You just need the right place and time—uh, maybe a mediator in your case."

"Fucking hell, dude. Just because you're happily married doesn't make you a shrink." I nod at the screen. "Any new info for us?"

"I've got some options out east, yes," Dexter says. "But we were still talking about you."

Damn them.

I drag a hand over my face.

Who knows if they're trying to help out or if they're just crapping on me for entertainment.

"Don't you start too," I growl.

"You were late over it, dude," Patton reminds me. "Over *Rina*."

Actually, the reason I was late wasn't because I was thinking about Rina. Sure, her storming back into my life was annoying, but it's Winnie who's crashed my day.

Miss Sugarbee keeps crowding my head like a weed.

The way she looked at me, all dewy eyes and heat and longing, like she *wanted* to be in my arms. Maybe she wanted more, the same hunger I sensed back at Solitude, when I held her too long and pressed her too close for common sense.

And fuck, maybe I wanted more, if I'm being brutally honest.

For an insane minute, I forgot who the fuck I was.

I forgot who *she* was and what we were doing.

If there's any silver lining to Hurricane Rina, it's that. My ex-wife reminds me how much I've already paid for woman trouble.

But I promised Winnie I'd talk to my brothers about her plight, and here I am. I tap the table. "Let's talk about St. Louis."

After groaning his disappointment, Dex presents his findings.

He suggests working our next place into a thriving green zone for people in the city center. Renewable energy, plants and flowers in the building itself, a smoothie and juice bar like the one Salem suggested in our Kansas City property.

We're eyeing a property outside an older part of the city, a concrete wasteland lacking a lot of parks and well-lit spaces.

It's in line with the direction the city council leans, plus it'll give us advertising you can't buy.

I have to hand it to him—it's not bad.

People love green plants and healthy amenities, now

more than ever. Even if Junie had a hand in encouraging him to go this route, it could catch on.

Even Patton doesn't object.

"It's decent," he admits, looking at the graph of projected revenue over a five-year period. "Not my style, but some people have no taste. If we can keep the branding, it's workable."

"You got The Cardinal in Kansas City. This one's mine," Dexter says pointedly. He turns to me. "What do you think, Arch?"

"Looks good, yeah." I run my pen through my fingers, blinking several times at the screen.

"That's it? That's all you've got to say? No ripping us a new asshole while you blow your stack over risks and why we should settle for safer growth?" Dexter blows a breath through his teeth. "Okay, man. What is going on?"

"There's one secondary issue I wanted to bring up." Now's as good a time as ever, I guess, and I might as well go for it. "You know Solitude?"

Patton and Dexter trade glances.

"You mean the cabin?" Patton asks slowly. "Yes, we're familiar."

"It's currently occupied and due to unforeseen circumstances, our current guest can't pay for the full stay they booked." I toy with how many details to give them, but my brothers are sharks. I can't afford to give them any blood. "This guest has a very serious personal situation. I promised I'd see what I could do to extend their time. They're an expert on bees and they've promised to help out in exchange."

"Bees? Hold on, I'm not following." Dex taps his pen loudly against the table like a drum. "Are you, Archer Rory, saying you want us to give this person a *free stay*?"

"Not free," I correct. "Apparently, the bee boxes our landscaping crew installed turned up something interesting. They produce rare honey. Supposedly. It's definitely purple, I've seen it myself. Sh—*our guest* knows how to extract the honey and says we can sell it. The stuff may get a decent price."

"Decent? How decent? Like does this purple honey outshine a barrel of oil?" Patton taps a few keys on his laptop. "Oh," he says, giving me a sly glance. "I get it now."

"What?" Dexter pulls the laptop closer, takes a good, long look, and grins. "Oh, wow. It all makes sense now. It's a *woman.*"

"Is she cute?" Patton asks. "Shit, I want to see her. She must be a knockout to turn Arch into Mr. Charity."

"Fucking hell, guys, this isn't about how cute she is. Knock it off."

"So she *is* cute?"

I glower at Dexter. "It's none of your damn business what she looks like."

"Okay. So Rina's back in town," Patton muses. "How's that going for you?"

"For fuck's sake, guys." I pinch my nose, wishing I could go back in time and start my own company. I could've taken the financial hit without ever speaking to these idiots. "This doesn't have anything to do with Rina."

"Doesn't it, though?" Dexter's grin makes me want to throw him off a cliff. "You're telling me you're *not* doing a fake-girlfriend thing to keep Rina off your back?"

"Hell no." *Not yet anyway.* "That's your territory."

"Worked out pretty well in my experience. Five stars. Would gladly find my wife again by pretending to date her first."

"That's not what you thought at the start of it," I snarl, then stop myself. "Look, I barely know the girl. She just wound up in a dicey situation."

"What kind of dicey? This better not have anything to do with mobsters or poisoned kids." Patton turns to Dexter. "But hey, it turns out he's got a heart. Who'd have thought? Christmas is saved."

"Fuck you entirely," I spit. "Look, this honey thing could be a potential gold mine. I did some digging. It's very rare when it's as neon-purple as this stuff and the markup on organic honey like this gets insane."

They both stare at me like bored cats.

I'm not convincing either of them. Hell, I'm not sure I'm convincing myself.

It's not like I'm doing this for the honey.

If Winnie hadn't cried—if she hadn't felt like heaven in my arms—maybe I wouldn't have been so determined to help out, but that's a strong maybe.

Hard truth is, there's something about her.

The vulnerability, the way she flinches away from certain things like they sting, it makes me want to fix this girl.

A new emotion, I'll admit.

I'm not the type of guy who walks around with a savior complex.

My brothers damn sure aren't used to seeing it, either.

I don't charge in and help people without good reason. Normally, I make the hard decisions in this business. I don't flinch at the consequences.

Shit, what if it's as simple as they say? The fact that she's cute?

But how many attractive women have thrown themselves at my feet over the years? Winnie hasn't even done that.

She hasn't done anything to indicate she wouldn't slap me silly if I tried to kiss her.

With her background in bloodthirsty politics, I'm just another rich guy. I don't stand out like a demigod who draws gold diggers.

Frankly, I doubt she knows who or what I am beyond Higher Ends, considering she isn't local. The Rory name means next to nothing in Springfield, let alone DC.

Except the way she looked at me earlier, when I comforted her...

Crap.

What the fuck am I getting myself into?

Patton tucks his hands behind his head again as he watches me, an unidentifiable expression on his face which can't mean anything good.

"Archer, you lucky dog, here's a bone. If Dex agrees, we won't kick your little honey out if she doesn't have anywhere else to stay. At least for a little while."

"We can take the loss. Maybe write it off as charity. I'll ask our CPA," Dexter agrees. "*Especially* if it means that much to you."

I don't bother correcting him.

I just clamp my teeth together and don't say a word.

Neither of these clowns will believe me. The more I fight back, the more they'll think I'm already fucking her nightly.

"Let's say a couple weeks for now," I say, slipping back into business mode. "After that, we can discuss it again if it's still applicable."

Patton gives me a shit-eating grin. "You mean when you know her better."

"Fuck you." I roll my eyes.

Though, somehow, I have a feeling he's right.

There's no way to do this good deed without getting more tangled up with this woman and the crazy she brings in her wake.

A woman like Winnie Emberly doesn't come streaking into your life like a comet without making an impact.

I just have to brace for catastrophe and hope the carnage isn't permanent.

IX: WANNA SEE YOU BEE BRAVE (WINNIE)

Maybe it's the emotional whirlwind I've been through these past few days, but I can't, for the life of me, figure out why Archer Rory wants to meet at The Sugar Bowl.

Don't get me wrong, it's a sweet place. Literally.

This cute little bakery lined with old photos of smiling people from floor to ceiling, scrumptious desserts, an adorable founding granny, and many, many awards they've won.

Archer wasn't too transparent when he texted me the directions.

From the minute I showed up, the neon lights and picture-perfect cakes and confections in the window told me this place is going to be good.

Of course, it's the same bakery I've been ordering my pity-party breakup boxes and unhealthy breakfasts from. My mouth waters just from stepping inside and inhaling the doughy air and so many other smells.

Chocolate. Cinnamon. *Miracles.*

If I'm being honest, I'd pop into plenty of bakeries in

Springfield and DC too. Holden used to call my sweet tooth 'unhealthy,' but I like to think it's sophisticated.

If people can be wine snobs, why can't they go to pieces over a heavenly eclair, or a bear claw so glazed you can skate on it?

I wish I had time to bake more myself.

I wish my parents let me, back when I lived at home.

I've watched so many episodes of *The Great British Bake Off* that I could lecture you about the best way to make macaroons.

This place has macaroons, too. Lavender and chocolate and lemon and—

Okay, focus!

None of this gives me a clue about why Archer summoned me here.

I spin around the middle of the floor, though, my bag clamped firmly to my side, just vibing in the carefree atmosphere.

There's a rack overhead with hanging plants draped through the slats. Tables are clustered together at friendly intervals, and there's so much wood and old-school tile walls.

Archer isn't here yet.

I check the time and pick a table in the corner. There's a menu already posted, a little leather booklet with gorgeous photos of desserts.

Yes, this place is magical.

Arriving early means I'm perfectly positioned to see Archer when he shows up. I don't have to wait long, and when he does...

You know how it is in movies when time slows down and dramatic music swells as soon as the immaculately dressed hero arrives with the wind tossing his hair?

It's that moment exactly, minus the background track.

And he walks toward the nonexistent camera after a quick scan around the room.

That moment, but real life.

This man is inhumanly attractive.

The whole big daddy package with dark hair brushed back from his forehead, piercing blue eyes, and stubble that would make every inch of a girl's skin tingle in the best way.

Today, he's gone casual with jeans and a white tee that shows off a tattoo wrapping up one arm.

Holy hell.

…is that a freaking eagle attacking a snake? No, the bird doesn't look quite right. It's smaller, shaped more like a cardinal.

I can't make out all the fine details, but I see enough. It's so whimsical and unexpected I smile.

Be still my beating heart.

And God, this man is sculpted. His biceps strain the sleeves of his shirt—which should be illegal, by the way—and I can appreciate the incredible Atlas-worthy breadth of his shoulders.

He really looks like he's ready to take on the world without a complaint.

He swings into the seat across from me and nods at the menu, giving me time to recover my wits and tuck my jaw back into place.

"Hey, Winnie."

"Hi," I say, thankful my voice still works and isn't dripping with dumb, flirty desire. *I hope.*

"See anything you want here?"

He's talking about the menu. *The menu, girl.*

"See anything I *don't* want, you mean? This place is divine." My face screws up with delight. "But honestly, I'm a chocoholic, so I'll probably try that volcanic brownie with toffee apple sauce."

"You sure you don't want the special?" He reaches over, showing off his designer watch as he hands me a smaller laminated menu I hadn't noticed before. "Honey cupcakes. With fresh honey and cream cheese frosting."

"Oh. My. God. Now I know why you brought us here."

I don't, but he smiles—an amazing smile, not just a ghostly switch of his lips—which makes me think I've never seen him truly smile before.

This one actually lights up his face.

Those dark-blue eyes of pure sorcery go from calm secrets to open night sky.

I think I stop breathing.

"My sister-in-law owns this place. Thought you might like it," he says.

"You're a little late to the party," I say, recovering my voice. "I've been ordering stuff from this place for days. I can't believe I missed the cupcakes, though. Honey cupcakes, *shit!*" I hold the menu to my heart. "Your sister-in-law is a genius. I bet we'll hit it off like besties."

I realize my mistake as soon as I say it. *I bet we'll hit it off like besties.*

Like we're going to ever meet.

Like there's a *reason* I should meet his brilliant baker sister-in-law.

"I mean, *if* I ever meet her," I garble, "which I won't, because... why would I? She sounds like a great person, though. I admire anyone who runs a place this cool."

Like he hasn't even registered my mammoth stupidity, Archer looks over the menu and waves to a server. She's a young, pretty girl with brown hair in springy curls and soulful dark eyes, a college girl, maybe.

Really, she's probably just a couple of years younger than me.

"Two honey cupcakes and an espresso, please." He looks at me expectantly. "What do you want to drink?"

I scan the laminated menu with the drink selection—sodas, coffees, hot chocolates, milkshakes—and settle on a Bittersweet Mocha with locally made dark chocolate and cane sugar. The girl takes the order and heads to the back.

Archer leans forward, bracing his tree branch forearms on the table.

"I spoke with my brothers yesterday. It's good news," he says, watching me intently.

"I can stay?"

"As our temporary resident bee specialist, yes. That's the deal. I told them you were going to tap the honey and help us get it analyzed, or whatever you do with the purple stuff."

I laugh. Honestly, the way he knows nothing about bees is kinda adorable.

Then again, adorable feels like the wrong word for a literal giant who inherited all the grumpy genes.

"Don't worry. I have *every* intention of getting my hands messy with that honey. There are labs that can help us figure out its medicinal benefits if we send off a sample. But did you tell your brothers it's purple?"

His eyes narrow. "I may have mentioned it."

"Aw, man, that's the best part! Don't you tell them anything?" I wag a finger. "That's half the selling point, until people taste it."

"I stressed how rare it is," he offers.

"And they just took your word?"

"I don't make lying a habit." His face tightens for a second, then relaxes. "Dexter and Patton know as much about honey as I do. Jack shit. I could've told them it was made from moon cheese and they wouldn't know better."

Okay, that wins him a snorting laugh.

I'm still laughing when a girl with hair redder than mine

comes over, though hers is much straighter and hangs in glossy waves. Archer gives her a relaxed, easy smile that makes him look almost soft.

"Checking up on me already, Junie?" he asks.

"I know how impatient you get when your stomach starts growling," the woman says affectionately. She might be a couple years older than me, maybe, and she's predictably gorgeous. Sea-green eyes, a lovely pale face that looks like it belongs on a marble statue, and a wide smile.

She sets our drinks on the table. I hate that my heart dips until he speaks again, wondering if these two have a thing.

"This is my sister-in-law, Juniper Rory," Archer says.

Sister-in-law? The owner? Oh, *thank God.*

Huge relief.

Junie, he called her. From the playful way she grins at him, they're on good terms. Certainly better than how he seemed to be with that woman who looked like she just stepped out of a play, still wearing her costume. His wife, I guess.

It's weird, trying to figure him out.

All the pieces don't quite fit.

But I've seen my share of unhappy, passionless marriages, so it's nothing new. I hope Arch isn't cursed with the same fate.

"This must be her, huh? Super nice to meet you," Juniper says to me with a bright smile. "My husband told me all about the mythical bee lady."

"Junie," Archer warns.

She flashes a mischievous smile. "Come on, dude. You know I had to see her for myself to know it was true."

Snorting, he shifts his gaze to me, an expression flicking over his eyes I can't quite read. "I'm sorry, Winnie. I promise you her treats make up for her attitude."

"You're lucky I'm busy, mister, or I'd fill your cupcake with gobs of cinnamon. See how you like it when you choke on a honey fireball. You're in my second home, so behave." Junie smacks him on the shoulder and gives me a grin before putting a brief, reassuring hand on mine.

Archer sighs as she disappears, leaning back into his seat.

"Mythical bee lady?" I ask. "They weren't sure I existed? Or do they have something against bees?"

"They know the bees exist," Archer says with a shrug. "They figured I wasn't lying about you. But the way I played up the honey, I'm sure they wondered."

"Well, I guess you have to see the stuff to get why it's special…"

But that doesn't explain the mythical part.

He grits his teeth, and for a second, I think he's upset.

But eventually, he says, "Frankly, they're not convinced this is about the bees. They suspect something else is going on."

"You told them about my dad?" I hold my breath.

"Absolutely not. But that doesn't mean they're stupid. I said you had a personal concern keeping you at Solitude and left it at that. They know there's more to the story than keeping you around to scare up purple honey."

I touch my bee earrings lightly between sips of mocha, trying to think past the weird feeling in my chest. Suspecting there's more to the story isn't the same as thinking Archer has any secret motivations beyond the kindness of his heart.

I'm getting carried away.

After everything that's happened over the past two weeks, I need to keep my brain in check. Especially with a generous, bad-tempered, flipping *married man* as drop-dead gorgeous as Archer Rory.

Before I can think too much about why that's so hard, Junie returns with our honey cupcakes. They look flawless.

There's honey drizzled neatly over the top with tiny flakes of sea salt. A little like salted caramel, I guess.

"Enjoy!" she says with a wink.

Archer scowls at her, but she doesn't give him time to think of a comeback before she sails away.

"You guys are on good terms. That's nice with in-laws," I observe, because that's safer than doing anything else. Like thinking about Archer and his motivations or what his brothers must think.

What he's not saying about getting raked over the coals thanks to my situation.

Holy hell, does his wife know he's asking for special favors and losing money over a strange woman?

"She's a nice girl," he says. "She makes my brother happy, which is a miracle I never thought I'd see."

"So he's like you? Grouchy?" He raises an eyebrow at me and I grin.

"I'm a serious man. Dexter just sucks."

I laugh. "Sure, sure, and I'm just a bee lady."

His lips thin and he takes a long pull off his coffee.

I do the same with my mocha, loving the balanced dance of dark chocolate and sweet sugar. It's like a symphony in my mouth.

I lick a dab of whipped cream from the side of the mug and glance up to find him staring.

My face bursts into flames.

"I'm sorry about the other day," he says abruptly. "When you ran into Rina."

Oh, crap, he's reading my mind.

But I guess we have to talk about it at some point, right? Since he's doing me a big favor, he has to mention the two times we got—way too close for comfort.

Any sane man would do the same and put me in my place, remind me that it can't keep happening.

"Your wife?" I whisper.

"Ex-wife," he growls.

What?

Oh. I never considered that.

But even though his eyes shutter at the mention of her, the tight pinch in my chest eases.

I haven't caused any arguments between husband and wife. He's not married.

Calm down, Win. Not married doesn't mean single. Let alone available and interested in you.

But it also doesn't mean covered in barbed wire and off-limits. I shake myself before I get carried away. Again.

"We don't communicate much. I haven't seen her in a long time," he adds.

"Really?"

"She travels a lot."

"Oh." I take a slow bite of my honey cupcake, quite possibly the best thing I've ever eaten. "Dear God, this is amazing."

The small moan that slips out of me almost kills me from embarrassment right there.

His eyes glow like sapphire discs as he watches me and says, "It's nice to see you smile again, Winnie."

At least his expression eases now that we're not talking about his ex-wife. Though I desperately want to ask him more about her—like when they broke up, why, and whether he's ever dated again—it's so not my place.

We talk about normal things.

Safe things.

There are a couple more cabins not too far from Solitude and one that's still under construction and not open for rentals yet. He says it's basically livable and I might be able to use it as a backup for a longer term stay if I need it.

I hope I won't have to burden him.

But I thank him anyway, and I don't dare mention how

much that means to me. I need every door open until I can find a real job.

First, though, I have to make sure the bees are being managed properly and find out what we can really do with the honey. I'm determined to pay back his generosity by taking this gig seriously.

We're going to make sure the Rory brothers wind up with the best streamlined small-time honey production outside North Dakota. Surprise, surprise, that's the top honey state in the nation. Producers are everywhere, big and small.

When we're finally ready to go, Archer clears his throat. "How'd you get here, anyway? I didn't see your car."

"Uber."

"Not driving?"

I shrug. "Technically, it's my dad's car now. His name was on the title since he's the one who bought it as a graduation present. I'm sure he'll have it tracked down and repo'd at some point. I don't want to cause more grief by driving it much longer."

Archer sends me a searching glance.

I deflect with a bland smile, trying to hide just how cooked my life is.

"Let me take you back," he says. "I know money's tight."

I should be embarrassed.

It's awkward knowing that a guy with *so much* money to his name knows exactly how broke I am. But something about the way he says it takes the sting away.

It's not condescension, it's *kindness.*

I've been around both long enough to know the difference, when someone's doing you a selfless favor or when they're only helping to put you in debt.

"Also, I'd like to get a better look at the bees without Colt around," he adds.

"You do?" I can't help it, I grin up at him.

"You promised me a gold mine and it's my duty to check it out. Thoroughly."

"You won't be disappointed." I practically skip over to his waiting Tesla SUV, which unlocks as he draws near. It's sleek and expensive and gorgeous.

I always wanted one, even if they aren't the most practical for the occasional cross-country drive to DC and back when my boss wasn't flying us.

I guess this is a good time to figure out if it's something I *actually* want one day.

Just like everything else in my life.

If there's ever been a time to reinvent Winnie Emberly, it's now.

As I strap myself in, I beam at him.

One corner of his mouth curls up into an easy, cool smile. On Archer Rory, that's a Cheshire cat's grin.

Without another word, he starts the vehicle and we set off.

* * *

If someone told me a few days ago that this no-nonsense, fussy lunk would make me double over laughing, I'd have called them a liar.

Yet here I am.

Breathless, sore, bent over and clutching my stomach, all while he eyes the bees with downright suspicion.

"They're so… loud." His nose wrinkles and he bares his teeth.

"Well, yeah. They're *bees*!" I gasp, trying not to fall into another laughing fit.

He really is a human bear, clumsily shooing them away with his large hands when they get too close.

Except here, they're always too close because technically we're in their space.

"Aren't you supposed to smoke them out or something?"

"Nah. Some keepers use smoke to keep them docile while they get the honey, but we're not doing that. We're just looking today." I catch his arm when he moves to shoo more of them away. "Don't do it. If you antagonize them, you'll get stung for sure."

"Isn't there a way to keep them the hell out of my face?"

"Dude, relax. Slow movements. No fear, no anger. If you scare them or show up flapping your hands around, that's when they consider you a threat."

"They're not bothering you." He glares at me.

I raise a hand, watching as the bees fly past. A couple land on my arm, crawl around for a few seconds, then fly off.

"See? No harm, no foul. You just have to wait and trust they won't hurt you."

"They sting, Winnie."

I laugh. "Archer, I'm aware. That doesn't mean they lash out for no reason."

A bee tangles up in my hair. I wait for it to figure out how to free itself.

Archer looks like he wants to help, but I shake my head slowly. He doesn't have my bee-whisperer skills or my patience.

Knowing him, he'll try to flick the bee out of my hair and get me stung right in the ear.

"I reached out to some other beekeepers in the area," I say once the bee flies off. "I sent them a few pics of the honey and they were pumped. Honestly, I don't think there's anything like this in the region."

His eyes are a dusky shade of blue as he looks at me, and I feel the full weight of his focus. Even the bees don't distract him now, and my throat tightens at the sight of it.

The sight of *him*.

"The color and sweetness could make it an attractive product. It'll have to be bottled up and branded, of course, but you're already a genius with that stuff," I continue. "And that's not taking the medicinal properties into consideration. We'll need the lab panel to determine that. There are plenty of private places, or maybe the local university could—"

"What the fuck." His eyebrows draw together. "Winnie, are you sure you don't have a PhD in entomology?"

"What? No." I feel my cheeks heat. "No, it's just a hobby. Something my grandma got me interested in."

I think he's going to drop it, but he tilts his head as he reconsiders. "She's into beekeeping too?"

"She had bees. I mean, she was rich enough to have gardeners and landscapers like you. She had a few beekeepers over the years. I was always fascinated by the way they'd handle the bees, even when I was a little girl. Whenever I'd go over to her place, I used to just sit and watch them for hours." I stop, a lump forming in my throat.

Going over to see my grandparents was always an escape. A release from normal life.

Between Dad demanding perfect grades and piling on extracurriculars, and Mom needing her pretty little girl to dress up, Grandma and Grandpa just wanted me.

Just Winnie, simple and unfiltered.

They're the only ones who let me be a kid.

Archer comes closer. There's still space between us, but less now, and the air vibrates.

"So that's where you picked it up?" he prompts.

"When I got older, Grandma told the beekeepers to teach me things when she saw how much I liked it. It was the one thing that was *mine*, not like the other stuff my parents decided I should do. All my life, I've been doing stuff because other people said I should. My dad told me what to study, what to believe. My mom used to pick out my clothes, my haircut, my shampoos and toothpaste. Everything—ugh. But the bees, they were mine, this sweet escape I had until the day my grandma died. My parents never knew until I was almost grown."

"Damn, woman, that's harsh. Sorry you felt like you needed one." His voice blurs gentle and rough.

The sharp glint in his eye says if he'd had a say, he would've done it differently.

Tingles.

The longer I stare at him, the more heat I feel, humming under my skin.

"I mean, it's fine now. It's nothing. Nobody has a perfect childhood, right? I'd rather figure out the rest of my life than waste more time blaming my parents." I wave a dismissive hand. Mostly because dwelling on it too long will make me cry, and I've done *more* than enough of that around Archer. "I think Mom still allowed it when she found out because she thought it was a phase. Something I'd leave behind after high school, but I've loved it ever since."

"It's admirable, Winnie. You loved something enough to pursue it for so long. Hell of a lot of people out there who never find that."

I smile softly.

"I wish you could convince my father." I sound bitter, so I force that smile to stay a little longer and gently brush a bee off his shoulder. "There. See how friendly they are when you're calm? You didn't even notice he was there."

"He, huh?" Archer narrows his eyes. "You saying you're an expert on all bee anatomy?"

"Oh, stop. I'm sure yours is bigger, if that's what has you worried."

Then it happens.

He laughs.

His lips split into a big, messy smile that makes my heart cartwheel, and I realize my hand is still on his shoulder.

Oh, no, I should move it.

Any second now, I'm going to move it and step back.

But his eyes flick to mine as his laughter fades. My breath catches in my throat and the rest of the world falls away.

I don't know when we started moving, but we're closer still, basically sharing breathing space. The height difference is so much I have to tip my head back.

His gaze drops to my mouth and I catch my breath.

Please kiss me.

Please just once.

The force of that illicit, insane thought takes me by surprise.

It doesn't matter if we're sharing bad jokes and bees.

He's a stranger. Older and rich and successful enough to make heads spin and ugly whispers fly.

There are definite reasons—very good ones—why we should absolutely *not* kiss right now if we value our lives. Especially the fact that we're total opposites and—

And okay, aside from that, maybe I can't think of any reasons. Considering the way his face is closer than it was a few seconds ago, I don't *want* to think of any.

This warm, fluttery feeling pulses in my belly. My hand on his shoulder clenches, fingers digging into his hard muscle.

"Winnie," he rumbles.

God, the way he says my name alone is an eruption.

And I know how crazy this is.

I know I've lost it as I stretch up on my tiptoes and put my hand on his other shoulder to steady myself in case my knees give out.

I know his hand lands on my waist, quick and possessive,

and his nose brushes mine with the slightest touch that still feels like a fireball.

I know I've never experienced a single moment this erotically charged.

Or a man like a human mountain, who takes his sweet time deciding if he wants to take what I'm offering in the most patient, painstaking way possible.

Like every brutal second is a challenge to overcome.

Like he needs to ask for permission with every movement.

Like he's testing the anticipation he builds, just to see if what's coming is truly worth the grief.

Oh, Archer, will you trust me just this once?

Will you be a little reckless?

Then his fingers flex on my waist and suddenly he's backing away.

My hands fall limply from his shoulders. Although the sun beams hot on my back, I feel almost cold without him there, fully hollowed out.

"I should go," he rasps, a thousand conflicts in his voice.

"Oh. Okay, sure." Pathetic. I try to collect my thoughts, scattered somewhere across time and space.

He doesn't meet my gaze, but I can see the redness on his cheekbones under his beard.

He's simply beautiful in this clean, masculine way. I want to wrap him in my arms and—

Yeah, and kiss him.

But he doesn't want that.

He won't kiss me.

The thought flash freezes the warmth that was spreading lower with every second we grew closer. He doesn't want me and that's cool.

Absolutely fine.

It's not like I *want* to kiss this man anyway, no matter how carried away we got in the heat of the moment.

I wasn't thinking.

I barely know him.

He wasn't that polite or gentle the first time we met. Even though he's been a lot nicer since, this whole situation feels too abrupt. Too sudden.

Too self-destructive for sure.

I follow him back to the cabin in grim silence, leaving the happy bees behind.

Archer's face is closed off, his eyes everywhere but on me. I make sure not to look at him after my first little glance.

Two can play this silly game.

"Thanks for the cheesecake," he says as we step into the kitchen. "It was delicious. Colt would've wolfed it all down in one go if I'd let him."

"Oh, yeah. You're welcome." I do my best not to imagine Rina, the ex-wife, eating it with them. "I just wanted to... apologize for the whole situation, y'know."

"No need. I'll be in touch." His eyes linger on my face for a beat too long.

"Okay." I'm crushed as I nod, forcing myself to stay where I am as he turns for the door.

Every part of me wants to say something to make him stay, but I bite my lip.

He's leaving.

He *should*.

This situation is explosive enough without introducing kissing and aching desire and mind-blowing sex, but I—

He pauses on the threshold, slowly glancing back over his shoulder.

Then he turns.

His hand tightens on the doorknob before he slams it shut and strides back over.

I only have time to blurt out "Wha—" before he's on me, guns blazing, one hand on my waist and the other sliding up my jaw, bracing me.

His kiss is all animal.

Rough, furious, greedy.

He gives me teeth and tongue and thunder, pushing a growl in my mouth that vibrates my bones.

He kisses like his lips have been aching to do it for months—for *years*—maybe for his entire freaking life.

I'm hit by a force of nature, swept back faster than I can breathe.

My back thunks against the wall and my hair spills everywhere.

I haven't even moved. That's all him, shoving me until I'm secure and held up, a willing victim just waiting to be pillaged.

Holy Mother of Lust.

His hands are rampant, squeezing and stroking and suddenly *everywhere.*

My hands are everywhere else.

I don't have time to think about it or time to give them direction.

They slide over his shoulders, his chest, admiring the hard cut of his muscles under his shirt, tugging him closer.

I need the burning air from his lungs.

I need his skin on mine.

I need him closer, *closer.*

I'm a silent demand, asking for so much more than this breath-thieving kiss.

He can have my whole heart.

He can tear my clothes off right here, right now, and bury his cock in me.

This man can have everything.

He can take me apart one fierce stroke at a time.

He can fuck my lights out just as long as he makes me forget.

Please, just make me forget I'm Winnie, the lost runaway bride with her life in ruins, and give it to me like a woman in full control of her destiny.

I'm smiling like a madwoman as I moan into his mouth, closing my eyes, surrendering in a way I haven't ever before.

Kiss by steaming kiss, as his tongue chases mine, I ask Archer Rory to demolish me so I can build myself again.

X: HONEY DRUNK (ARCHER)

God fucking damn.

How is she sweeter than that purple honey?

This woman is a human drug.

Small, yet all-consuming.

Shy, yet brave enough to make demands.

Broken, yet still boiling with passion.

When she opens her mouth, tongue sliding against mine, I react on instinct, pulling her closer, stealing another moan from her lips.

Yeah, fuck, she tastes as good as she feels under my hands.

I swear I want to maul her.

My hands sweep lower, grabbing her ass. I don't care how hard I squeeze those cheeks.

I'm already drunk on this Sugarbee, devouring her one messy kiss at a time, both of us breathless and making noises that aren't human.

Her body kills me.

Lush hips and full, heavy breasts that seem strange on her small frame. I've been seeing her naked in my head since the first day we met.

And since that first almost-kiss? I haven't jerked off so much in years, throwing myself under ice-cold showers, only to have Winnie's pussy invade my mind. Fucking hounding me until I fist-pump ropes of come from my cock.

Now, those ropes may wind up where they belong.

What the hell is wrong with me?

This sickness, it isn't me.

It's just making out, one long mistake we should stop any second, as soon as we come to our senses, but my entire body *burns.*

I rub a thumb along her breast and she gasps in my mouth. Her soft arms cling to my shoulders, pinning her to me.

I sink my teeth into her bottom lip, biting her again.

It's like she doesn't know how mad she makes me, how fucking sexy she is.

In hindsight, there's no way I could've resisted the way she bit her lip as she watched me leave. A guarantee with another billion dollars, ten more years of life, and three more inches on my dick couldn't have turned me away.

Resisting Winnie in the garden was a feat alone.

I don't know how I managed.

She shreds my self-control with a single green-eyed glance and she doesn't even know it.

That's the best kind of seduction.

My favorite kind.

The kind where she's oblivious to her own vixen power. It's spontaneous, natural, and so fucking potent I worry I've lost brain cells in charge of my reason.

No, it's not just the fact that I haven't had so much as a quick hookup in years. Living like a monk for Colt, for my business, that's been the norm.

It's not this earthquake rippling through my life that's taking me apart.

It's *her*.

I forgot what pure, unfiltered woman feels like, and Winnie reminds me with every whimpering kiss, every caress of her round tits against my chest.

Holy shit.

I'm snarling hellfire through my teeth as I press her to the wall, shifting my hips so we're aligned, my cock throbbing so hard it wants to knock me out cold.

We've been kissing for two minutes—hell, maybe two days for all I know—and I'm ready to rip right out of my pants.

If we don't stop now, we never will.

It's the uncontrollable nature, the feral animal inside me, that makes me breathe like my lungs are torn.

Her leg sweeps around mine, just enough to push her pussy against my thigh, so hot and slick even through the fabric.

"Archer, please. Anything you want," she whispers. "Anything."

That last little promise with her voice shaking, so brittle and helpless, jolts me back to my senses.

I throw myself back before I can't, breaking free from her siren clutches.

We both stare at each other for a second in disbelief, our chests heaving.

Her green eyes are wide and dark.

Her lips look like they've been stung by one of those bees out there.

Somehow, I've done more damage than any hornet ever could.

I kissed her.

I fucking kissed her.

I fucked her lips with my tongue, promising one new obscene disaster after the next.

More than anything, I fucked myself, sending my soul—or at least my conscience—straight to hell by treating her like a toy.

Archer Rory, you colossal jackass.

It doesn't matter how bad I want to kiss her again. I'm about to lose my mind and what tiny thread of self-control I've gotten back.

"I should go," I grind out.

Her mouth drops like she wants to say something, but I can't wait to hear it. Because the instant she asks me to stay, I'm going to march over and strip that shirt off over her head, and then—

No.

No, I can't take advantage, even if she's absolutely willing.

So I wheel around and storm back through the front door, damn near panic running to my SUV and setting off fast enough to kick up gravel.

When I dare to look back—big mistake—I see her standing in the doorway, all haunted eyes.

Dust finally obscures her face. Thank God.

I don't need more heat or confusion or blinding lust.

Not now.

My hard-on jerks uncomfortably against my jeans, cursing me to my grave. I have to adjust myself, wondering if my balls are bluer than Papa Smurf.

Holy fuck, I need a cold bath or three to get her out of my head.

Then I need to forbid myself from ever winding up alone with Winnie again.

* * *

IN THE TWO days since I kissed her and signed my death warrant, I've held three Higher Ends meetings, signed more contracts and stupid damn documents than I can count, and dreaded seeing Rina at this lunch at Mom's.

Any one of those things should be on my mind. Especially Rina and all the bad memories she brings, along with stale suspicion.

The divorce was messy.

The marriage was hardly any cleaner, and although I wouldn't change a thing about Colt, I have enough regrets to fill a mountain.

Failing that, this new project in St. Louis should be taking up some grey matter. Dexter is determined to push on, and I know a lot of this is due to Junie and that brotherly rivalry we've got going on, but still.

It's a big deal. We can't jump the gun and wind up making errors.

Usually when these plans come up, I'm the guy who stops that from happening.

I'm not doing that today.

Instead, my brain stays glued to the bee-obsessed honey trap who's living rent-free in my property and in my head.

This fucking blows.

Mom grins at me from the other side of the living room as Rina babbles over how tall and handsome and smart Colt is. He's too old to enjoy anyone fussing over him, but I guess because it's his mom, he takes it in stride.

"You've gotten so big. You're going to be taller than your dad in another year or two," she tells him for the fifth time.

"Uh, we'll see. I'm still growing."

"You'll make it. Your uncles are tall guys too. If you want a break from trying to blow yourself up in labs, you should try modeling." She reaches over and ruffles his hair.

"Mom, stop. Jeez. I wouldn't be caught dead doing a runway walk."

I force a smile even though the sound of her voice feels

like a cheese grater on my soul. The sooner we're done with this farce, the better.

"Did I tell you about my carvings?" he asks, grabbing his phone and scrolling through his camera roll. "Dad helps me a lot."

Rina shoots me a look like she can't believe I'd help develop his passions. I glare back at her flatly.

He's my son. For him, I'll stand around at the most boring-ass art fairs all day.

Thankfully, wood carving is far from dull. It keeps the mind and hands busy, and I have to admit Colt's gotten pretty damn good.

"Oh, wow! Colt, honey..." She takes the phone and looks at the screen. "You made all of these birds?"

"Those are my early ones, yeah. Look, here's one I finished last week."

It's a small wooden fox. The ears were the hardest part; the boy was in a panic for two weeks thinking they'd break off if he shaved them too thin.

Her eyes widen, and her reaction sets something off in my gut.

It could've been so different.

If she'd just been here, taking an interest in his life before now, she would have *known* about his art.

Just like she'd know he plows through advanced math well beyond his grade and he eats up everything related to science. She'd know he's a regular at Mom's art shows and we even started hiring out a table to sell his carvings in the summer.

People buy his stuff, too. I let him keep most of the profits for a little spending money and throw the rest into his college savings account.

I may be rich enough to make his future education a rounding error in my accounts, yes, but a kid should always have some of their own skin in the game.

Also, this is all new to Rina because she's been an absentee mother for almost his entire life, only popping in when she feels like it with a gift and an unfulfilled promise of more to come.

More presents, more pop ins, more *her*.

To no one's surprise, it never happens.

"Is that a cardinal?" she asks, beaming from ear to ear.

"Yep! I made it for Grandma." Colt smiles too, all pride as he glances at Mom, who watches with the usual indulgent smile she reserves for her grandkids.

"Lucky Gram," Rina says, keeping her smile pinned in place. "Do you think you could make something for me?"

For a second, he hesitates.

This is actually pissing me off, the chance that this could be some new head game.

"Uh, sure. What would you want?"

"Maybe one of you? Can you carve people?" She smiles. "Photos are nice, but having my boy in 3D would be pretty sweet."

Why? Because she's about to fuck off until he graduates high school?

I tense but keep my tongue in check as Colt considers her request before nodding.

Of course, he does.

There's no way my kid will turn down a special request like that. Not from his mother, who he still loves like the good boy he is, even when she's the last person alive who deserves it.

Eventually, he sits back and looks at the blue sky wistfully. He needs a break from all the coddling and unexpected praise.

I don't blame him.

"Hey, why don't you head outside, bud?" I suggest. "Looks

like a beautiful day out there and Grandma could use some help with those weeds in her garden."

"Okay, no prob. Is the trampoline still up?" he asks Mom. He might be thirteen, trying to be all mature, but he's still a kid at heart.

"Not right now, but I can get it out for you."

"Mom, don't—"

"I can handle it, Archer," she tells me, pulling her silk scarf off and tossing it on the sofa. "I might be old, but that doesn't mean I'm too over the hill for a little exercise. Come on, Colt, let's go."

She gives me a knowing look that tells me I'm free to talk to Rina privately.

And maybe, despite the fact that she invited Rina here today, she wants me to talk to her, too.

"Have fun," Rina whispers. There's clear disappointment on her face as he sprints outside behind my mother.

Guess she didn't get the memo. Active, healthy teenage boys don't want to sit around and gab all day with moms who barely acknowledge their existence.

As soon as the door shuts behind them, I lean forward, resting my elbows on my knees.

"Okay, Rina, cut the crap. Why are you really here? I want answers."

"Huh?" She looks at me, familiar antagonism written on her face. "Archer, don't talk to me like that."

"Is it money? Do you need some help again? You know I'm reasonable." Or maybe it's some inner angst, another relationship with some fuckboy gone to pieces, realizing her own mortality. Wouldn't put it past her.

"Oh, please. I hate groveling for money, especially to you. I only ever asked when I had nowhere else to turn. Energy work and art don't pay like real estate," she spits. "It's more like you pay me to get rid of me. I never got together with you for your money, Archer. You know that. I'm not here because of it now."

"Yes, you're a saint. You don't give a fuck about the money." I have to admit, it's half-true.

She only comes calling when she's in a bind, realizing she can't support herself off erratic art gigs and astrology consultations alone.

I've always topped her off generously when she needs it, despite no obligation.

It's for the family. I won't have Colt worried sick about his mother, broke and living out on West Coast streets or wherever the hell she's living now, dodging violent junkies and rusty nails or whatever.

"Can you give me a *little* credit?" She holds up two fingers with a sliver of space between them.

"Not with this. You haven't given two shits about Colt since the divorce, and now you're here fawning all over him. Why?"

She huffs loudly, rolling her eyes like a scorned teenage cheerleader.

"So this is how it's gonna be?" Rina asks. "We can't discuss this like adults? I see some things never change."

Fuck her discussions.

I said I wanted answers.

I also hate that something about Rina's presence brings back the hotheaded young man I used to be in my past life. Back before Colt, when her wildness attracted rather than repulsed me.

Back before I thought it would be anything serious. Back before I *wanted* anything serious and only gave in because we made a kid.

That's not who I am anymore.

I'm better than Old Archer, who wanted to keep playing

with fire after his dad died and he saw how short life could be.

I need to *be* better for my son.

That's the whole-ass reason why I dragged myself away from an epic romp with Winnie Emberly, isn't it?

"Fine. Talk," I growl. Rina blinks sadly. Well, that makes two of us. "Should we rehash the facts? You moved to Portland with that art collective and you never came back for him. You never put in effort. Forgive me if I'm skeptical if I think a tigress never changes her stripes."

Rina takes an angry breath. I think she's going to bawl me out, but she just releases it then, long and slow.

"We were so young, Archer. We made so many mistakes," she whispers, sounding genuinely sad. Like she isn't just saying it for the sake of flapping her mouth.

Can't disagree with her there.

One of the biggest mistakes was being together in the first place—and that's a fuckup I would never change since it's the reason Colt exists.

"We did," I say. "Look, I won't deny it. I'll be the *first* to admit I made mistakes. We both did. But Colt, he's my son. Our son. I had to figure out my shit and fast to look after him alone."

And you didn't.

I don't say it, but the words hover over us like a sword.

Her fingers braid the knitted shawl she's wearing over an oversized yellow shirt. "Yeah, you're right. I know. I kept fucking up after he was born."

Not just after—basically his entire life.

Thirteen *years* of mistakes.

The biggest was not being there to see how she'd perform as a real mom.

"I want what's best for Colton. Simple as," I tell her. "If he wants his mom, I won't hold him back. But that also means you have to *be* his mom, Rina."

"I know! I'm not stupid." Agitated, she stands and paces across the floor, her shawl falling to the floor. For the first time, I get a good look at the sleeve of tattoos across her right arm.

And there, smack in the middle, I see the word *Colt* in cursive script. Bold and decisive. That's definitely new.

The sight swings a hammer at my heart.

She just had to go and do that shit.

Get her son's name tattooed on her arm. I'm not against tattoos when I've got a few myself, but I've always made it a rule to never wear anyone's name.

People are too transient, fading in and out of life.

If I'd tattooed Rina's name on my flesh, I would've carved it off rather than keep staring at the bitter reminder.

Back when we were together, I know she felt the same way. My name's nowhere on her body—I can guarantee that.

But now she's gone and branded herself with Colt's name permanently.

"You of all people should know how hard it is to swallow your pride and admit you screwed up," she snaps. "But here I am, doing it. Trying to, anyway. Doesn't that count?"

"Depends."

"Depends on *what*?"

"Why you're actually here, swallowing your pride. The motive matters. It depends what you *want* out of this, Ri." I stand in front of her, appreciating for the first time how small she is.

Winnie, she's short too, but the coppery red hair and her boundless energy somehow make her seem taller.

Rina has folded in on herself, her eyes drilling through me. She stands like one more wrong word could break her.

"I've done a lot of growing up over the past few months, you know," she says quietly, looking up at me like I can see the truth in her face. "A lot, okay? The last few years were rough. There's a ton I regret. I just want to know my son before he's a grown man. Before it's too late… Is that really such a crime?"

Fuck me.

She's saying all the right things, plucking the old heartstrings like a banjo. But there's still that muddy ball of distrust she built over years of disappointment. I can't just blink and shove the dirt aside.

If I believe her, if I give her another chance, it's too likely she'll let me down again—and more importantly, let Colt down, too.

I can't let that happen.

My boy isn't a grown man yet. He's still a kid, susceptible to heartbreak and bad decisions. Having his mother abandon him for the fiftieth time when he's old enough to understand it might scar him for life.

Fuck that.

Colt deserves better than a part-time parent who ghosts in and out of his life whenever she pleases. A parent who says the right words but doesn't follow through.

A parent who only loves until she gets bored.

Yes, I get it.

Being a parent of any kind is fucking hard.

I learned that lesson better than anyone, and even though I've tried my best, I've made my mistakes. Now, I just don't want to open him up to more hurt.

Only, the way Rina looks at me, all big eyes and that wounded expression, makes me think maybe I'm misjudging the situation.

She's spent enough time away from us, living her life. What if she *has* come to her senses?

What if she just wants to be a positive force in his life before it's too late?

Part of me thinks it already is.

Then again, if it was too late, Colt wouldn't be hanging out with her like this. He wouldn't answer her questions so gently, so freely, chatting up his accomplishments and smiling at her stories about beautiful beaches in Oregon and California.

He *wants* a mom.

Before I can say anything, or even figure out what the hell to say, Mom comes strolling back in the room.

"Trampoline is up and he's jumping his heart out," she says, all smiles and pleasantry.

It's insane how she manages when she might just hate Rina more than I do.

Back when we first got together, she told me not to go through with it. The marriage, the counseling when the relationship was hanging by a thread, the everything.

The past is the past, though, and Mom's mature enough to figure maybe there's something more going on.

Adelaide Rory is a forgiving woman. She always gives people the benefit of the doubt, even when Rina Desmona only ever lets people down.

I guess that's why I'm so damn protective over her, trying to keep away people who might exploit her generosity. It happens every year at her art shows and it pisses me off.

I'll be fucked if Rina will be one more of those people.

She gives me another glance and smiles awkwardly at Mom. I think she knows as well as anyone that Mom doesn't like her standing here, barfing up her heart.

"I'll head out and find Colt, then. Make sure he doesn't hurt himself."

We don't speak until after she leaves the room. Then Mom sits on the sofa and looks at me.

"This could be a good thing, Archer," she says.

"You really think so?"

"Yes. Rina moving on and getting her act together means a lot for Colt. He's at such a tender age. More importantly, it gives *you* a chance to move on."

I snort impulsively.

Rina coming back won't help me move shit—not that I need to move on, anyway.

If we weren't psychoanalyzing my love life, it wouldn't be a visit with Mom.

I've dated other women since Rina left. Even if those dates were more like coffee and a quick fuck. Enough to scratch an itch a few times a year when Colt goes away overnight with Mom or friends, never enough to mean anything, and that's exactly how I like it.

It's not like I've been celibate for a decade, pining away after my demented ex.

"Archer—"

"Mom, we'll see," I say. "Time will tell. I don't trust a word she says."

"I'm not just talking about Rina, honey."

"Then what?"

"Why, the lovely young woman who's been staying in your cabin. I heard you had a dessert date with her."

Oh, shit.

This day just got better.

Damn Junie and everyone else who's been leaking my personal crap to my mom of all people. Will I ever catch a break?

But Winnie dredges up the thought of what happened last time we met.

Try like hell, I can't escape the memory. It stabs me in the head every time I have a spare second. Sometimes even when I don't.

A three-minute make-out kiss never affected me like this. It never wrecked me before.

Sometimes, when I'm alone, I think I can still smell her.

"Colt showed me the honey," Mom explains. "It looks very special and very sweet. It was nice of her to give him some."

Yeah, because in the brief time I've known her, Winnie hasn't learned how to be anything but 'nice.'

Maybe if she was meaner, bitchier, and more selfish, she would've avoided this entire mess. She could've told the dickwad who chased her away to take a hike, and she could've stood there in that pretty wedding dress with a worthy man who cherished her.

Still, I'd never change shit about that woman.

I just don't want to think about her honey-sweet, sunshiny personality and the way it goads me into wanting to defile her.

"Yes, well, she knows what she's doing with that. The girl's obsessed with bees and honey harvesting." I fold my arms, trying to steer the conversation away from how nice she truly is. "And for the record, it wasn't a 'date,' Mom. It was business, plain and simple."

"Oh? My, that's too bad. Junie said you two looked cute together."

I shake my head ferociously.

"It's *Junie* we're talking about. She lives for gossip and matchmaking. Do you remember that girl three months ago she tried introducing me to?"

"I do. She gave up after you turned her down three times for a date. I think you scared the poor thing away," Mom says soothingly. Like that changes the hard fact that my scheming sister-in-law, roughly ten years my junior, thinks I need her help setting me up with women.

Bah.

"That's not the point, Mom. I don't need Junie's help, or anyone's. I can handle my love life just fine, thank you. And for the last time, Winnie is *not* part of it."

"Ah, Winnie, yes, that's her name." Mom snaps her fingers. "I couldn't remember."

"You don't need to," I bite off. "There's nothing going on."

But Mom just smiles back like the happy mind-reading elf she is until I want to groan and hide my face.

Fucking hell... is it that obvious?

Am I that honey drunk, hung up on a woman who's every kind of wrong?

The ever-widening smile on Mom's face tells me that's a big fat *yes*.

I fight the urge to start punching the wall.

XI: BEE-DAZZLED (WINNIE)

There are few things better in life than a homemade meatball sub.

This one has everything. Meatballs, onions, savory red sauce, and a nice dose of gooey cheese. I'm in seventh heaven before I've taken a single bite when the phone rings.

The sandwich goes everywhere as I make a grab for it.

It's so embarrassing how desperate I am for Archer's attention. Apparently, I'll move with sandwich-destroying speed.

A human travesty.

Especially when I spent way too long finding the perfect recipe, cooking the meatballs and sauce from scratch, and assembling the whole thing. Now, half of my precious meatballs are on the floor with the other half scattered across the table.

Oh, plus one on my lap.

Fantastic.

The name on the screen isn't even Archer's. Disappointment stabs me in the gut until I process the name.

Lyssie, my bestie from Springfield. The disappointment

fades into a mix of nerves and cautious excitement as I swipe to answer.

"Hey, girl."

"*Wynne Abigail Emberly*, holy shit! Do you know what you've done?" Lyssie hisses. Guess it's serious, then—she would never use my full name otherwise.

"Fled my wedding? Yep, I was there, Lyssie."

"On the day *of*."

"Ah, thanks. I wasn't aware."

She laughs awkwardly and then goes stone-cold silent again.

"…was it the dress?" she whispers. "It was gorgeous, don't get me wrong, but it looked like a beast to climb into."

"It *was*. That's why I cut it off. With scissors."

She gasps. "Winnie! Are you serious?"

"Why not? It's not like there was a man around to help take it off."

"Well, no. But where are you? No, wait, don't tell me…" She pauses dramatically. "I should have a little plausible deniability. I didn't think you'd actually pick up."

"So they've been hounding you about me? I'm sure they have."

"Yeah, only about five million times. I'm guessing your dad knows you're still alive. I'm pretty sure he would've sent every State Trooper on payroll after you if he didn't. They're kinda furious."

I wince.

My stomach gurgles, angry because it isn't full of meatballs and marinara, but I'm a little relieved that's not the case.

"Tell me something I don't know, Lyssie."

"I've been worried sick, Win. They've been hitting me up about you *constantly*, which is the only reason why I haven't called more. I kept hitting you with texts, figuring you'd answer at your own pace. But would it have been so terrible to reply? You still have thumbs, right?"

"How do you know? Maybe that's why I fled," I deadpan.

"Pssh, like you'd give up your opposable thumbs. How would you ever deal with bees? Thumbs are the best body parts."

My nose scrunches.

"Wouldn't be easy. And the best, huh? Hmm, I don't know, I can think of a few other—"

"Okay, okay! So we have a few other goodies, but I stand by my claim that opposable thumbs are our greatest asset, and in this case, you could have used them to message me. Just once, a friendly 'hey, I'm not dead' message. Just so I knew you weren't rotting in a ditch somewhere."

I exhale slowly through my teeth, closing my eyes.

My head dips forward until it touches the table—only to find I've put my forehead in a patch of tomato sauce. *Beautiful.*

I jerk up again.

"I'm sorry. How are things back home?"

"You wanna know the truth?"

That can't mean anything good.

"Um, yes? I think so... No, maybe not. If you're talking about Dad cussing me out behind my back, I already guessed that."

"Oh, no. *Publicly,* he's been making all sorts of excuses, surprisingly." Lyssie's voice is dry. Of everyone I know, she's basically the only person who understands how I felt about the wedding and Holden and the entire gross situation.

"And privately?"

"Well, I heard from my mom that your parentals have been seeing Holden every day. *Apparently*—and take this with a grain of salt—Holden has vowed to hunt you down and bring you home."

"Holden? What the hell? I can't imagine that man hunting anything." I snort and shake my head. "Also, I'm not some sort of deer. But if he wants to come at me with a rifle, I guess I get it."

My bitter laughter hurts.

Honestly, I didn't mean to leave him holding the bag in a public humiliation ritual, even if I don't love him and barely tolerate his existence.

But a big, nasty confrontation with my lame ex feels like the last thing I need to worry about. Holden hasn't ever shown much passion for anything besides his crypto portfolio or his dad's mixer events with the rich and famous.

"Well, I imagine he's bringing his ego, which could be just as dangerous. No one gets why you left, by the way. Like, I think I do, but"—her voice turns deeply sarcastic—"who *wouldn't* want to sign away their life to a catch like the glorious Holden Corban?"

"You've got me."

"Anyway," Lyssie says, and I can hear a microwave ding in the background that makes me smile. She has this gorgeous apartment with a fabulous kitchen, but she prefers instant meals and junk food over real cooking. "Tell me everything that's happened since you've been gone. At least tell me you found a cool hideout?"

Unfortunately, like it's done a thousand times since he left, my mind jumps back to Archer and the way he pinned me to the wall and kissed my soul out. My toes scrunch up.

"The hideout is really nice. Just a little dull since I haven't been out much. What makes you think much has happened?"

"Um, your choice. Spill it, girl. Do you already have a rebound dude? Is he hot?"

Oh, God.

"What? No!" Unless Archer Rory decides he *wants* to be my secret lover. I don't think I'd mind rebounding with him one bit. "I didn't run away from the wedding because I'm in love with someone else or dying to hook up with randos, Lyssie."

"Okay, good. I would've been so pissed if you hadn't told me first." Her lips smack between words as she chews. Knowing her, it's probably one of the instant pho cups she heats up or a giant frozen burrito, her usual obsessions. "So what's going on with you? No rebound man?"

"I'm not that lucky. Things are... kinda complicated." That's true enough. "Dad cut me off from my trusts, so it isn't peachy on the money front."

"Oh, what! Oh, shit. Winnie, do you need me to send you a little extra? I don't mind. I know you'll pay me back. And even if you can't for a while—"

"No, it's cool. Actually, the guy who owns this place let me stay here for free. He's really generous."

"Guy?" I swear Lyssie has a superhuman antenna for sniffing out entire volumes from words, and she latches on immediately. "*Please* tell me he's hot and this is a sexy roommate situation."

"No flipping way." But there's also *no way* I can effectively lie my way out of this one. I close my eyes. "If you insist, he's handsome, I guess. So there."

"You're *totally* crushing. I can tell. That's exciting, Winnie."

"Liar. You're just saying that because *you* want the sexy illicit roommate situation. Me, I'm happy to keep him at a distance."

"You suck so much," she says flatly. "So, he's hot *and* nice and he's not staying overnight. Why is he letting you stay there for free? Are you sleeping with him?"

"Lyssie, *no*. It's not like that at all." I inhale slowly. "There are bees here. I'm staying on as their official beekeeper for the time being."

"...bees." Dead silence until she speaks again. "Lady, if you were anyone else, I'd know you're making it up. Ugh." There's real disappointment in her voice.

"No, it's a good thing." I launch into telling her about the purple honey and what a cool experience this is.

Everything I ever wanted, even if I am leaving a big heap of chaos at home burning in my wake.

"Okay, fine," she says, amused. "The purple honey sounds cool enough, so I know you're having fun. Just lay low until I can visit, okay? And whatever you do, keep it light. Maybe your hot landlord guy can help with more than just your glow in the dark honey."

"Don't push it, Lyssie."

She laughs. "Okay, whatevs. I'll leave you to your hot girl beekeeper life and buzz off. Just remember, older guys can be *fun.*"

My face heats.

"How did you even know he's older?"

"Oh, let's call it intuition."

I call it freaky.

She's always been able to do that, reading people between the lines like cards. It's a skill that makes me jealous.

The call cuts off and I sink back down in my chair, realizing I must have stood up at some point. Back to reality, starting with cleaning up the kitchen and my meatball sub massacre.

I can't stop smiling, and it's not just because of Lyssie.

There's no good reason this exile needs to be torture.

I should have some fun, even if that has nothing to do with the snarling unpredictable man-bear who's moved into my head full-time.

* * *

AFTER ANOTHER FULL day of being ghosted by Archer, I'm feeling a lot less smiley and far less confident.

There's a decent chance he considers The Kiss to End All Kisses the biggest mistake of his life.

A hot mistake, sure, but nothing more.

That's a sane reaction. It shouldn't leave me moping around like it does.

The knock at the door comes in the evening when I'm almost ready to curl up and watch some bad reality TV.

I just know it's him.

Call it intuition or the fact that I know the sound of his vehicle parking or just the way he needs to *hit things* when he knocks—either way, I know.

I take a second to check my hair in the mirror in the hall before throwing the door open.

Just as I expected, he's there, tall and broad and filling up the doorway with his imposing size. He's in his usual formalwear, minus the jacket, a starched white shirt unbuttoned at the collar with a red tie.

Yes, I could eat this man alive.

But he's been ignoring me for three whole days after our kiss.

Although I've been dying to see him, something about the mere sight of him here makes my throat tighten and heat flood my cheeks.

The last time we saw each other, he kissed me like he meant to steal every future breath. I kissed him back like he was oxygen.

When I don't say anything because I'm lost in the moment, he clears his throat. "Hey, Winnie. How are you?"

"Good."

His eyes trace over my face before dropping down to where I've folded my arms. I'm not sure whether I'm pumped he's here or annoyed he's been ghosting me, so I settle for cautious excitement.

It's an easier emotion to manage.

"It's been a busy few days," he says, already making excuses for blowing me off.

"Um, right."

"You remember Junie at The Sugar Bowl? She wanted to check out that honey and see if there's any to sample."

I open the door wider and let him in. "They're your bees and your property, dude. You don't really need my permission. Let me grab you a jar."

Once he's inside, he feels too big for this space, even if it's perfectly accommodating. The man just has this way of sprawling into my personal bubble without even noticing.

Does he have to be so tall? So intense? So scowly?

I don't remember his eyes ever looking so dark before, shifting to blue-tinted coal in the dim, soft light.

"As it happens, I collected a lot of honey the other day, so… give me a sec." I rush past him before he notices me staring. I'm practically drooling, for God's sake.

"Take your time. I'm glad I'm getting my money's worth," he says, leaning against the kitchen island, his tie hanging crooked over his very large chest.

My toes scrunch. They're very good at doing that when he's up in my head.

Or maybe it's just the thought of why he's here, armed with so many lame excuses and small talk.

Is he nervous like I am? But why?

He made it crystal clear he isn't interested.

I open a cabinet over the sink and pull out a jar of purple honey. Every time I see it, I'm amazed just *how* purple it is. The stuff really glows at night.

Not like that chemical solution inside a glowstick, but it's there, more like a cozy candle with a dim flame.

"How do you mean? I'm sure you're still taking a loss on me, no matter how much this stuff brings in long-term."

"You're organized. You don't slack off. That's a nice start."

"I'd better not." I shake my head. "You're giving me free shelter and letting me mess around with bees. It's the least I can do when it doesn't feel like real work." I tilt my head as I look at the honey. "Did you think more about that lab we mentioned? They can analyze this stuff and pinpoint anything that'd be good for natural supplements or research. Of course, you might need to bring in somebody who knows about that sort of business if that's the route you decide to go, but stranger things have happened."

"Good point. I'll have a sample sent off." There's something warm in his eyes as his face relaxes and he gives me a small smile.

"Right. Yes." I hand him the jar and our fingers brush.

God, it's like static on steroids.

The shock jolts up my arm so fast I rip my hand back, making a small noise in the back of my throat.

And now he's staring.

Awesome, awesome.

That means we'll have to talk about it, the hundredth awkward conversation I never needed with this man. But I figured that was coming because he's here, all piercing eyes locked on mine and his big hand wrapped around the honey jar.

That's probably why he decided to show up at all, to clear the air so we won't suffocate in each other's presence.

"Archer, look, about last time," I start, "The kiss was—"

A knock at the door stops me mid-sentence.

Honestly, I'm a little glad. Maybe Colt came along and got tired of sitting in the car.

Or maybe it's my dad—finally sniffing me out and paying

me a visit—ready to roar his demands to come home or wind up forever penniless.

My stomach hurts at the thought. But if I have to face him, I won't be alone.

"Hang on, I'll get it," I say, holding up a hand.

Archer stays silent and watchful as I hurry to the door. I pause and pat my hair again because it tends to frizz when I'm stressed in this midsummer heat, then I throw it open for the second time this evening.

One look turns me to stone. Medusa, eat your heart out.

It's definitely not Colt or even Dad standing on the front step. I can only wish it was just my father.

It's *Holden*.

He's scowling, his ice-blond hair slightly ruffled in the evening heat and his suit crumpled. His eyes are dark with resentment, deep shadows carved underneath, and something else moving on his face.

…is that sadness? Over *us*?

I think I'm scared.

"Winnie, thank God," he growls my name, his voice clipped. Instead of waiting for me to invite him in, he shoves his way inside, brushing past me. "I didn't think you'd really be here. Do you know what a nightmare it's been? What a fucking pain… You've been impossible to find since you ran off." He sighs and shakes his head.

"Holden—"

"What the fuck, Win? Tell me one thing." He steps forward, crowding me back against the wall.

It's not that I'm truly scared of Holden.

I can't imagine he has a violent bone in his body, but he looks like he's holding himself together with the force of a paper clip.

I've never seen him like this, bristling with emotion, and I don't know what to do with that.

And after everything, I don't need him here.

I don't *want* him here.

"Why, Winnie? What the hell were you thinking?"

My breath comes too fast.

How did he find me?

I thought I was safe here, that no one knew if Dad couldn't figure it out. That was the whole reason I didn't give it away to Lyssie either, and she knew not to ask.

But she warned me, didn't she?

She said Holden was *hunting* me down. I should have known he'd have the money and influence and high-tech crap to find me eventually.

God.

I swallow thickly.

"Isn't it time to come home?" he demands, rubbing his eyes. "Enough games. Everyone's worried sick. Your mom thinks you've had a mental breakdown. She's worried, and it's not fair to just cut her out like this."

Then it happens.

Holden Corban hugs me with real energy.

Not another one of his awkward cousin-like hugs I'm used to, just a formality for a man who never felt anything for me.

And when he leans in and whispers in my ear, I'm stiff as a board.

"I missed you so much. Come on, Win, let's go pack your stuff. If we start moving, we can make it home before midnight and—"

Archer appears then, this huge shadow towering over Holden. I use the shock to step out of his arms, forgetting how to breathe.

Archer, though, he hasn't forgotten anything.

He pushes Holden back with one giant hand, placing himself protectively between us.

"Cool it, little man. Did she say she wants to go with you?" he snarls, an edge to his voice like a sharpened blade. He glances at me, taking in my expression.

I don't deny it.

What else can I say? Even if this has me sick and confused and stunned, I'm not ready for this conversation with Holden.

I'm definitely not ever going home with him again.

Archer must see the hesitation on my face, and he knows.

His mouth thins into a hard line of judgment.

Holy hell.

I've never seen him look so feral before, like he's perfectly ready to start breaking bones to get his point across.

I want to cry out, to tell Holden to leave and go home without me.

Just *go*, before he winds up with a broken nose.

But I'm beyond words as Holden stiffens, glowering back at Archer like a mean alley cat, wild fury replacing the shock in his dark eyes.

"Who the hell are you?" he snaps. "Last I checked, this is between my fiancée and me. Nothing to do with you."

"Ex-fiancée. She's made that very clear. I'm her landlord," Archer throws back.

I almost laugh at how he says it.

I *want* to laugh, or maybe scream. I gave up the fiancée title the moment I left Springfield, and there's no way I'm taking it back now.

"Oh, her *landlord*! Excuse me." Holden gives a cruel, disparaging smile. "Seriously, man, move the fuck over. You're getting in the way. This is between us."

Archer tenses in front of me, his back straight and ready for war, harder than a mountain. "The second you threatened her and got in her face, you made it my business."

"Fuck off. I'm not threatening anyone," Holden snaps, and

tries to sidestep Archer to catch my eye. "Listen to me, Win. You need to come home now. If you just come back, we can still fix it. Everyone gets scared on their wedding day, right? It's not the end of the world."

But it is.

That was the day the Winnie Emberly everyone knew died a fiery death.

"I'm not going back, Holden," I strain out. "Leave."

"What? For fuck's sake..." He snarls out a frustrated breath. "Is this because of the tiara? Look, if you want to wear the stupid thing, fine. Just come—"

I don't let him finish.

My laugh rips out of me, high-pitched and half-insane. "The tiara? The *tiara*? You honestly think I left you because of a dumb fucking tiara?"

He's cold, frozen, just watching my eyes spin.

I'm sure I look manic and I don't care.

"All I know is I texted you about it, then you disappeared." Holden does his best to barge past Archer, but Archer throws up another hand, and Holden halts in place, scowling. "What the hell is it about if it's not that? Is this like an actual nervous breakdown? There are pills and doctors for that, you know. Good ones."

Classic Holden.

Another quick fix he thinks he can solve with money.

For the first time since Archer showed up, I think I can breathe again. Something in my chest relaxes as I look at the man I almost married—the man I despise like nothing else on this planet.

"I said I'm not going back with you," I say evenly. "Not tonight. Not ever."

He shakes his head wildly.

"So, what? You're going to piss your life away here in Kansas City? Away from all your friends and family and your career? Everything that *matters*? Jesus. Your parents should have *dragged* you to a shrink the minute you took that leave of absence from my dad's office. Even he couldn't believe it."

Ah yes, the all-powerful, all-knowing, upright senator I don't work for anymore.

He's falling back on his gobs of money and influence and legacy back-scratching. But they can't help him with this.

"And what's here for you?" he continues, oblivious to the hardening mountain of muscle he lacks between us. "Do you have any clue how much you've upset your parents? And mine? Winnie, you've freaked out everyone."

Yes, I knew.

I knew the second I took off that everyone would be livid, and no one would even try to understand except Lyssie.

And I still made my decision despite the avalanche of crap guaranteed to roll over me.

A decision I'm still making, standing my ground, unmovable and determined to put myself first for once.

"I like it here," I tell him, lifting my chin. "It's quiet and peaceful and there are bees."

"Bees?" He laughs bitterly. "Seriously? Again with the fucking bees. I hoped you'd grow up when we got engaged."

"Funny. I thought you'd be less of an asshole."

His face hardens. I'm ready for him to come at me, barking empty threats, cursing my riches to rags.

But Archer moves faster than either of us.

One second, he's immobile.

The next, he has Holden by the arm and he's throwing him out the still-open front door.

"Time to leave, you yappy goddamned prick. You don't get to insult her on my property," he growls. "Leave. Right the hell now before I call the police."

"The police? For what?" To my surprise, Holden holds his ground. The porch light outside gilds his hair, casting sharp shadows on his face from his tormented grimace. "She's my *fiancée*, you asshole. I should call them on you."

"I'm not your anything, Holden. Not anymore." My voice is amazingly steady. "I left you the ring. It's over."

His face wrinkles.

It's like he's on a spring when he jumps up and lunges forward, but Archer steps up and catches him with ease, slamming a hand into Holden's chest that spins him off-kilter again.

"Off my property. Final warning before I get you booked for criminal harassment and trespassing."

"Fuck you, man. You don't threaten me with cops. Do you even know who I am?"

I can't see Archer's face with his back to me, but I can imagine the expression—cold, unyielding, terrifying, lethal.

I saw it when he jumped between us, and it made my blood run cold.

"Why the fuck do you think I care?" Archer spits.

"I'm Holden Corb—"

In one smooth motion—almost too fast to even see—Archer takes Holden's arm, twists it behind his back, and shoves him violently toward his car. The movement throws Holden off-balance, leaving him face down in the dirt.

"You're leaving. End of discussion," Archer finishes.

Without hesitation, he marches forward, rips Holden up, and perp walks him to the sleek black car he drove here before he releases him again.

"Are you insane?" Holden whispers.

I run outside, sharp gravel dragging against my feet.

"Archer, no, it's not worth it! Don't get yourself in trouble. Not for him," I whisper loudly before raising my voice. "Holden, just go. Stop fighting. Go home and tell Dad—tell him I'm not coming home."

Crap, I'm going to cry again.

Why is my defense mechanism *crying*?

And why does it always have to happen around Archer of all people?

Looking back, Holden glowers at us both, his gaze fixed on Archer and his fists balled up for a second too long before he finally slides into the driver's seat.

I want to run up and start pelting his car with rocks, but none of my limbs are working.

If he found me, Dad will be right behind him, I'm sure. Especially when Holden delivers my message back home.

I know he will. He's never been the subtle type.

Just not the part where I said I'd never go back.

Not the part where I gushed about the bees.

Certainly not the part where Archer gave him a sorely needed ass kicking for my sake.

He might just claim Archer assaulted him. Another lie, of course.

Nothing about the way angry, bitter Holden tried to box me in that caused this scuffle.

But that wouldn't stop him from bending the facts to fit his narrative. When you grow up in politics and big money, it's hard not to master that skill.

As Holden's car disappears down the road, Archer turns back to me. His face is angular, cheekbones sharper in his rage, and when his gaze drops to my bare feet, he curses, low and harsh.

"Fuck, Winnie. Your feet. Get back inside before you step on something sharp."

"I'm… I'm so sorry." I think I'm trembling. Or maybe we're having an earthquake. That would explain my irrational reaction and the way I think I'm shaking. "I'm terribly sorry about this, Archer. I never thought he'd come here and stir the pot like this. I thought maybe—"

"Winnie, enough."

Even my chin trembles, but I do my best to clamp my teeth together and face him.

Here it comes.

"You can't stay here another second with assholes like him prowling around. Not one more *second*," he says, plunging daggers ringing in his voice. Rage burns his eyes, a hot blue flame that threatens to consume me.

I nod limply like I knew this would be the response.

"I get it. I know. I'm sorry and I'll go."

He glances away with his lip curled, staring into the night where Holden's car vanished, even though we can't even hear it anymore.

"Go? No. I'm taking you somewhere safe, Sugarbee. No arguments. Somewhere you won't be harassed by that sorry shitlicker." He raises his fist, brandishing it like the fearsome weapon it is. "He's lucky I let him limp home."

"Archer... what? I don't understand."

He sighs, low and torn. "Winnie, I said I'm taking you home. My house."

Oh.

Oh, crap.

XII: MURDER HORNET (ARCHER)

*W*ell, shit.

This is what happens when you let instinct jump in the driver's seat and take the wheel.

I'm not sure logic has had a single say in my decisions ever since I got to Winnie's house. Seeing her ex barge in like that, belittling and threatening her, turned my vision red.

Before, I wasn't sure what to think about him. Sure, she didn't want to marry him, but that didn't mean he was an absolute subhuman worm.

That just means they weren't meant to be together.

She didn't want him for good reason.

It's not like she ever went into great detail, and I didn't pry.

Damn good thing she didn't.

Because I might have been tempted to blow into Springfield to make sure he understood the concept of distance. And yes, maybe to fuck him up a bit for good measure.

If I knew he was an abuser who talks like he owns her, I never would have let him set one foot on my property.

Logically, it's irrational as hell.

That's bully fists-first caveman shit speaking, not a man who stakes his entire life on rules, laws, order.

Winnie Emberly is not my fiancée.

She's not my anything.

She's just a girl who's showering down the hall and singing hideously off-key. Meanwhile, I'm in my room, fighting a hard-on, because even though I'm pissed as all hell at her abusive ex, I can't make myself unsee her showering in my head.

Water curling down round breasts and peaked nipples.

Her soft stomach, hips, and long, long legs.

Soap suds foaming across that softness, running down toward her—

Fuck.

I'm so hard I think my heart has migrated south, throbbing like mad.

How can a woman this strange and annoying rile me up so much? I barely even mesh with her as a person.

I kissed her, yeah, but that just means I find her sexy.

That was base biology speaking, and nothing more, even if she flips my switch in a way it hasn't been flipped in years.

I shake my head and snort, dropping my face into my hands.

Who the hell am I kidding?

There's something about Winnie that *demands* I like her.

Almost like this hurt calling to me every time she speaks. I'd sooner cut off my ears than be deaf to it.

She was so quiet earlier, so wounded, even when she apologized like it's *her* fault, having her fuckboy ex coming at her like that.

I had to step in.

I had to act.

I just didn't need *this*.

My house? Shit, I could've paid for her stay at any hotel in town.

Yet my angry, horny, dick-dragging buffalo brain decided to bring her here, into my home.

I haven't figured out what I'm going to tell Colt.

The water stops.

I do my best not to imagine her stepping out of the shower, glistening with droplets, tiny rivulets tracing her curves before she dries off with a towel.

Yeah, this is not going well, and it's barely the first *hour*.

No matter how much I try to focus on moldy sausages and the last time my little nephew Arlo stuffed himself with too many brownies and barfed on Mom's Turkish rug, when Winnie barges into the room, all the gross shit in the world can't undo the awful truth.

I'm still hard enough to cut diamond.

And when I look up, seeing her standing there in nothing more than a towel, I know it's a lost battle.

It's modest enough, yes, covering everything important, but it stops mid-thigh like a towel should. I want nothing more than to skate my hands all the way up her leg until she's gasping and wet—in an entirely different way from the shower.

I focus on her face and try not to look down. She gives me a small smile.

"Hey, Archer."

"Hey."

Her eyes flick down and almost immediately snap back to my face. Hopefully she hasn't noticed the tent in my pants.

"I'm sorry about this whole thing, you know. I just wanted to tell you again."

"I heard you the first fifty times, Winnie. It's fine."

In fact, we're living the opposite of *fine*.

"You can call me Win like everybody else. If you want to, I mean..."

I blink at her.

Bad, bad idea.

Take down too many of the flimsy barriers left between us and I don't think I'll be able to stop myself from touching her. It's already all I can think about, a steady roar between my ears and in my cock.

Hell, I've already started calling her Sugarbee, releasing that name I only kept in my head. Another mistake.

"Okay," I say after a second. "But you need to stop apologizing."

She swallows hard and drops her gaze to the floor.

I hold in a sigh.

Even if I'm currently being tortured by one of the sexiest women alive in my master bedroom wearing a towel and nothing else, I know this was the right decision, getting her out of there.

My bathroom has the best shower in the house with steam and dual rainfall heads. After the shit Holden pulled, she deserved max comfort when she said she wanted to clean up.

She's so delicate, so fragile, so beautiful inside and out despite her obnoxious singing. I want her to feel safe, dammit.

Then she presses her hand to the towel's knot under her arm and blushes something fierce.

"Oh my God," she says, squeezing her eyes shut. "I'm so sorry. You... you didn't have to let me use your shower."

"I insisted. Rainfall makes anyone feel better. Tell me it didn't."

She tries to hide her grin but can't.

"Sorry," she just whispers again.

"Keep apologizing and I'll have to give you something to

apologize for." Bad idea. I can't just say that. I can't just *do* that. Even if the only thing I want to do is march over, rip off that towel, and pin her to this bed until she's fucked senseless.

Her eyes widen and she sucks in a breath, her neck bones standing out in sharp relief, glistening with water beads.

She missed a spot when she dried herself.

Holy fuck, I didn't know it was possible to be this aroused.

"You can have the guest room. I put your stuff in there," I say, trying to force this conversation back to safety.

"Okay, sure. I don't want to be any trouble."

"No trouble." Total lie, but if she apologizes one more time, I don't think I'll be able to help myself. "This is about the safest place you can get. No one's getting in here without permission. That's why I have a gate."

"Only if you're sure." She sucks in another breath, but this one sounds different. "Thank you, Archer. I appreciate it."

"And if you want to see the bees and work with them, all you have to do is say the word. I'll take you over there. We'll both go. If Holden comes back, I'll send him away on a stretcher."

She laughs roughly, like she's a few seconds away from tears. "You almost did that this time."

"I gave him a warning."

"Hopefully he listens. Just don't get yourself in real trouble. He's not worth it," she says, and this time her laugh is a little stronger.

She smiles at me, and I return it.

The moment lingers, heavy and potent in the air. The longer I hold her gaze, the darker it gets. She wets her lips and I track the movement.

Goddamn.

I don't think she knows how sexy she is, how much I want her.

Raging need pounds through my veins. I subtly fist the duvet to keep my hands from being too tempted to touch her.

Touching her is absolutely the only thing on my mind right now.

It fucking dominates my senses, this demanding itch I can't ignore—especially with the hooded looks she gives me now.

If I storm over and seize her lips, she'll melt like butter.

She won't deny me for a second.

She kissed me back at the cabin. Hard, too.

Her mouth was as needy as mine, starved for attention. And she pulled me closer, tangling her tongue with mine like she's been lost in the desert, dying of thirst.

When I think of her fuckface ex, I get it.

I also get angry.

She's never had a real man in her life, and this woman desperately deserves one like a blooming cactus deserves rain.

Holy fucking shit, having her here was an epic mistake.

If I can't stand five minutes of this without my brain going sappy and poetic, how will we survive days together? Possibly weeks?

If she's in my house, the only thing I'm going to be thinking about is tasting Winnie, making her moan, discovering that beautiful body inch by inch, pushing her up against the wall and wrapping her legs around me and thieving her voice until she's hoarse from coming.

Winnie clears her throat loudly, tucking a wet strand of hair behind her ear.

"So what do we do about Colt?" Her question throws a metaphorical bucket of cold water on my head.

Yeah, that.

There's nothing like thinking about how you'll explain this to your brilliant, insanely curious son without sounding like an animal who just wants to get his dick wet.

"Leave him to me. Don't worry," I growl.

Good advice I wish I could take.

I'm already very fucking worried.

* * *

THE NEXT DAY, I shut myself away and mostly succeed at losing myself in work.

So effectively that by the time I resurface, my stomach keeps growling like a bear.

Fine.

Probably dinnertime, which also means time to figure out what's happening with Winnie.

My back aches as I stand up from the chair, launching into a long stretch.

Mom claims forty is young, but it's rapidly approaching like a boulder heading straight for me, and I can feel the pain.

I'm thirty-seven and now I get stiff as a board whenever I sit too long.

I snort at the thought.

If I could've seen this ten years ago, I would've laughed myself silly. But working a job where you're chained to a desk all day fucks your body over, no matter how much you work out or try to step away for walking breaks.

As I head upstairs to the den, I hear voices, and I pause just outside.

That's Winnie talking, delivering the gospel of bees to a chorus of young voices pelting her with questions.

Colt's there, of course, and so are his two sidekicks by the sound of it.

Damn.

When did I *say* he could have people over and leave solitary confinement for nearly burning down my cabin?

Still, I peer through the door.

Winnie's curled up on the sofa with Colt beside her. Briana and Evans are lounging on opposite sides of the other sofa.

The TV's going, but no one's watching it.

Colt has a block of wood and a tray under it for catching shavings, whittling it down into a big, round shape that looks suspiciously like a bee.

Figures. I think all this bug shit is getting to everyone's head.

But Winnie laughs loudly, her face flushed pink.

Her wild auburn hair curls around her face like a girl cut from a Rubens painting, too beautiful for life.

She holds up her hands, telling them about Japanese hornets between laughs. Pretty deadly by the sound of it, and since they're little punks, they're fascinated by the morbid side of nature.

"...that's why they're also called 'murder hornets,'" she says. "They can wipe out an entire hive of ordinary honeybees in no time. Washington state's been chasing them for years before they do too much damage, ever since they showed up there. They're one nasty invasive species."

"Damn! Ice-cold," Evans whispers excitedly.

"Do they attack people?" Briana asks, leaning on the edge of her seat.

"Not typically. Only when they feel threatened like most things." Winnie holds up a finger dramatically. "*But* they're arguably the most dangerous animal in Japan."

"How come?" Colt looks up from the wood he's shaping.

"They're big disruptors in Japan's honey industry. Did you know as few as *ten* murder hornets can kill off an entire farm? That's tens of thousands of bees. Farmers can lose their entire investment for the season if they aren't careful."

"Holy crap, that's wild," Briana says, examining her black and purple nails. "But can't they, like, use their numbers to defend against the hornets? Like, selective breeding or whatever."

"You're thinking of natural selection, Bree," Colt says. He turns to Winnie. "We learned about evolution in biology."

"Oh, right." Winnie takes a cushion from the couch and hugs it, almost infuriatingly cute with that hair and bright smile. Those big green eyes that were so haunted after Holden hollowed them out sparkle today. "Well, it's a different situation, but they *have* evolved a way of dealing with the hornets. It takes some luck and a quick response."

"Like what?" Colt asks.

I smile, hearing the old boyish curiosity in his voice. I worry growing up might strip that away one day, but it hasn't happened yet.

I lean against the doorframe, unseen, just watching them.

This is definitely new.

Colt can be a shy kid, even if he's been perfectly socialized. I didn't expect this version of my son, letting down his guard with a stranger in our house, but it makes my heart rattle like a rock.

"Well, the bees surround the hornet and kinda beat their wings really fast. The air gets trapped and they create a tight ball of heat around the intruder. A little like a heat ray." She flutters her fingers, smiling ear to ear.

"Savage!" Evans gushes, glancing at Briana for confirmation this is cool. Or *savage*, I guess. "So the hornet dickhead dies off, right?"

"With a little luck, yes," Winnie confirms. "That doesn't always mean the hive will survive, unfortunately. Sometimes there's more than one murder hornet or the bees aren't fast enough."

"Screw murder hornets!" Colt pumps his fist in the air.

And then they're all yelling like the kids they are, plotting an entire species' gruesome extinction with lasers and bee-sized hunter-killer drones based on Winnie's testimony.

She covers her face in good-natured horror, one hand sliding over her mouth as she giggles.

For a second, it's too perfect.

My son, his goofy friends, and the stranger who inspired this outburst of passion lighting up the entire room.

I don't know what the hell I'm supposed to be feeling right now, but *confusion* is a very big part of it.

"How can we destroy them?" Briana demands, curling one hand into a claw like a menacing kitten.

Always the big questions with her.

Winnie hesitates, biting her bottom lip between her teeth as she thinks.

"Guys, hold up. Just because they're big and mean doesn't mean they don't play a role in the ecosystem. We just want them to do it at home, not here."

Before the kids burst into violent protest, I step into the room to help her save face.

"That's enough talk about killing under my roof," I say harshly.

"Dad! How long were you there?" Colt beams at me. "Didn't you hear how horrible the hornets are?"

"I heard. I also heard Winnie make a good point. You can't just go around planning to obliterate an entire species." I fold my arms. "If we could wave a magic wand, a lot of people would do away with mosquitos, too. But you do that, you rob a lot of interesting animals of food. Bats, turtles, fish, you name it. I read about it in an article on my last long flight."

The kids go silent, guilt etched on their faces.

Winnie looks like she wants to jump up and kiss me.

Shit, we definitely don't need more of that.

I can't help myself, though, and I smile at her anyway. She lets her bottom lip drop as she smiles back.

Goddamn, that frigging smile. I could stare at it all day.

"How about some pizza while you're pondering the universe?" I drop the most important question.

"Yeah, cool, Mr. Rory." Evans punches the air again. Briana almost smiles at me. "Are we ordering or are you making it?"

"Please say you're making it, Dad. Your pizza blows away all the chain stuff."

"What? You make your own pizza?" Winnie's gaze drifts to me, her eyebrows raised.

"Deep dish," Colt says proudly.

"Guilty as charged." I hold up my hands in mock defense.

"Wow, and here I figured you had a personal chef like my parents." She uncurls from the sofa, revealing long, bare legs and a pair of short white shorts. "Need some help?"

I don't, but I nod anyway.

There's no sense in leaving her stranded with these teenage monsters.

I barely have time to contemplate how I'll keep a lid on my urge to rip her shorts off as she follows me to the kitchen.

XIII: BIRDS AND THE BEES
(WINNIE)

*W*elp.

It turns out making pizza is a deeply sensual act. Who knew?

I certainly didn't until Archer led me to his kitchen—enormous and gorgeously modern with high-end appliances, by the way—and pulled out his pre-made dough.

Pre-made dough.

As in, this man *made his own dough*. Like, from scratch.

Just to check, I prod it and say, "You really made this? From flour and stuff?"

"That's dough, yeah. All mine. I threw it together a little earlier," he confirms.

Oh my God.

It almost feels like he's breaking a cardinal rule of being rich and handsome, but I'm here for it.

I didn't think rich people like Archer existed when my parents barely lift a finger to prepare their own food. Neither does anyone important in the rapid power rush of DC, where takeout competes with prepackaged meals and artisan chefs for the stomachs of the nation's capital.

It's just like that British baking show except this is Archer Rory.

Archer, with his huge tattooed arms and a business that's doing scarily well.

Archer, with his dark stubble and midnight-blue eyes and thick hair.

Archer, who mysteriously looks like he's equally at home in a suit working at a desk or wearing a t-shirt while he beats up idiots like Holden.

That Archer made flipping pizza dough from scratch.

"Surprised?" he asks when I continue staring at the dough like it has ancient Sumerian written all over it.

"Maybe?" I laugh and force my shoulders to relax.

Hardly the first time since I showed up.

The things I felt when he walked into the room while Colt and his friends were spouting off about the hornets…

Even now, the butterflies storming my belly haven't settled down one bit. Neither have the indecent, intrusive thoughts that keep bleeding in every time I look at him.

He stands beside me now, our elbows almost touching, chopping an onion with near professional precision on a bamboo cutting board.

"I'm a single dad, so I'd better know a thing or two about food," he tells me. "And when I say Colt was fussy as a kid, I mean it."

"Really?"

"Yeah, and not like most kids are. You know, the ones who turn down their veggies and live on nuggets and mac and cheese."

"I'm familiar, yes." When I was a kid, classic box mac 'n' cheese was my favorite. My mom and her hired nannies had a fight on their hands to get me to eat *anything* else, including pizza, ironically enough. "What did he like?"

"Grapes. The boy used to eat them by the vine. He'd eat

fries, but only if I made them myself with seasonings he liked. Bread, he'd only eat when it was warm out of the oven. Never knew kids could be so damn fussy."

I smile. "What did you do?"

"Got real good at making bread for one. I also found ways to expand his palate, sneaking grape jelly into his bread and pairing it with healthier stuff." He snorts. "The first few years were rough."

"Oh, I can imagine," I say quietly. "He's a good kid, though."

"I'm glad that phase ended. Now I could feed him nothing but chips and salsa and he wouldn't even notice. The kid's a bottomless pit, he'll clean out my groceries in two days if I'm not careful."

I hide a smirk as I sprinkle flour on the counter and spread the dough.

Archer finishes chopping and he throws the onions in a pan, soon followed by chopped tomatoes, garlic, and a variety of herbs I don't catch.

I barely think to hand him the containers and pick up a few scraps for the trash. I'm too busy staring at him working.

Open-mouthed, blank-eyed staring.

There's nothing else in my brain except *Archer*.

The man can cook. No one who wields a knife with his gracefulness is an amateur in the kitchen.

"How about you, Winnie?" he asks. "What's your favorite food?"

"Um, pizza?" I say it without thinking. Just as our elbows brush again and I have to focus very hard on not making an embarrassing noise.

Here I am in Archer's kitchen, making pizza.

There's an entire expanse of counter space the size of the Arctic Circle around us, but he's still close enough to touch, cooking up a tomato sauce on the enormous stove with his massive back turned.

"Then you're in luck," he says proudly. "This might be my signature dish if you ask Colt. Let's get started on the stuffed crust."

Unlike the man standing beside me, I'm no cook.

Don't get me wrong.

I can make some things like meatballs or cupcakes by following a nice recipe on my phone. But I'm hardly a natural in the kitchen.

I can't just see something and know how it'll taste.

Archer doesn't seem to have that problem. He throws ingredients together without thinking, all muscle memory moving his large hands like the pizza artist he is.

He reaches into the wooden cabinets and pulls out his deep-dish pans.

I follow his lead, helping spread the dough into them, pressing it in evenly. At one point, I step back to look at him, the way his forearms flex as he works.

Dear God.

He's a walking billboard for sex and he doesn't even know it. Or if he does, he's crazy subtle.

I rub my cheek, wishing I could slap away my stupor and wondering how on earth I wound up here and what I'm going to do about it.

What I'm going to do about *him*.

Neither of us have brought up the kiss yet, but we need to.

Preferably before someone implodes from the simmering tension in the air.

Before I do, I mean.

If we can just clear the air, figure out where we stand, maybe I can get past feeling his eyes strip me naked with every glance.

"Have you always lived around here?" I ask awkwardly, desperate to find *something* to talk about besides his hands in that dough, or how much I wish he was kneading me instead.

"In Kansas City or this house, you mean?"

"Both, I guess."

"Kansas City, born and raised, but we moved in here about... seven years ago now?" He pauses to think, pushing the pizza dishes back. The sauce is bubbling on the stove and he stirs it almost absent-mindedly. "Yeah, seven years sounds about right. I needed a fresh start with Colt after—you know."

No, I don't.

But I think I get what he's not saying.

"It's a cool house. You have a great sense of style," I say flatly. I almost ask about his ex-wife, but that feels too much like prying, plus I don't care to ruin the moment.

Another moment we should *not* be having, I mean.

"I got lucky. It took a lot of back and forth with my designer to figure out the finishing touches. Even my mother weighed in—she can't help herself. Thankfully, I didn't cause her a fit like my idiot brother when he decided to install a massive fish tank in his place." He glances at me and frowns as I smile.

Those blue eyes hold mine, magnetic as ever, and he reaches up and touches my cheek, skimming his fingers over my skin.

I stop breathing.

"You had flour on your cheek," he says, but his fingers linger.

For one stalled heartbeat, I think he just might be stupid enough to kiss me again.

Suddenly, no matter how large this kitchen is, it feels too small for us and the ridiculous tension making the air thick enough to chew.

I want him to be stupid.

I want him to kiss me.

Desperately.

I want him to say screw it, push me against this counter, maybe lift me up onto it, and bury my lips under his until I can't remember my own name.

But Archer exhales a loud, ragged breath and stomps away to a wine fridge, pulling out a bottle.

"In true Italian style," he says, holding it up.

I force a laugh and gesture to the dishes. "I hate to break it to you, but there's not much Italian about this. The guy I worked for was on the Trade Committee. He had so many dinners with Italian officials from the EU last year."

"Chicago style, then." Humor replaces the hooded darkness of want in his eyes. "There's beer if you prefer?"

"Wine's good. I'm not a big beer drinker."

"If my little brother heard you say that, he'd have your whole life figured out." He fetches two wineglasses and fills them. "Patton thinks a person's drink of choice is their whole personality."

"Better than astrology, I guess." I laugh. "You get along pretty well with your brothers, huh?"

"They're complete assholes, but still decent guys when they need to be. We're closer than we used to be, I'll admit." He brings out toppings of all kinds—mushrooms, peppers, red onions, pepperoni, prosciutto, the works—and turns the sauce down to a simmer. "What about you, Winnie?"

"No siblings. Just me and my folks." I don't mention how lonely it was growing up in that big house with two control freak parents who were too busy for their daughter.

Mom had nannies from the day I was born, for heaven's sake. But when I got older, she cut them loose. I think she was too paranoid about Dad having an affair like so many other rising stars in politics.

My childhood was a constant churn of new faces. Superficial relationships and glad-handing and smiling for Dad's campaign ads as he climbed the political ladder.

More than anything, it was being fabulously alone and learning to cope with it.

Maybe that's why I like Solitude so much.

I've been *conditioned* to be lonely. I just didn't think too hard about it until now.

"I wish I had a sister, sometimes," I say into the silence. Archer watches me intently, and I'm not sure I want him reading any of the deep melancholy thoughts drifting through my head. "You know, someone my age, or maybe a little older."

"With two jackass brothers, I'd say you were lucky. Siblings are hard work."

"*Brothers* are hard, but sisters do stuff together. They can actually bond." Even as I say it, I know it's wishful thinking.

Maybe I *like* the idea of having a sister because Lyssie is basically a sister from another mister, and I always wanted something like that.

"Have you always lived in Springfield?" he asks, shifting gears.

"I mean, yeah. I traveled around a bit. DC and Virginia, you know. Lots of trips across the country and sometimes abroad. I spent a few months in New York once while the boss hobnobbed with his old-money donors."

I enjoyed it, too, but I don't think I'd like settling there. It was a massive change, going from a big fish in a small pond to feeling like plankton in the ocean.

New York City eats you up and spits you out, even if you're a United States senator. If you're a staffer, you're total fish food.

After a while, I hated the anonymity in the city, this huge, teeming place where it felt like no one cared. What started out as my big adventure became pure claustrophobia.

Just give me my little house somewhere with my bees, please.

Peace and quiet and cool fresh air.

If I'm lucky, a family to go along with it, and a man to come home to who's huge and bold and kindhearted, a man like—

No.

You're doing it again.

Winnie, you are not *settling down with Archer Rory.*

"My mother liked the honey," he says, surprising me. "She tried it, actually."

"That's good to hear. Have you tried it yet?" I help assemble my pizza, putting way too much pepperoni on top. What can I say—I like some spice and balance has never been my thing.

"Not yet."

"Not even on toast? Man, what are you doing with your life?" I roll my eyes and cluck my tongue at him.

With a quick sly smile, he opens the fridge and pulls out the small jar. There's only a little purple left, but it's beautifully strained, just as bright as I remember.

"If you want to force-feed me, I won't stop you," he says deadpan.

Holy crap, is he joking?

But his face is set like stone.

The image of feeding Archer Rory that purple honey hooks into my head and doesn't let go.

…I guess maybe I *could* put it on a spoon and pass it over without bursting into flames.

Unless he makes a big show of licking it off.

My toes scrunch like caterpillars.

He wouldn't dare… would he?

I know I'm being silly, thinking he'd ever want to make me imagine licking it off his hard, punishing body.

Time to put my fantasies to bed and do something less erotically charged.

"I have another thought," I mutter, practically stuffing my head inside his giant fridge.

I find sriracha, garlic, ketchup, and soy sauce, and start mixing them together in a small bowl. Finally, I add a dab of honey from the jar.

"We'll just give it a little drizzle, if that's okay? Or we can set it aside as a dipping sauce for the crust," I tell him.

"Sure we can. How did I know you'd find a way to pair that damn honey with the pizza?" Archer chuckles.

"Hey now, honey goes with almost everything if you try," I say pointedly.

"Don't know why I ever thought anything else."

My ears burn, still stuck on double meanings.

"Smart-ass." I take another small sip of wine, knowing if I have too much, it'll lower my defenses dangerously.

"Not the first time someone's called me that."

Maybe not, but I can't imagine many people have insulted him to his face.

The more I get to know him, the scarier he seems, especially with the big dark military tattoos creeping down his arm.

With the wine putting courage in my blood, I reach out and trail one finger along them.

"I like your ink. Says you've got a good reason for being such a grump," I say, and he stiffens. "An eagle and a…"

"Caduceus. For medicine," he answers roughly.

"Huh." I tilt my head as I consider. "You were in the army?"

"Special Forces Medic. Almost drove me to medical school when I was younger." He puts the pizzas in the oven and leans against the counter, facing out into the kitchen.

From downstairs, Colt and Evans yell something unintelligible, probably caught up in their video games.

"Impressive," I say, watching his face as a shadow crosses it. "How come you didn't stick with being a doctor? Real estate seems more boring."

"Because I learned to make the pizza." There's a gruffness in his voice that makes me blink.

"Come again?"

There's a sadness in his eyes now as he slowly looks away.

"I'm not such a hardass about making the pizza perfect just for Colt's sake. For me, it's about honoring a mentor—a friend. We called him Big Frank. He was a Chicago guy, and he made the best goddamned pie I ever had, working miracles in mess halls from a few ingredients and MREs. If you tasted it, you would've had to strap yourself down not to take flight. He was killed in an ambush. Syria was fucking chaos, too many different sides and special ops the public never knew about. Officially, we were never there when it happened. He took shrapnel to the neck. I tried like hell before we were extracted, but I couldn't save him."

My heart crumbles.

Even now, there's a hint of panic on his face behind the brave, stoic mask.

I see this young, wide-eyed, heroic Archer coming out who's so human it hurts.

He's always been like this, I guess. The natural protector, and when he couldn't do what he does best, when he let his fallen friend down…

God.

"So that's why you have the tattoos."

"Yeah." He nods. "As for the rest of it, why I came back—" There's a fraction of a pause where he bites back whatever he was going to say. "I had to come home and figure life out fast. Being a father wouldn't wait ten damn years to finish medical school. I couldn't be away from Colt that long, not with the situation with his mom."

He looks away.

I have *so many* questions. But I'm also not stupid or cruel, and now obviously isn't the time to pry at his marriage.

"I'm sure you did the right thing," I whisper.

I hate that my eyes are stinging again.

I've always been a huge sucker for these wounded warrior stories, though. It's the only thing that ever seemed *real* in politics, the times when we'd show up so the senator could pay his respects to military families.

The flag-draped coffins always tore my heart out.

Especially the ones that came back from the places just like he said—the invisible, background wars and special missions no one thinks about.

The ones where good men die for mysterious causes.

Nothing changes the tears, hot and real and shed by loving families.

Even now, I want to flipping hug him, but I don't know where the boundaries are anymore.

I just know they're blurred like staring into murky water, and I kinda wish they'd just get messier.

"That's really kind, you know. Making food to honor Frank and keep his memory alive. I'm just sorry you had to go through—"

"That was that, Winnie." He cuts me off. "You can't change the past, and there's a certain point where there's no use in crying about it either. Me, I'd rather fucking eat."

Somehow, that makes me laugh.

"Well, I'm no expert on parenting, seeing how my parents never did much when I was a kid. But from what I can see, Colt's a very lucky young man."

"He's not a proper man yet, but he's on his way. More wine?" He smiles and refills my glass. I'm a little shocked when I see I've finished it. "We'll just see how well he handles it once he figures out you've moved in."

Scrunch.

There go my toes again.

And I ever-so-slightly regret the hot honey sauce I mixed up when my body temp must be well over a hundred degrees.

* * *

According to Archer, the kids don't usually stick around to eat with adults.

Normally, they retreat back to their hole with plates piled high with pizza to continue their gaming marathons.

Today, though, they settle around the table.

"This honey sauce slaps," Evans says as he drags his crust through my sauce until it's totally marinated.

The purple tint makes it look a little weird, but it tastes yummy.

Oh, and the pizza is incredible.

There's no doubt Archer Rory can cook with heart and soul.

"It's an easy sauce to throw together. I think the honey might be a tad sweeter than the usual kind," I say.

"See, Dad? I told you it'd be big. Don't you ever listen?" Colt says impatiently, reaching across the table for another slice.

"Yeah, but this is proof," Archer says. "It's decent enough to ignore the fact that it's purple."

Archer grins at me from the other side of the table.

I wrinkle my nose, biting back a smile.

This is kinda fun, being caught up in a family moment

like the kind I never had at home. If we ate dinner together as a family, there was no joking.

Dad would be stuck on work, and Mom would be worrying out loud about her next big dinner party. Or—and this happened more often—dinner *was* the big fancy social engagement and work project rolled into one fake, miserable event.

Lucky me.

Talking about Dad's work or Mom's dress or the stiff, stilted small talk of those dinner parties wasn't thrilling.

Maybe discussing the nuances of purple honey isn't the most sophisticated subject, but it's warm. It's friendly and authentic and fun.

The two enormous deep dish pizzas Archer assembled go down amazingly fast with five people attacking them. I'm glad I put together some extra garlic bread.

The teenagers are machine eaters, and there's a weird pleasure from seeing them sit back in their chairs and talk about how full they are by the end.

"Tell me about your wood carving. You're pretty into it, aren't you?" I say to Colt as the other two push their chairs back, take their plates to the sink, and scamper back through the house.

"Yeah. Dad helps me sometimes, but I do most of the work."

"That's great, Colt." I nod at the bookshelf behind him, which is decked out with several pieces clearly shaped by his skilled hands.

I see a globe, a scarecrow, a windmill. The last one even has tiny shingles etched on it.

"I'm seriously impressed. How long did it take you to do the windmill?"

"Oh, uh, forever! Definitely a few days to get all the little lines just right. It was only my second time using this new craft carbon knife for precision." His face lights up.

"Keep it up, no matter what you do for school or work," I tell him. "You never know when it'll come in handy—or when it'll be a ticket to a date with some pretty girl."

I can't resist laughing at how he flushes.

"Aw, Winnie, you're as bad as Dad. That's what he says all the time."

"You're destined to be a ladies' man, boy. Just not too soon. You've got my genes, after all," Archer says smugly.

My laughter amplifies.

Colt rolls his eyes like marbles, but he grins and laughs.

Yeah, this is new and rapidly addicting.

The warmth, the teasing affection between father and son just reinforces everything I thought about Archer being a good dad in a normal family.

And it's sweeter than any magic honey when it makes me feel like I'm part of it, rather than the weirdo alien bee-girl dropped into the middle.

Archer holds out a hand for Colt before he goes barreling past us with his plate.

"Hold on, bud. There's something we need to discuss."

"Oh, crap. Evans staying over? Dad, I promise you we're gonna study a bit. You can even call his mom. She asked me to help bring up his math grades this summer before—"

"Not that. You've been behaving yourself, so you're no longer thrown in solitary," Archer says.

"Oh, cool." With a huge sigh, Colt stops and leans against the table. "Okay, so, what is it?"

"There's been a problem with the Solitude house and my other places are booked up. Winnie can't stay there right now, and since we know her, she's going to be staying with us for a few days. Not too long, just a temporary fix until we find her something else," he says. I can't thank him enough for keeping my secrets close to his chest.

Colt purses his lips and glances at me. His eyes widen.

The kid isn't stupid.

He's thirteen. He probably senses something going on, but I look away before I can blush and give everything away.

"Uh, okay. No problem," he says quietly.

"Also, don't tell anyone for now. Keep it between us. Not even Uncle Pat or Uncle Dex or even Grandma. You hear me?"

"Yeah, sure. Because you're worried they'd get the wrong idea?" Colt asks, a knowing grin spreading across his face.

"Exactly," Archer clips. "Promise me, Son. I know no good deed goes unpunished, but this time I'm trying to avoid the hit."

"Gotcha. I'll zip it, Dad."

"Keep it down, too, and make sure Bree gets picked up at a sensible hour," he commands.

Colt nods and sets off to rejoin his friends, pausing in the doorway to look back at us. "Oh, and I meant to tell you, Mom called. She wants to take us out to that new park this weekend to fly my drone. Will that work?"

My stomach tightens.

Archer's expression darkens, a hint of the grim, angry face I saw with Holden resurfacing again.

Wow.

It's such a dramatic shift I almost flinch.

Was his ex really that awful?

Not that he'd be alone in the terrible exes department. Holden Corban could probably give her a run for the money any day, but if she's such a monster, why is he even keeping her around? Yes, I know there's all sorts of legalities with trying to separate a boy from his mother, but still…

I don't know the nitty gritty details, I guess.

My parents should've gotten divorced years ago, but they stayed together for money and image. I can't remember the last time they showed each other any affection that wasn't staged for a photo op.

"I'll think about it," Archer says after a moment. "But I should talk to your mother first, okay?"

"Okay." Colt beams and runs off while Archer stares at his plate, lost in stormy thoughts—and from the look on his face, none of them are good.

* * *

It's late.

Almost midnight, according to my phone, and the house is dead quiet except for the distant thump and laughter of Colt and Evans still gaming. Briana left a few hours ago, saved from any new drama erupting with two teenage boys on a summer night.

Understandable, since I think they both have a crush on her.

I pad across the almost-silent landing, my robe wrapped tight and my hair tied in a messy bun, ready for bed. It's almost automatic where I'm going.

Same for where I finally come to a stop.

Really, I shouldn't be here, standing in front of Archer's bedroom door for the second time today.

The sensible thing to do would be to walk away.

Just go back to bed in the softest robe ever and sleep.

He loaned me one he had left over from a spare box in storage, surplus robes for men and women from their properties, all embroidered with the Higher Ends logo.

I wish it made me saner than I feel.

I wish it stopped me.

But the heavenly robe can't control my hand when it moves.

I knock.

Gently at first. Then with more force when he doesn't respond.

I wait, heart beating in my throat, but there's nothing. No response to suggest he isn't asleep.

Honestly, that's fine.

I'm the clueless idiot disturbing him.

I should know better, considering the disaster of the past kisses, yet here I am, rocking up to his bedroom door like I *want* something to happen tonight.

My toes are probably white from being scrunched inward by now.

I count ten seconds before I turn, ready to race back to my room like the startled mouse I am and lick my metaphorical wounds. But just as I turn my back, I hear the door click.

"Winnie?"

I swivel around. My jaw drops when I see him.

Effing magnificent.

That's the only way to describe Archer Rory in his tight green army tee and athletic shorts that leave little—yet still too much—to the imagination. My eyes flick to the bulge underneath the valley of his abs for the slightest second.

It's like staring at the sun, but it also takes crazy effort to push my gaze back to his face.

"Um. Hi."

"Everything okay?"

"Yes! Yes, everything's fine, Archer. I just—" *I want to fall through the floor and erase your memory of you ever finding me like this.* "I was just up and feeling a little restless. That's all."

He holds the door open for me.

"There's a view from my balcony," he says, and when I step past him, he leans over me to shut the door.

Holy hell, the smell of him alone ignites my senses.

If I wasn't already climbing half out of my mind with lust, his woody, manly, dangerous scent would leave me stranded in crazy town.

For a second, his head turns toward me, and he stares down at me, close enough to kiss.

The air froths with energy.

Oh, this is bad.

My body floods with wicked heat. But just as I think he might close the distance, he pulls away.

I don't know if I'm relieved or disappointed.

At least his butt looks great as he leads me through his large master bedroom to the balcony. Just as he promised, the view is incredible, even if it only takes my mind off Hercules incarnate for a few seconds.

The neon lights of downtown Kansas City glow like another world in the distance. The air is still balmy, sticky even, and I can see a few faint lights from ships snaking along the Missouri River.

"Pretty awesome. You can see most of the city from here," I say.

He rests his arms against the metal railing as he stands beside me, close enough to feel his warmth bleeding through my clothes.

"What's up with you, really?" he asks. "Somehow, I don't think you came here to just admire the view."

"Yes. No. I mean…" God, why is this so hard? I huff out a breath. "I just came to talk. If you want to, I mean. After dinner, you seemed kinda bothered. It's not my business, but…" I dip my head, not wanting to look him in the face. "Look, I appreciate what you did with Holden. I'm super grateful for all your help, really, and I want you to know that if you ever need an ear, I'm here. For you and Colt both."

He's dead silent for so long I wonder if he hears me. I

glance up to see him staring at me with a crooked smile, so close and so striking I can't remember how to breathe.

"What about a mouth?" he whispers, his voice low and gruff and raspy. "Frankly, that would help me a lot more than an ear tonight, Winnie."

A mouth?

I frown, my frazzled brain trying to parse what he means.

Until he grabs my shoulders.

Until he pulls me closer.

Until he makes his words crystal clear with a demand disguised as a kiss.

Holy hell.

There's no gentle pleading, not tonight.

No hesitation.

He knows what he wants, and he goes for it.

I don't hesitate, opening my lips and tangling my tongue with his, matching him stroke for stroke.

My body is so hot and tense I can't stand it.

And I run my hands down his shoulders, his chest, his stomach, until he groans.

He kisses me again, deeper than ever, his tongue moving against mine with a fury, speaking silent words.

I moan into his mouth so loud it's almost embarrassing.

But I can *feel* his erection, thick and hard, pressed against my belly.

Wanting him this bad isn't a passive thing.

It's an entire storm, just as demanding as his kiss.

Just as consuming as the feel of his thick, coarse hands running down my sides.

His thumb swipes under my breast, tracing the curve until he winds up to my nipple.

I break away to gasp.

"You're perfect," he tells me. "Fucking perfect. Men will kill to be inside you, Winnie."

Right now, I think he's killing me.

Because this is what I've craved.

Filthy truths pouring from a man's mouth. From a man who actually cares.

But Archer doesn't need to sweet-talk me into bed.

For him, I'll go down willing and eager.

For him, I'll open my legs and give it all up to a *man*, not an immature little boy.

My lips tingle from the scrape of his stubble.

Flipping delicious.

When he turns his attention to my neck, stamping hot, rough kisses that pull at my skin when he sucks, all I can think about is how he'll feel between my legs, the wild contrast of his hot tongue and the animal friction that's imminent.

Sighing, I press my thighs together and almost gasp at the sensation.

I'm so wet it's insane.

His hands skim down my butt and his fingers grip my cheeks.

Closer.

Closer, his grip says, and he holds me in place so he can grind against me. The shorts are thin and molded to him, so tight I can feel every inch of him.

Yeah, there's a very real chance I might just combust and set his house on fire. I don't know how he'll ever explain the ashes to the police.

And I'm even more baffled how I'm still standing as he pulls my robe open and sucks, hard enough to mark me, just above my nipple.

I fall against him with another moan, completely in shambles.

"Let me hear you, Winnie. Tell me you want this," he growls between kisses, sucking and pulling with his teeth.

Oh, sweet hell.

His breath feels furious against my neck, pure dragon smoke condensed into a whisper.

My robe hangs open.

Answering, I undo the knot around my waist, tugging it open.

Sadly, I'm not completely naked underneath, but I sleep in a tank top and a pair of loose, silky shorts that skim the curve of my ass. Not deliberately, but right now I'm glad I didn't opt for my ratty tee and boring cotton panties.

But from the way Archer growls his approval, I think he'd still love me if I was wearing a paper bag.

He slides my robe the rest of the way off, tugging until it pools on the floor.

My nipples pebble in the night air and he circles a peak with one hand, wrapping his other around my waist, the better to make me a willing captive.

Before I can wonder what he'll do next, he lifts me up and carries me inside.

I wrap my legs around him, rubbing across his length.

Fuck me, that's good.

And that's exactly what I want, what I need—for him to take me now.

No barriers. No slow caresses. No hesitation.

This doesn't have to mean more than one reckless night. For now, that's enough.

Because I've wanted every sexy inch of him ever since he first walked into the cabin and growled in my face.

He tosses me on the bed.

I land with a bounce and a startled giggle.

When I turn to face him, he's standing in front of me, all angry god.

He looks down like I'm his property, a feast laid out for his taking.

I'm pretty sure this man is all muscle. *Let's face it, I am.*

All mother-of-God, bona fide, delicious *man* I want to gulp down like cold sweet tea on a suffocating summer day.

"Fuck," he rumbles, his voice hoarse with need.

"Yeah. Couldn't have said it better myself."

His gaze skims down my body now.

I can practically feel the weight of it dragging past my breasts, across my stomach, landing between my legs.

God, if I have my way, he'll go to town tonight.

His cock jerks in his shorts, and I watch with rabid enthusiasm as he looks on at his offering.

Of course, he's enormous.

Part elephant.

The kind of huge that I know might hurt a little when he enters me, at least until my body adjusts to his size.

I also know that means it's going to be the best fuck of my life.

I mean, *just look at him.*

If there's anything this guy knows besides pizza and being father of the year, it's sex.

And weightlifting, I guess. With biceps like his, he could throw me across the room.

Or just pin me down and leave me begging until I pass out.

In one swift motion, he pulls off his shirt, but before he can reach his shorts, I sit up again.

"Wait." I reach out, running my fingers along the waistband. "Let me do the honors."

Without seeing his face, I touch him through the shorts. He groans.

"Woman, I didn't invite you in to tease me," he says as I run two fingers along his length, feeling it throbbing under my fingers.

God.

I lean in and breathe against it, and he sucks in a rough breath of his own.

"I know."

"You don't have to do this. If it's too much, too fast, we can stop right now, even if I'll need to spend the rest of the night in the tub, buried in ice."

"I don't, Archer." I smile up at him as I cup his balls. "But I want to taste your come."

"Winnie—fuck!"

It's so on.

My brain sticks on all the little details as I pull his shorts down to his knees and open my mouth for the first few inches of his massive cock.

He's so girthy it's inhuman.

His abs are granite, inhumanly well defined as he inhales sharply.

His pecs are broader than mountains.

The tattoo on his arm swells as he flexes, and I notice more ink on the right side of his chest.

A poppy, I think, standing dark red against the black of what looks like barbed wire. There's a date, too.

It must be for his friend. Big Frank from Chicago who never came home, and the thought unlocks something in me.

Doesn't make me less horny, no—I don't think anything could stop me from wanting him right now—but there's this tenderness, too.

Plus, unholy appreciation, because tattoos on a man like this would make any red-blooded woman feral.

I show it by dragging my lips down his cock, dangerously close to gagging when I take him, and I'm still not even *halfway down*.

Worth it.

So worth it.

"Good girl," Archer rumbles, sliding his fingers through

my hair, holding me against him. "I like how you struggle. Keep sucking. Take what you can."

With pleasure, I do.

My pussy aches from how intense this is, even when it's an exercise to keep breathing between the slow, rhythmic thrusts of his cock.

He's sexy and bossy and so fucking hard I want him to slam into me right now.

I'm so wet, I've soaked my little shorts. When he looks down between my legs to see, I know he notices. His eyes darken as I come up for air.

"Will you come in my mouth? What do you want next?" I ask, licking my lips.

It's not that I need to be commanded, but Archer has such a voice, and it would be a crime if I didn't let him use it.

When he doesn't answer, I slide my fingers up his thighs, stopping short of reaching where I know he wants me to go.

On reflex, he thrusts his hips, and I grin.

"You have to tell me, silly."

"Never had you pegged for a dirty girl," he mutters, his fist tightening in my hair.

"What do you want, Archer Rory? Tell me."

He groans. "Just put your mouth back on me. Fuck, I want to taste your pussy. You make me want a thousand things, all hard to decide, Winnie."

When I pull his shorts fully down his legs, I shiver. His cock leaks on my fingers as I stroke him slowly, engulfing him again with my mouth.

When I lick the moisture off the tip, his other hand fists my hair harder, drawing me into him.

I take him fully in my mouth this time, pushing until he's back against my throat.

It's not tender, not sweet, not like two new lovers should be.

NICOLE SNOW

This is fully sensual, a concert of skin and moans.

Sex doesn't always have to be a slow burn. I'm not the kind of girl who expects flowers after letting a man plaster her face.

Of course, that's what my parents wanted. The good girl, their picture-perfect pawn on the chessboard of money and power.

Mom still thinks I'm shy and guarded, protecting my body like it's a sin to be wanted. Kept pure until marriage to the dullest man in the world.

If I'd married Holden, I know how it would've been. Sex would have been a chore like cleaning the kitchen, the same as our whole lives.

In all the time we 'dated,' we never once slept together.

It didn't take long to figure out he preferred his phone to real women. I noticed when he passed me his phone a couple times to look up restaurants or directions and he had a dozen porn tabs open.

The whole time we dated, Holden never took me back to his bed even once. But being sexually compatible didn't matter, not when we were supposed to be soulmates politically.

Another pawn.

Another prop.

Another wasted life.

But with Archer, there's no doubt he makes this feel electric.

This thing between us is unhinged, dirty and demented and volcanic.

We're teetering on knife's edge of losing our minds and I *love it.*

Logically, yes, this is a bad idea we'll regret tomorrow. But I can't bring myself to care when he's gripping my hair and thrusting this hard.

One hand guides my head.

His other slides down my body to my breasts, palming them roughly, possessively.

I lean into his touch, giving him permission to use me.

Any way he wants.

Anything.

Because I'm not the shy little wallflower Mom wanted.

I'm not waiting until marriage, and I've had other hookups before, most of them young boys in the DC circles who talked a big game and blew it in bed.

But I know what I like.

And I'm happy to show him exactly how he can please me by pleasing himself.

Archer doesn't seem to need much encouragement, though.

He groans low in his chest, the sound vibrating through him. He's not content to sit and take what I'm giving him.

Growling, he tugs at my nipples, testing my reaction, feeling what I like.

Of course, I moan louder the harder he goes.

Soon, I'm a complete mess, sucking his cock, wondering when he'll fill me until he pulls out and pushes me away.

He eases me back on the bed with azure hellfire in his eyes.

All the better to give him access as he pushes a hand under my shorts, his fingers skimming to my slick center.

Every part of me narrows to that bundle of nerves.

He flicks his finger, feeling how wet I am.

"Fuck, Sugarbee," he whispers, so guttural this time. Almost like he can't quite believe his own senses.

He slips a finger inside me, hardly needing to try, and his finger feels so big, filling me already.

I try to think past the raw sensation, focusing on what I'm doing, but it's so hard. *Pun intended.*

"You're so fucking tight." His hand tightens on my hair, pulling like reins. "Winnie, do you want this? Can your pussy take me?" Then he inserts another finger, and I roll my hips on him, fucking his fingers.

"Y-y-yes," I stammer. "Archer, please!"

He answers, pushing his dick back in my mouth.

Oh, I could come like this.

Honestly, I *might* come if he doesn't stop, even though he's only just started.

My body comes alive, riding the high of him in my mouth, fingers inside me, Archer all over me even though he's barely giving me these slow strokes with his fingers.

I choke on a gasp as this seething heat settles in my core.

Another groan rips out of him, and the knowledge he's close tips me over the edge.

Ecstasy floods me, coming in devilish waves.

I moan around him, losing control of my mouth, my tongue. But I think he likes it because I hear him groan again.

"Archer!"

And I start overflowing.

My vision goes white and the harshest orgasm of my life plows through me.

Coming!

He pulls out of my mouth just before I'm done, holding me in his arms as his fingers work every last bit of pleasure from me. I let my head tip back to look at him, and he wipes spit from my jaw.

"This won't last long, but it'd be a sin not to use your pussy," he tells me. His voice is all growl, but his hands are so gentle.

"I... I don't mind."

I truly don't.

It's not about how long it lasts, but how good it feels

while it does. And from what I've seen so far, I think it'll be pretty amazing.

He crosses to the other side of the room while I peel off my panties and wait for him on the bed, splayed out for his delight.

Eyes fixed on me, he unwraps a condom and slides it on.

I'm breathless with awe.

"Treat me like your fantasy girl tonight. It must get lonely without a woman," I say as he crawls over, pressing me into the mattress without a word. His cock teases my entrance, his big head dragging over my clit. "Rough, hard, whatever you like…"

"You *are* my fantasy, Winnie. Every honey-sweet inch of you." He edges himself against my clit again, *almost* inside me.

I swear, that 'almost' is going to be the death of me.

I arch my back, chasing the tantalizing pressure of his cock.

His next kiss is hard and punishing. I love that he doesn't feel like he needs to hold back.

Not with me, maybe not with anyone. I don't know much about his sex life, but I also don't care.

This isn't about our past.

This is our present.

Our moment.

Tonight was made for us.

When he still doesn't slide inside me, though, I wrap my legs around him and give him what he needs.

"Please," I whisper.

"Louder," he whispers. "Beg louder because I can't fucking hear you."

I shiver.

I guess this is payback for wanting to hear what he wants. He needs to be in charge and I like it.

Even though this is new for us, I love the give and take, the frantic chase of flesh and words and explosive passions.

That's what good sex should be—give and take.

Later, we can figure out specifics.

Later.

"Please," I hiss again, rubbing myself against him. "I want you inside me."

With a satisfied smirk, he finally grabs his cock and pushes inside, slowly and firmly.

A good thing, too—he stretches me like I knew he would, almost splitting me open. It's a good pain, the sensation of being filled so completely I can't breathe.

I need more.

More, more, more, until he's fully inside me, and he releases a breath that's more like a torn sigh.

His soul exiting his huge body, maybe.

"Does it hurt?" he asks, brushing my hair back from my face when he's finally seated in me to the hilt.

"Only if you stop."

He chuckles, this gritty whisper through clenched teeth, and then his hips start moving.

Oh.

Oh, God.

Now, it's my turn to feel my soul take flight.

In all my years, all my messy hookups, I have never, ever felt a cock built like a battering ram.

But it's not just the wonderful way he wields it with every greedy pump of his hips.

It's the full ensemble that takes me apart shockingly fast.

The weight of him pressing against me every time he goes deep.

The intimacy, the way he looks at my face like it's the sunrise.

The unbearable, almost killing friction of his cock moving in me.

This time, when I come, it's an avalanche.

I clench around him, throw my head back, and let out this hitched scream that splits the night.

And I'm only halfway through when I feel him tense, when those bed-breaking strokes deep inside me suddenly stop and he holds his cock so, so *deep.*

Archer erupts inside me, pouring himself out with a curse, filling me with a molten heat I swear I can feel through the condom.

Holy flaming shit.

And later, when he pulls out reluctantly and we're spent, lying there with the dim moonlight streaming through the window, it feels different from the other times I've had sex.

It's hot and sweaty and primal, yes. But as he rolls off me and cooler air dances across my skin, I feel something new.

Without him, I feel empty.

And when he clambers back into bed after disposing of the rubber, tucking me into his side like going back to my room isn't even an option, the feeling eases.

It's slowly replaced by this liquid warmth that's so different from the delirious heat still chasing itself around my veins.

Sleep finds me quickly in his arms.

But before I go under, I feel his lips pressed against the soft skin behind my ear, a whisper without words.

Winnie Emberly, you are in trouble.
You're so fucking mine and there's no going back.

XIV: UNBEELIEVABLE (ARCHER)

I don't think I've woken up this happy in the past ten years.

At first, I don't even know why.

It's like I've been drenched in the most glorious honey scent and I want to drown in it.

Then she wiggles her plush little ass against me and my dick reminds me exactly why I feel like a billion dollars.

Winnie.

Stifling a growl, I slide my hand around her waist and between her breasts.

Her hair is a delicately tangled maze of curls. She smiles and blinks like she's dazed.

"Morning."

"Damn good morning," I growl back.

Like a satisfied cat, she stretches, grinding against me again.

My cock is truly awake now, and I catch her hip as I grind against her sweet ass. Neither of us bothered to put on any clothes last night.

If I had my way, I'd keep her here like this forever, naked and all mine.

Her body feels just as perfect as I imagined.

Better, even.

Her breasts are small and pert with pink nipples like ripe cherries, made to tease a man, and her skin feels impossibly soft.

"Careful, I have morning breath," she protests.

I kiss her anyway.

Fuck morning breath—I need her again.

It's insatiable, this hunger she's stirred awake.

Before Winnie, sex was mechanical, an urge like an itch I'd scratch once in a blue moon.

Sure, I wanted it.

A man has needs, and I found women to fulfill them. Always at their place, and rarely twice in a row. They'd go back to being nameless memories the very next day.

Plus, with work being what it is and Colt getting older, even quick and dirty hookups have gotten less frequent.

I started to think that was just part of aging, the carnal desires taking a back seat to life, probably for the better.

But no, not anymore.

Not when I want to *devour* this woman, to savor every part of her. From what I discovered last night, she tastes like licorice and honey.

It's already fucking constant, this addiction to Winnie Emberly, the way my hands still ache to touch her even when she's right in front of me.

It's hot need, pure and simple.

I pinch her nipple as she moans, low and demanding.

Another thing I love—she knows what she wants in bed, and it's sexy as hell.

She doesn't wait for me to initiate, either. She goes for what she wants.

Her long legs wrap around mine and she grinds against me again, teasing me.

Growling, I push my fingers against the nub of flesh between her legs, already soaked, and press.

She gasps.

She's so wet for me I instantly lose my mind.

Always so ready.

Fuck, I could slip inside her right now and I'd fit like heaven because she wants it that bad.

"Archer," she whispers.

This shit is unhealthy.

It's honestly *sick* how much I love it when she moans my name like a prayer. I'm addicted, and I slip my fingers inside her, catching her moan in my mouth, when I hear footsteps.

Not coming to the room, no, but plodding around downstairs.

Loud voices, young and adolescent, just on the cusp of puberty rattling them to lower octaves. Colt's voice is slowly getting deeper, but Evans has that rasping, nasal quality of a voice always about to break.

Shit.

I remove my hand from her at the same time she rolls away, her eyes wide.

"Colt," she mouths.

Double shit.

What now?

He shouldn't know we slept together.

With my other hookups, I was careful to a fault, never letting any of my flings intersect with his life. He doesn't know I see women, and that's how it should stay.

Especially because this thing with Winnie is—

Shit, I don't know what this thing with her *is*.

All I know is I want her more than my morning coffee,

which is sacrosanct. The day doesn't start before coffee strong enough to strip paint pries my eyes open.

Raking a hand through my hair, I ponder what to do.

"I'll go downstairs and start breakfast," I tell her. "Wait a little to make sure the coast is clear."

Her hand is cupped over her mouth, but although her eyes are wide, they're filled with laughter. A breathy giggle escapes.

She's still naked, the little minx, showing off this tiny roll around the base of her stomach when she sits up.

I love that too.

Winnie isn't bird thin. She has real curves. Her physique reflects the carefree spirit behind those big green eyes.

Goddamn.

I don't know what I did to have a woman like this fall into my bed, but I'll pray to any deity who can keep her here.

But first, Colton.

I jump up and throw on a pair of jeans and a white tee, hoping to hide the hard-on from Hades that refuses to behave.

When I head down, the boys are on the sofa, laughing at some dumb streamer on TV screaming like a girl while he games.

I heave a sigh of relief.

Okay, disaster averted.

No, I didn't get to see Winnie ride me this morning, but I saw plenty last night. In the moonlight, she looks like a goddess coming for my soul, and I was set to hand it over.

I snort at the thought.

A fucking goddess?

Who am I? Where is Archer Rory?

While Evans and Colt laugh themselves red over the streamer's antics, I get started on breakfast, beating the pancake batter together and frying up some bacon on the side. I've just about regained my composure when the doorbell chimes.

Weird. Someone at the gate at ten a.m. on a Saturday? I pull out my phone, check the camera, and my heart stops.

Of course, it's Rina.

It had to be her.

Shit!

What did Colt say again?

Something about his mother wanting to take them to the park?

Naturally, I forgot like the sex-crazed lump I am today. I was so taken up with Winnie that I never gave Rina the time of day.

I didn't call her like I meant to. I never even made a final decision about this outing.

And Winnie's still upstairs.

Fuck.

At least Colt hasn't realized she's not in the guest room. If I can just tell Rina to come back later before Winnie comes down, this whole mess might be averted.

But when I buzz her through and open the door, she breezes past me like she owns the place.

"Pancakes," she says as a greeting, inhaling sharply. "You always were good at those."

"What the hell are you doing here, Rina?"

"Visiting Colt, obviously. You know I'm not here for you. Didn't he tell you we have plans?" She sails into the kitchen and I follow, gritting my teeth and hoping Winnie doesn't choose this instant to pop in. "I want to take the boys out to the park to fly their drones."

"Why didn't you call me?"

"Must I run everything past you to see my own son?"

My glare could melt through solid granite.

"I'm his dad," I remind her, folding my arms.

In this space, I'm painfully aware of the fact that Winnie was here last night, cooking with me while our elbows touched. The lightest brushes were a soft breeze, bringing the storm that came later.

The air feels different in this kitchen with Rina today. *Colder.*

"When it involves *our* son, I have a right to know."

"And I'm his mother. Are you saying you don't trust me to look after him?"

"I'm saying you gave up your right to just skip through his life when you walked out." Yes, my temper is off the rails. I suck in a low, slow breath. Hard to believe we were ever anything more than two strangers bristling with suspicion. Did I ever love her?

She sighs and shakes her head.

"You should've called me, Rina."

"I told Colt to run it by you. I figured he did. He says he wants to go."

Yeah, I know because he told me. And it wouldn't have pissed me off so much if I hadn't forgotten about it.

Predictably, Winnie chooses this very second to waltz in.

She's cleaned up well, decked out in a green skirt paired with a white shirt that clings to her curves. Nothing inappropriate, but still hot as fuck.

Her hair is piled in a messy bun, and she beams like the morning.

At the arched entryway, she stops, staring at Rina like she's seeing double.

Rina stares right back.

If these were two cats crossing paths, they'd be blowing up like furry balloons, if they weren't already ripping and biting each other.

"Oh. Crap." Winnie rips her gaze away from Rina to look at me. "Sorry, I didn't mean to intrude."

Rina gives a sickly smile I don't believe for a second.

"I'm the one who's intruding, believe me. I didn't realize I'd interrupt your precious time playing house, Archer."

"It's not like that, Rina," I bite off.

My vision goes red.

She's too good at pushing my buttons.

"Oh, I think I know exactly what it is. No need to hide it. You're a grown man and you can do what you want." Her eyes flick between us both. The worst part is, she's not wrong. Winnie looks healthily fucked and *happy*. "I just didn't know you were bringing your girlfriend around Colt, Arch."

"Rina, enough," I spit.

Winnie forms up beside me and throws her arm around my shoulders.

It's so unexpected I almost jump.

A gesture of support. Possessiveness.

Back off, she says with her pose. *He's mine.*

I shouldn't like it, but I do.

That's when I know my mind is fully gone.

"Sorry," Winnie says, her voice saccharine. "I didn't mean to step on any toes. I didn't know you guys needed to discuss it first? Does Archer need your permission to date?"

The fact that she's just casually taken on the role of my girlfriend bowls me the fuck over.

I'm speechless.

My girlfriend.

My *girlfriend*.

I haven't had a girlfriend since my divorce. This is new, and I have no idea what she's doing.

None of this should be happening right now in any sane universe, but I'm not denying it. I don't *want* to deny it, which is even more ludicrous.

"Oh." Rina blinks, and fuck, why does it feel so good to

see the woman who made me so miserable lost for words? "Well. It's not... It's not that you guys can't be together. Around Colt, I mean." She pulls herself up. "But you probably want some alone time, right? I'll go say hi to Colt."

It's a good save, honestly.

I might have respected her for it if she wasn't Rina. *If I didn't hate her guts.*

Winnie tilts her head as she looks at me, waiting for me to make the next move. Although she's stepped up with this little act, this is ultimately my son. My choice.

That alone is enough to make me want to kiss her until she forgets her own name.

"Rina, wait," I say, because the wretched woman's right about one thing—I desperately want some alone time with Winnie. Twice last night wasn't enough. I'm painfully obsessed, and my whole cock burns just thinking about it. "You can go—as long as Colt checks in and you bring them back before it's too late. I'll text you the number for Evans' mother."

Rina smiles, pleased at having won this round.

It unsettles me, but there's no point fighting this when I have so much to gain, too.

"Okay, cool. I'll get them out of your hair soon."

I have to bite my tongue.

I hate her smarmy-ass insinuation that Colt is a burden in any way, but I need to pick my battles.

She's Colt's mom.

No matter what else she is, I can't escape that fact.

"I'll call them over," I say, even if leaving Winnie alone with Rina screams bad idea. A spitting match with Colt in the house is the last thing I need. Even so, I head over to the great room. The two boys look up from their streaming. "Hey guys. Your mom's here, Colt."

"Sweet." His face clears. "You're cool with letting us go to the park?"

"As long as you check in. Every few hours at least, okay? If you don't, I'll come and find you."

It's not that I don't trust Rina.

But I *don't* trust Rina.

"Sure!" Damn. The kid's too eager to appease me so he can go with her.

That invisible knife stabs me in the heart.

I hate that she's done this, making him believe she's here to stay, and now I feel like the bad guy for being suspicious.

"All right, bud. She's waiting in the kitchen."

"Evans, let's go."

Colt grabs his phone and sprints off the sofa. Evans follows, nodding awkwardly at me as he passes, and we head back up together.

To my relief, Winnie and Rina aren't talking.

Winnie rummages around in the fridge for some orange juice, then pours herself a tall glass. Rina watches her with barely concealed irritation.

I don't know what the hell is going on, but seeing Rina flustered like this feels satisfying, like rubbing salt into an old wound.

For once, it isn't mine.

Then she sees Colt and her face lights up. She smiles like he's the only person in the room, me and Winnie long forgotten.

"Hey there, kiddo. You guys ready?"

"Do you guys need lunch money?" I ask, sounding like a dick.

Rina's expression tightens. "I've got it covered, thanks."

Colt, because he's astute for a kid of that age, glances between us with a slight frown.

I force a smile.

"Okay, you can handle it, Ri," I say. "Remember, Colt, check in."

"Dad, I *know*. Gah." He lowers his voice as he glances at Evans and mutters, "Sorry he's so uncool sometimes."

Uncool?

For fuck's sake, I never thought I'd be branded Satan in teenager-speak.

I fold my arms and catch Winnie's expression, which she's trying to hide behind her juice glass. But she's grinning all the same.

"Let's go!" Rina drapes an arm over Colt's shoulders, though it doesn't look as comfortable for her as it did a few years ago, back when he was shorter. "I'll bring him back at a decent hour."

"Sure. Thanks, Rina."

The awkwardness feels palpable, but the three of them head out and the front door closes, a little harder than necessary.

I turn to Winnie, who's no longer smiling.

"What the hell was that, Sugarbee? My girlfriend?" My confusion makes my voice sharper than intended.

Any other reaction would be impossible.

"I'm sorry," she says, putting her glass down. She's shy again now that she's not playing whatever role she had mapped out in her head. "I didn't mean to freak you out. If I upset you, I'm—"

I cut her off right there, pressing her against the counter with a kiss.

Her hot breath catches, the rest of her words swallowed in my mouth, and she kisses me back, digging her hands into my hair.

With me, she's not soft. Not delicate.

And fuck, it's hardly been thirty minutes since I left the

bed with her in it, but I've wanted her all that time, and it's been driving me mad.

She's just as eager as I am, tugging at my shirt and hurling it to the floor, then exploring my chest with her hands.

She hasn't asked me too much about the tattoos yet. At some point, she will.

Now isn't the time, though.

The only thing that matters is skin and sweat and stricken moans.

My hands graze down her thighs and lift, hitching her up so she's perched on the counter. Her legs wrap around me, and she rubs against my erection, moaning pure honey into my mouth.

She feels so fucking good even through my jeans.

When I press a hand between her legs, rubbing her pussy, she's soaked all over again and so responsive.

I could play this woman like an instrument.

Some notes, I only discover by touch. Every time I do something she likes, she lets me know. *Loudly.*

I can feel my dick throbbing in my head.

I've never heard anything as erotically charged as Winnie's voice when my thumb brushes her clit or when I let it linger, gingerly massaging her to the brink.

"Th-there! Archer!" she gasps, dragging her nails down my back. "God. Right. There."

What a good girl.

I keep going, reading her breaths and ragged moans and the way her tits grow heavier against me. I suck her nipples, bite her neck, kiss her until I'm drugged with her flesh, all while she fumbles with my belt.

Her hands are so small and warm against my cock.

I groan.

Usually, I pride myself on being able to last, but something about her strips away my self-control.

It's all I can do not to blow off in her hands as I bring her closer, claiming her pussy with two fingers pushing deep, the better to stroke that sweet velvet that's already mine.

Before I take her there, when her body tenses around me, ready to come, I push myself free from her clutches and crouch down in front of her, spreading her wide and tasting her.

Licorice and honey.

Goddamn.

She smells and tastes incredible, dripping with desire.

It's smeared across her thighs, and when I bring my face down to suck, she damn near jumps off the counter.

"Archer—shit!"

My tongue goes to work, tasting her, lapping and thrusting until her hot, sweet cunt becomes my world.

When her legs tremble, that's my cue to pull her closer.

I hold her down, fusing her to my face, making her ride my beard. I know what that friction does, and I can't wait to feel her come on my mouth like fucking fireworks.

"Ah-Ah-Archer…" she whimpers my name, tensing her shaking hands on my shoulders.

I stop and look up. "Do you want to come for me, Winnie?"

"Do you want to fuck me?" Her laugh is more of a rasp.

"I asked you first."

"Then yes. Make me come."

"Say please."

"*Please.*" Her nails dig into my head as she scratches through my hair. "Please make me, Archer."

Music to my ears.

"Good, good girl." Time for her reward.

I slide another finger inside her, loving how hot and tight she is, and pull her clit between my teeth, bringing her off with that brutal yet delicate tongue work that will have her dreaming about me for the next decade.

Her orgasm hits like a desert storm, sweeping through her with sudden, shuddering fury.

She's damn near ripping into my scalp with her nails, moaning so loud it's a good thing there's no one else around.

Her pussy convulses, squeezing my fingers so tight it's almost uncomfortable.

My cock nearly blows in my pants, jealous as hell it isn't in her.

"Now," I whisper after she slumps with eyes half-closed, drifting down from the high with her legs still wide and open for me. "Now, I'll fuck you."

"Every time you're in this kitchen, you'll think of me," she says, her voice low, almost lazy.

Honestly, I'm afraid she's right.

Every move I make that heightens this addiction seems destined to backfire tenfold.

Snarling, I unwrap a condom from my pocket and roll it on as she arches her back, offering her tits to me.

This woman is unreasonably perfect, reducing me to a depraved wildebeest.

"Don't think of later. Stay in the moment, stay with me," I tell her, pushing inside. Her heat welcomes my cock like coming home. "Think of now."

Message received.

She wraps her arms around me, pressing her chest against mine, and there's something so ungodly intimate about the way our bodies connect.

I pick her up and carry her to the sofa in the living room.

I need better leverage than the counter. Hell, if I have my way, I'll fuck her in every room in this house a hundred times over.

She braces herself against my shoulders as I sit, holding her on top of me, still seated inside her.

"I've never been carried off by a caveman before. No guy ever did that…"

"It's bad taste to bring up past partners in the middle of mind-blowing sex, Winnie," I growl, jealous as hell that anyone else had her before me.

"Sorry!" Her head tips back as she laughs, a bright sound that comes straight from her belly. "Sorry. I guess I don't know sex etiquette too well."

There's something damnably disarming about this woman. It pushes past the stupid, primal jealousy at the idea of her being with other men.

"Right now, the rule book says less talk, more riding my cock." To encourage her, I press my thumb against her clit again until she grinds against me.

Incredible.

Her smile beams wicked delight. "You made me beg for it, Archer Rory."

"And you loved every second."

"Your turn." To illustrate my point, she shifts her hips again and takes my bottom lip, biting gently.

Prickling heat flares through me, adding to the gently building pressure at the base of my cock, stirring fire in my balls.

Oh, she'll get me there like this, no question. But it'll be slow, like the incoming tide, not the crashing apex of a mighty wave.

And I'm hungry enough to want the wave.

But this won't be that easy.

If she wants me to beg, she'll have to work for it.

"It's cute that you think you can make me." I trace my fingers down the dip of her spine.

She gives me green eyes dark like the forest at dusk and grins. "Oh, don't worry. You will."

The next ten minutes are the longest divine torture of my life.

For a while, I indulge her, letting her play at being in control. She always gives back that slow, dick-teasing glide, holding back whenever I thrust too hard and deep.

When we're both torn to shreds with desire, panting and groping, damn near mauling each other and fighting for this fucking release, that's when I move.

I grab her and pin her down under me.

Then I fuck her like a mountain coming down, dragging my pubic bone against her clit until she explodes.

Her screams echo off my high ceiling, filling the house with our music.

And my ears are ringing when I come so hard in that honey-sweet pussy my soul leaves my body, pouring myself out in this little splash of madness, wondering if I'll ever find myself again.

XV: DOMESTIC BEE-LISS (WINNIE)

*S*o I've always been an active participant in bed.
Let's just say I've always known what I want from sex, and usually it's something my partner can't deliver.

It's not like I'm enormously demanding.

I don't expect him to be Mr. Hour Long Pound or Sir Jackhammer, or even to carry me from room to room like I don't weigh anything. I'm not expecting a man with a ribbed and dotted dick hot off the assembly line for my pleasure.

But I do expect enjoyment.

To come just once, even if there's no guarantee.

To feel *wanted*.

I think Archer Rory just set a new gold standard.

He makes me feel like the only woman in the entire universe. When he's looking at me, he can't see anything else.

There could be supermodels dancing naked around me and he wouldn't notice.

And he toys with my body. *All of me.*

Not just the usual parts—although he worships them plenty too—but other things as well.

He nips at my earlobes and kisses my neck and the back

of my knees, my sides, my feet, everything he thinks I might like.

He knows when to give and take.

Just like he knows when to ask and when to surprise me.

Honestly, that's a freaking miracle in and of itself. A lot of younger dudes don't have the *ego* to ask, much less improvise.

Not just 'do you like this, babe?' but 'do you like it when I touch you here, or here?' He's mastered the art without words.

And holy hell, do I like it.

This scary, sexy, slightly deranged man makes me come like I never knew I could. I'm pretty sure my soul has transcended matter into pure orgasmic light.

I may have seen whole lifetimes flash before my eyes.

Right now, I perch on the counter, just like I did when he licked me so good, as he picks up making the pancakes he started before Rina butted in.

Rina, the ex-wife with a severe case of resting bitch face.

That's almost enough to pierce my happy afterglow. *Almost.*

I don't know if I have the courage to bring that up now—he mentioned bad sex etiquette before—so I just nod to the expert pancake flipping going on.

"I bet you could hire a whole team of chefs."

Just like my parents did. My mom probably hasn't made anything more complex than toast in years.

Archer glances at me. "You didn't like having a cook growing up, huh?"

"I—" At his knowing look, I stop. "How did you know?"

"Call it intuition." He grins at me when I purse my lips. "Also, you wrinkled your nose."

"The food was always good, I mean. It wasn't horrible."

"But?"

"But they were *paid* to feed me. Every meal was made with precision, not love. But that doesn't make it bad." I shrug because I don't mean to sound bitter about my upbringing all the time, especially to a man who's probably richer than my father. I'm guessing Archer also grew up ten times as privileged. "And say you're ill—it's not your mom bringing you homemade chicken soup and ice cream. It's the happy chef who plates it up with a smile and doesn't stick around for story time."

"That's why I learned to make pancakes."

I laugh. "Is that Colt's sick food?"

"No, I want him to feel like I'm invested. I'm always his dad, even when I'm busy with work." He winks then, and it's so different from the uptight grouch I first met that it strips my voice away. "I'll admit I'm a sucker for takeout, though. The damn apps make it too easy these days and it saves us time some nights."

"Me too," I admit, like we've just shared a dirty secret. "I had an apartment in Springfield. Mostly because I wanted to escape my family. I'm pretty basic with cooking. I just haven't had much time to practice."

"You're never too old to learn, Winnie. Making food isn't air traffic control." He slides some pancakes onto a plate. It's beautifully weird that such a big man gets so tender and gentle with cooking. And, on occasion, with me. "Want to flip the next one?"

"Hmm. I think I like watching you do it better."

I lean up to kiss his cheek. Then I stiffen, because even though it felt right in the moment, was it really?

Oh, God.

Yes, we're having amazing sex, but I don't know if I'm overstepping boundaries.

How does a gentle peck on the cheek somehow feel more intimate than sucking his dick?

But if Archer notices, he doesn't comment. He just flips another pancake.

Once, twice, three times in the air before he catches it again.

"Show-off." I laugh, but Rina flashes in my mind, and my smile dies.

We haven't known each other long. I still haven't asked him much about his ex-wife. Every time I've touched it with the longest pole, he's dodged the subject.

I get it.

She was a mistake.

She hasn't been around a lot.

She isn't important to him anymore but he lets her see Colt because that's what divorced parents do.

It's kinda endearing.

Really, everything about this man is, from knowing he used to be an army medic to the way he makes pizza and pancakes to die for like it's a daily occurrence.

But the fact that Rina was *here*, and my first instinct was to claim Archer right in front of her, to make it clear he's *mine*, feels worrying. Especially considering I don't know anything about their relationship or why it didn't work.

I don't even know why they fell in love in the first place.

At a glance, they couldn't be more different. Maybe that's part of it.

The whole opposites attract thing isn't always as glamorous in real life as it is in romance novels.

...but aren't we basically the same? Opposites?

He's a certified grump, older and wiser than I'll ever be, and a no-nonsense money-driven suit by day.

I'm just—Winnie.

And Just Winnie doesn't seem destined to be more than a fleeting love interest in the long, winding line of women falling at his feet. I'm sure they exist.

But as he piles pancakes on a plate and drizzles maple syrup over them, I wonder.

I need to keep my craziest thoughts to myself.

For now, brunch is enough.

It has to be when the rest of this situationship is too precious, far too fragile to be mowed down by hard truths.

* * *

WE'RE NOT IN A RELATIONSHIP—NOT explicitly—but if we were, it couldn't be going more smoothly.

I've semi moved in, although we've both stressed it's a temporary thing. A quick fix to keep unwanted company at bay.

What we're not saying is how good it feels.

Spending time with Archer feels natural. Too easy.

It's the same for his son. Colt might be one of the easiest kids ever to get along with.

And the sex—oh my flipping God.

We take advantage of every second Colt leaves to defile new surfaces of his spectacular house.

The library, the dining room, the living room (again), the hallway, the shower…

He's insatiable. So am I.

It's like being together taps into this secret well of rabid need that's been building for years.

But unfortunately, real life also happens, duties and doubts waiting to disrupt paradise.

I wish it didn't, but no matter how explosive we are in bed, time keeps ticking by.

I promised him a beekeeper for free rent. I'm not skimping on my end of the deal. That's why we return to the cabin together.

Solitude.

It's such a perfect name for this tranquil place. Without my woes seeping in, it's an oasis in the woods where all worldly cares melt away.

We've been back a few times since I started staying with Archer. Every time, he accompanies me with this protective edge in his voice.

I'm afraid he'll wreck Holden's face if my dumb, selfish ex is stupid enough to show up again.

But the bees are doing well.

At first, I was concerned, like leaving the place vacant could open them to some shocking disaster. But no, they're thriving.

The honey looks just as royal purple as always, and it seems like there's more of it every visit as the summer wears on.

"Can you pass me the hammer please?" I hold my hand out behind me. I feel something cool and metallic settle in my palm a second later and I wrap my fingers around it.

"You sure you've got this?" Archer asks.

"Oh, yeah. I've built more than a few of these over the years." With the back of my hand, I wipe sweat from my forehead.

It's already August with the late summer sun blazing, but the effort is worth it. This extra box will give the bees plenty of space to expand before the season ends and into next year.

My phone buzzes again and I push my hat back as I stare at the screen.

Another missed call from Mom.

Sigh.

I listened to her last voicemail in the bathroom so Archer wouldn't hear it, and it was predictably needy as hell.

We've reached the begging stage of her manic guilt trip. The part where her world starts imploding with a huge Winnie-sized piece of it missing.

Mom *pleaded* with me to come home.

She needs me, she says.

Dad needs me, she promises, even if he won't admit it to her face.

Without me, their dutiful and loving daughter, the family isn't complete.

Same old manipulative crap I've put up with my whole life, whenever I was on the verge of striking out on my own and cutting ties.

Seriously, why listen to another word?

My answer is the same no matter how much her voice breaks, no matter how much she goes to tears at the end and gurgles, *"Winnie, we love you so much... you don't even know."*

"Everything okay?" Archer asks, laying a hand on my shoulder.

I blink at him.

"Sure." I stick my phone back in my pocket. "Just a few funny TikToks from Lyssie." Which isn't a lie when she's been spamming me since this morning. Wedding fails worse than mine mixed with the usual antics of crazy cats.

"The best friend?"

I nod. "She's the only best thing in Springfield."

He hums and I go back to assembling the new box.

It's quick work since his maintenance crew left some spare wood lying around in the shed and he figured we could use the boards. I definitely don't mind.

Especially when he looks like this, staring on in silent approval and catching the way I twist while I work.

The man's eyes are always so hungry it makes me blush.

But I kinda like it.

I finish hammering two more planks together and then let him take over when he pushes past me, signaling me to take a break.

For a rich guy with a real estate empire, he's insanely

good with his hands. And he's really rocking the lumbersexual vibe today with a saw and a checkered shirt he's rolled up at the sleeves to reveal his forearms.

God, I could watch him work all day, his brow glistening with sweat.

A bee zooms around his head, but instead of swiping at it, he slows down and lets it check him out before flying away.

"Nice and calm. You're learning," I tell him approvingly. "You'll be a beemaster yet."

"Don't hold your breath. Getting this close without swatting the damn things is about all I'm good for."

"You're very good at it."

Although he doesn't look at me, a tiny grin quirks his lips.

I smile down at my hammer and the pile of nails in a small plastic container. As soon as this box is finished, I might just jump his bones right here.

But my phone buzzes again with persistent notifications, shattering my temporary peace, and my smile melts.

Okay, don't panic.

It's either Lyssie calling to remind me my life could be worse with shark attacks and hot dog eating competitions held at gunpoint and asking me more questions about Archer, or Mom.

Or it could be Holden.

I have a bad feeling when I finally cave and glance at the screen.

This is a mistake, he tells me. *Just hear me out?*
When can we talk?
Winnie, please.

This is the third message he's sent ever since Archer practically catapulted him off the property.

The first two messages were angrier, long walls of text chewing me out for having the *audacity* not to welcome him

THREE RECKLESS WORDS

back with open arms, and standing by while a brute assaulted him.

He still doesn't get he's half the reason I fled.

The man isn't the brightest, no matter what his pedigree and fancy degrees say.

I guess now that he knows it didn't work, he's going for the whole soft apology route. An ugly good cop-bad cop routine packaged into the same person.

I delete the message, wincing sourly.

There's no way I'm falling for that song and dance.

Besides, reality doesn't look so nasty with a sweaty, dirt-smudged Archer stripping off his shirt in front of me.

That's a welcome distraction that means I can push it aside for a little longer.

"Don't you have some work?" He catches me staring and grins.

"I'm doing plenty." Um, I'm pretty sure thirsting after the hottest billionaire daddy in Kansas City is a valid job.

Like always, I trace his dark tattoos with my eyes. They hug his massive body like ornamental war paint, giving him this feral look that electrifies the most primitive parts of my brain.

Before Archer, I never indulged in ink-dipped men.

The educated, affluent boys at college and the cute dorks I'd find in DC kept their tattoos small and discreet.

Last night, I worshipped Archer's chest with my tongue, wondering how it still feels like skin. They're so dark and detailed it gives me this optical illusion, like I should be able to sense the texture.

"Do you ever miss it?" I blurt out. "The army, I mean."

"What brought that up?" He pauses what he's doing and lowers the saw.

"Just wondering."

"It was a different life. I was a different Archer," he says eventually, meeting my gaze. "There are parts I miss, sure, but life's better now. I'm not spinning along like I was those days. Losing my dad in a plane crash really fucked me up for a while. Happened not long after I left the service."

My eyes widen. I stretch up and put my hands on his shoulders, squeezing gently.

"I'm so sorry, that must have been hard. Was it a big accident? Like, a passenger plane?"

"Nah." He snorts. "Dad had two hobbies—reading bad poetry and flying. One got him into trouble. He had a pilot's license and everything after deciding it was something he wanted later in life. He had a grandfather who grew up in Seattle, always told him stories about the early days at Boeing, and I guess they stuck. Most guys settle for a flashy sports car or a woman half their age when they go full midlife crisis, but not Dad."

I smile wryly.

"He just had to get his own wings as soon as he had his lessons down. He kept at it while everybody else told him he was out of his mind. Mom was always on edge every time she knew he was going up. It got better with time, the more flights he put in—until one day, he never came home." He chuckles bitterly.

"That's so sad."

"That's life, Sugarbee. Shifting sands, light and dark, and you either find your footing or you sink. These days, that's a lot easier. I have Colt, my brothers, my business. The army gave me discipline I wouldn't have picked up anywhere else. Plus, I had a chance to put my country first. There's value there, getting invested enough in your people to give up your life if duty calls. You serve a higher cause, even when damn near everything goes against you."

The man he couldn't save, he means. Big Frank from Chicago.

I bet Archer would've traded places with him in a heartbeat.

Maybe he tried and it was all in vain.

God, maybe Frank traded places for *him*.

Heavy stuff.

The thought makes it a little hard to breathe.

"Hey!" A loud voice comes from behind Archer.

I switch my gaze to a tall man in a burgundy shirt and tan slacks, hands in his pockets. He's standing by the house, watching us both with an amused expression.

At first glance, this guy could be Archer's twin, minus the thinner dark shadow around his jaw that isn't quite a beard. He's handsome enough and younger, with nearly identical piercing blue eyes that shine out from a distance.

He's also just as well-dressed as Archer usually is.

Archer also turns, giving me a view of his sculpted back.

I've seen him naked plenty of times, but I swear I will never get over how good this man looks shirtless.

"What are you doing here?" Archer grumbles, his face darkening.

The stranger approaches, pausing to give me a wicked smile before shifting his attention to Archer. Now, he's closer, and I see his hair looks a tad more rusty and he's certainly younger. "Is that any way to greet your favorite brother?"

Archer snorts. "I can't believe you think that's you."

"Well, we both know it isn't Dex. Mrs. Potter said you'd be here." The man's posture doesn't change, unaffected by the snarl in Archer's voice. It's amazing how he flips from warm and teasing to hard and tense in a heartbeat.

A muscle jumps in Archer's jaw. "What's the point of having a receptionist again if she gives away my location to every asshole who asks?"

"Manners, for one. They never hurt anyone, Arch. And you know the office would suck without her."

"Like you'd know. What're you doing here, Pat?" Archer folds his arms, flexing his biceps. I snap my jaw shut before I get caught in a dogfight between brothers.

"Two things. First, I wanted to see the place for myself. You said there were bees, but I didn't know how many." His gaze lands on me again. I get the feeling *I'm* what he wanted to check out the most. "Also, I wanted to talk about the St. Louis numbers. You've been avoiding my calls."

For the first time, Archer glances back at me. "This is my brother and business partner, Patton Rory. He's a complete jackass, so you won't be seeing him long."

"Pot and kettle," Patton says, totally unruffled. He strides forward on his long legs and offers me a hand. "Nice to meet you. Wynne, is it?"

"Winnie or just Win," I correct. Wynne is my birth name, but I've always hated it. "Nice to meet you."

"Right back at ya." He gives me another once-over, smirking.

"Leave her alone, Pat. She's working," Archer growls.

"Yeah, okay. So, if she's busy playing beekeeper, do you have a minute to talk about the figures? You pulled the report at least, right?"

The way Archer flexes again tells me he doesn't want to waste another second on this.

But he also has no choice.

I bite back a smile. There's something adorable seeing the two brothers interact.

There's a wedding ring on Patton's hand, too, so I shouldn't have to worry that his interest is anything but curiosity.

"I skimmed. Regrettably, I haven't had time to give it a full read-through," Archer admits.

"Wait, what? You? *You* haven't had time to read a business report?" Patton rubs his eyes in disbelief.

"Did I fucking stutter? You heard me," Archer throws back.

"Man, are you feeling okay?" Patton presses his hand against Archer's forehead before Archer jerks away. "You got a fever or something? Replaced by an AI clone to simulate what it would be like if you were nice?"

"Fuck off, Pat."

"I'm serious. It must be bad for you to stop working. Is Colt sick? Where is he? Like, what the hell else could break your focus?" Patton looks at me with a knowing smile. "He's a workaholic freak. This just isn't him."

"Prick," Archer spits.

"Your favorite prick, yes. Well, *second* favorite." He looks pointedly at Archer's crotch as Archer curses him roundly. I press a hand against my mouth as I watch, trying not to giggle.

"You didn't have to come all this way to talk, you know. You could've sent an email."

"Is that how brothers talk? Like we're stuck in 2004?" Patton tilts his head. "You weren't answering my calls. What was I supposed to do?"

Archer scratches the back of his head. "Leave me the hell alone?"

"Too easy, big bro. And turning in your homework late, you don't get rewarded."

"If you *must* know, I've been busy here," Archer says, gesturing at the box we're constructing and all the other bees flying around. "They take up a lot of time."

"Right, right." Patton laughs. "The sacred bees. I forgot you wanted this place to have culty vibes."

"The honey's really rare," I cut in, feeling like I should help. Patton clearly doesn't know Archer and I are—together.

Which is already a complicated label. "I don't know if you've looked into it, but it might give you guys some unique opportunities."

"Opportunities, huh?" Patton snorts, looking like he's just been handed a big one. "I think I can imagine what sort of opportunities you guys have been getting up to. When's the wedding?"

"Patton, enough. I'll get back to you as soon as I have that report read, and it'll happen a lot quicker without you standing here, running your mouth," Archer says, pointing to the front of the cabin sternly. "Leave."

"Ah-ah. It's cool, Arch, I get it. You had good reason for playing hooky from work. So many things you could get up to here in this beautiful place," Patton muses. "So many... opportunities. With honey, too. I wonder how it tastes when you lick it off someone's skin?"

"Patton." His blue eyes flare like gas flames.

"It's amazing stuff, if you'd stop being so buttoned down and—"

Archer takes a swing.

Patton ducks so smoothly I almost gasp, not even taking his hands out of his pockets. It's rare to see Archer so flustered, and I watch as he glowers at his brother.

"Why are you still here spreading misery, you fuck?" Archer growls.

"Because. I wanted to see you, dear brother."

"You have proof of life. Now get your ass moving."

Patton winks at me. "Have you seen his ugly side? If not, I'm doing you a favor. Run while you can."

"Patton, I will beat your ass."

Laughter spills out of me as I brush my unruly hair back from my face. "It was nice to meet one of his brothers, Patton."

"Wow, she remembers my name. None of the Mr. Rory

crap most people go with. I like her," Patton says, chuckling at how Archer grits his teeth audibly. "By the way, Arch, you better clear some space in your *very busy* calendar for Mom. Because when she finds out you're dating a *beekeeper*, you won't live it down."

I'm actually worried.

Archer looks like he's about to blow a blood vessel in his head.

So with another smile and a wave—Patton is almost offensively charming and so different from Archer it's weird how similar they look—the younger brother leaves.

"Sorry you had to suffer his crap." Archer grabs his shirt and mops his red face with it. "Pat never learned how to pick up on subtlety. Or a brick to the face."

"Lucky he has you," I tease, "seeing as you're so good at subtl—I mean, bricks to the face."

He smiles, but his gaze lingers on Patton walking away, and I know he's thinking about what his brother said.

Dating.

Holy Mother of God, he said *dating*.

And I'm not sure if we'll ever live it down, if he even decides to acknowledge the insane truth at all.

XVI: THE BEE'S KNEES (ARCHER)

I have no clue how to get out of this.
Much less how *this* came to be.

I've only known Winnie Emberly for roughly a month. We've been—I don't fucking know what to call it because 'fuck buddies' doesn't feel accurate—for less time than that.

But here we are now, sitting in my vehicle outside Mom's place, just a few days after Patton's contrived ambush.

She twists her hands idly in her lap, a hint she's as nervous as I am. More, probably, because at least I know my mother and what to expect.

Come to think of it, that's more reason why I should sweat bullets.

I don't know what Patton told Mom, but she's bound to get carried away.

She always does. Anytime she thinks I'm involved with a woman, even when it's never been a thing and I'd rather chew porcupine quills. I've had to dodge dinners and surprise outings with women I have zero interest in, or else give in for an evening of drab tightrope walking where I try to humor Mom without making the girl feel like hot trash from my total disinterest.

Only, with Winnie, it *might* be different this time.

Maybe that's why I feel so damn uptight about this, almost disembodied, hovering outside myself and watching as I try to keep my shit together.

I drum my fingers against the steering wheel. She glances at me.

"We can always do this another time," she says quietly.

"That would be worse," I tell her.

"Worse?"

Shit. *Poor girl.*

"Canceling on Delly Rory isn't a walk in the park. You'd better have a damn good reason. To her, hosting comes only second to family."

I wonder if it reminds Winnie of her parents from the way she inhales and her nostrils flare.

But Mom, no matter how much she wants to be part of our lives, knows we're adults. She sees we're capable of making our own choices. Of course, she wants to be part of those choices.

She definitely wants to make sure we carve out a space in our lives for her, but that's different from wanting to micromanage us into arranged fucking marriages like the unlucky woman next to me.

As Winnie starts picking at the skin around her nails, I reach over and take her hand. "It's fine. I told you, we'll keep this simple. We go in, talk about bees, I bring up Colt as much as possible, and we get out with a smile and a good night."

"And cardinals, right?"

"Sure, cardinals." Mom does love to talk about birds and the family symbol that shows up in so much of her art. It's harmless, really, and Winnie seems to like the whole idea.

"Oh, and I'll play down whatever dating stuff your brother told her," she promises, squeezing my hand.

"Yeah. Thanks." I should be thrilled.

Instead, I take a moment to let that sink in. Weirdly, even though I *know* Mom will be all over it to everyone's annoyance, the fact that Winnie feels like she needs to downplay it bothers me.

Which makes absolutely no sense.

We're not *dating*.

Not for real.

Not properly.

I haven't asked her to be my girlfriend, either, and though I'm pretty sure we're exclusive with our odd little arrangement, it's not because we agreed to anything.

I'm not ready for that step yet.

At least, I didn't think I was, but now I'm here with her, and this visit feels less terrifying than I thought.

Remember, jackass, you're not dating her. You're setting your mother straight because your shit-flinging little brother opened his fat mouth and lied for kicks like he always does.

I need to stake that thought in my head before I forget.

Before I fall into easy laughs or innocent touches with Winnie in front of Mom.

Before I make this insanity too painful to quit.

We get out of the car and head to the front door, very much not hand in hand. I do that deliberately.

She keeps a few generous inches between us, really hanging on to this 'just friends' ruse. I don't let that bother me, though.

Inside, whatever's baking smells good.

Always does, but I think Mom has upped her game.

That's Junie's influence, giving Mom off-the-cuff lessons ever since she and Dexter tied the knot, and Mom has really taken it on board. Today it's a fruity dessert smell, maybe cinnamon, too, though I'm no expert.

"I think she's busy cooking," I say when no one jumps out to welcome us. I tilt my head, angling my ear to the faint blues music bleeding from the kitchen. Safe to say she's dancing in there too. "Let me give you a tour while my mother's occupied."

"You sure?" Winnie glances around and gives me a sharp, amused look. "We don't have all week to make her think nothing's going on."

"Very funny."

"I thought so." She snickers.

I take her hand without thinking. So much for fucking appearances.

"Come on, I'll show you the library first. You'll like it."

"Library? You have a whole *library*? In your *house*? Has anyone ever told you that's excessive?"

"No, little smart-ass."

Smiling, she holds up her free hand. "Hey, I come from money, too, okay? I know what wealth looks like, but I bet your library is next level."

To be fair, the shelves in Mom's study have been cultivated over generations. Books that belonged to my great-grandparents still live on the shelves, filling the room with the cozy smell of long-lost memories the instant they're opened.

This house has been in our family forever, and the library is one of the few things each generation has actively added to. Dad's additions were the last and best, I think.

There are still times I'll steal a book or two to bring home to Colt, poems Dad made me appreciate. I wasn't born with a literary bone in my body, but my old man made me grow a few.

Winnie's mouth drops open when we head inside.

"Holy—oh, wow. You weren't kidding when you said library." She breathes, taking a second to drink it in. "I haven't felt this book drunk since I'd walk through the Library of Congress."

"Book drunk, huh?"

She grins sheepishly.

I try to see it from her perspective.

When I was a kid, the bookshelves were all ancient mahogany. Then Dad had them painted this pine-green color and the whole room has felt lighter ever since. A door leads out onto the lawn, and it's open a crack, leaving the white curtains fluttering in the breeze.

The shelves, the paint, the colors have changed over generations. Yet there were always heaps of books, giving it so much soul.

Smiling, Winnie pulls her hand from mine and walks over to the photos on the wall. They're in prime position, display pieces plastered on the wall so everyone who sits on the cozy plush seats will notice them.

"Your family?" she asks, reaching out like she wants to touch the frame, then drawing her hand back.

"Yeah. It's a family history of sorts, starting with my great-grandparents."

"Holy shit, Archer," she whispers.

I shrug. "Honestly, no big deal. Just a bunch of dead people on a wall."

"But you guys still put them there. Ghosts on your *wall* with their own lives, their stories."

"Is that so shocking?"

"No, my parents are just weird, I guess. They never wanted to hang a single photo that wasn't perfectly staged. Where I grew up, it was art. My father changed our wall art every few years, updating to whatever seems more popular."

"To buy votes by acting like he shares the people's taste," I growl.

"…pretty much, yeah. Gross, right?"

It is.

I'm also sorry as hell a girl this sweet grew up living with an image-obsessed weasel.

"These are really beautiful, though," she says. "You can totally feel the history here."

I squint at the pictures again. Most are black-and-white. Some of the more recent additions show my parents in color, along with me and my brothers as kids. In the last photo, my father stands there next to the small plane he used to fly, smiling proudly.

The passion took his life but I doubt he regretted a damn thing.

We don't keep secrets very well in this family, I suppose. It's all hanging out in the open.

Winnie gasps. "Is that… President Truman?"

I knew that was coming.

When you grow up in Kansas City, you recognize Give 'Em Hell Harry like the back of your hand.

"He was a big deal in this town back in the day," I say. "My great-grandparents knew him before he was president. They had a hand in getting him to the Senate before he climbed his way up the chain."

"Wow." Winnie clamps her mouth shut, like she wanted to say something else but doesn't know how. She steps back, finger combing her mass of auburn curls, twining the hair tightly.

I grab her wrist and pull it away.

"What's wrong?" I ask.

"Nothing." Wide eyes flick to mine and away again. "We should look around the rest of the house, though. And say hi to your mom."

I take her on the abbreviated tour—the conservatory, the lounge, the game room, the basement gym, the little room upstairs with spacious windows where Mom paints—and finish with the bedrooms.

Specifically, *my* childhood bedroom.

"This is so cute!" Winnie laughs when she sees the pictures of Spider-Man on the walls. The original and best Spider-Man, Tobey Maguire. "It's weird thinking of you as a kid."

It's weird being back here, honestly.

I live so close I haven't crashed here in ages, and when I do, it's usually after a long holiday where I've had too much to drink and Colt's stuffed with pie and zapped out on the sofa.

Some things never change, though.

I still see my old books on shelves, the classics and silly B-movie horror pulp I used to read growing up. My PlayStation sits in the corner, untouched since the last time Colt played with me for nostalgia.

There's still old homework and papers I wrote packed away in boxes under the bed. The edge of one peeks out.

"I don't know why she keeps half this stuff. Too much ancient history here," I mutter, picking up an ornament of a cardinal and looking it over. I found it in my Christmas stocking one year and put it on top of my bookshelf so Mom wouldn't get sad.

"Moms like to do that. Normal moms, I mean." There's no hiding the melancholy in her voice when she looks at me. "But you said ancient? I think you meant *prehistoric*."

"Shut it, brat." I snort.

"Did you have a happy childhood?" The way the question comes out makes me stare.

It feels like it was bubbling under the surface, waiting to

emerge, oozing with the grim hint that Winnie's own childhood was anything but enjoyable.

"Happy enough. I mean, Dex and Pat were annoying pricks, but that's what any older brother deals with." I look at her sharply and the awkward way she's hugging her stomach. "You okay?"

"I'm *fine*, Arch." Like hell. The emphasis she puts on 'fine' says the opposite. "Your mom's done, I think. Let's go meet her. I'm starving."

Surprisingly, dinner isn't set up in the formal dining room.

Mom usually hosts there because it's bigger and grander, but I guess because it's just the three of us, she's decided to keep it simple in the kitchen instead. I lead Winnie in there.

"Winnie!" Mom says, kissing her on the cheek. "It's *so* good to meet you at last."

"Great to meet you too, Mrs. Rory," Winnie says politely.

"Don't you dare call me anything but Delly." Mom beams at us. It's clear Patton talked this up, which means I'm going to have to punch his face in. "Sit, sit, both of you. I hope you like chili, Winnie? It's a creamy white chicken chili recipe, a southwestern classic with a Midwestern twist. I kept the jalapeños on the side in case you don't like much spice, dear."

"I love it. I can handle a few peppers." Winnie smiles as she sits, poised and confident. Just the right warmth glows on her face.

All her usual nail-picking nervousness is gone.

I shouldn't be surprised she can rein it in when she's grown up at political dinners where there are five damn forks at your place and you look like the biggest moron in the room if you don't know how to use them.

"Perfect!" Mom quickly ladles chili into bowls and launches straight in as she serves them up. "I must say, I've been so excited to meet you, Winnie. I've heard so much about you."

"Really?" Winnie glances at me. "I only met Patton once."

"Oh, not just Patton, though of course he talked you up. Actually, Colt's the one who's been singing your praises for some time now."

Shit. How could I forget?

"Of course he has," I say dryly. "Turns out, he's a big fan of the bees."

All thanks to Winnie, but I don't say that part.

"And of *you,* Archer," Mom says so abruptly I almost choke on my soup. "But tell me about the bees."

Winnie goes into way too much detail, telling her about the brand-new boxes we set up for expansions, honey extraction, how much she's expecting to yield this year, and the rare plant the bees are making their purple gold from.

But Mom doesn't mind her passion.

Not at all.

She watches Winnie like the girl's a celebrity as she eats, hanging on every word, nodding with a smile every time Winnie looks up.

Goddammit.

I can't stop gawking at her for very different reasons.

Not because of what she's saying when I've heard it all before. Rather, it's how she lights up when she nerds out about her precious little honey farm.

She's human glitter, radiant as hell when she's caught in the one thing in the world she loves unconditionally above all else.

It makes me wish her idiot parents or that jackal ex would never take this away from her.

If I had my way, I'd leave her with bright, happy eyes that could rival the moon and the widest grin to go with her clumsy, gesturing hands.

I'd make sure she gets to be this fresh-faced, excited young woman when she talks about honey without another care in the world.

I'd find a way to keep her grinning because it's so fucking endearing.

That's because you want to kiss her again, idiot, I tell myself.

Apparently, when she's around, my sex drive doesn't have an 'off' switch, but when she's like this, there's nothing I want to do more than kiss her sweetly, tenderly, and press my teeth into her plush little lip to whisper what she needs without words.

Woman, it's going to be okay. I promise.

Your damn bees are all you should ever have to fuss about.

Shit, I'd even listen to her ramble for hours.

As long as it takes to know that emptiness in her eyes isn't waiting again as soon as her family injects more misery into her life.

What the fuck is happening to me?

I really wonder as she runs out of words and stops motormouthing to breathe.

Then Mom turns to me. "My, no wonder Colt's taken such an interest in beekeeping. How could anyone be bored of this?"

"Yeah," I say. "I think he's planning a whole biology project on it."

"Biology? He isn't busy enough with his summer math classes?"

"For fun," I say with a proud snort. "He and that Evans kid are going out to document the lifecycle of our local bees and enter them into some big national app for bee studies. If it keeps him out of trouble, I can't complain."

"Pure genius," Winnie says warmly. "God, I wish I had half his brains when I was that age. It would've saved *me* a lot of grief."

That age honestly wasn't that long ago for her when she's only twenty-five.

Sometimes I forget the age gap between us.

It doesn't impact us when we're together, but when I step back and think, it's a glaring reminder that this madness we've fallen into can't last.

There are rules to life, just like dating.

This is an ongoing hookup with a damsel in distress, and I'm the ass clown with the calcified brain breaking every one of them by keeping it going.

"Mrs. Rory," Winnie starts.

"Delly, remember? No stuffy formality around here, darlin'."

"Delly... Would you mind if I used your bathroom?"

"Certainly. Right down the hall and to the left. Big white door. Can't miss it."

"Thanks!" Winnie pushes her chair back and leaves the room.

Mom smiles after her, waiting for her footsteps to fade before jabbing her fork at me.

I already know what's coming before she utters one word.

"I like her," Mom proclaims. "She's a sweet girl, very authentic. I have a wonderful feeling about this one, Archer."

"This one? You talk like I have women coming out my ears, Mom."

"That's only because you won't let them, boy. How many times did I have to drag you into this house to sit down with a pretty girl?"

"And it was a big mistake every time," I mutter.

Her gaze sharpens.

"You know how I feel about mumbling, Archer Rory. Takes me right back to your moody days as a teenager. You were always the sullen one, even if Dexter gave you a run for your money." She purses her lips before she continues. "But your Winnie, yes, trust me when I say she's a good one. Do not screw this up."

"Mom, she's not mine. The whole point of bringing her here was to show you we're just friends." I stop and bare my teeth in the most strained smile of my life. "So you can stop getting carried away every time you hear I'm hanging out with a woman."

She sighs roughly. "Is it such a grave sin if I just want to see my oldest son settled and *happy* for once?"

"Yes. Because it isn't *like* that." I don't elaborate when I don't know what the hell it really is.

If Mom knew we were sleeping together without putting a neat label on it, she'd probably call this an 'interlude' or some shit. Better than 'situationship' and other dumb things the kids say, I guess.

Really, it's a fling.

A little taste of summer wine before stone-cold reality comes ripping it away like a ruthless wolf pouncing on a happy drunk.

"Okay," Mom says flatly, "but why can't it be like that? Why won't you open your mind a little, Son?"

"Mom, you know why. Do I need to sit here and give you all one thousand reasons?" I scratch my neck. My whole face itches. This conversation always makes me want to rip out my hair, but this time it makes me want to pluck every strand one by one.

Anything would be better than listing the many reasons why Winnie and I can't work in gory detail.

"Give me one—one good reason—and don't you *dare* hide behind Colton like you always do."

I grit my teeth.

"Rina, for one," I say, and I know I've hit the jackpot because her lips thin. "All the crap with that. You know what happened with her, what a snowballing disaster it was. I'm almost forty damn years old. I don't need that much drama in my life. We've been getting along just fine without it, thank you very much."

She frowns. "If it was a different girl, perhaps I wouldn't push. But Winnie isn't like Rina or the other women I tried to set you up with. You're smart enough to know that."

Damn.

I *do* know, but that alone isn't enough reason to shut her yap.

"Colt," I say, holding up a hand. "I'm not using him as an excuse. You know I can't just go wandering around taking on girlfriends when he's still a kid. Especially not when he's at the age where he'll be figuring out what dating means soon enough. If I can't set healthy examples, I shouldn't set them at all."

"Oh, please." Mom huffs a breath and rolls her eyes. "Archer, it's not like you send women through a revolving door. We're talking about *one* young woman who makes you smile. Don't even think about denying it when I've seen the way you look at her."

"Not the point. Stability comes first. I'm not tripping over my own bad decisions and screwing up Colt when he's walking that tightrope into adulthood right now. He won't be like me, Mom. He'll grow up *better.*"

She fixes me with the same glare she used to give us as kids whenever we'd step out of line.

"So, that's it? You're digging your heels in and deciding this can't work before you even give it a try? All so you can commit to being a hermit and say it was for your son?"

"So I can finish raising my son right, yes. And that's not even getting into how I'd complicate Winnie's life. She's too young for me even in the rosiest circumstances."

"Oh, Archer. Your poor bruised ego..." Mom shakes her

head. "Age is a number. Nothing else matters when two people hit it off."

I snort. "Nothing and everything for a lasting relationship. How many times do I need to say you're asking for the impossible?"

"About as many times as I need to remind *you* there's nothing wrong with a positive attitude, dearie," she tells me, tapping her nails on the table. It's pretty obvious where Dexter got that habit. "If you believe it can work, if you'll stop shooting down a good thing before it has a chance to bloom, miracles *can* happen."

"Miracles. That's great," I mutter. "Or maybe I'll go and get everybody's hopes up only to blow everything to pieces. I can let you down and confuse Colt with one stone. Brilliant idea."

"Like you're doing now, you mean?" She stares through me. "Not every woman is another Rina, Archer. You can't let the divorce ruin the rest of your life."

Knife, meet guts.

That's Mom, though. Always willing to strike deep with brutal precision out of love.

I exhale slowly, refusing to show how deep it cuts.

"Rina," I spit. Her name alone damn near gives me hives. "I don't even know what she's doing in our lives again. I'm sure you heard about it from Colt. Needless to say, I don't trust her."

Mom looks at her nearly empty bowl, her expression unreadable, before she looks up again. "She came around here yesterday, you know."

"What? Again?" I can't hide my outrage.

"Watch your tone."

It's an effort to moderate it, but every single turn this conversation takes just makes me more frustrated.

"Why did she come over here again? To beg you to hand over a piece of the family fortune? To kidnap Colt?" I'm only half joking. She's been gone so long I don't trust her intentions.

"Actually, she wanted to apologize," Mom says, laying her cutlery down so she can look me full in the face. I fold my arms.

"Apologize for what?"

"She knew you wouldn't hear her out, so she came to me."

What. The. Fuck.

Hearing that hits like a buffalo stampede.

I push my chair back and pace the room, too restless to stay put.

"Damn right," I growl, raking a hand through my hair. "Some nerve. After everything she's put us through—all the money I've pumped into her accounts just to keep the peace, raising Colt alone—and she *still* had to pester you with some big fake apology?"

"Archer—"

I shake my head, snarling. "See, this is what I mean. *Exactly* why I'm not getting involved with another woman. The drama, it never goes away."

"Archer—" Mom raises her voice.

"I don't care how sweet Winnie is or how good you think we'd be together." I'm running my mouth in a way I haven't in a long time, but I need to get this off my chest. "You need to take whatever bullshit Patton told you with a boulder-sized pinch of salt. Stop fixating on relationships that aren't happening."

"Archer." Mom watches me with hooded eyes. "Sit down."

Her eyes are deadly serious.

I sigh.

"Are you listening now, at least? We're friends. Nothing more." I slice my hand through the air, drawing an invisible line that feels weak even as I say it. "She's nice and I'm helping her out of a tight spot. I promise you that's it. We're not dating and we will *never* be anything more."

"Okay," Mom says, her voice softening.

You could chew the thick silence between us.

I'm panting, I realize.

I'm getting fucking *winded* over this, my shoulders tight with stress.

"Sit down, darlin'. I didn't mean to wind you up."

Grumbling, I drop back in my seat and lean back, the wood creaking under my weight. It's been a long time since I've been this pissed.

I already regret half the shit I said, sure.

Especially about Winnie Emberly.

It's almost enough to make me forget she's still in the house until she comes back in the room.

She flashes us a shy smile, tucking her hair shyly behind her ear.

It isn't fair.

It's cruel that she looks so gorgeous I could feast my eyes on that pretty face all day. Before I met her, I didn't think I had a 'type.'

Now, I do.

Her.

Every little detail from the soft freckles dusting her cheeks to her maddening hips to the way she laughs like a song.

"Winnie," Mom says with relief—probably because she didn't walk in a split second earlier. "I was worried you'd gotten lost, hon."

Winnie's face splits into a wide, buttery smile as she retakes her seat.

"It's a big house. You almost need a map." That's all she says.

When she glances at me, her smile looks strained, like

she's struggling to keep it in place. It doesn't quite reach her eyes.

That's the first hint I've fucked up royally.

When she doesn't look at me again, I know beyond all doubt.

XVII: BEE-FORE YOU GO (WINNIE)

We're not dating and we will never be anything more.

Archer's 'never' echoes in my head for the rest of the visit.

When his mother asks if I want dessert—one of Juniper Rory's famous creations—I remember the way he told her nothing would *ever* happen between us.

Now I know what it feels like to get shot and have shrapnel lodged deep in your flesh.

When we retire to the living room with coffee after dinner—because that's what rich people do—I replay his words.

Never.

Never.

Never anything more.

Okay, fine.

It's not like I ever thought we were truly dating, even if he acted like we were most of the time. Holding my hand. Who even does that with fuck-buddies?

He's old, though. I'm not sure he knows how casual things get with younger people these days.

I even told him to his face I would play down the suggestion we were dating to his mom, and he agreed.

So, it shouldn't bother me.

It shouldn't be such a big, nasty surprise.

I have no claim on him and I never pretended I did.

But he sounded so intense when he vowed I'm just his latest charity case.

Like there was never a chance it could ever be more.

Like the notion of just being with someone like me is *ridiculous*.

I try to stop obsessing over it and just enjoy the moment, the easy conversation with Delly as they laugh about Colt.

Only, the second we leave and get in the car back to his house—which I'm still living in—I'm stuck on that single killing word.

Never.

It's so flipping grim.

Not just 'probably not,' or 'I don't think so' or 'don't be silly.'

Never is a killshot.

Never means *never*.

I'm grateful for everything he's done for me. And just because we're having amazing sex doesn't mean we're soulmates destined to ride off into the sunset with Just Married painted on the car.

Logically, it's cool, and I've been telling myself that ever since I overheard him.

So why does it flay me open everywhere?

Why does it make me tear up like I'm back in that stuffy dressing room before I fled Holden and the wedding from hell?

When I came back to the kitchen and heard him growling about how impossible we are, it felt like someone threw me on a bed of broken glass.

Maybe because I've heard it all before.

My allergy to 'never' didn't originate with Archer, no. How many times have other people used that word like a weapon?

Dad used to bellow it every time I tried to step out of line.

You'll never make it on your own.

You'll never make a living as a beekeeper!

Never think about leaving DC again. Your life is here, Wynne.

Don't tell me you want to break things off with Holden. You'll never find someone like him again. He's your future, the glue between our families, and you're being ridiculous.

Our families.

Not me.

Never me.

And there's that 'never' again, digging deeper every time with sharp, gnawing teeth.

We get back to Archer's place after nine, just as the sun sinks below the horizon.

"Want to do anything else this evening? A movie?" he suggests as he pulls into the garage.

"Thanks, but I think I overate." I put a hand on my stomach and force a dead laugh. "Your mom really took Juniper's baking advice to heart, huh?"

"She cooks for ten people when it's only three." His laugh sounds a lot more genuine than mine. "Are you just wanting to head upstairs, then?"

"If that's okay."

He gives me a strange look.

"Of course."

Great, now I'm being weird.

But the longer I'm with him, the harder it is to pretend everything's fine and dandy.

I just need space.

Time to process the unchanging fact that this whole arrangement has an expiration date.

"I'll see you tomorrow," I say as we head inside. This time, I don't kiss him and just head upstairs, leaving him standing in the hall staring after me.

For Colt's sake, we've tried to sleep in different rooms in the early mornings, though of course in reality we've been in the same bed most nights.

This time, I head straight to my guest room.

As soon as I'm there, I pull out my phone and call Lyssie.

"Hey, babe. How are you holding up?" she says when she answers, bright and cheerful and everything I'm missing.

My eyes fill with tears I blink away.

"Those silly TikToks of wedding meltdowns you keep sending are definitely helping."

"Hey, it's important you see how bad it could've been. You got off light." She laughs to herself. "Anyway, what's new?"

"Besides running away and ruining my life? How do you know there's anything else?"

"I've been your friend forever, Winnie. I know when you're BSing me." She sniffs loudly. "And I can smell it now."

"I don't know why I even bother talking to you."

"Because you love me?"

My laugh sounds brittle because it's true. "Okay, fine. So basically, there's this guy—"

"I knew it!" she says jubilantly. "Landlord Daddy? The guy you were telling me about before?"

"Maybe."

"Bingo. Two for two." There's a pause, and I lie back on the bed, staring at the ceiling as I listen. "And you have a crush on him."

It's not a question.

I close my eyes. "Yeah. Something like that."

It's so embarrassing to admit it out loud, but today just confirmed it in the sickest way.

I have officially progressed beyond 'attracted to' Landlord Daddy and flown into obsessed-with-Archer land.

The fact that I'm this *hurt* over his honest, perfectly reasonable opinion shared in private with his mother proves it beyond any doubt.

"So what's the problem?" Lyssie coaxes in that voice she has—the tone that drags my secrets out. "There is a problem, isn't there?"

"Yes, there's a problem." I sigh. "He's emotionally unavailable."

"Oh. Oh, shit." Lyssie sighs. "You really know how to pick them, Winnie. You've gotta break that pattern."

"Tell me something I don't know. But he's not another Holden, at least. This guy, he's divorced. Older. A lot of real, valid reasons to be leery of getting closer." I pick at a loose nail before I catch myself and pin my hand down under my head. "Be honest, Lyss—how dumb am I being? On a scale of oops to chronic sponge brain?"

We won't mention the fact that I've jumped in bed with him.

Some secrets are too precious to share, even if Lyssie's BS radar probably tells her already.

"You're not being dumb," Lyssie says. "At least, not *crazy* dumb. It's not like you slept with him or anything. Just don't get too attached, okay?"

Yikes.

"Um, right. I think my manometer broke after the wedding," I mumble.

"You're not in a good headspace yet. That's expected. *Who* would be after that gross engagement lasted for so long? You haven't really had a chance to meet normal guys yet. Nice ones, I mean."

Right.

I think I'm broken.

Archer Rory is anything but nice and that's the whole reason he makes me tingle.

I let out a small wail, rolling over so my face gets buried in a pillow. "How does that help? What am I supposed to *do*?"

"Keep your space. Be nice to yourself. Be sensible. Slow down, smell the flowers, take some walks, adopt a puppy. There are good and bad ways to get over Holden, you know."

"Oh my God, I'm on team puppy. But I was never *into* Holden," I hiss. "I never loved him. You know that."

"Sure, but you still left him *and* your old life behind. You're not grieving the wedding or him. You're mourning the old you."

"Ugh."

She's too good at this.

"I know, being right all the time is hard work. You'll buy me dinner to get me back when we hang out again."

"Have I mentioned how much I hate your advice column?"

"All the time," she says, a smile in her voice. I can't help but smile back. "Look, it's not as bad as you think it is. You've just had a lot going on. You're emotionally vulnerable. So keep your guard up and put yourself first."

I am.

And yet I also just let Archer waltz in and sweep me off my feet.

Maybe Lyssie *is* right.

Maybe this is a rebound with teeth and claws.

I wanted validation and affection since I never got any from Holden or Dad, so I picked the first gruff, gorgeous, unavailable older man who came along.

Sigmund Freud, eat your heart out.

"You gonna be okay?" she asks after a long silence. "You

know I can come down there. It's only a couple hours' drive. Just say the word."

Tempting.

But if she comes here and sees Archer and the way I feel about him—if she sees I've freaking moved in with him even if it wasn't on a whim—she'll probably haul me off to therapy the next morning.

"I'll be okay," I say. "Don't worry about me, Lyss."

"Nope, I'm gonna worry. But I also know that if anyone can look after themselves, it's you. And you've still got your bees, right?"

"Yup. Thank God for one good thing."

I press the phone tighter against my ear, imagining her here with me. Aside from the whole Archer situation, it would be amazing to pig out on tacos and watch K-dramas and just vibe with her.

"Miss you."

"Miss you more. Keep the updates coming."

"I will." I end the call, tossing my phone aside.

The house seems oddly silent. I kick myself for imagining Archer coming to check up on me.

But why would he? After everything he said to his mom and the abrupt way I ran off the second we got home…

Oh, this is brutal.

Sighing out a long breath, I change into my pajamas, which are deliberately modest so Colt doesn't suspect anything if I head downstairs for a snack later. I sit on the edge of the bed, marooned in my own thoughts.

Asshole or not, Archer Rory has good reasons to be closed off.

After all, he's a single dad, and there are clearly big issues with his ex, even if he won't talk to me about them.

I can't stay mad, especially when I was eavesdropping on his private conversation.

Not deliberately at first, but when I realized they were talking about me, yes, I may have slowed down. I hung back around the corner for over a minute.

What girl wouldn't want to know what her—what the guy she's crushing on says about her?

It's not his fault I didn't like the answer.

And I haven't even *thought* about that old-world Kansas City history the Rory family is just marinated in.

It should feel like I'm escaping one powerful aristocratic family just to fall into another, even if the Rorys don't seem to touch politics.

Groaning, I drop my head in my hands.

Getting involved with a family like his should be at the bottom of my list.

New Winnie, she's not interested in prestige and politics and names with big reputations.

But the thought doesn't help.

Even hours later, when I'm yawning and hurting alone, his words still sting.

I don't know if I can take Lyssie's excellent advice.

I don't know if I can ever learn to just turn off my heart and breathe.

* * *

I ALSO DON'T KNOW I've fallen asleep until I feel hot lips on my temple and warm breath dancing down the side of my face.

I stir awake just as Archer scoops me into his lap.

He's already hard, but his hands are gentle.

"What time is it?" I reach for my phone, but he captures my hand and kisses a finger.

Heat flashes through me.

"Almost eight."

"What? In the morning?" My eyes flip open and I see the sun glaring through the blinds. "Shit. How did I sleep in so long?"

"Don't know, but Colt's out this morning for math class." Archer kisses me again, his tongue sweeping into my mouth possessively. "I thought we'd make the most of it since you conked out early last night."

Crap.

From what I remember, when I fell asleep—on top of the covers, apparently—I was still thinking about Archer.

I faded off with some half-assed thought that I should end this before we get more involved and more hearts get broken.

But now that he's here with his mouth on my skin, I'm much less sure.

The damage he's done hasn't made him any less addictive.

I stretch languidly on the bed, relishing the feel of his huge body on mine. He's here now, and maybe he won't be in the future, but doesn't that mean I should enjoy the moment more? Why shouldn't I make the most of it?

Can't a girl *breathe* by having a little fun?

If experience has taught me anything, Archer knows how to enjoy the now without a worry in his head.

Wet and bothered, I shift my weight so I can straddle him properly, wrapping my arms around his neck.

He's perched on the edge of my bed.

We kiss again, deeply and chaotically.

His cock twitches against me.

"Okay," I say with a small laugh. "I'm awake now."

"Feeling better? Your stomach?"

"What?" I jerk back at the concern in his voice before I remember the excuse I gave him. "I'm fine. I just needed sleep."

"You had it, brat. I missed you last night." His hands find my butt and squeeze. "And I *really* fucking missed this."

God.

He growls it so easily, but I guess to him it doesn't mean anything special.

Maybe he even feels it in the moment—maybe he did miss waking up in the night to find my ass grinding against him.

The thought makes my throat tight, but I just smile.

"Well, it's not getting any earlier. You better make up for it now."

As his arms wrap around me, he stands, and I link my legs around his waist.

We stumble to his room like drunken teenagers, kissing and groping until I can't breathe.

He definitely can't see past my curls.

My back collides with the wall, and he tugs at my pajama top until it comes off.

"Much better," he rasps, bending his head so he can suck my nipples.

My top lies on the floor, forgotten, and I rub myself against him, loving the way his breath comes fast and hard against my bare skin, pelting me with desire.

With Archer, it's always so raw.

That's what makes it so good.

It's never a secret how much he wants me or how much I turn him on, and I'm pretty sure I could come just by looking at him.

When it's over, I'm going to miss that. *A lot.*

But I'm not thinking about over now—the only thing that matters is the way he's touching me, pushing my thoughts from my mind.

"Are you gonna fuck me right here?" I pant, running my hands through his hair.

"Why not?"

There's no good reason, except I want to see Archer in bed, hands digging into my ass as I ride him.

After last night, I want a little control.

"Take me to bed first," I whisper, running my lips along his throat.

He chuckles roughly and takes my nipple in his teeth.

I'm pretty sure my lady parts have been scattered to the seven winds by now.

"As she wishes," he snarls. "My bed."

So sexy.

So is the way he carries me into his room, one hand on my ass moving me up and down against his cock, rubbing me against him.

I'm pretty sure even through two whole layers, he can feel how wet I am.

By the time we reach the bed, I'm already close.

Totally ridiculous, because even though we've been sleeping together for a while, I'm still not used to the spell he casts on me.

It must be magic, simmering my blood and turning nerves I didn't know I had into purring violin strings aching to be touched.

He tries to lay me down on the bed, but I keep my legs locked, and he tumbles down after me.

We both laugh, breathy and gasping.

For a second, I just absorb the magnificent feeling of him on top of me, his weight and heat and strength.

Yeah, this man couldn't be disgusting if he tried.

The king-sized bed feels as huge as always, so I roll, pinning him under me as we strip away the rest of our clothes. His cock springs free and as I look up at him through my lashes, I take him in my mouth.

He groans.

I *love* that sound.

Just like I love it when his head rolls back, his jaw working like he's trying desperately to keep himself under control.

That's the hottest thing, when I make him go to pieces.

When *I* make him lose control.

I might not have him forever, but I can guarantee he won't forget this.

When I sink down on him, he grasps my hips, his fingers digging into my skin greedily, wanting to move me, to control me, to *break me.*

"No," I whisper, taking his hands and linking our fingers. "Hold tight."

"Sugarbee." He groans that nickname, his hands locked around me so tight it's almost uncomfortable. "You feel so fucking good."

"I know." I rock my hips, doing everything I know he loves, bringing him to the edge.

I throw myself into it, riding him *hard,* the better to push him to the very brink and then pull back when he's about to explode inside me.

No condom this time.

Holy shit.

I don't know if he just forgot in the dizzying heat of the moment or if we're that crazy to feel each other with nothing in the way.

But my pussy feels his veins, every glorious thrust, and it's impossible to control my movements.

"Shit, you're… you're going to come inside me," I grind out.

His eyes sharpen.

Not with surprise or denial.

With unbridled lust.

"You want that, woman? You want the man who fucks

you this good to take every bit of you that's left?" His breath hitches. "You want me to flood your little pussy?"

Oh, God.

I bite my lip so hard it hurts, so lost that all I can do is nod.

My own orgasm rolls in like a fast-moving storm, aching to feel us come together so bad.

Another moment.

Another delusion.

Another bittersweet memory, maybe.

But right now, I don't care.

I'm that insane, writhing on his cock, if I'm still moving at all and it isn't his hands flinging me up and down on his shaft.

Holy hell.

Yes, it's temporary, this feeling of belonging, but I crave it desperately.

I crave him like oxygen.

But that's a thought I shut away for another time as I lose myself in midnight-blue eyes.

"Winnie, goddamn!" Every muscle against me turns to granite, his skin slick with sweat.

"I'm close," I tell him. My words are clipped but soft. "Archer, I'm going to come!"

"Fuck, fuck. Come on my cock, Winnie." He holds my gaze like lightning splitting the sky.

I do, and he flexes under me as he gives in to his animal need, swelling deep inside me as I tighten around him.

He's a human wave, a groaning storm, a tsunami slamming my body against him.

I feel his echo in my bones.

The way he twitches, the rattle in his chest, the way he rasps as he buries his cock to the hilt and unloads.

Coming!

Then there's just white-hot ecstasy burning away my senses.

Every shattering moan and rough grunt as he erupts deep inside me feels like the darkest enlightenment.

Yes, I think I get it now.

If this is a beautiful delusion, don't ever bring me home.

If this is how it has to end with Archer Rory, I'll suffer for every second we have left.

* * *

His hands hold mine so tight I can't feel my fingers when I open my eyes again.

It feels divine to just enjoy the afterglow.

Almost as good as the orgasm itself, this weird intimacy that still lingers between us when I roll off him and start cleaning up.

"Come here first," he says, holding out his arm. Tucking into his embrace feels a little too normal, a little too easy. Like walking back into a familiar room or smelling the specific muted scent of his laundry.

I close my eyes, listening to the thud of his heart.

"When will Colt be home?"

"Not before noon at the earliest."

"That's a long math class."

"It's a whole college course crammed into a couple months. He's meeting his mom for brunch, too." He sighs against my head. "I said he could go."

Dang.

This is opening him to so many questions, but I don't dare ask.

Not like this.

Not now.

After the nightmare yesterday, it feels good to just *be*, with no big expectations or fears or anything.

I don't want to ruin the moment with thoughts of Rina.

His phone buzzes beside him, though, and he frowns, reaching to look at it and accept the call.

"Hello?"

The voice buzzes on the other end of the line.

Then his face settles into hard edges and grim lines. I know whatever he's hearing must be bad news. Nothing good ever makes someone's face age in an instant.

"Okay, yes. We'll be there," he clips. Brisk, professional, emotionless.

He hangs up abruptly and I slide out of his arms.

"What is it?"

"That was my maintenance boss. He was called out to Solitude this morning by one of his crew," Archer says slowly, holding my gaze. "He says there's been some damage."

"Damage? What kind?" My heart catapults and lands in my throat.

"He said we should see it for ourselves, Winnie. Let's get cleaned up and go."

XVIII: SWARM BEFORE A STORM (ARCHER)

Well, fuck.

I'm staring at a disaster that has me stunned. It's like a whole pack of ferocious Pooh bears hit the bee boxes in search of honey, tearing apart every last one of them.

There's wood scattered everywhere, bits of purple honey splattering the ground, pieces of honeycomb littering the flower beds.

Before I have time to process the massacre properly, Winnie throws herself at me, burying her face in my chest.

"Who… who would do this? *Who?*" she demands between sobs. Her whole body shakes.

Only Winnie Emberly could get this emotional over a few destroyed beehives, but honestly, she has good reason this time.

The police officers who showed up just before us are still poking through the debris, but I already know the verdict.

Nothing.

No clear evidence.

Whoever did this *knew* the property was empty. They knew there was no one else around to worry about.

They were also savvy enough to use gloves and not leave any obvious prints or DNA around, even in the unlikely event this went up the forensics' chain.

Still, there's no denying it's a targeted attack.

I just don't fucking get it.

There's plenty on this property that's far more valuable to destroy, if someone came here with an axe to swing against me.

Hell, the whole damn cottage, for starters.

Yet, it looks like it's been left untouched. The doors are securely shut; there's not even a smudge on any windows.

The bee boxes, on the other hand—some hyperactive little perp sledgehammered them to pieces.

How they avoided getting stung unconscious, that's another mystery, but I have an idea when I see the door to the shed hanging open.

The lock's been broken.

They took the goddamned beekeeping equipment.

They used a bee suit to destroy the bees.

The nasty discovery kicks hot rage through my gut. I grit my teeth to keep it from my voice.

What kind of fucking animal does this?

"They… they were *just* bees. Oh my God!" Winnie bawls into my shirt.

I can't find the right words to soothe her. Not when I'm bristling with murder like this.

Sighing, I stroke her hair, hold her closer, squeeze her so hard her chest strains to breathe. But she just clings to me more, fisting her hands in my shirt.

How did we get here from mind-blowing sex in the blink of an eye? In the space of an hour, life just unraveled, and I don't have a clue how to fix it.

"We'll find who did it," I promise, resting my chin on the top of her head, staring at the carnage.

The mess, the financial damage, that's not what I give a fuck about.

No, the way this feels like a pointed attack on Winnie personally, that's what makes me see blood.

Who else cares enough about her fix on bees to invade my property and smash them this violently?

I have one very good guess.

And I already regret not punching his ass out cold when I had the chance, consequences be damned.

I hear rustling and turn to see the lead officer picking his way through the debris field to us. His name is Paul Higgins, but he told us to call him Paul when he arrived. His deputy heads back to the car, a bulky tablet tucked under his arm.

Sniffing, Winnie pulls away, trying to pull herself together for the cop.

"I'm awful sorry about this, Mr. Rory," Paul says, addressing me after an uncomfortable glance at Winnie. "Did y'all say you had cameras up?"

"Over the entrance, yes, but not facing the back gardens where we installed the boxes." A huge annoying oversight.

"Well, any footage should be useful. There's only one way in if our suspect came by car. If you can pull the video and send that over, I'd be glad to have a look."

"Of course, Officer. I'll have my assistant at the office pull it from the cloud as soon as she can." I give him her details and fire off a quick message to let her know Paul is waiting, and it's urgent.

Then it's just us, alone with the catastrophe.

Simon Chance, the maintenance manager, follows the cops back to the station, presumably to give the statement he volunteered and do all the official shit. We're the ones left cleaning up this mess.

I swipe a thumb gently over Winnie's tear-streaked face.

Seeing her in ruins makes me want to punch something, but a caveman eruption won't help anything right now.

"Hey," I whisper. "It's going to be okay. Leave the cleanup to me if it's too much."

"Archer, no. How can you even say that after they did *this*?" She stares blindly across the smashed boxes.

Not many bees are around now. I guess they dissipated in a hurry after their homes were obliterated.

How many of them died in the attack?

I've seen a few crushed bees around, but I don't want to think about it, even if the swarming bugs themselves creep me out a little.

I let Winnie wander through the wreckage, taking it in, mourning her happy work.

I'm still getting a leash on my anger when she shouts behind me.

A surprisingly happy shout, I think. Did she find some good news in this mess?

"There!" she whispers, pointing to the forest. "They missed the one in the woods, I think."

Before I can say another word, she takes off, sprinting across the garden lawn and heading through the tall wild grasses where the forest begins just past the farthest ruined boxes.

Just like she thought, there's a box the attacker missed.

"Hey, babies," she murmurs to the bees as she falls to her knees next to them. "Hey, hey. You guys made it. Y-you're safe." She's crying again, but I'm pretty sure these are happy tears.

A few bees hover up, drifting lazily around her hair and occasionally landing before they take off again. As usual, she doesn't mind.

Winnie damn Emberly, the patron saint of purple nectar.

The best friend on two legs a bee will ever have.

I stop a little ways back, not wanting to get too close to the small swarm, but she just glances back at me, her face slick with sweat in the balmy air.

"There's still one left. We can keep this going."

"Great. When I'm through with it, we'll turn it into Fort goddamned Bees-Knox, Winnie," I tell her.

It's the least I can do.

I'm not used to feeling powerless after I've been assaulted.

I hate this shit down to my bones.

I failed to protect my own property, knowing bad actors might come sniffing around.

Worse, I failed to protect her heart.

Her body, her life, maybe.

But what would have happened if she'd been here when the prick who did this showed up?

The thought chills my blood, forming a burning boulder in my throat.

There's nothing else I can say, so I move toward her, mentally pulling together what we need to protect this last box.

"Cameras, barbed wire, fencing, whatever it takes. If they come back, they'll be on camera this time. I'll have access to the app and automations set up to notify me and the police before they get too far."

"Y-yeah." She sniffs again, wiping her nose on the back of her hand. She slowly leaves the bee box to rejoin me.

The bees' distant buzzing gets louder. I swear it sounds unsettled, but she doesn't make any quick movements, and eventually the last insects unhook themselves from her and rejoin the group.

Yeah, I don't think I'll ever get used to bugs crawling all over me. Especially ones that sting.

But the fact that they mean so much to her means I'll guard them with my life.

"I don't know, Archer. It's a nice thought, but will it make a difference?" She looks into my face. "Whoever did this, surely they won't be back again. Assuming they got away with it."

"We'll find out soon. The front camera might turn up a license plate number, a vehicle type, but—"

"I don't mean that." She sighs, taking my hand and looking down as she twines our fingers together. "I already know who did it."

"Yeah. I didn't want to say it out loud with no evidence." I massage my temples.

"...it makes sense, though, right?" Her eyes are clear green pools now, no sign of the tears she shed before. "This is *just* the kind of shitty, petty thing Holden would do."

"Fuck Holden Corban." I snarl the words like the man hit *me* with a sledgehammer instead of the bee boxes. "If we find proof, I *will* nail his dick to the wall. All the trespassing and destruction of property charges known to man. Hell, maybe terroristic threats if they'll apply."

"We'll see what turns up." She smiles sadly. "But I really hate looking at all this mess. Can we try to put our lives back together?"

She's talking about the crime scene, but I read more into her words.

That's why I nod, roll up my sleeves, and head for the shed.

* * *

It takes a couple hours to clean up the disaster zone.

I offered to call in a couple maintenance people to help before we got started, but she insisted we handle it ourselves.

I think she wants to feel every single piece of hurt in her own hands.

As if it was *her* fault some weak little bastard couldn't take the hint that she didn't want to marry him.

Knowing she almost went through with it and married a thin-skinned, passive-aggressive little skidmark makes my blood boil.

I don't condone murder, obviously, but I wouldn't shed a tear if he drove himself into a tree.

This shit was a step too far, well beyond any petty acting out.

I have my on-call driver bring Colt over after his math class and brunch with Rina. There's no use hiding what's going on when he's at that age where he'll just find out anyway.

He arrives around two o'clock, heading into the back garden where we're gathered.

When he sees what's left of the devastation, the bee boxes gone, he stops in the middle of the pathway with his eyes like marbles.

"Shit," he says.

Usually, I'd correct him for his language, but this time it's warranted.

"Shit," I agree.

"What happened, guys? Are you all right?" He looks innocently at Winnie, who's so pale, so fragile in the bright sunlight, like the vivid hurt of this chaos has drained away her color.

"I'm fine, Colt," she says with an unconvincing smile.

"Hey, bud, you're just in time. Help me convince Winnie she should go inside and take a break? A nap wouldn't hurt." The place probably doesn't feel safe anymore, but she's worked through her misery enough for one day.

I don't want her cleaning the rest out here.

Winnie makes a face. "No, I slept for a million hours last night."

"You'll sleep some more."

Colt glances between us. "…are you guys hooking up?"

Fucking hell, this kid and his mouth.

"Colt," I say sharply. "You don't just ask people that."

"You do when it's obvious," Winnie quips and grimaces. "Sorry. Not that I'm saying it's—"

"Whoa." Colt frowns at her. "I mean, that's cool and all. None of my business. I just—"

"Damn straight," I growl. "You were about to shut your mouth and help me bag some trash."

"It's okay." She glances at me and hesitates. "You know what, I think I will head inside for a break. It's pretty hot out here and I'm already burned. Should've brought sunscreen."

"Good idea." It will get her away from my son, who clearly needs another reminder not to run his mouth. "If you need anything, just give me a shout."

"Sure thing." She shades her face with her hand and gives me a small, sad smile that makes my heart twist before she walks through the sliding doors inside.

Goddammit.

I turn on Colt. "What the hell was that?"

"What, I can't ask?"

"No, you can't. Worming your way into someone's private business makes them uncomfortable."

"She wasn't *that* uncomfortable," he says. "I mean, you're the only one acting like it's a big deal. It isn't, Dad, you're just another guy. I get it. You guys can answer a question or two without freaking out."

"I don't need to answer anything. But for the record, it's not like you think."

"Cool, more vagueness." He snorts and shakes his head. I

watch him grab the gardening gloves Winnie left on the ground. "So, what *is* it like, then?"

"None of your business, for one." I grab a bulging trash bag and haul it to the gate. I'll have the maintenance crew pick them up later. "How was brunch with your mom?"

"Awesome! I had eggs Benedict with lobster at that new place. She asked me about summer school and we talked about the bees." He shrugs. "It was nice to talk to her. She said I should come out west later this year in the fall and she'd take me up to the San Juans or Vancouver Island."

In other words, a long fucking way from home for my son and his irresponsible mother.

"Mm-hmm," I grunt, barely biting my tongue.

This is the part I hate.

Being a parent means manning up and moving past the drama so you can co-parent effectively, yes. Only, no one tells you how fucking hard it is.

Or how much you want to shake your kid sometimes because you can't shake the hell out of your stupid, conniving ex.

Rina's done this before.

She's raised his hopes and then left me to pick up the pieces, to explain why his mom has a screw loose that stops her from ever growing up and following through on big plans.

Sure, Colton deserves a mother, and I will never hide her from him, but he should get to walk into this with his eyes open.

"Is she heading home soon?" I try not to sound too hopeful.

"Dunno. Sounds more like she's going to stay in town for a little bit. She said she wants to come to the next parent-teacher conference, to meet all my teachers and see how I'm doing." There's pride in his voice. "Oh, and I promised I'd carve her something."

"Right."

He looks at me. "Are you mad?"

"No."

"But you're mad at Mom."

That doesn't deserve an answer. I don't want to lie to him.

Yes, I'm angry at his mother for charging in like this after ghosting him for years. I've been angry at Rina over that shit for years, and there's still no good reason to believe this time will be different.

"So you had fun?" I ask flatly.

"Yeah! Did you know she makes TikToks? Just product reviews and some lip-sync videos showing off her art, but they're sorta funny."

Sure.

Simply hilarious when Rina always was a master manipulator, and it seems like the perfect place for her smoke and mirrors. Also, her latest desperate attempt to relate to a kid she's actively chosen not to care about until now.

He grabs an overstuffed trash bag and grunts as he picks it up.

I know better than to suggest I carry it.

At his age, he's sensitive to every suggestion that he's not strong or capable enough, just like every boy.

He's a fit kid, too, even if he's always put brains over athletics.

If I'm being honest, after what he's been through, he's stronger and smarter than I was at his age. Like it or not, my boy is halfway to being a young man.

Fucking terrifying.

"I get it, Dad," Colt pants as we lug the bags to the gate. "Why you're mad at Mom, I mean."

"Did I *say* I was mad at her?"

"You didn't need to. It's kinda obvious." He rolls his eyes and drops the bag. It clatters against the fence and he dusts off his hands. "Like, it makes sense. She ghosted you, then turned up out of the blue, stealing me away. You're pissed. Fine, whatever."

She didn't just ghost me—I could've lived with that.

The trouble is, she ghosted *him*.

"Why do I have a feeling there's a but?"

"Well, but... isn't it worth giving things a shot? It's been so long." He sounds so sincere. So sure that what he's suggesting is the right thing. "Especially if she's changed."

I turn that over as we head back to the debris and start piling more wood into another bag.

"Trouble is, Colt, I don't know that for sure. Hanging around a few weeks and picking you up for parks and lunches doesn't prove much." And I hate myself for saying it even though it's the stone-cold truth. There's too much bad history to just walk blindly into the future.

"Why? What proof do you need?" he demands.

Shit.

For a thirteen-year-old, he's a hell of an inquisitor, always homing in on questions that make me squirm.

"Because. A leopard doesn't change its spots overnight. They need bleach for that." A fucking lame cliché. Real nice.

What does that even mean?

I'm frowning because I sound like my father, speaking in rhymes meant to sound more profound than they are, even if my heart's in the right place. All that poetry from Dad rubbed off too much.

Didn't I loathe that shit he'd give me when I was Colt's age? Like I needed riddles because I was too young to handle a real human conversation.

My old man was wrong then, and I have a sneaking suspicion I'm wrong now.

"You know, Mom isn't even weird with you and Winnie," he says, not looking at me. "Like, you guys being together, she just laughs it off."

"We aren't *together*," I snap. "I'm helping her out. Temporarily. Case closed. As soon as she's found a new place and once this bee thing is back on track without any surprises, Winnie will get on with her life and so will we. So don't keep acting like she's a fixture now, okay?"

Colt stares up at me with a frown.

He shrugs, his thin shoulders jerky, and looks away again.

"Whatever," he huffs. "So you don't care about her. Got it."

Damn.

"Colt, I didn't mean—"

"Dad, it's—whatever!" He tears an empty trash bag off the roll and heads back into the last of the mess to start raking it up, surly and wounded.

My heart sinks like lead.

Everything keeps coming out wrong and it's fucking me up royally.

Colt's old enough to have an adult conversation about this stuff—and he deserves to be let into parts of my life now that he's getting older. Especially when it concerns his mom and the woman I'm sort of maybe with.

But no, I go and blow up at him because talking about either of them feels like tearing open fresh wounds.

And that's not accounting for the mess Winnie's ex-fiancé left behind.

We had an unhinged intruder on my property destroying her stuff. All because she turned his ass down, and he never learned to respect a woman's wishes.

Oh, I'd love nothing more than to wind up alone in a room with Holden for a few minutes with no cameras.

But I hate how violent it makes me feel, how impossible it

is to deny my gut feeling for Winnie—or how hard I'm running from the truth.

The similarities to how I handled the late Rina situation beat me in the face.

It sticks in my head like a burr. No matter how hard I try to focus on cleaning up, I can't stop thinking about it.

Winnie and Rina.

Rina and Winnie.

Two very different women.

Both bringing pure electric chaos into my life.

By the time I've faced the long-delayed truth they bring, cleaning up Solitude might be a cakewalk.

XIX: WORDS LIKE HONEY (WINNIE)

You couldn't keep me away from Solitude with a flamethrower.

Archer persuaded me to come back and sleep at his place, yes—and that's fine, after Holden wrecked everything, it didn't take much persuading—but I head back early the next day to sort it out.

I know it's crazy, but I feel weirdly responsible.

If I hadn't come here with my raggedy life and questionable decisions trailing behind me like a flimsy caboose, none of this would've happened.

Holden wouldn't have shown up to mess with Archer's property. He wouldn't have destroyed those poor bees.

It makes me tear up even now. The implications are brutal.

Too personal.

Too cruel.

Too flipping heartbreaking.

Every time I stop to think about it, my throat closes and I forget how to breathe. It's this odd defensive thing where my body shuts down and falls into stabbing pain all over, from head to toe.

I just have to sit and wait it out.

Wait for my lungs to start working again and remind me I don't have to lie down and die.

I still have a chance to make it better.

Right. Back to work then.

First, I work on planting new flowers even though it's getting late in the season. Next year, they'll come up nice for sure.

Archer stays busy with the new cameras he's putting up around the place. I try to figure out ways to make the property more appealing for the bees without ruining its commercial curb appeal.

Of course, there aren't many around here now.

Most of them escaped when their homes were hammered to pieces, but there are still a few around, and we're going to bring them back.

The bees will prevail, and so will we.

And what if there's that teensy-tiny chance it was a random attack? Hard to believe, yes, but we still have no proof.

Maybe the new cameras and large surveillance sign and a proper fence around future bee boxes will be enough to keep anyone else from attacking them.

Just in case, though, I wonder about putting more boxes closer to the forest. The attacker overlooked that one. Maybe they'd be safer with more natural camouflage, even with all this technology.

Plus, it would put them closer to the kudzu and black locust trees. Maybe the honey would turn even more purple.

I'm on my knees, replanting some of the disturbed flowers, when I see it. It's a tiny thing, really, barely noticeable if I wasn't brushing plants and leaves aside.

A gum wrapper.

It's small and pink, with the words 'berry bomb' on the front in a goofy retro font.

My hands start shaking before I even pick it up.

My body does that thing where it forgets how to breathe.

God, there's no mistaking the truth now.

I've seen this brand, this exact flavor of gum so many times I couldn't miss it.

Fucking. Holden.

I always knew it was him.

No one else would've made the journey here from Springfield, and no one else is petty and spiteful enough to do something this vindictive.

Dad wouldn't come in swinging a hammer, much less get his hands dirty with petty destruction. That's not his style.

He's already cut me off, taking the legal route.

But Holden is a spoiled child, no matter how much he pretends otherwise.

Here's proof—and a warning that he throws a bigger temper tantrum than I thought.

God, what *else* will he do with his temper?

My vision blurs.

I hear my own breathing in my head as I stand, the world spinning, that stupid gum wrapper fluttering in my fingers. Thinking Holden did it abstractly and having absolute proof he did are two different things.

I've never hated anyone in my life.

Not like the way I hate him now.

It's almost explosive, this ugly feeling throbbing under my skin.

I want him to pay.

I want to hurt him.

To take his balls and twist because he just destroyed the

homes of so many precious bees, and for what? To get back at me?

Sweet Jesus.

I'm not thinking straight as I yank my phone out and dial his number. There's a cooler breeze today, but I'm flushed, sweat running down my back as I stand in the flower beds he ruined and listen to the sound of it ringing.

"Winnie," Holden says softly when he answers. "Hi."

"Don't give me that crap. Why did you do it?"

"I wondered when you'd call." He blows right past my question. Typical.

"Holden, how *could* you?" I snap. Everything is shaking—my hands, my voice, my bones. I feel like I'm about to shatter. "How dare you."

"Oh," he says, his voice hollow with disappointment. "Yes. I thought you might have had a change of heart."

"Change of heart? Go to hell." I'm so mad I'm spitting. I start pacing across the crumbling soil of the flower beds. "I know what you did and you don't get to deny it."

"Winnie—"

"No. You listen and listen good. If you ever come here again, it's all-out war. Do you hear me? Do you understand?"

He sighs. Just like he has a thousand times before when I complained, like I'm some petulant child burdening him. "You're confused. I don't know what you're talking about."

"The fuck you do."

"You're really going to swear at me?"

"Why not?" I mock through acid tears.

I hate how I cry when I'm angry—it takes the edge off my rage. No one takes a crybaby seriously.

"Let me guess, it isn't *proper* like nice young ladies are supposed to be for a senator's son? Newsflash, Holden. I'm not nice. But I'm still a thousand times kinder than you."

"You don't need to tell me twice after you fled our wedding."

"Then why are you going around destroying other people's property in some sick, stupid attempt to get me back? I don't do threats." It's laughable, really, the fact that he thought this could bully me back into line.

Is that all I am to him? To my family?

A throwaway who's easily intimidated.

No!

Actually, I'm so angry I can't see straight.

"Winnie, I didn't do whatever you're accusing me of," he says.

I laugh, high-pitched and scornful.

There's a chance I might be losing it, but I don't care.

"Save yourself the gaslighting, Holden. I know it was you. And FYI, there's *nothing* you could do to ever convince me to marry you again. I told you, we're done. You were a rotten boyfriend and you would've been the worst husband."

"Like you were perfect?" he snarls, then hesitates, like he remembers he's supposed to be winning me over. "Look, no one's perfect, not all the time, but—"

"All the time? You want to know what it was like dating you? It felt like looking across the table and seeing my father. Cold, indifferent, obsessed with his image and his next career move. You never loved me."

"That's… that's not true," he sputters.

"Isn't it? You put your career first, second, and third." It feels good to get this out while he's struck speechless.

Cathartic in a way.

I've never said any of this to his face, and he deserves to hear it.

I want him to know how shitty he was, even if the memories make my throat tight.

"You're remembering things wrong," he whispers, back to his practiced tone, numb with the endless patience.

"And you're patronizing as hell," I snap. "You're belittling, you're childish, you're selfish. Worst of all, you're a coward, Holden, lashing out like a kid when you don't get your way. You never *once* made me feel special, you know. You *never* put me first. And looking at you, I could see my future... I'd wind up just like my mother. No thanks."

"Your mom is—"

"Miserable." I'm full-on crying now, yes, and it's gross. All snot and tears and those heaving panicked breaths I can't control. My body doesn't know what it's doing today. "My mom is miserable and lonely and a pushover. That's not me, Holden. Go find yourself another doormat."

"Doormat? Hold up—"

"No. Why don't you just *admit* it?" I practically scream. "The only thing you care about is your fucking career. I embarrassed you and you want to make me pay. You don't even want me back at all. Say it."

Holden yells something through the phone, unintelligible and garbled, and the phone flies out of my hand.

I don't know what happened until I look up.

I never saw Archer approach, but he's here now, a stone expression on his face that's ready for murder.

If Holden was here, there would be blood on the ground, I'm pretty sure. And I'm not sure I'd mind seeing it.

"You're blocked, asshole," Archer says. He has no right sounding so menacing when I was—and still am—falling apart. "You're not breathing another word to Winnie. Not today. Not fucking ever."

More incoherent buzz from the speaker.

Holden hates it when people talk down to him, and Archer is so clearly the dominant man in this situation. Holden will hate that even more.

Serves you right, I think viciously.

"If you ever show up on any property I own again, I will hunt you down. Pressing charges will be the easy part," Archer growls, pausing. "You'll get them in spades, then I will turn your fucking skull into honeycomb. Understand me?"

This time, I catch the gist of what Holden says. "You're threatening a senator's son? Are you stupid?"

Archer snorts.

"I don't give a shit what you are." He hangs up, following through with the block setting in my contacts.

It's a load off my mind, knowing Holden can't contact me again unless he comes here.

And I don't think he will.

Holden is many things, but brave is far from it.

Sure, he risked a little of his skin breaking and entering, but that was before he got caught. Before Archer knew it was him.

I don't have time to think about anything else before he's on me, his big hands on my face, pulling me into a kiss.

His mouth is so possessive, so demanding, and he doesn't seem to notice there's still snot on my face or that I'm hiccupping and crying.

But that's fine by me.

What I really need now is a distraction, and Archer obliges.

When he's kissing me, there's no room to think about anything else. When he pulls me against his body, he squeezes out everything else, all the poison.

Holden, my dad, my stupid wedding, the bees.

Everything is smothered in him.

His smell, his taste, the way he holds the back of my neck. There's this primal, jealous edge to the gesture, and I love it.

Call me sick.

I don't care.

Even if he has no reason to be jealous. Only a total fool would choose Holden over him. It's the difference between a little boy who's full of himself and a man who drips life experience.

Archer's thumbs swipe at my cheeks, wiping away the tears that keep falling as he holds me.

I can't seem to stop them, but that's okay.

With him, everything is fine, even when it's not.

"I'm... I'm sorry," I force out, and he shakes his head, wiping my face with his sleeve.

"Don't apologize, Winnie." His voice is hard and hoarse, and he kisses me again, one arm locked against my waist. "Don't ever apologize for him."

"O-okay."

I could get used to this version of Archer.

He's normally a man of few words, but right now, he's giving me everything I could ever want to hear with his hands, his mouth, the way his breath catches when I grab his shirt and pull him closer.

We kiss harder, until I know my lips are swollen.

By the time we come back up for air, a haze of emotion and throbbing need, Holden and his destruction are already forgotten.

He's the past.

Archer Rory is my present.

And if I don't have my future figured out yet, he's part of that too.

I don't care if we're destined for a storybook ending or a great big nothing.

With him in my life, holding me together, I'll survive.

"Let's go," he whispers so gently, brushing my messy hair back from my face.

I gladly listen.

* * *

I EXPECT him to take me home.

At first, we're heading in that direction, but before we're too far down the road, we turn off down another minor road surrounded by leafy trees. Archer's hands are white-knuckled, tight on the wheel, and he doesn't say much.

Every so often, though, he puts a hand on my leg.

It's this silent, sweet assurance he's still here.

Still thinking about me.

Still checking in.

It makes my chest feel like it's too big for my body. Like if I'm not careful, I might just pop like a balloon from too much feeling.

The route he's chosen leads deep into the forest, and I watch as the trees swallow the landscape.

It's gorgeous, this path through dense greenery that feels like a well-kept secret, just as quiet and tucked away as Solitude itself.

Maybe that's the point. Archer, he's like me—he craves the silence, peace without worries and no one else around to tangle you up in their woes.

I'm not used to feeling this about another person.

Even Lyssie, as much as I love her, can get annoying sometimes. She's a great friend, but she's not a perfect puzzle piece who instantly snaps in to complete my life.

If I wasn't scared he'd bolt like a frightened rabbit, I'd be tempted to tell him how much this means, how *connected* I feel.

Right now, we're two halves of a whole. Whatever corny phrase doesn't feel as devastating as 'soulmate.'

But I *am* scared.

Scared he would dump me on the side of the road if I

confessed my feelings and hightail it back to Kansas City, so I wait until he's driven deeper into these woods.

Of course, he's way too much of a gentleman to do that, but the jittery rabbit in my brain won't let me ruin a good thing.

There's a little parking space off the side of the road, a rest stop of sorts made from a mix of dried mud and gravel. He pulls over there.

The vehicle shuts off.

In the silence, I look at him again, very slowly like I want to hide behind my hands.

In the dappled light coming through the trees, he's a patchwork of sun and shadows, the human version of a mountain catching the sun.

For a second, I freeze.

My irrational side reaches peak self-loathing when I'm actually terrified he might lay down the law right here and end things.

What if that kiss was a goodbye? And now here comes the breakup in this calm, beautiful place he's chosen to soften the blow.

I inhale so sharply I almost choke.

But his big hand on my leg lingers, screaming reassurance.

It's so *gentle*. That's not what someone who's about to go full heartbreaker does, right?

Not that I'm his partner or girlfriend or we're technically together. He made that clear with his mother.

I'm sure that whole mess gives him plenty to regret.

There's a growing list, and my ex breaking in and destroying his property is probably at the top, soon followed by the hard reality that I've infiltrated his home and his life.

"Winnie?" he asks, his blue eyes flashing with concern. I

realize my hysterical laughter must be bubbling close to the surface if he can see it.

My eyes water from the effort of keeping it in.

That breakdown is coming, faster than I thought.

"I'm fine," I rush out. "Why did you bring me here?"

He hesitates. "Walk with me?"

How could anyone say no to that? Anyone who's not afraid of being axe-murdered, anyway—which I'm not with him. The grim, intrusive thought is just more hysteria because that kind of cartoon evil almost feels preferable to him gently letting me go.

I get out and we follow a narrow trail into the forest. He reaches out and takes my hand, gingerly holding it the entire time.

We walk into a silence barely disturbed by birdsongs.

I'm afraid to break it.

While the sweet hand-holding suggests he's not about to smash my heart like an ornament, it's not like I haven't caused him a lot of trouble.

Infinitely more than he bargained for.

We come to a fallen tree, mossy and ancient and kind of majestic. He leads me to it, holding on as I stumble over the uneven ground gnarled in rocks and roots, urging me to sit.

We're in this little fairy-tale clearing with the blue sky above and birds flitting in and out of branches.

Breathtaking.

A little slice of heaven—or as close as you can get in Missouri, just thirty minutes or so away from a teeming city.

"I'm sorry for crying all over you back there," I start before he has a chance to speak. "And I'm *really* sorry for what Holden did... coming to Solitude and destroying the bees like that? God."

"Will you stop apologizing for him?" His voice hardens.

Eek. I don't know how to stop.

If my lovely parents ingrained anything, it's the guilt trip—and apologies are how you get demanding people to forgive your mistakes. And I've made a truckload of errors since moving here.

"Sorry. It's just, you don't need this." You don't need *me* is what I really mean.

But he shakes his head fiercely.

"You think I brought you here so I could listen to you apologize for shit that's not your fault while you rake yourself over the coals?"

"But—"

"Winnie, no. We're here so I can tell you something." His grip on my hand tightens. "I need you to just sit and listen, okay?"

Sit and listen.

Okay.

I can do that.

"I couldn't care less about this 'trouble' you've caused. That's part of keeping you safe," he rumbles. "I want to be honest with you, and I haven't been. No, that's not fair." He searches for the right words. I hold my breath, unsure where this is going. "What I mean is, I haven't been open enough with you. That's my fault, and I want to be."

Listen, listen.

He told me to listen so I'll keep my mouth shut, but it's hard when his words are so heavy and I want to kiss him, to tell him he doesn't need to go out of his way to confess whatever it is that's eating him up.

I'm trying not to cry again.

"I was very young when I met Rina, and it moved way too fast," he says. "I didn't have my life figured out before she got pregnant, before we were even serious. I tried to make the impossible work."

Yep, the tone of his voice alone means I'm definitely going to cry now, but I keep listening.

"On paper, I did all the right stuff," he says, bitterness creeping into his voice. "I proposed. I gave her a big-ass ring, quit the army, came home, and tried to make a family. Everything was for her and my boy. Then she grew restless. She put her dreams over our family—and it fucked me up because I let it."

"Archer," I whisper.

He shifts, pivoting until he's looking at me.

"This life I put *everything* on hold for was over, and I blamed her for years. Maybe it wasn't all her fault, but the fact is, she left. She ran away from me and her *son*. And I don't think I ever got over it."

"I'm sorry." I put my other hand over his and squeeze. "That must've been so hard. But I... I don't understand. Is that why we're here? So you could tell me about Rina?" And the fact that he's not over her haunting him.

That stings more than it should.

"Not Rina. Not specifically." He makes an impatient gesture with his free hand. "I brought you here because everything that's happened lately peeled my blinders off. Having you around showed me how much I've let Rina fuck me up, Winnie. I let her put chains on my life without even being here, and I'm done with all that."

"Done?" I swallow.

"Yeah. Done with letting the past have any power over me, Winnie." He touches my face, tracing where the tears traveled half an hour before. "I'm done with dancing around the damn elephant in the room. I'd rather be trampled than keep pretending I don't want to be with you for real."

My laugh comes out startled and definitely snotty. "You mean... Are you being serious right now?"

"I am."

"You want to be with me? For real?"

"How many times do I have to tell you, woman?" He tugs me closer and our lips graze. "I want that fuckhead out of your life. Permanently," he growls. "I also want to make you forget he ever existed."

Holy hell.

This might be it.

The moment for me to say it, to gush love all over him like the crazy idiot I am, but I just wrap my arms around him and kiss him like my life will end if I don't.

Right now, it might.

He kisses me back just as fiercely, and in the middle of the forest, with just Archer, it feels right.

Like this is meant to be.

Not just a distraction, but destiny.

Archer Rory tastes like home, my very own nest of honey-sweet words and ferocious muscle, and the realization doesn't scare me.

If he's not afraid to be with me, how can I be scared to love him with my whole heart?

XX: BEE OPEN (ARCHER)

I'm no optimist.

I'm sure everyone I know would consider me a blackhearted certified pessimist from the day I was born, but lately, there's no denying the truth.

Things have been going remarkably smoothly ever since I spilled my guts to Winnie.

I told her the hard truth, almost everything, all the reasons why I walled myself off. And now, things are—well, they're damn good.

Like all I needed to do was break down the last unspoken barriers between us.

She wasn't expecting me to go there.

To talk about Rina, to cough up the past and the ugly way I feel about life.

If she were anyone else, it never would've happened.

But holding that broken girl in my arms with her wrecked hives must've rewired my brain, or at least woken me the fuck up.

Now, it's undeniable.

There's something about Winnie that's worth lowering my shields.

The weirdest part is I'm not scared shitless. I have no regrets.

There's only one last nagging talk I dread, but it feels almost manageable.

I've chosen a small café away from anyone connected to us. I want privacy for this.

No Junie eavesdropping over my shoulder—however well meaning—and no memories of anywhere we used to visit back when we were young and stupid.

Nothing but the present.

Just two people, who we are now, Rina and me.

It's high time we sorted our shit out for good and leveled with the truth, assuming she's as determined as she seems to be in Colt's life.

So I choose a small independent place on the other side of the city with clean round tables and a small pastry case that might've looked impressive a few years ago. After Junie and The Sugar Bowl, it's hard to get excited over anyone else's sweets.

I'm nursing a cup of hot dark roast when Rina walks through the door, her shoulders tight and her brown eyes wary. I know that look.

I lift a hand, gesturing. She comes over to join me after a pause.

"Hey," she says cautiously, taking the chair across from me.

I nod at the menu.

"You want a drink?"

"Oh, yeah. Just an iced vanilla latte, extra espresso."

I smile as I get up because it's the same drink she'd always order. Some things never change. But others do, and there's that nervous hand around my throat again, stalling my words.

Fuck, I need to do this as soon as her coffee comes.

The barista is a slim girl with glasses too large for her face and an apron tied tightly around her waist. I put in the order and she makes idle small talk as she gets it going.

With Rina's latte and a fresh refill of black coffee for me, I head back to the table.

She's made an effort today, I see. I wonder why.

Even if we didn't have a history between us that's pure dry rot, after Winnie's curves, I could never go back to anything else. Rina's slim frame always verged on bony.

Modelesque, I used to think, back when I was younger—until she had Colt and blamed him for destroying her figure with ten or fifteen pounds of baby fat she could never lose.

She wouldn't accept the changes to her body gracefully.

She wouldn't accept a lot of things.

At the time, that wasn't something I gave much thought. It wasn't like we were having sex by then anyway.

Dead bedrooms crop up like weeds when no one's looking. You grow apart with petty arguments and work and bigger fights you *should* have.

Then one day you wake up and find a roommate wearing your ring, barely putting in the effort to play house and wife.

You know she's pretending just as hard as you.

You know you'd both rather eat a bowl of live fire ants than make love.

Today, she seems to carry herself different. I can't quite pin it down.

Either she's gotten back to where she wanted by dropping a few pounds or she's finally stopped giving a damn. Because with her soft earthy colors and only a splash of her usual sea-green turquoise, she looks fine. Bird skinny doesn't turn my crank anymore, but plenty of guys will eat it up.

Her figure aside, I think she's been taking care of herself.

The dark hollows and puffiness I usually find under her eyes aren't there.

She hasn't gone for much makeup, but what little there is smooths her skin and makes her amber eyes pop in the light.

She always did have big eyes.

Once, I loved them.

Now, I watch her disinterestedly as I slide her sugary coffee across the table with the ice cubes clinking softly.

Too much has happened for me to find Rina Desmona pretty the way I used to.

That's not why we're here.

"Here you are," I say. "Dripping with enough vanilla to choke a buffalo."

"Thanks!" she says, taking a long sip as she looks around. "Gotta say, I can see why you like this place."

I don't really, but that's not the point.

"I think it's only my second time here. I've been expanding my horizons a little, changing it up with the local coffee scene."

"Since your brother married that baker, you mean?"

"Yeah, Junie ruined pastries for good. It's all about the coffee quality now."

"God, Dexter married! I can't even imagine." She nods and sips her coffee. Her eyes close, then open and fix on me. "So, let's get to it. Why are we here, Archer? Why this place?"

"It's neutral territory. Not my place or yours."

"But why? Why are we meeting?"

"I wanted to talk. We haven't done much of that since you came back to Kansas City." I lean my elbows on the table.

"Okay. So talk." She watches me again with those big eyes in that birdlike face, but where they were swarming with secrets before, now they're all caution.

She shrugs.

Easy for her to say. I take a swig of my coffee, searching

for the right words, the script I've tried like hell to rehearse in my head.

"You know, when you first showed up again, I didn't trust you one bit."

Fuck. Not exactly the right words, but they're true.

I know I'm doing this wrong, but there's so much in the air.

Too much baggage.

Too much history.

Too much *Colt.*

"Uh, yeah. I figured," she says evenly. "You made that clear. I get it, Arch. I do."

"The thing is, that attitude isn't helpful. Not for Colton and not for us." I sweep a hand through my hair. "The mistrust—that's what I'm talking about. The way it feels like we're trying to make him choose."

Rina looks at me, her thin lips pursed like she's trying to read me.

Once upon a time, I guess she could—when we were together, she knew me better than anyone. At least, the version of me before I spent a decade hunkered down, raising a son and building a company instead of chasing wild dreams like she did.

"I was thinking that, too," she says quietly. "I don't want to fight anymore. I'm so over that. And you're right, I don't want to make him choose."

"We can be better, Ri."

Her brows crease as she frowns at the old nickname. "Do you know why I came back?"

I guess I'm about to learn.

I sit back, letting her talk.

"When I left Washington and went off to California and Arizona, I did a lot of reflecting. What I wanted. Who I'd become."

I nod, taking another sip.

I think we've both done plenty of reflecting over the years—and if hers was anything like mine, it couldn't have all been positive.

"I worked in Sedona the last few years," she continues, "and the energy in the earth, the way people would come there to heal, it really made me think about my choices, my priorities. I had a son, but I hadn't even seen him in a year." Her eyes fill with tears. "My son, Archer. It's like I woke up."

Damn.

It's like watching what happens after a light switch flips, changing her from the confident person I knew to someone so vulnerable.

But there's nothing I can say.

She brought this on herself.

She's not Winnie—if she was sitting in front of me, looking so pitiful, I'd have ripped apart the world to protect her.

With Rina, her pain is self-inflicted. It feels like watching some addict stranger on the street, a slave to bad habits, still begging for money.

You feel pity, sure, but it isn't personal.

Is that what love is? This desperate need to shield Winnie from the crap in her life versus this melancholy heartache at Rina waking up to her own self-destruction?

She's right, of course—she had a son she never fucking bothered to see.

I don't tell her the last visit was well *over* a year ago.

There's nothing I can say to make that better, to take back time.

It's a harsh truth lodged in my throat the same way it's blocking hers.

"I realized how screwed up my priorities were," she says. "They were so wrong for so long... but I want you to know

I'm serious. About coming back here and all, sorting out my life. Making things work. Being in Colt's life."

I nod once. "I'm glad. I want this to work out, too. For Colt."

"Yeah." The hint of a smile touches her mouth. "But you know, your instincts are pretty sharp."

The warmth creeping through me stumbles.

Her tears have stopped welling, but there's something else in her glassy eyes now.

Tension.

"What do you mean?" I ask warily, taking another slow sip of coffee.

"I mean, you were probably right not to trust me. Why would you after... after so many things?" She lifts one shoulder in a half shrug. "It's not like it was deliberate, but Archer, you have to understand—I'm *mad*. I wasn't seeing straight. I hate that I lost so much time. I let so much slip through my fingers and it made me a little crazy."

I release the coffee cup so I don't accidentally crush it.

"Crazy about what? What are you talking about, Ri?"

"I... I was there at your cabin that day," she says. "Your mom mentioned the place. I think she was happy for you, but hearing the way she talked about you two—like Winnie was some *gift* dropped into your lap..." She snorts. "I knew about the bees."

My ears are ringing.

My head feels like it's about to implode like a tin submarine plunged too deep.

"You?" There's a sinking boulder in my gut. "It was you?"

"No, not exactly. Not like—" This time when she shakes her head, the movement is jerky. She's bitter, but it's aimed at herself, I realize. "You know, I almost didn't come here to meet you and tell you."

"Don't fuck with me, Rina," I say, my voice low. "Tell me what you did."

All this time, I was so sure it was Winnie's ex, but if the great bee massacre was fucking Rina this whole time—isn't that what she's working up to?

Fuck.

My stomach churns with bile.

"I was trying to psych myself up to do it," she whispers. "I... I had a whole box of poison canisters. I was going to spray them down one by one. Figured that would teach your little girlfriend to mess with this family—and you." She laughs, but the sound is empty this time. "No, this isn't about you, Arch. I don't give a shit who you date, even if she's half your age."

The bitterness in her tone says she cares more than she lets on.

It's a Herculean effort not to yell, not to throw my coffee over her head, not to stand up and roar at her to never show her face anywhere near me again.

"Leave Winnie out of this, Ri—or I swear to God you'll regret it."

"I already do! That's what I'm trying to tell you," she flares, her eyes brimming with tears again. She blinks them away impatiently.

I watch, impassive, unable to bear the idea of her hurting Winnie like this.

That's when my brain turns back on.

She said poison, didn't she? The bee boxes were smashed. There weren't even many dead bees mixed in with the debris.

My brain struggles to make sense of it.

"It was Colt who pushed me over the edge." Her voice cracks. "He... he kept talking about Winnie like he already knows her better than me, his own mother. And you, being around her, looking so happy like you're just bursting with glee… I was losing my family."

"A family you walked away from." My voice is raw, wounded.

"I know! And… and I regret that more than you can *ever* imagine, Archer. Seeing you all together, hearing Colt talk—God, he won't shut up about her—it just made me rage. So I went out there. I was going to spray those stupid bees and let her find them dead in their nests." She heaves a sigh so heavy it sounds like an exorcism. "But I couldn't do it."

"Fuck you mean?" I'm snarling every word.

"I was there and I—I just couldn't make myself kill them. Not because it's a crime, but because I realized how insane I was being. But then I was about to go and I saw this man pull up. He was wearing thick gloves and he looked really angry. He walked in like he owned the place, carrying this giant hammer. First, he broke into the shed, and I think you know the rest. He did it all for me. I put my anger out into the universe and the universe answered. Even if I didn't lift a finger, the bees were destroyed, no different than if I did the smashing myself."

Holden. So it *was* that entitled little fuckwit after all.

But that doesn't stop my anger, knowing she sat me down and put me through all of that, dragging it out for her own damn pity party. And then having the gall to attach some New Agey moral to her story.

Even the pain etched on her face can't stop me from spiraling.

One look at her face and the way she's pressed her lips together, the way her eyelids flicker, tells me she wasn't doing this for fun.

I don't give a damn.

She drew this out because it was too fucking hard for her to tell me straight.

Yeah, she knows me, but I know her, too.

The little things—the things that don't change, like the sound she makes when she cries or the way her eyes crease when she lies.

She's not lying now.

"Why did you tell me?" I demand, my voice gruff. "Rina, what the fuck?"

It's too much.

Finding out my ex-wife hates my new girlfriend so much that she was seconds away from destroying the one thing Winnie loves more than life. It's the most ridiculous shit I've ever heard and I'm pissed as hell.

"You asked me to come here because you wanted to tell me that you've forgiven me, right?" she says. "Or at least, you're trying to. Isn't that it, Archer?"

I go still.

That's *not* what I was telling her.

Or hell, maybe it was at first, in my own muddled roundabout way.

"So, what? You figured you'd give me some crazy story about how you almost broke Winnie's heart?"

"I gave you the truth. It's all you deserve and all I can offer. You have a family now—a normal one—and my feelings are the last thing that should get between you and your happiness. Or Colt's, or even Winnie's." Her gaze slides to the side. "Look, I know the way I left. Some things can't be undone after that. I know, Archer."

Just like before, I don't know what to say.

My throat feels parched with hot rage and I don't think more coffee will fix it.

"I want you to be happy," she says. "In time, I just hope we'll have an understanding. I hope you'll feel more comfortable with me being in Colt's life again."

After everything she's said, I don't know if that will ever happen.

On the other hand, she told me. A horrible secret she could've easily kept to herself.

I'm so fucking conflicted it feels like my head might pop off.

When I say nothing, she gets the hint, standing and excusing herself.

With burning eyes, I watch her leave, the bell ringing over the door.

I keep staring even after she's out of sight, waiting for this whole situation to start making sense, and hating that it won't.

* * *

My phone blows up with voicemails before I reach the office.

All from Dex, weirdly angry, rambling on about some regulatory notice.

What the hell? I listen twice, but I'm way too busy thinking about Rina's meltdown to really comprehend his message.

The fact that she told me all this shit about the bees and Winnie…

I can't decide if it's a huge red flag or a green one, or whether I'd be the crazy asshole to leave Colt alone with her in the future.

When I finally get to Lee's Summit, still consumed with Rina and Winnie and Colt, Dexter and Patton are waiting in my office.

Pat's pacing and Dexter stands there like a statue.

Both of them stare at me as I head through the door, right before Dexter slams a thick printout onto the table.

"Explain this," he demands.

I pick it up and skim the first page.

It's a notice from the Attorney General's office, Carroll Emberly III. A legal notice announcing an antitrust probe against Higher Ends. A big old stack of legal bullshit no doubt explaining all the ways Carroll Emberly intends to fuck me very personally by proxy for preventing him from controlling his daughter.

"What the hell?" I flick through the pages, working deeper, even though I can guess what it's going to say.

A lawsuit.

A dick-shitting lawsuit.

All because I went and pissed off Mr. Big Shot AG by giving Winnie breathing space.

"Holy shit." Pat resumes pacing when he sees the worried look on my face. He's usually the more relaxed one, armed with ten dumb jokes, so the fact that he's this agitated says everything. "Holy fucking *shit*, this is bad."

"Who does he think he is?" Dexter says. "This is bullshit."

"What are we going to do, guys?" Patton tugs at his hair. "What right does this asshole have to throw this at us?"

I lean against the table and pinch the bridge of my nose, trying to figure out a way we can get around it. Unlike the other two, I have some idea why this is happening.

"If this succeeds, it's going to be hell to pay," Dexter fumes. "Do you know how much we could lose? Even if we win, the legal fees alone will drag us down, and it could go on for years."

"Let's not get carried away," I say, holding up a hand. "It's going to be all right."

Patton turns on me. "Easy for you to say, Arch. There's no quick fix for this shit."

Believe me, I know.

But between Patton and Dexter I'm the calm one, the

older brother who's intelligent and in control. I do my best to play the part, even though the only thing I want to do is rip something apart with my bare hands.

Fuck!

"Listen to me," I say loudly. To my surprise, they both stop and stare. "We set our legal dogs to work. We're going to pad our team with as many lawyers as it takes to shoot this down out of the gates. We won't let it get off the ground. You hear me?" I slice my hand through the air. "No way."

"No way in hell," Patton repeats.

I shake my head.

The temptation to punch something is almost unbearable.

Pushing away from the table, I pace across the room.

"What a bitter, controlling little troll her old man must be to pull this," I mutter. "I can't even imagine one man being so petty."

"What?" Dexter says, his voice quiet. "Whose dad?"

"Do you need to ask, Bro?" Patton laughs harshly. "Little Miss Honeybee. It's obvious. She comes along, kicks up trouble, and then daddy swoops in to sue the blood out of us."

Dexter looks at me, waiting for confirmation. "Her father is Carroll Emberly the fucking Third?"

I nod. No point in hiding the truth now.

"Goddamn, Archer!" he snaps. "Didn't you think it might have been useful to know that before?"

"And the fact that she's in a family feud," Patton says, slapping the back of his hand against the pile of papers. "This kind of shit follows you like a vulture."

I fold my arms. "It's none of your business, boys."

"None of our business?" Patton narrows his eyes. "You're calling *this* none of our business when it's lighting our entire company on fire?"

"We'd have helped her anyway," Dexter says with a sigh.

"We wouldn't have turned her away. But fuck, man. At least if we'd known, we might have been prepared for this."

My cheeks balloon as I let out a sigh.

Maybe these two clowns have a point.

I told Winnie my brothers and I are close. Her private life is none of their business, but the fact that her father is after her definitely is now.

"I'm sorry." I hold up my hands. "I should've told you sooner."

"Damn right." Patton's still seething, and I can't blame him.

"Did you know this was coming?" Dexter asks.

"No, of course I didn't." I scrub my face with my hands. "If I'd known, I'd have told you, all right? I'm not that big an asshole."

Patton snorts, and Dexter leans his hip against the desk.

"We need a plan, Arch," he says. "How do we combat this?"

"We own a billion-dollar company." I keep my voice calm even though I want to hurl things at the floor. Maybe scream down the phone at Carroll fucking Emberly for going full vengeful psycho. "We have money to throw at it. We can beat it."

"Money doesn't make this shit go away," Patton says. "Politicians and lawyers, they don't care about profits. They'll drag it out for years just for the misery factor, never mind flexing their dicks."

I fucking hate that he's right.

If I stay in this room with them any longer, though, I'm going to lose it.

After coming back from the damn meeting with Rina to this, my nerves are too raw.

I need to deal with this, but not fucking *here*.

THREE RECKLESS WORDS

A text pings my phone and I look at it absently. It's from Colt.

Winnie took me to Grandma's art fair. There's a craft stand with bees and carvings!!! Can you meet us at the river market soon?

It's a flimsy excuse, but it'll do.

"That's Colt. I've got to go," I say, pocketing my phone again.

Both Dex and Patton glare at me like I'm number one on their eternal shit list.

The last thing they need is me bailing when I'm the reason this fire started. I never bail unless they're being stupid.

Always a first time for everything, I guess.

"Look," I say, losing some of my cool, "I know I fucked up. I made the company a target and that's on me. I'll make sure I un-fuck it, too. I'll get started tonight."

Before they can say anything, because they're my brothers and don't know how to keep their mouths shut, I walk out and let the door slam shut behind me.

"Fuck," I hear Patton yell.

Yeah, fair enough.

My head aches as I head back to the car. I don't usually feel like this when it comes to Higher Ends, but this is one crisis where I have no idea what I'm doing.

Logically, I do. I know the next move. But this whole thing isn't run by logic alone, and neither are my feelings.

Holy shit, what a mess.

And right now, it's a disaster I can't clean up.

I slam my hands against the steering wheel.

Colt's text sits accusingly in my pocket.

Goddamn, I knew it was too good to be true.

Over the last few days, I thought everything with Winnie was settling down, but now this veneer of normality—the fucking art fair—feels like having a time bomb ticking away under the dinner table.

What will having a real relationship with a sweet, innocent young woman do to the people I love?

What the hell will this attraction to Winnie Emberly cost me?

XXI: BUSY LITTLE BEES (WINNIE)

I wasn't sure what to expect when Colt first told me about Delly's art fair.

After meeting her and seeing her love for cardinals, I figured it would be stuff like that. Paintings, mostly, although he promised me bees.

But when we get there, the whole thing takes my breath away.

It's that adorable.

Sure, there are tables and stands with more traditional art, but this time, Delly has brought an entire group of bee people. The stands take up half a block. Honey and wax makers and special handmade gift sets of balm people can take away.

The wooden carvings pump Colt up the most, but I get to talk to bee people all day. There's no end to them, and it feels like the best thing to happen to me since the wedding—

minus Archer, of course.

Not that I tell them much about the purple honey.

With the bees in such a fragile place with just one hive left, I don't want to risk attracting more attention.

Maybe next year, when they're doing better, after the colonies are thriving again.

Then I catch myself.

'Next year' is a whopping promise I'm not sure I should make.

Even if Archer and I decide to explore what we're meant to be, that doesn't necessarily mean I'll still be living here. I have a whole life to figure out, including a new career since I'm done with the DC scene.

"Did you say your dad could meet us here?" I ask Colt.

"Yeah." Colt looks unbothered. "He said he would."

I check the time on my phone. Archer said he'd be here a while ago, and that's okay, seeing how we hit him up on such short notice during a workday.

We're all sprawled out on the grass by the river, resting on Delly's thick handcrafted blankets.

I bought myself a beer and Colt a milkshake. I've got a thick handful of leaflets about beekeeping in northern Missouri in my bag.

If Archer were here, it would be perfection.

A minute later, he is, sitting beside me like he just materialized from my thoughts.

"Hey, you two," he says with oddly low enthusiasm. "How's it going?"

I kiss his cheek, but there's something reserved about his voice.

Something cold that isn't normally there.

My stomach sinks.

Is he having second thoughts?

Rejection always tastes the same, no matter who it comes from. Didn't Colt say he was meeting Rina earlier today? Maybe it didn't go well.

Or maybe it went *too well.*

My jaw clenches as my brain spins through horrible possibilities.

Lyssie's parents were divorced for ten years before they reconnected and ended up getting married again. These things happen, especially when they share a kid.

Especially when a kid gets to be Colt's age and they're approaching early middle age—just in time to reevaluate life. The idea of being a family is a tempting one, I'm sure.

At least, it could be.

It's not like I'm an expert with knowing what normal, loving families look like.

But Colt chatters on about all the cool carvings he's seen and how excited he is about them. The latest piece from some place called Redhaven leaves him awestruck. It's a giant crow, painted white, and the guy selling it couldn't shut up about how he got to work with some famous local guy named Gerald Grey on it.

I stare at Archer's hand, willing it to land on my leg like before.

I think he knows I like to feel him touching me, warm and secure and always sexy.

But it doesn't.

No matter how much I stare, his hand doesn't move.

Call it stupid that I'm disappointed.

It's laughable that something so small could open this pit inside me, but it does.

"That sounds great, Colt," he says, but there's still this flatness in his voice. Something empty that makes my chest ache.

"Winnie had fun talking about bees," Colt says proudly. "I thought it would be a good idea to bring her here."

"And you were right." My laugh sounds forced, but neither of them seem to notice. "There are so many bee people here. I've found my tribe."

Neither of them laugh, though I think it's because Colt gets distracted by some guy walking past in full medieval armor. It wouldn't be an art market without a few eccentrics who think the renaissance festival is a year-long event.

Archer just stares at the grass to his side, plucking blades absently.

"What about you? Rough day?" I ask.

Maybe a little desperate, but hell, I am.

"Huh?" He glances up, but there's no mistaking it this time—there's something closed off in his expression. His eyes are shuttered. "No, Winnie. My day was fine."

Fine.

Nothing about him screams fine.

If he stays this tense, he might just permanently set into stone.

But from the way he's looking at me, then glances at Colt, he's not going to say anything about it here.

Okay, Archer. Later it is.

I look down at the lazy river and eventually Colt suggests we go for a walk.

Fine. I grab Archer a beer and he holds it loosely in his hands as he looks at the carvings Colt points out.

It's a good mask, I'll admit.

He's saying the right stuff, going through the motions, and it's convincing enough for Colt, who just wants his dad here to share this with him.

But maybe I'm more discerning, or just insecure.

Colt's position in Archer's life is guaranteed, for heaven's sake. He's his *son.*

Mine is far less guaranteed.

We haven't really talked about the future, and things have been good, but that doesn't mean they're official. They're not *unbreakable.*

Yeah, I'm overthinking.

I bite it back, though, until Colt goes off with some woodcutter guy who knows way more about carving than anyone else. I follow Archer down to the riverside walkway with a growing cactus in my throat.

"So," I say after a few minutes of standing in awkward silence. Weird how after we've been so close—and I mean really freaking close, considering he was inside me just this morning—everything feels so distant. "You can't keep avoiding me, you know."

He barely looks at me. "I'm not avoiding you."

Right, and there's a giraffe in my pocket.

"Archer, please. Let's not pretend everything is cool when it obviously isn't. I got that enough at home."

The word 'home' reaches him. Now, he does look at me.

Cold and distant like unblinking blue stars.

"Fuck, you want to know? My company got a notice from your father's office," he says.

What?

Oh my God.

...I'm going to murder my father.

Scalding blood rushes to my face. My eyes sting as I reach for my phone. "No way. I'm going to call him right now and—"

"No. This isn't your fight, Sugarbee," he snaps, catching my hand. It's the first time he's touched me since he left to see Rina.

His fingers feel warm and slightly calloused around my wrist. Despite everything, it sends electricity zinging through me.

"What do you mean? My stupid dad did this. He's a child." And all because of me, though I can't bear to say it. Anger burns into guilt that tastes like ashes in my mouth. "Please, Archer. You have to let me help."

He still hasn't let go of my wrist and he's closer now, his

body almost pressed against mine, eclipsing me. I want him to take the final step and wrap me in his arms, but he doesn't.

The Archer this morning would have done it in a heartbeat. Why does everything feel so hard now?

"I'll handle it," he says gently. "You've already been through too much with this asshole."

Tears prick my eyes.

I thought we were safe, past the worst of it with Holden's little stunt, but now my dad had to butt in, making my issues a burden again.

He talks about what I've been through, but what about him?

Not to mention all the drama he's gone through before I entered his life.

My father launched a lawsuit—a flipping *lawsuit*—because he can't stand me having a shred of free will.

I don't have words to convey how much I hate this, so I step closer into Archer's embrace. Thankfully, he hugs me this time, holding me against his chest.

"I'm so sorry," I whisper. "He's just mad, lashing out because he can't control me anymore and he knows it. He's a toxic control freak."

"Let him have his fit. I'll deal with it, Sugarbee."

"I still want to help you. Any way I can."

One of those big, rough hands strokes my hair, such a relief that I close my eyes, blinking away the surge of tears.

"You don't need to worry, Winnie. You've done enough of that."

A messy laugh cuts through the silence and we break apart.

Then I look up and see Colt standing with Delly, who's holding a lump of wood I think *she* tried to carve. It looks like a mangled bird with one wing.

They're both doubled over, laughing their heads off.

Ugh.

It's not just Archer my dad's attacking. It's this family, Delly and Colt too—good people I'm growing to love. Innocent people who should be able to enjoy a day out with everybody happy.

Seeing them like this, oblivious to the knife at Archer's throat, just makes my heart hurt.

No, there's absolutely no way I'm going to sit back and let the monster who raised me walk all over the entire Rory family. They mean too much.

Archer waves at Colt and my heart pinches again.

Holy shit, this man is putting on one hell of a front for his son.

For me, he tried, but I know him too well.

As soon as I'm home, I'm calling Dad and sorting this out.

Even if it kills me.

* * *

I WAIT until I'm back in my guest room at Archer's place before I pick up the phone.

Archer's been consistently on edge all afternoon, and who can blame him?

It's a wonder Colt hasn't picked up on the bad vibes, but he's been busy talking to wood artists and laughing with his grandmother. Thankfully, he hasn't noticed anything off.

I'm happy for him, honestly, but it just makes this whole thing harder.

Predictably, Archer shut himself away in his office right after dinner, muttering about documents to review. Probably an excuse, yes, but it leaves me free to act.

The sound of the phone ringing in my ear makes me feel sick.

"Hello?" Mom answers the old home landline. Just

like always. There's a pause where she checks the caller ID and then her voice changes. "Winnie, honey, is that you?"

"How could you let him do it?" I swallow thickly, hating that I already feel like I'm shutting down. It's a warm evening, but I'm shivering. "Mom, how *could* you?"

"What are you talking about? You should come home, sweetie." Like always, she's soft-spoken. Outwardly unrattled. No wonder she lets Dad stomp all over her. If she ever had a spine, it's melted into pitiful compliance jelly after years of his crap.

"That's not happening, and I think you know it." I tighten my fist in the comforter. "You never stand up to him. You let his worst instincts take over. You always stand by while he savages other people."

"Oh, Winnie, really, I don't know what has you so upset," she lies. Still oh-so-gentle and deferential even though I'm her own daughter. "You know your father doesn't discuss his legal affairs with me."

I hate that it makes her confusion sound sincere.

"You really don't know?" I sigh. "You never bothered finding out what Dad's been up to ever since he cut me off?" Somewhere deep inside me, there's raw emotion, but it's so choked off, so cold, I can't feel it. "You mean you never *asked*? Not once?"

I shouldn't be surprised.

If Mom's good at one thing, it's living in her own bubble of fake suburban perfection.

There's another voice in the background then, sharp and authoritative, and I hear Dad take the phone.

"Wynne," he clips. "It took you long enough to call."

"How dare you." I'm trembling when I say it.

For a second, he hesitates before he says, "If this is how you intend to speak to me—"

"No. *No,* you don't get to play victim. How about you stop trying to *sue* Archer Rory?"

"Sue? I don't know what you're talking about," Dad says, his voice as glacial as mine. "If you mean Higher Ends Incorporated, well, that's a state matter now. This has nothing to do with a personal dispute and everything to do with enforcing fair business practices."

"Like hell!" I'm standing before I know it. Some of the coldness has left me now, replaced by boiling heat, the kind that I know will reach my eyes soon. "I'm not stupid, Dad. Can you stop bullshitting me just once?"

"Watch your language, young lady."

I laugh painfully.

"Watch *my* language? Listen to yourself!" My throat hurts. A sad part of me wonders why I bother with my next question. "Have you ever wanted to be my father at all? Even if I'm not useful to you?"

"Winnie… I was the first one to hold you when you were born. Do you expect me to dignify that with a response?" There's a pause, only for a fraction of a second. "Do you have any idea what you've done?" he asks. Hard, angry. "Your boyfriend, threatening your fiancé and a senator's son with assault. A very powerful senator, mind you, who used to be your boss, and who can make and break careers in this state at the snap of his fingers. This isn't something we can brush aside, Winnie. This mishap has teeth, and my goal is to make sure they don't chew up this family."

Oh, God.

There's a lot to unpack there, so I go for the easiest one. "He's not my fiancé anymore, Dad. Or did you miss the memo? We're *over.*"

"That isn't my point. The fact is, the man you're with now threatened Holden, and frankly I don't feel confident you're safe in his care. Never mind the political ramifications, this is a nation of laws. You simply can't have Neanderthals stomping around and attacking law-abiding people when they show up for a basic conversation. You're a smart girl, Wynne. Don't be stupid."

"Stupid? You want to know what stupid is?" I clench my teeth. "Keep pushing me and you'll find out, Carroll."

"Carroll?" Anger seeps into his voice now. "Now see here—"

"No. When have you ever acted like a dad to me? There's no point in calling you that anymore."

"I understand you're very angry—"

"Fuck *yes,* I'm angry. But if you don't stop this, if you don't stop protecting that abusive little creep because you're scared for your career, I'll do some lawyering up myself. I promise you, I'll seek a full restraining order against Holden, and you can bet the media will hear about it. Along with the disgusting way he trespassed and destroyed Archer's property."

As soon as I say Archer's name, I regret it.

Dad doesn't need the gory details from me, no. I doubt he'd believe them anyway.

Of course, he just clucks his tongue. "Find your brain soon, young lady. I'm imploring you. Otherwise, you will make a grave mistake. I suspect an antitrust probe is hardly the worst of Higher Ends' issues."

My heart nosedives.

"What do you mean? What are you getting at?" For the first time, panic stabs through me. Dad would do this if he's decided to fight, turning over every rock until he finds vulnerabilities his lawyers can go after.

"Since you're an insect aficionado, you'll love this." Victory creeps into his tone like poison. "I decided to take the matter of those bees up with a contact in the Department of Conservation. Evidently, there are a few rare subspecies of honeybee in this region with federal and state protections. They're prone to producing that royal purple honey I'm sure you admire. If you think Holden Corban is such a threat—well, wouldn't it be wise to protect your specimens by re-examining Higher Ends' claim on the land and its property? Perhaps the company failed to do proper environmental research before it developed the land."

"You wouldn't." My voice is a whisper.

"I think you know there are no limits to what I'll do for the law. If you want a war over this, sweetheart, I can gladly deliver."

My heart clenches.

Jesus, he really is insane.

Fleeing a bad marriage for my life wasn't a declaration of war, it was an escape. Not just from Holden, but from a life filled with this type of drama and my control freak father throwing his weight around.

But I should have known better.

Dad never takes losing well.

Having me slip out from under his thumb after I torched the arranged wedding he staked our entire future on hits like a slap in the face.

Not because of me.

Never because of me.

It's the principle, losing control.

"Don't do it," I whisper. "Don't bring the bees into this."

Don't use my one love against me.

"The law is the law, my dear. Perhaps you should have thought harder before your friend attacked Holden."

"Dad, please!" Here it comes. I'm going to pieces, fighting to strain out words around my closing throat.

"Next time, I sincerely hope you'll weigh your choices more carefully." And the line goes dead.

I stare at it, waiting for my screen to light up again.

But it doesn't.

That's it, conversation over.

My heart plunges so low in my chest I think it might drop through the floor. Dad has me over a barrel and I hate it with every fiber of my soul.

But what I hate even more?

The horrible reality that this endless family shitstorm has trapped me yet again—and now it's trapped Archer too.

XXII: MAD AS HORNETS (ARCHER)

The next few days blur by in a hell that feels like a time-robbing fever dream.

Conference calls and lawyers and so much legal horseshit I hardly know how I'm wading my way through it without drowning. I promised Dexter and Patton I'd take the reins, so everything goes through me personally.

King Carroll Emberly III has plenty of lawyers at his disposal, which comes as no surprise. Although he's loaded and friends with damn near every high-powered attorney in the state, he doesn't have the financial war chest we do.

And I'm ready to throw it open.

This is our only advantage and I'm not about to waste it.

"The last thing you want is a protracted court battle. We'll do what we can to prevent it from getting that far," Brian Hennessy, my lead attorney, says patiently.

"I'm aware."

"Right now, we need to buy you time. Time means a better defense to pushback. We'll work on appeals to stall the data discovery first."

"Appeals." I snort. "Will even one succeed?"

He sighs, and I know his answer before he gives it. "Frankly, Mr. Rory, I wouldn't hold out for any miracles. The state AG's office is harder to thwart than any competitor or basic civil suit with a customer."

"If we can't buy time, you'd want to settle out of court?"

"Better that than the negative press, I'm sure you'll agree. If it goes to court, I don't like our chances."

My fist clenches.

The whole thing is utter bullshit.

We're hardly the monopoly on the luxury rental market like the antitrust suit claims.

Still, if we have any time left at all, I want to attack this on more than just the legal front.

"I need dirt on Emberly," I growl. "Every skeleton in his fucking closet, find it and pull it out. Got it?"

"Yes, sir, that's your prerogative. There's no rule saying you can't do a little off-record data discovery yourself or enlist a few private investigators to help. Just please make sure you keep your nose clean and ensure they're fully licensed with solid reputations."

"I'll have them report to you. The second they turn up anything, you call me."

"But—"

I end the call and lean back in my chair, rubbing my face. Hennessy doesn't like dealing in anything that isn't a document, but he knows better than to fight me on it.

Three days of turning over our own records, crafting every single legal defense we have, and I'm exhausted.

When I close my eyes, I see grim-faced judges and lawyers with assassin's eyes in my future.

This could fucking kill me, and my brothers too.

Everything we've built...

Fuck, it's already gouging our expenses like a hungry bear.

Yes, we can afford it, but that doesn't mean I want to hemorrhage money for months thanks to Carroll goddamned Emberly.

The office door creaks open.

I sit up in my chair.

"I'm on it," I start, but when I see Winnie's fiery mass of curls, I stop.

She's pale in the midday light, but just as beautiful as ever. Seeing her knocks the air from my lungs.

It's incredible how she still does it, even after we've been to bed more times than I can count.

If I ever stop and wonder why the hell I'm suffering this torture, there's my answer, writ large in big green eyes and hair that teases at a glance.

"Sorry to barge in. I know you're busy," she says, hands tucked behind her back.

"Not for you, Sugarbee." I reach out an arm, and when she comes over, I settle her on my knee.

She fits there too perfectly. I take a good, long breath of her, inhaling honey and something floral and delectable.

This woman always makes my mouth water while my dick turns to diamond.

For her, I'm insatiable, never too upset to not want to be balls deep inside her.

I kiss her neck, feeling her melt into me.

For a second, I actually relax, trailing one hand up her side.

"You came to distract me?" I whisper. My cock swells in my pants at the thought of bending her over this desk and fucking her right here.

Let the phone calls from hell wait.

"Actually, I came to ask you a question," she says breathily, shifting on my lap and making my hard-on pure steel.

"Can't it wait, Winnie?" I nip the tender skin under her

ear and she gasps. God, she's sexy. I'll never get over how gorgeous she is. "Ten damn minutes. That's all I'm asking."

"Archer..."

"Use your mouth first and it'll be five."

Laughing, she squirms away from my lips, straddling me as she turns to look up at me seriously.

"No, I mean it. I need to ask you something."

Too bad.

A sweet distraction would've helped, but I sigh and nod, settling both hands on her thighs. She's wearing hip-hugger jeans today and they accent her shape. I'm sure they look even better on her ass.

"Okay, go," I tell her.

"Have you heard from the conservation people?"

"Conservation people?" I frown at her, honestly perplexed. "You mean the specialist from the state? She called earlier, wanting to come out and look at the bees, but I figured it was your doing."

Her face whitens. The slim hand on my shoulder tenses so much it hurts.

"Are you kidding?"

"No. Winnie, what's going on?"

"It's a trap," she hisses. "Another hit job from my dad. I just thought... I thought maybe he was kidding, or maybe he wouldn't do it, but he already has. He *has* and I'm so sorry."

My vision shakes.

"Wait, wait. You talked to your dad again?" I do my best to keep my voice under control, but my earlier lust dissolves into pure frustration. "Winnie, I told you not to call him, didn't I?"

"Yes, while you sit up here in your office, stressing over how my family keeps destroying your life." She sighs, flipping her hair. "I had to do something."

"It's not your battle."

"But it is." She shuffles back off my lap and I let her.

She may be eerily beautiful when she's mad, her coppery hair static and her eyes flashing like angry seas, but that's not enough to distract me from the fact that she's complicating this fuckery when she doesn't need to.

I told her to let me deal with it.

Any legal crap is out of her league.

Not because she's stupid—no, quite the opposite—but because this isn't something she has any experience with. If her old man wanted to approach her and fix this with a family talk, he would've done it by now.

But he didn't.

He's using his office to go full scorched earth, and that's how I have to respond. Winnie doesn't have the expertise, and now there's a very real chance she's made it worse.

"This is my problem," she insists, her voice choking. "It's *my* father and this is all because of me. Because he wanted to marry me off to that scumbag and I said no. Because you tried to protect me."

"It's my company and my problem, Winnie." I stand, too. She seems so small suddenly, this fragile slip of a woman I'd risk the universe for. "Let me fix it."

"Archer… I know you mean well," she starts, but I shake my head, cutting her off.

"This isn't about meaning shit. It's about dealing with the problem in the most effective way, head-on."

"I can't just sit on the sidelines. Sorry, but I can't. I've been doing that my entire life and that's what got me into this mess." She reaches out to brush my cheek, delicately feeling my beard. "For the first time in my life, I'm standing my ground. I'm not running. That shouldn't destroy me. And I certainly can't let my problems destroy you either."

I push her hand away, irrationally annoyed at this destruction talk.

Carroll Emberly hasn't wrecked anyone yet.

God willing, he won't, if I have my way—and I will.

Compared to feeling your friend's heart stop while he bleeds out in your arms on Syrian soil, this is a high school drama.

"You worry about your damn bees. Leave the legal crap to me. That's what I pay my people through the nose for," I say, my voice too harsh. She flinches back. I see it, but I can't stop myself. "And if your old man's so corrupt he's willing to step in and protect the bastard you got away from, I'll bring him down, too. I'm not scared, Winnie. I'm not afraid to fight."

She stills, and for a second, I'm sure I've said the wrong thing.

Whatever else he is, he's her father.

Then she exhales and shakes her head. "I know. I just wish you'd let me help."

"This isn't something you can help me with."

"Please don't push me away, Archer," she says, her voice smaller than ever.

"I'm not pushing. I'm protecting you, protecting both of us."

She sighs.

"But that's *exactly* what you're doing right now. I want to help you face this head-on, not hide away like some helpless little doll you put on a shelf."

"Don't you think you've done enough?" I snap, and she flinches back. Shit. "Look, I know you tried when you called him up, you had good intentions, but—" I exhale, frustrated. "Can't you see I'm doing this to help you too? I need you to trust me."

She folds her arms. Her hair almost seems like it's bristling.

"Actually, sometimes I can't. If you just shut me out, if you insist it doesn't concern me when it clearly does... Archer, how can I trust anything you say?"

I stare at her, my nostrils flaring.

"If you can't trust me, then maybe none of this is right."

Fucking hell.

As soon as it's left my mouth, I want to claw the words right back.

Her face whitens. I think she might cry again.

But I guess that's not what she does when she's hurt, because when she looks up at me, her wide eyes so full of agony it rips at my heart, she's calm. Composed.

"Wait—" I start, but she waves away my words.

"Maybe you're right."

"I didn't mean it."

"But you did," she says coldly.

What is happening?

I want her to break down, to rage at me, to put me back in my place for running my mouth, but she just looks lost now. All this venom and agony deep inside her where I can't reach.

It fucking hurts watching her.

Like she's so used to being tossed aside, she knows how to handle the rejection.

"Winnie, I didn't mean it. I was just frustrated."

"You don't just say something like that and take it right back." She sniffs. "Especially when you... you meant every word."

Damn.

I know I can't undo it, I know it's not that easy, but this is shredding me. I don't even know what the fuck I really meant. I was just spouting off because I was pissed, scared at the thought of her suffering.

The look on her face screams pain.

"I know you're angry, and I know you said it because

you're mad," she says, still quiet. I reach out to her and she steps back. "But you're right. This isn't working."

"You can't mean that," I rasp out, feeling like she's shot me through the heart.

Her lip quivers, sadness filling her eyes.

"Wouldn't it be easier than fighting him? I walk out, I go somewhere he can't find me, and then he has no reason to come after you." She gestures between us, her hand shaking.

When I reach out to grab her, she sweeps back to the door, leaving before I can try to mitigate this train wreck. And yes, I'm the idiot conductor who ran it off the rails.

"Wait," I call after her. "Winnie, come back and talk to me!"

"No." She shakes her head. "Not now. I just need... give me space, Archer, okay?"

Space.

How can one mundane word feel like a guillotine?

I don't know what the hell to say to that or how to make her stay. Just like I know I can't go after her or take back the mindless dribble I spat at her.

She closes the door behind her with a small click that's so fucking anticlimactic it's laughable.

Insane.

Why couldn't she burst a lung screaming at me like Rina? I'd rather feel her slap me across the face than this.

Of course, my phone picks the shittiest time ever to go off, but I don't look away from the door and I don't pick up.

Winnie doesn't return.

The call goes to voicemail while I stand there in silence, stranded between love and regret.

* * *

To no one's surprise, Dexter and Patton agree that this conservation case could be a slow-moving catastrophe for Solitude and the other cabins there. Let alone any future expansions.

Just one whiff of 'endangered species' will freeze our properties in legal limbo for months, possibly years. They'll sit vacant while scientists and professors come pouring in.

Talk about a total loss.

"It gets worse. One proven violation could endanger our plans elsewhere in the state," Dexter says, tapping his pen against the table. "Like the St. Louis project. We won't have the investment capital if we blow it all on legal fees, let alone the zoning approvals and permits if our name turns to mud in Missouri."

"Shit, guys. We better step back, pause the expansion before anything goes further," Patton says miserably.

It's his baby and I've just drowned it in the bathwater.

I grunt in agreement, hating that I need to.

So much for fixing things.

My brothers are both adults, but in my head they're still the same kids who used to stumble along after me when we were growing up. The same brats I'd save from neighborhood bullies when they stepped on too many toes, before they could get their asses beat.

Patton is the impulsive one, the risk-taker.

Dexter has the bones of a real businessman when he can keep his temper out of the dealings.

I'm the smart, levelheaded human compass who keeps us focused, always heading in the right direction.

Until today.

It's stupid, I know, but I can't help feeling I'm letting my little brothers down, throwing them into the fire instead of bailing them out.

Especially knowing they did nothing to cause this mess.

"I'm sorry," I whisper. "The company shouldn't shoulder all the legal fees. I can throw down some of my own money to soften the blow."

"Excuse me?" Patton raises an eyebrow. "Did you miss the part where Emberly is suing the *company*?"

"Because of me. It's personal."

"Because of that girl," Dexter says. "Who, by the way, is the first person who's made you smile since the Wicked Witch of the West flew off on her broomstick."

"Bullshit," I say, more forcefully than necessary. "I've smiled plenty since then. I have Colt."

"*Bull. Shit,*" Patton mocks back, jutting out his lower lip.

I remember why I shouldn't feel too guilty over these pricks.

Dexter points his pen at me like a dagger.

"It's different and you know it. I don't know what this Winnie means to you, but if she's helped you get over Rina, she has my respect."

"Helps that she's hot," Patton adds with a chuckle, shrugging at Dexter's glare. "What? She is. Nothing on Salem, obviously, but who is? For runner-up, she's not bad."

"Runner-up? And you're saying my Junie gets fucking bronze?" Dex growls.

"Goddammit, guys, not now." I groan, dropping my head into my hands.

However hot she is—and she could beat Helen of Troy with a beauty stick—it doesn't change the truth.

I fucked up massively and she's probably not going to be hot for me any longer.

But you're right. This isn't working.

Her words float back to me like angry ghosts.

"We're going to fight this," Dexter tells me, tapping the table again to get my attention. "All of us, not just you. And not for the company, but for you. Fucking hell, Arch. How many times have you fought our battles?"

"Like when Dex screwed up that deal with Haute?" Patton dodges the swipe Dexter aims at him. "Look, it's not like you're the only one who ever stepped in it here. Even Mom didn't see it coming when Arlo got sick."

I shake my head, wishing we'd never speak of that insanity again.

"Yeah, but this is next level, Pat."

"So what? We'll get through it like we always have." Patton leans back in his chair and spears me with a look. "Whatever happens, Bro, just promise me you won't screw it up with Bee Lady. That's my one condition. You gotta keep getting laid. It helps your mood."

"Cute," Dexter deadpans.

Too late, I think bitterly, but then I shake myself.

What the hell am I still doing here listening to my brothers squawk?

I could be trying harder, fixing the gaping hole I cut in our relationship.

He's right.

I need to move my ass and patch this up before she walks out the door forever.

And knowing Winnie and how willing she is to flee when things seem hopeless, it's probably going to be sooner rather than later.

"I need to go," I say, and Patton smirks.

"That's the spirit. Go get her, Arch."

"We've got this," Dexter says, waving me to the door. "Just go home and relax. Remember to talk to her like a normal human being. You'd be surprised how far it'll get you."

"Fuck you guys," I mutter on my way out.

They both dissolve into laughter.

My brothers are adults, yes, but they still behave like punk-ass teenagers with me.

Even so, I'm grateful for their shit.

If it wasn't for them, I'd probably be paralyzed, rather than driving home, looking for Winnie's heart.

I have to see her.

I have to apologize.

I have to undo this and show her she *can* trust me.

I just hope it's not too fucking late.

XXIII: HONEYPOT (WINNIE)

I didn't think it was possible for a human being to cry so much.

Aside from blood, which remains in my veins, I never knew I had this much fluid to lose. Scalding tears leak from my eyes. My nose runs in an ugly stream that no amount of tissues seems to help.

I guess when they say the body is like fifty percent water, they aren't kidding.

But when I fled my own wedding, I didn't cry half this much. When I left my entire life behind for the unknown, I just had the occasional weepy fit.

It wasn't this.

And this is a full-blown Winnie meltdown.

Disgusting and wet and body-shaking. Shuddering breaths, breathy sobs, red cheeks, the works.

It makes it harder to see to pack my stuff, but I'm working on it.

Archer went to another meeting, I assume, probably stomping through the mess I left him in. I need to take advantage of the opportunity to get the hell out of here and save face while I still have a chance.

Before he comes back and one look at his gorgeous face makes me crumble and want to stay.

Before I talk myself into ignoring how much my very presence hurts him.

God, it's so *weird* breaking up with a man you were never really with, but who still means the world to you.

Archer can say whatever he likes, but when he told me I should just shut up and trust him, everything snapped into place.

It's not right.

And I don't mean *he* isn't right for me when he's perfect, possessive, and kinder than anyone I've ever known.

But this situation...

No matter how magical it feels with him, I can't ignore the risk that I'm costing his company millions and running it straight into the ground. That's not just him at risk or even his brothers, but everyone they employ, not to mention the customers who enjoy such beautiful places.

All because he stepped in to play hero and Dad's ego couldn't handle it.

I hate this.

I toss an empty box of tissues to the side and frantically dab at my eyes. Crying this much shouldn't be possible.

I should be a shriveled husk right now, drained of all moisture.

But somehow the tears keep coming, the eyeball equivalent of dry heaves.

At least fitting all my stuff into my bags goes faster than I thought. I leave the new clothes he insisted on buying me last week hanging in the closet.

It's not too late to return them, and I'm not going to make him waste another penny.

I even leave the shirt I've been sleeping in, torn between throwing it in the washer or abandoning it. I can't waste too much time.

Also, it still smells faintly like him. In a moment of weakness, I press it to my face and inhale him.

Yeah, leaving a man I'm totally wrong for shouldn't hurt this much.

He even made it perfectly clear we weren't ever together, didn't he?

Not really.

But then there was that whole conversation in the woods, where he said without really saying it that we *might have a chance.*

There was also a heap of drama with his ex and stuff with Colt and it was—it was nice while it lasted.

Now, it's over.

Someday, I hope I can look back on my time with Archer Rory as an innocent mistake, a 'loved and lost' that was never meant to be. He was everything I needed in my darkest hour, and everything I had to let go before I plunged him into night.

I throw the shirt in the hamper—no one should touch that again until it's clean after my snotty face was on it—and then I haul my stuff downstairs.

I march out to my vehicle and stuff the trunk full.

Then it's back to the kitchen for the finishing touch.

A goodbye note to Archer.

I can't ghost without saying something.

I scribble fast, hoping he can read my handwriting. I keep it short and simple because I don't have time and my heart can't bear a whole essay on why I'm leaving or the thousand and one ways it guts me.

. . .

Dear Archer,

This summer with you and Colt has been wonderful, the best weeks of my life. No lie.

But I think we know it's reaching its expiration. I don't want to ruin your life more than I already have, so I'm taking myself out of the equation.

I wish you and Colt the happiest days ahead. Please move on, please don't wait for me, and please remember how to smile. You look so good when you do.

-Winnie

Okay.

Okay, so there *might* be a few telltale drips that I smear away and smudge the writing slightly, but it's good enough, right?

I need to get out of here so I can hash out a real escape plan to my future. But before I can make a long drive anywhere, I need to clear my head, and the woods are calling with fresh air and pretty birds and shining stars.

After this last heart-ripping day, I desperately need some time alone with nature.

I leave the note on the counter and turn to leave—only to have my heart fly up my throat when I see who's there.

Colt, standing in front of me.

He's holding something out to me. I have to blink several times to see what it is.

Something wooden? A carving?

"You're crying," he says in the petrified tone of a boy who doesn't deal with crying adult women very often.

I sniff, wiping my eyes with my sleeve.

"Um, I—it's nothing. What's that?" I croak.

"A bee," he tells me, setting it gently on the console table in the hall so I can pick it up for a better look. "I've been working on it for a few weeks." His face screws up. "Technically, Dad still has me grounded and limits my time with the TV and phone, so…"

He shrugs so nonchalantly and pushes his glasses up his nose.

I can't help it, I laugh.

This is pure Colt.

Just like his father, he's a giant sweetheart pretending he isn't.

The bee is fantastic, of course. Sanded smooth where it counts and detailed with tiny lines in its wings. Even the eyes are crazy realistic.

"This is fricking amazing," I say roughly. "Thank you, Colt. Can I give you a hug?"

"Yeah." He submits to my manic hug, and I squeeze him tight because I'm going to miss him, too.

I'll mourn the crazy family dynamic in this house and this sweet, shy boy for a long time.

When he pulls back, his eyes flash with worry.

"What happened? Are you leaving?" he asks. "Do you want me to call Dad? I can get him in here ASAP."

No!

Panicked, I hold up my hand, forcing a smile.

"No, don't worry. It's… it's an adult thing," I say, shaking my head. "Your dad and I had a disagreement. We just… we need some time to sort things out."

"Oh. Oh, shit." The dramatic way he says it sounds almost comical, especially when he folds his arms and rolls his eyes. "Winnie, what dumbass thing did he pull on you?"

My smile breaks, but I do my best to hold it.

"No, Colt. It's my fault, actually. That's the problem. He's been trying to help me out because he's a great guy, but I'm here causing a lot of issues, and I can't keep getting in his hair. So, yeah, I'm going to head out for a bit."

He cocks his head, studying me like he can tell this is goodbye. I suppose he's old enough to know the truth.

"Where are you going? Not back to the last guy?"

"God, no! I'm not crawling back to my old life, that's dead and buried. And I have you and Archer to thank for that."

Instead of saying more, I pull him into another hug.

He's *such* a great kid.

My eyes mist over again and I squeeze them shut, counting to ten until I think I've got myself about under control.

"Bye now. Take care of your dad," I manage, turning my back and hurrying out the door before another look from his sad blue eyes changes my mind.

* * *

Well, crap.

Despite loving nature a ton, Mother Nature doesn't always love me back. She's kinda demanding and one-sided like that.

I've been comfy enough camping in the Ozarks and a few other parks, but it turns out that those places you go where people strike windproof tents and where you always have fluffy beds and full canteens and endless instant foods—that isn't real camping.

At least, not the sort of camping I've gone for this time.

I bought all the equipment secondhand off a guy on Facebook Marketplace before I realized not only am I not the best person to be doing this—aka, a total clueless idiot—but this isn't remotely easy on your own.

I picked the forest near Solitude because it felt appropriate, the other side that must be a few miles from the cabin.

I couldn't set off from the property itself. That would have hurt too much.

Instead, I picked a parking lot farther up the road and headed for the trail winding into the woods.

I'll only spend a night or two here, I decide. Just a nice healing breather, surrounded by pretty trees, then it's back to real life.

At some point, I'll call Lyssie to help plot my next move, and try to line up a rental car before I blast off from Kansas City.

It's funny how walking makes time melt away.

I hike along until my sneakers rub and my legs feel like rubber and my shoulders are killing me from the hefty backpack I brought along. I leave my car behind because I'm sure Dad will have it repossessed soon enough.

It's only as the sun sets and soaring trees start casting shadows on every good camping spot that I stop and realize I have no earthly clue how to set up this tent.

Or make a fire without a portable burner.

Or do… anything.

Brilliant, Winnie.

In the end, after panicking for a hot minute, I just toss my sleeping bag on a bare spot of ground, tent abandoned, and dig into cold chili from a can.

Yes, it's as gross as it sounds.

To settle my stomach, I flop back to watch the night sky, so obscured by those big crisscrossing branches overhead that I can only make out the occasional star.

In another life, it might be peaceful, but my legs ache like mad from a few hours of hiking over rugged ground.

My heart lurches at every single noise—and there are a lot of them tonight.

This is a forest, after all. I should've realized how spooky and *busy* forests get at night. Every second, another bush rustles or some animal calls out.

I have to bite back a scream.

It's dark and cold and I'm exposed.

I have to do serious convincing to reassure myself there's not a murdery axeman with a pyramid for a head threatening to kill me, or even a bunch of dumb teenagers with fireworks. No rabid foxes or werewolves around these parts, no sir.

But there could be a bear...

Black bears still roam around some parts of Missouri, and I think they get *really* hungry in late summer before they bulk up for winter hibernation. They're pretty rare around Kansas City, I think, but sometimes a straggler with a growling belly strays this far north.

Jesus, I don't know.

I never learned much about bears, and now that I'm here on their turf, it feels like an oversight. Wasn't there something about standing still if one approaches? Or are you supposed to run? I can't remember.

God, everything here is *so loud.*

The many eerie noises aren't helping me think.

Even if I could sleep, I'd still be pissed at the noise. It's insects mostly, although sometimes I hear a muffled grunt or a twig snapping from something that totally can't be a bear.

If I hear an earsplitting howl, I'm out.

So I dig into my sleeping bag, feeling every bump and stone under me.

If I'm honest with myself, the worst part of this whole situation is the fact that I walked away from Archer in the blink of an eye.

Yes, he started it.

But I couldn't stand to hurt him a second longer.

THREE RECKLESS WORDS

What else is logical when you tell someone you're not right together—and you know it's the terrible truth.

It wasn't about trust.

If he couldn't see it was unreasonable, wanting me to keep my nose out of *my own* business, then yeah, it wasn't right.

Just like it wasn't right to let my stupid, belligerent father come trampling mud all over his life, his family.

Removing myself like a plague rat made sense. I'm bad luck.

But damn does it hurt.

About as bad as I feel right now with fresh brush scratches, pulverized muscle, and feet turning into swollen bricks.

Leaving Holden didn't feel half this awful.

I just felt like I had to get away before he could rope me back into a marriage I never wanted. I was scared he would chase me down and force me into the life I didn't choose.

Now, a tiny part of myself *wants* Archer to come and force me back into the life I can't have.

I must be insane.

But even though I can see him and Colt every time I close my eyes, I know it's not wise. I've lost the right to beg for Archer Rory to come charging to my rescue again.

He couldn't find me if he wanted to.

I don't think I could find myself on a map.

Just in case, I roll over and find my phone, plugging it into the portable battery that the guy on Facebook Marketplace *assured* me was working perfectly.

Guess what?

My phone charges less than five percent before the battery sputters out. Then nothing charges at all.

This is fine.

I'll just head back into civilization tomorrow and pretend

this never happened. I'll get back in my car, try to pawn this stuff for gas money, and go straight to Lyssie.

She'll gladly take me in.

I'll sob all over her and we'll eat ice cream, and then she'll beat me over the head with a pair of reindeer socks—she wears them year-round—until she forgives me.

A few glorious months from now, it'll be like none of this ever happened.

I can regroup for a few days in Springfield, laying low, and run away with a better plan.

If only those cicadas or whatever they are weren't so loud, I might actually be able to get some sleep. I duck under the hood of my sleeping bag, which has the added benefit of making sure said bugs don't crawl all over my face.

I'm lying *on* the tent, but still. *They can crawl.*

And I'm still willing my brain to shut out the creepy crawlies when this weird moaning sound comes from my left.

I bolt up.

Okay, Mother Nature.

Not cool.

We are about to have some serious words, because this is *not* what I signed up for when I went on this stupid camping disaster without thinking it through.

The next moan comes closer.

I fling myself back in my sleeping bag, finding my shoes and putting them on. That's it—I'm heading to the RV park I saw a little ways from here. At least over there, I'll find people around.

Light and familiar noise.

A little community where I won't just magically disappear alone.

It takes me way too long to stuff the tent and its doohickeys back into this oversized bag. Then I'm on my way in the dark, my phone in my pocket and the light from the moon guiding the way.

Or rather, *not* guiding the way.

As time ticks by and I clamber over rocks and fallen branches and twigs reach out to scratch my face, I'm coming to the worst conclusion possible. A perfectly rotten close to this disaster of a day.

I am lost.

Totally and utterly.

I wander around for about an hour before giving up and checking my phone to see if I can call emergency services—only to see my phone has ten percent left on its battery. And the service bars look weak, fading in and out as it tries to find a tower.

Holy shit.

I don't think it's even going to hold out to call anyone, so I send a quick Snap to Lyssie, taking a picture of the dark and captioning it, *Guess where I am! If you find out, please tell me because I have no clue.*

There.

Not too panicked.

Nothing embarrassing.

I don't want to worry her, but also, I am freaking out.

The only thing I can do is press on, though.

Only now I'm facing a different, scarier problem than the one I tried to flee from.

My stomach knots as I push through the dark, hoping I'm going in the right direction, desperately looking and listening for any sign of the RV people.

XXIV: LOST HONEY (ARCHER)

I read the letter Winnie left for the umpteenth time.

I practically know it by heart at this point, but I can't stop looking, even when every word feels like a toothpick in the eye.

It's the saddest fucking letter I've ever read in my life.

Winnie, thinking she's brought so much chaos she's deleted herself from my life. In her heart, I'm sure the math made sense.

Because I'm the prick who told her.

I fucking *told* her it wasn't working, demanding her trust and barking shit, and of course she took that literally.

How many times has she been pushed around by men with egos bigger than their brains? And I went in and threatened to abandon her if she didn't fall into line.

Now, I'm another name on her long list of disappointments, and I can't blame her for taking the one way out she had.

She left.

The worst part is, I know what she's feeling.

I know how she feels about rejection.

Her entire family, her stupid ex-fiancé, the career she had in politics, they all made her feel like *less.*

Now I'm standing here, gobsmacked that I followed in their footsteps.

Colt shuffles into the kitchen, sees me standing there reading the letter that Winnie stained with her tears, and walks back out again.

What does he know?

"Wait," I say, lurching after him. He's been home all day—he probably saw her leave. Maybe she talked to him or said something, or at least—

Goddammit, what? I don't even know what I want besides having Winnie back.

Colt stops in the hall, folding his arms.

"What do you want?" His voice has an edge that says he's hiding something.

"Did you know she was leaving?" I demand, not caring that I'm too heartsick to be Mr. Calm Upright Dad of The Century right now.

He shakes his head. "Not until she came into the kitchen with all her bags and that letter. She was *crying*, Dad."

Hearing that knifes me deep.

"Did she say where she was going?"

"No. She didn't say much, just that you guys had a fight." He stares at me sullenly. The kid's got a point.

I'd be thinking the same thing if I was him, wondering how my old man could fuck up such a good thing.

"So what was it? Don't tell me you chickened out." He sighs.

"Work stuff," I bite off. "It doesn't matter."

"Work stuff? Lame. And yeah right, it must matter a lot if you're shitting things up with an awesome girl," he throws back, shaking his head again, this time in disgust. "I can't believe you."

Me neither, kid.

Snarling, I lean against the counter and pull out my phone, which has been buzzing frantically in my pocket.

For a brief second, I'm able to hope it's Winnie until I see it's my brothers, checking in. Patton wants to make sure I'm okay and Dex is close behind him.

I don't have the heart to answer them.

And I don't the rest of the day, either.

Instead, as Colt shuts himselfself away in his his room and ignoreses me, I mope around the house in the hopes she'll call or come back or—fuck, do something.

Just tell me you're okay.

I read your letter and I know you had your reasons. We can still talk.

I hate that I only realize I'm being desperate and clingy after I send those texts.

No matter what I do, though, I can't shake the feeling that I'm missing something vital. That uneasy hollow in the pit of my stomach doesn't fade, and I'm positive it's there thanks to Winnie.

Look, I'm not like Rina. I'm not the New Agey type who believes in premonitions or sixth senses or what the hell ever.

Right now, I'm just a man who's brutally worried because she left and I don't know how to get her back.

The best thing that's ever happened to me, and she's gone in a flash.

Patton and Dexter turn up at seven o'clock sharp, just as I'm plating up a spicy pasta dish Colt promptly grabs and takes to his room so he can go right back to ignoring me.

I damn near bite my tongue off, choosing to back down and let it slide.

If I force him to eat with me at the table like a civilized

person, it'll turn into a fight for sure, and neither of us need to turn on each other more.

Too bad my brothers had to come. I don't know if it's to save me or toss me straight into the fire.

"So, did you talk to her yet?" Patton asks when I let them both inside.

"You've been ignoring us all day," Dexter adds.

Yeah. I think I'd rather wrestle Colt to the dinner table than take love advice from these two.

"And naturally, you thought the best way to handle the situation was to barge in here and pester me?" I snort.

Patton smirks, his favorite expression. Like always, I hope his nerves misfire and it gets locked on his face.

"It's not like we were getting anywhere with hoping you'd get back to us."

Shit. I'm trapped with a pair of hyenas.

"Since you're here… dinner? I can set a few more plates." I gesture to the table and the pasta still on the stove.

"Nah," they say in unison.

"Junie's making that chicken with the mushroom cream sauce when I get back," Dexter says smugly.

"Where did you bury your inner health freak after you killed him, Dex? You must've put on ten pounds since the wedding." My lip curls.

"Lucky man. I'm on dinner duty when I get back," Patton says.

"You can cook?" Dexter raises an eyebrow.

"Better than you. It's amazing what a wife and kid will do for your food game."

"Your game is recycling the same six recipes biweekly. You wouldn't know a cookbook if the whole library in Mom's pantry fell on your head," I growl.

As happy as I am for their domestic bliss, I don't need them rattling on about it in my dining room right after I detonated relations with the only woman I've wanted to cook for in ages.

So I fold my arms and lean back in my chair, studying them slowly.

I don't have time or patience for this shit.

"If you're not going to say anything useful, get out. I'm not in the mood tonight." I glare at them.

"Damn, Arch, Winnie never had a prayer when you're just dripping in charisma," Patton deadpans.

"I mean it, dickhead." I set my jaw.

"Okay, so let's talk about Winnie since that's why we're here. Colt told me you crapped the bed," Dexter says. "What happened? I thought you were going to smooth things over?"

"I was," I say. "But she wasn't here when I got back."

Patton's forehead creases, his smirk gone. "What, she left?"

"I mean *she left,* Captain Oblivious. Left me a Dear Archer note saying she'd ruined my life enough, so she was taking herself out of it." I sigh.

How is this happening to me?

Long ago, I told myself I was done with women and relationships. It was just Colt and me.

Now, he won't even speak to me.

"Shit," Patton says. "What did you do?"

"I don't know," I tell him, which is the truth. At least, partly. "I fucked up, of course. I know that. But where she's gone or what her plan is now? No clue."

"What about Colt? Doesn't she talk to him?" Patton asks.

"He doesn't know where she went, but even if he did, I don't know if he'd tell me. I'm his favorite villain now." I look down at the plate of food I've barely touched, not remotely hungry. Talking about this doesn't feel useful like it's supposed to. It just adds to the dead weight in my chest. "He's pissed and I can't blame him."

"That's because she was fucking good for you," Dexter huffs.

"You've got no clue at all?" Patton presses. "No hint where she'd go if she's mourning your dumbass?"

"I don't know, Pat," I snap. "She's a runner. It's part of her instinct. Hell, that's how I *met* her. She wound up at Solitude after the wedding fell through with her bastard of a fiancé. For all I know, she could be back in Springfield. She must have a few friends there."

Friends, yeah.

Plenty of folks she never wants to see again, too.

Aside from that? The world is a big fucking place and Winnie could be anywhere.

"What about her vehicle?" Dexter asks, opening his phone. "We can track down her plates, maybe. You know I'm in good with the cops."

"Dex, no. She's not a fucking missing person. She just decided she's had enough of my bullshit," I grumble. Dex has his police contacts, yes, but that's too intrusive. "It's not like there's something wrong. It's no crime to breakup and dash."

"*You* know something's wrong," Patton says. "You've been glowering and scowling all evening. I know that's like your signature move, but it's worse than usual. Also, you always answer your emails except for the rare Colt emergency—or when you're worried about her."

Guilty.

Dexter's face is unusually grim, even when he says nothing.

I don't like it.

My brother must feel that same heavy shadow in his gut, the inexplicable sense that something's off about this mess.

Or maybe he's just picked up on my vibe.

That's easy enough when he says, "We'll find her, Arch."

***

They stay all evening.

They'd never admit they're there for moral support—and I wouldn't let them—but deep down, having company that has my back makes me feel slightly less shitty.

It isn't long before the crowd grows, too.

Junie shows up, and then Salem and little Arlo, who's growing faster than Colt did at his age. Maybe it's the weirdness of only finding out you have a new nephew after he's older than a toddler.

Junie throws together a huge batch of that hybrid chicken parm with the stroganoff-like sauce for everyone. There's no denying it goes down faster and easier than my pathetic fire pasta.

The women and Arlo lighten the atmosphere, letting me melt into the background while they talk and laugh and tease.

Fine.

As nice as this impromptu family gathering is, I can't shake the stress drenching my bones.

Dexter keeps quietly making inquiries. Patton does his best to distract me, prodding Arlo to talk everyone's ear off about his latest additions to their fancy aquarium. I don't think they'll ever have enough cuttlefish.

Still, all I can think about is her.

Winnie, crashed in a ditch somewhere, smoke billowing from her crumpled car.

Winnie, bleeding by the side of the road.

Winnie, captured and gagged by some mean-eyed fuck who likes to lure women into the trunk of his car, an easy target.

She's a fighter, but she's too gentle.

Her world isn't violence and pain and aggression. She

grew up sheltered with parents who didn't give a damn what her world became.

The only fighting she knows how to do is with words.

The hours crawl by.

I do my best to focus on anything but Winnie's fate. Salem smiling as she gently rests on Patton's shoulder and Junie gazing adoringly at Dexter isn't helping one bit.

Eventually, I get up and face the inevitable.

I grab my phone, hit Winnie's contact, and listen as the call instantly disconnects.

What the hell? Did she block me?

I stare at the screen in disbelief, my last fucks to give about today slipping through my fingers.

It's getting late. The stars peek through the thick clouds. There's a full moon, or close to it, which I'm unreasonably grateful for. Not that it's much light if there's someone alone out there, desperate for help.

Not Winnie, I'm sure.

Considering the other reasons why her phone might shut off like that, I *hope* she blocked me out of spite.

"Do you want us to get out of your hair? Or can we help you find her?" Junie asks gently.

She swings her hair, and the movement reminds me of Winnie, too.

All I can think about is how depraved I am for blowing this to kingdom come.

"No," I say. "You should get home. She's probably just hiding out somewhere. It's not your problem." Even as I say the words, I know they're lies. But Junie smiles, accepting my usual no-nonsense logic.

"You'll see her soon, Arch. Give it time."

Yeah, *time*.

If Winnie ever shows up again, I'll be the happiest idiot

alive, and I'll do everything in my power to make sure I never lose her again.

"I'll keep you guys posted."

Dexter holds my gaze. "You mean you'll actually call her? Brave man."

"Don't be an ass." I don't tell him I've already tried calling and received the worst response. *Silence.*

"Don't deserve it, then." He pulls me into one of those half arm-wrestling handshakes brothers do. "Call me the second you need anything."

Patton fakes a yawn beside me. "Don't call me. We've got an early morning with Arlo, big karate tournament here."

"He'll kill it. What's he up to now, third degree black belt?" I smile at the little boy, who's already passed out on his dad's shoulder.

"If anything comes up, call anyway," Salem says. "I'll make sure his phone stays on."

"Hey!" Patton protests. "You can't make promises when a guy needs his beauty sleep."

"I can and I will." She lowers her voice ominously. "He's your brother and he *needs* you."

"I'm right here," I say dryly. "Kindly pray for me if I need help from this bozo."

Salem gives me a knowing smile.

"Don't be a stranger, Uncle Archer," Arlo pipes up, suddenly awake and rubbing his eyes.

Everybody laughs.

"Right. Now get lost, all of you," I say.

They've done enough for one night, coming over here and keeping me company until it's almost midnight.

I wait for them all to leave before trying Winnie's number again, breathing around the worry in my throat.

Just like before, there's nothing on the other end.

That boulder of worry snowballs into a mountain.

As if on cue, another call comes in, this time from Higher Ends' head of security. She's a newer hire after our old guy retired, just brought on a couple weeks ago.

Janine, I think. Frowning, I swipe to take the call.

"Hello?"

"Mr. Rory? I'm sorry to disturb you so late, sir."

"It's fine, Janine. What's going on?"

"We've been barraged with calls at The Cardinal from a young lady in Springfield who insists on speaking with a Miss Winnie Emberly. She wouldn't let our manager off the line until he promised we'd try to contact you personally. She believes you can help her. Miss Emberly's name comes up in the system as a guest, so I told her I would forward her number to you."

Holy flaming shit.

Springfield, huh? I'm instantly suspicious, knowing how Winnie's family treats her, but Janine said 'young lady.'

Winnie never mentioned a sister or nosy cousin or anything.

I close my eyes and press the phone to my forehead before answering, my voice husky. "Yes, send the number along. Right now. Thanks."

"You're welcome, sir. Again, my apologies for bothering you this late."

"Don't apologize, Janine. Just enjoy the bonus on your next paycheck."

She's smart enough to leave it there.

We keep a security help desk open twenty-four hours in case there's an emergency at our properties. If this is a clue about Winnie's whereabouts, I don't care if nothing comes up for a year—it will have paid for itself ten times over.

My phone buzzes with a text as the number comes through and I call it immediately. A slightly sleepy voice answers.

"Is this Archer Rory?"

"Speaking. What happened to Winnie?" I can't hide the ruthless demand in my voice.

"That depends. Are you..." Her voice sharpens as she inhales. "Are you the dude she was seeing?"

"You know about that?"

Fuck.

"Not all the details, no. Winnie never spills about stuff like this over the phone—you have to pin her down in person and squeeze, but still, I know enough." She seems to realize who she's talking to and coughs. "Um, do you know where she is?"

Huh? That's not the question I expected.

"No, I thought you called me because you'd know. I've been trying to get in touch with her."

"Oh, man. Oh, crap." She's quiet for a second before saying, "So, I got this weird picture from her about an hour ago. Winnie asked me to guess where she was. If I figured it out, she told me to tell her because I think she's lost. She wouldn't show up on the map at all."

"Picture? What picture?" I growl.

"I don't know. It came through on Snapchat. Just darkness and trees. I thought she was joking, but she wouldn't pick up and her phone seems dead. If she's lost or kidnapped..." The girl breathes harshly. "I don't like it one bit. I've tried calling her, but it's like her phone got disconnected. I thought about just calling the police, but after everything with her family, that's my last resort."

"You think the phone died? The battery?" I say flatly.

"I mean, I don't know what else could've happened. And listen, Mr. Archer, I don't know you, but if you give a crap about my best friend like she thinks you do... you should find her. You're the only person she seems to trust in Kansas

City. If she's out there in the middle of the woods, lost and alone—" Her voice chokes as she breaks off.

I have to remind myself to breathe.

Believe me, it's an effort after feeling the word *trust* plow through my chest like a bullet.

"Who are you again?" I ask.

"My name's Lyssie. We've been close for years and I'm really worried about her."

Shit.

Winnie told her friend about me, and now I'm this friend's last option.

If it's as bad as it sounds, I need to find her before it's too late. My mind won't process what could happen if I *am*.

"She has to be out there somewhere. Do you know any big parks or anything around there?" Lyssie asks.

"You think she's in the woods?" I try to keep my tone calm.

"Maybe. Whenever she wants space to think, she goes outside. I looked around and it looks like there's a lot of forest around the city. She's been camping before, so it wouldn't be the craziest idea. Then again, I don't know if she's ever really done any big-time camping. Like the kind with no outhouse."

Great.

My poor, beautiful Sugarbee is lost somewhere in countless acres of woods in the Kansas City metro area.

That's a big fucking haystack to sift through.

I don't know where to start, especially if the forests are dense like the stretch that backs up to Solitude and—

Wait.

Solitude.

…she wouldn't be that obvious, would she?

But she *does* love her bees to death, and she's had a taste of those woods.

"I have an idea. I'll get back to you soon," I say. "I have to go."

"Okay! You go get her. Let me know the second she's safe." She exhales a long breath. "Oh, and Mr. Rory?"

"What?" I can barely focus on the conversation as I run to the mudroom and pull my shoes on.

"She likes you a lot. You'd better not let her down."

* * *

Normally, I'd be happy to have Colt back on speaking terms.

If I couldn't see how white and scared his face looks in the glaring light from passing cars, I'd be thrilled. I only gave him the basics, yet he insisted on coming along the second he heard the news. Even so, it's enough to scare him shitless.

He's still a kid, but he knows how dangerous the forest can be if you're lost and alone, and how hard it gets to locate anyone in miles of dark, dense growth.

After Lyssie called, I spent a frenzied hour calling up park rangers and state troopers before heading out, armed with every lantern and flashlight I own. I have to try finding her myself.

Now, here we are.

Patton and Dexter camp out at two different nearby parking lots, scouring the forest. One call and they dropped everything, stunned that I was desperate enough to ask for their help.

If it brings her home, I don't care.

I head to the lot farthest away from Solitude, not far from that beautiful clearing in the woods. The same place where I let her dream I wouldn't morph into a total jackass.

No such luck so far, but it's early.

A ranger told me there's an old hiking trail that leads into the woods from there.

I don't have anything better to do tonight. I'm certainly not sleeping.

I've been surviving on pure caffeine and adrenaline since yesterday, and if I'm not careful, I'm going to start seeing double.

Still, my nerves are too frayed to let me do anything except keep moving.

Find her.

Fix this shit.

"Dad? Do you think we'll find her?" Colt breaks the silence that's been strangling me.

"We will," I promise roughly. "Even if I have to knock down every tree in this forest."

He nods and goes back to looking out the window.

I swerve into the parking lot after taking another quick pass through the small winding roads that weren't gated off.

There are hints of light on the horizon, dawn barely approaching.

The light helps me look for Winnie's vehicle, ready to be disappointed again.

But there it is, tucked away in the corner by some brush, parked slightly crooked like she just pulled up and only meant to stay a few minutes.

Another sucker punch.

She was so upset by everything that happened.

She wasn't even thinking straight enough to park properly before she wandered off.

That's not the considerate, lovely woman I know.

What the hell did I *do* to her?

With my breath stalled, I pull up beside her vehicle and screech to a stop, not caring about my parking, either.

She was here.

She was here and she meant to come back.

With Colt still in the passenger seat, I leap out and check her doors.

Yes, they're locked.

There's nothing inside, either. No purse on the passenger seat or stray camping gear she planned to come back for later.

Nothing to tell me where she intended to go.

A few feet away, there's a big park board mapping the trail, which snakes on for miles across these woods.

If she took this route, she could be miles away by now.

Hell, she could be anywhere. It would take an army to look for her.

But I know she was here first.

Inhaling the night air, I force back the urge to rush in after her blindly.

That won't help anything.

Plus, with Colt along, it's not practical. I don't have the right equipment—food, water, anything I should've brought if I was going to start scouring the woods.

But I want to. I want to follow her like a bloodhound, knowing she's probably still here somewhere.

"Dad?" Colt asks quietly from behind me. "What are we going to do?"

"First, I'm going to call your uncles and tell them we found her car. Then we're going back to the visitor's center and updating the rangers. They'll have enough cops here to help us soon."

Like it or not, the police are involved now. I couldn't care less if it ever makes it back to the assholes in Springfield who helped send Winnie into the wilderness.

He looks at my face, back to being a little kid. It's the same way he used to look at me when I seemed like the bravest superhero in the world.

"Then what? We should do something."

"Then we're going Winnie hunting. We're just a few hours from morning. The light will make this a lot easier."

I hope.

"Okay." He nods, face pale and jaw set. "Just tell me what to do, Dad. I want to help."

"I know, Son." I drop a hand on his shoulder. I don't think it's possible to be prouder of him than I am right now. "You'll get to as soon as we've got everything ready."

It's almost sunrise by the time I pull back up to the visitor's center where there's a bustling command center assembled.

Someone pulled in a Search and Rescue unit, swarms of cops from three towns over, and a big, well-dressed man with an entourage buzzing around him. I assume he must be the top dog managing everything, even if he's not wearing a badge.

"Stay here," I tell Colt as I get out of the car.

As I approach, the man turns and looks at me with pure derision.

I don't understand when he sniffs, holding out a cautious hand like he recognizes me. I've never seen this guy in my life.

Unless—

"Archer Rory," he clips, his eyes wary. I look at his hand, but there's no way I'm about to shake it as I realize who I'm dealing with. "I'm Carroll Emberly, Winnie's father."

"I *know* who you are," I spit.

His gaze flits across my face, sizing up my expression. He holds up his hands defensively, oozing a heavy sigh.

"Before you punch me in the face, please hear me out…"

XXV: TO BEE OR NOT TO BEE (WINNIE)

I think it's getting dark again.

I've watched the sun moving through the breaks in the leaves. It feels like watching an hourglass running out.

Out here, time means nothing and also everything.

I can barely remember if this is the first or second night.

The only thing I do know—and I really do know it—is my body hurts.

It feels like being plugged into a dull electrical current.

What started as a drumming pain became a steady, deep ache that makes it hard to think. When I blinked my sore eyes open this morning, I was damp and confused and so, so tired from having wandered around all night, totally lost.

And I do mean *totally*.

If there was ever a path in this part of the woods, there's no sign of it now, buried under years of thick brush and debris. Every step I take feels like the wrong flipping way.

So yes, now it's getting dark again.

My legs are wet spaghetti and my stomach gurgles. I really should've thought harder about what to pack for food instead of doubling down on dried fruit and instant oatmeal. I only had chili the first night because I thought I'd be settled by now and I didn't want to lug around tons of cans.

I'm so tired I could pass out cold, face down in the dirt.

I blink, force myself to yawn, trying to figure out which way is up and forward, and press onward. Overhead, the rustling leaves block the last scraps of daylight.

I'm slowly resigning myself to death.

Then my stomach flips over again, threatening to heave up my guts, and I change my mind.

I'm so not ready to die.

There's nothing I want less than to slowly run out of food and die out here, feeling my life draining away like I'm sinking in the world's slowest tarpit.

Plus, being eaten alive, one mosquito bite at time.

Another little vampire comes for me, landing on my arm and instantly stabbing into my skin.

I never said I liked *all* bugs.

I grit my teeth and slap at it, but the momentum makes me wobble and I tumble back against a thick tree. Rugged bark scrapes my shoulder.

Ow.

I'm too old for this crap.

Or is it too young?

As the forest wakes up with ominous night sounds, I pause and think.

I am definitely too *something* for this adventure.

Too alive, maybe.

Too sheltered.

Definitely too soft.

My stomach cramps again, even worse this time. I heave from the sensation, bending over to cough up stomach bile into the brush next to me.

I haven't eaten since last night, honestly.

There's nothing left for me to throw up.

One more mistake among many.

I never should've left my nice, comfy sleeping bag and gotten *more* lost.

Instead of staying put and letting myself dehydrate like a normal person while I waited for another hiker to stumble across me, I just had to get thirsty. Then I had to go and drink from that little stream.

It looked clear enough, but what do I know?

Not much, apparently.

Now, my entire body rebels, determined to speed up my doom by dehydration.

God, this really might be the end.

I need to focus, though.

Just sit down. Relax. Breathe.

Doubled over, I walk over to the tree that scraped me and slump down against its trunk.

Civilization feels like a far-off dream. Did it ever exist at all?

I can't remember what sleeping in a real bed feels like.

All I know is dizziness and pain and the never-ending chirps and humming of the forest.

My legs ache, demanding water and electrolytes, reminding me that all I've done today is float around in circles.

But... but if I stop now, if I shut my eyes too long and drift off, I'll never find my way out.

I *have* to keep going.

Keep moving.

Keep—

My fingers dig into moss and I blink, trying to process the info relayed by my own senses.

Somehow, I've gone *sideways* without noticing, and now my nose is about two inches from the ground.

Oh, this is bad.

The kind of hanging over the edge of a cliff bad that has me scrubbing at my face to dislodge the fear, the confusion.

Even my breathing feels erratic.

I wince and clear my parched throat, wishing I had the words to curse the people who put me here.

Holden.

My stupid parents.

Archer.

No, not him. He might've trampled my heart, but at least he had reasons that aren't completely selfish.

Mostly, I want to curse myself.

There's a deep ringing in my ears, and I suck in a long breath. Then another. No matter how much I breathe, I can't shake the weird buzzing sound that only amplifies.

Am I on the verge of passing out?

Groaning, I push myself up, hugging the tree for support.

Come on, one, two.

One, two.

One little step at a time.

I'm plodding along like a drunken camel, but at least I'm plodding.

If I just keep on going in one direction, one shaky step at a time, I *should* reach the edge of the forest eventually.

Logically, that makes sense.

A Hail Mary that gives me just enough hope to bargain with the universe.

"I don't want to die," I rasp. Ridiculous, sure, but I have this weird urge to hear my own voice. "How do you think Archer would feel?"

My heart twists, thinking about him and Colt both.

If I never make it out of here alive, they'll beat themselves up forever.

Archer, he'll blame himself for chasing me out here, an

unforgivable failure when all he ever wanted was to protect me.

And Colt, being the sweetie that he is... he'll never get over being the last person to talk to me. He'll think he could have said *something* to put the brakes on my stupidity.

Even poor Lyssie, the unlucky recipient of my last dumb joke.

I can't give up.

I can't give up for them because fighting for myself isn't enough.

I just wish my throat didn't feel like I've gargled half the Sahara, but the pain screams *I'm still in this.*

"Come on, pick yourself up. You're gonna live. You're going to survive. You have to," I whisper. My knees aren't playing ball, so I crawl forward, falling over a few times until my nails dig into the dirt.

I'll never clean it out at this rate, but they're half-destroyed, anyway, chewed to bits.

Pain becomes my mantra with every step.

Guilt becomes my courage.

The evening gloom drapes over the trees, the late summer air hanging thick and stifling. Somehow, I'm still drenched in sweat after feeling like I've shed half my water weight.

That frenzied buzzing in my head gets louder, more insistent, more worrisome.

Sighing, I shake my head, but that won't make it go away.

Something lands on my arm—thicker than the mosquitos that keep plaguing me.

I squint down.

"Work, brain," I slur.

It's amazing how everything can hurt and feel numb at the same time. None of my senses work.

But my eyes finally focus on the small creature crawling up my arm.

…a bee?

Yes, a perfect little honeybee.

And I realize that droning buzz isn't just in my head.

That buzzing, it's—

Holy shit.

Bees!

My heart rockets straight to the sky, flooded with emotion.

Happiness. Relief. Awe.

I choke back a sob as I crawl on my hands and knees, closer to the buzzing sound, a lopsided smile twisting my face.

This is worth the agony. The achy limbs, the nausea, the impending death.

This is worth my very real fear of dying out here, because if I hadn't come out all this way, I never would have known the bees made it.

Holden didn't kill them by leaving them homeless when he scattered them to the winds.

They're here, alive in the woods, safe and hidden.

The next sound that escapes me is guttural and raw.

I'm sobbing.

Real, rib-cracking sobs.

I curl up on the mossy ground and vent my feels in a messy explosion of sound that hurts to expel.

I can't be certain, but I'm pretty sure these are the same bees from the bee boxes. There are never any guarantees bees will make it when they're violently evicted from their old homes.

But I think these guys did.

They're *alive*, busy, and so close.

Slowly, I clamber forward until I can just about make out the hive in the darkness.

It's huge, built into a dark shape bigger than a tree. Some

sort of ancient, half-collapsed shed or wooden hunting blind, I realize.

The air is thick with bees, and their loud droning echoes in my bones.

It reminds me of good things, of home, of Grandma, of Archer and his kisses, and it's such a sweet relief I almost pass out.

But I won't until I see them.

Closer, closer, until the noise surrounds me like dull static.

They're dormant at night, but a few lazy blind bees tangle in my hair, landing on my arms before lifting off again.

I don't care.

This is the miracle I needed.

Almost all the light has bled out now and we're well into gloom and shadows.

My hand shakes as I reach the side of the shed, peeling back a piece of rotted board to take a piece of the honeycomb.

The buzzing turns deafening and the bees sound angry.

They really don't like bandits coming for their goods at night.

Crap. I need to get out of here soon or I might win the most ironic death ever.

Even if I'm friendly, to them I'm a threat, and there's nothing to protect me if they get riled up enough to attack.

No, they can't see well in the dark, but a few hundred drones will find their target if I'm right on top of them.

Grunting with effort, I work quickly, breaking off a small chunk of honeycomb to take.

"I'm sorry, guys. You know I'll get you back someday, I promise."

The buzzing intensifies. A few bees flit past my head like screaming bullets.

But I stagger backward, retreating, whispering more apologies.

Maybe they're still about as exhausted as I am from having fled their hives and built up busy new ones. Or maybe it's just the dark.

Either way, they don't chase me into the night.

I'm clumsy, though.

It takes too long to put some healthy distance between me and the hive. Finally, after a few parting stings for my trouble, I stumble off to safety.

I set the honeycomb on my lap and rip a couple leftover stingers out of my skin.

My fingers are sausages. I have to try several times before they're out.

Six pulsing stings add to the cacophony of pain bouncing around my body. But I have the honeycomb, and that means I have precious food that won't upset my stomach. A little sugar, simple to digest, which hopefully means the energy to avoid passing out.

When I run my tongue cautiously across it, I make another discovery—one which means almost as much as the bees.

This has to be the purple honey.

It's too dark to see it, but the taste gives it away even before I notice that dim telltale glow.

I spent half the summer loving this flavor. There's something distinct about it, rich and sweet without being overwhelming. It's almost like fine wine or chocolate, and it cleans the foul taste from my mouth.

And I realize any healing properties it has won't magically save me, but right now I need all the help I can get.

A little glucose to keep my brain working, plus whatever enzymes are in this stuff.

I *will* survive.

My hands are greedy as my nausea lifts and the hunger hits again. I break off large bits of honeycomb and cram them in my mouth. Soon, I go full hangry Pooh Bear, wiping honey off my chin and licking it off the back of my hand.

No, I'm not pretty right now.

I'm determined.

Luck hasn't been on my side lately, but this tastes a little like destiny.

I'm feeling more lucid by the minute as my body pumps glucose into my blood, more aware of my surroundings than I have been since yesterday, even as the night gets denser and the woods turn eerie.

A soft summer breeze blows through the trees. Aside from the creaking branches, it helps everything feel a little less stifling.

I should keep moving with the wind literally at my back.

"Don't give up. Not now. Not ever," I whisper.

Though maybe I should rest just a few more seconds to keep up my strength.

Also, now that I'm fed, I'm impossibly tired.

We're talking bone-deep exhaustion that could send me smacking into a tree. I'm not sure I'd even notice.

I slouch down against another huge tree trunk, my feet screaming at me.

Okay, okay. Just a minute or two, then we're moving again.

Colt would love this cool secret nest.

Archer would shake his head and warn me how dangerous it is.

The thought drops in my head like a pebble on a lake. Every time I imagine Archer and Colt, my heart twists tighter.

If they could see this place, I bet Colt would cook up a whole new biology project. Archer would hold his son back from the bees, and I'd loan Colt a bee suit to keep him safe, and then we'd hang back, holding hands while the teenager explored to his heart's content.

Oh, that hurts.

There's no running away from them, is there?

I can't just zoom in and out of their lives like a lost little bee without expecting to leave a trace.

If Archer was here, you'd ask him to put a new cabin deeper in the woods, and he'd tease you for wanting him to build this deep in the forest just so you could live next to the bees.

Despite everything, a tiny smile curls my lips.

I can just imagine him, all gruff words and shining blue eyes—outwardly grumpy but really just a softie. Indulgent and sweet.

Big daddy perfection to the end.

I miss him.

I miss everything—except for the gigantic tangled mess of my family's drama.

The mess I caused.

The smile slips off my face.

The world resumes throbbing again, my vision wavering.

I'm hugging my shoulders.

It's weird because it's definitely not that cold tonight.

Yet somehow, I'm shivering.

I wish I had a kiss with a bad-tempered man to warm me up.

I would not mind it if he used that mouth.

He knows what he's doing with his tongue, and I can almost feel it now, the searing, sharp heat flowing through me. I let my head roll back.

This is what I want, what I need.

But I can't have it.

Reality picks me up and hurls me back down.

I can't have it because I left, and that was the right thing to do. *It had to be.*

If only good morals didn't hurt so effing much.

Every time I blink, it's like the world reassembles itself in a slightly different way.

My eyes dart around. I think I hear voices, but it's just the trees whispering, the leaves shaking and murmuring with the wind.

Win-nie, they say.

Winnie!

I start laughing. Trees don't talk and they certainly don't call your name.

Even if they could, I'm not important enough for them to know me. They don't care.

It's a little sad.

Archer cares—or at least he did.

The little family I had, the one who adopted me—and I know I'm stretching the truth but God I don't care—they cared plenty.

I frown because I keep pinging on the ugly truth.

I ran away from them.

I didn't even wait for an adult conversation.

Some coping mechanism.

I'm sure Lyssie will dig me up and kill me again once she finds out how dumb all this is.

God, I'm a mess.

Maybe it's the fever giving me these teeth-chattering chills. Can some bad algae from a tainted stream poison your brain, too?

I go to look it up, but remember my phone's dead. My hand falls uselessly against the ground.

No phone.

No hope.

Right.

Heat pricks along my limbs and sweat seals my clothes to

my neck. I'm shivering with the heat, and it's almost impossible to string a single coherent thought together.

The only thing that stands out in my delirious mind is Archer Rory.

I miss him so much I can almost see him standing in front of me.

And I must be terminally sick because my hallucinations look real enough to touch when he appears in front of me like a guardian angel.

Is this how it works?

Do you get to see your favorite people before you die? Even if they're still alive?

"Hey, Archer." I grin up at him, still tasting sticky honey on my lips.

He answers by sweeping me up in his arms and flinging me over his shoulder.

Don't pinch me.

If this beautiful delusion is my grand finale before the lights go out, I never want to know when the fireworks end.

I never want to wake up when he holds me, cradling me, his eyes so bright with love and concern.

"Winnie, stay with me. I love you," he whispers.

Love you too. I try to mouth back those three reckless words.

But I think I'm too far gone.

I pass out smiling, ready for the great beyond.

XXVI: TAKE THE STING OUT
(ARCHER)

"Winnie, stay with me. I love you."

Those words sear my throat like a prayer to a God who won't listen. I know what it feels like now when a man throws himself down, begging for divine intervention, everything hanging by a thread.

And all I can give her right now is the truth.

Truth and a smile.

Even when she's worn ragged in this terrifyingly fragile state, she *still* tastes like honey. Hard to believe, but she settles against my chest like she's content to stay there forever, a small smile on her face.

Seeing her like this with her hair matted, scratches and bug bites all over her arms, her face too pale and still somehow flushed, it's enough to turn my insides liquid.

I fucking found her.

If it wasn't for those bees making noises that could rival a jet engine, I might have lost her for good. I searched for hours, tracking deeper into the woods, far off the trail, using an old historic map on my phone from the days when a company came out here clearing trees and looking for coal to mine.

The paths are long overgrown, but barely traceable in some areas if you stop and look.

When I heard that racket, I followed, mostly out of curiosity.

Now, I press her face against my shoulder, loving when she sighs.

"You... you smell like Archer." She slurs her words.

"I am Archer, Sugarbee. I'm here," I tell her, but either she doesn't hear or she doesn't process.

She just lets out another long, slow, chest-heaving sigh.

"I miss Archer."

"I missed you too," I whisper, knowing she won't hear it.

I don't care.

There'll be plenty of time later to laugh about how out of it she is, after we've escaped this damn forest.

At least I've got the extra gear, courtesy of her old man bringing in the best police search and rescue resources in the whole state.

I hate to admit it's made this hunt easier.

Yes, Carroll Emberly is still a first-rate fucknut for helping cause this disaster, but he's also man enough to own his mistakes. Possibly just in time to save his daughter's life.

"Winnie?" I say when her eyes close, shaking her gently. I'm no doctor, but I can tell she's gravely ill, and you can't let people this sick fade before they get medical care. "Stay with me, woman. Don't sleep yet."

She stirs, nestling closer, but at least she's still conscious.

Still breathing.

I try to stop myself from imagining what might have happened if I *hadn't* gotten here in time.

I'm doing a terrible job of it.

The only thing I can picture when I close my eyes is what would've happened if we'd lost her for another night.

She's fucking burning up. Her skin feels like clothes just out of the washer, clammy and hot.

"Stay with me," I urge, climbing over a large fallen branch as I head back the way I came. At some point, I'll have to shift her onto my back.

I'm about a mile out from the nearest group and real help, but I like having her here, cradled against my chest.

I guess it appeals to my insane inner caveman, the lunatic who needs to hold her, to feel her, to have her warm sweet breath against my neck so I can know she's alive.

I'm not her knight in shining armor.

I'm one more culprit who drove her away, and now I'm racing against time to save her, to put her back together so I can apologize and tell her she's everything.

She is my gravity.

And even if she decides she can't be, if I've hurt her too much... she still needs to hear it when she's lucid.

I need one chance—just one—to tell Winnie Emberly she's turned me into a madman.

Forever obsessed.

Forever lovesick to my soul.

Goddamn.

I'm just glad I noticed that boot print before I turned off toward the distant buzzing.

When I radioed my findings back to the command center, the sheriff in charge told me it looked old, stamped into the ground for days.

Thank God I followed my instincts instead.

Winnie stirs again.

Her auburn hair hangs damp with sweat.

"Am I dead?" she asks.

"No," I tell her as gently as possible. "You're in heaven."

"H-heaven? This feels like a dream."

"You're awake, sweetheart. You're alive and well." I risk a look at her to see she's gazing up at me, her eyes unfocused. She sees me, yes, but she's not registering that I'm really here holding her.

She reaches up to trace my jaw under my beard, the palms of her hands burning.

"You're so handsome," she whispers. "Why lie to me? You... you can't be here."

"No lie," I tell her again, but it's no use.

She's trapped inside her fever and whatever hallucinations started before I swept her up.

Hot tears are swimming in her eyes.

I want to wipe every single one of them away.

Her voice cracks as she speaks.

"I... I love you, Archer. If I got to spend the rest of my life with you, if I could marry you, if I wasn't dying... I would. I'm sorry," she whispers.

It floors me.

Absolutely short-circuits my brain.

Shit.

If I wasn't hauling her to safety as fast as I can without tripping, I'd have to stop and stare into space to process what she's saying. It's too fucking enormous.

The rest of her life.

Not just a few weeks, a month, a year.

Not just the hottest, strangest summer of our lives, bursting with stolen kisses and fatalistic pleasure.

Her whole *life*.

Fuck me.

The sweat pouring down my face in this heat must be getting in my eyes. They sting like hell.

"If my dad would just buzz off," she slurs, "and if my life wasn't a wreck, I would choose you. Always. Every time."

"Winnie." My voice breaks.

This wasn't where I planned on making a big declaration of love—hell, I hadn't planned on any declaration at all—but the words throttle my lungs and I need to get them out.

Right the fuck now.

Her breath flowers across my neck and she grabs at my shirt.

"I'm so sorry for pushing you away. I was wrong, Winnie. Shutting you out was dumb as hell. I see that now, I—" I'm not good at apologies, even when I know there's a decent chance she won't remember this once she's better.

Goddammit, though, I need to say it anyway.

Especially when I already told her the rest once.

And once wasn't nearly enough.

"I love you," I growl. "I *love* you because you're a free spirit. Whether you know it or not, you came and set me free, and I love you for that. I'll never forgive myself for seeing it so late, for putting you through this, but fuck."

She shifts in my arms. The tip of her nose feels oddly cold against my throat when the rest of her is fire.

It's damp, and when I glance down, I see she's crying.

"I don't make the same mistake twice. If you'll have me, after this is over, I'll keep you, Sugarbee. I'll keep you for the rest of your life." I don't care if it means I have to bend time and space and science to keep her alive.

I'll be here for every breath she has, all her days.

I'll be the man she can count on to never let her go.

Next to Colt, she's more important than anyone else in the world. I know she shares that feeling, and I don't care if she's too sick to say it or even comprehend it right now.

She understands, though, and I love it.

Just like I love her.

It's stunning that it took a wake-up call this horrible to beat some sense through my thick damn skull.

Before she went missing, I was walking around with my head in the clouds, adoring her and needing her and wanting her but never knowing how much I loved her.

If it takes me ten years, I will find a way to prove it.

Every day, I will fight for her.

But she's still crying, and I hold her tighter.

"What's wrong?" I whisper softly. "Tell me where it hurts."

"No, it's just… why does this have to be a *dream?*" Her voice hitches. There's such anguish it almost stops me dead.

"Winnie, listen. You're not dreaming. I'm really here, holding you, taking you to get some help." I shift, propping my leg against a rock and freeing an arm so I can cup her cheek. "I'm as real as my beard, sweetheart."

Her fingers feel so small and warm as she clings to my hand, her cheeks slick with tears.

Her chest heaves.

If taking her pain ten times over would ease her anguish in the slightest, I'd do it in a heartbeat.

"I was dreaming, though. I dreamed you'd say that for so long. I wanted you to say it, to tell me you loved me. But now you did and it's all in my head." Her crying intensifies, wet sobs that rack her entire body. "I wanted it for real."

"It is real. Winnie, look at me." I turn her head to look into her eyes. "Do you see that? I love you. This is real."

Her eyes are wide and her cheeks are glazed with tears as she looks up.

"I hope I never forget your face." She laughs.

It's no use.

The sooner I get her to a hospital, the faster she'll have her brain back.

I'll tell her a second time, and she'll believe me. It'll be easier after I've done it once. I test the words again.

"I love you."

Those three words are so fucking heavy they almost break me.

I've said them to Mom, of course, but that's an old habit. A kiss on her cheek, a quick 'love you' at her house before I grab Colt and go.

Back when Rina and I were together, I said it to her, too.

Not often, admittedly.

More at the beginning, when we tried to convince ourselves it was true and our cursed relationship could work. Back when we were naïve.

Then it faded and stopped.

I don't know if I was the first one to give up on that magic phrase or if it was her.

Regardless, the love ended before our marriage. I haven't said it to another woman since.

Over ten damn years without conjuring those words, and here I am, sputtering my love to a girl who's barely conscious.

If my heart wasn't pounding through my chest with real fear thudding through my veins, I'd find it funny.

"Hang tight, just a little while longer. I love you," I tell her again.

She's practically asleep now. The crying probably exhausted her, but the ghost of a smile touches her lips as she whispers, "I love you, too."

* * *

It takes too long for her to wake up.

Too many hours where I'm stuck by her side in the hospital room—like hell I was settling for the waiting room and her family didn't fight me—watching IVs stuck in the back of her hand as she lies under a thin blue sheet.

I only break the silence to text her friend, Lyssie, letting her know the nightmare is over.

The whisper of her breath is the only sound in this room.

I count her breaths, too, because they're my only assurance she's still alive.

The nurse said she was horribly dehydrated. She'd gotten a nasty stomach bug from some water she drank. They gave her meds and now they're replacing her nutrients or something.

I don't know. I'm not a doctor.

All I know is I'm not moving until she wakes up.

My own exhaustion kicks in and I nod off a few times into the morning. Grey light filters through the blinds when I lift my head from the corner of her bed.

She's awake, watching me with a tired smile.

Relief floods my system.

"Hey, Sleeping Beauty. How you feeling?" I pull up my chair and take her hand, giving it a gentle squeeze.

"Hey, yourself. How long have you been there?"

"A few hours."

"All night, you mean." She rolls her eyes. "You look rough."

"Nice to see you too."

Another tiny smile touches the corner of her mouth, and her fingers tighten around mine. "I didn't think you'd ever come."

"You couldn't have kept me away with a chainsaw. I was ready to cut down every square foot of that forest until I found you."

"I didn't take you for a big outdoorsman." Her smile widens.

"Neither did I until you went AWOL." I stare at her face for a second, reassuring myself there's color in her cheeks. "You scared me shitless."

She purses her lips. "I blame the tent."

"What?"

"The reason I got lost. The stupid tent. If it didn't suck so much because I bought it used, I would've just stayed there all night instead of trying to find that RV park." She grimaces, and it's so damn cute I have to stop myself from kissing her. "I'm sorry if I worried you."

"*If* I was worried?" I thread my fingers through hers, and though she tenses at the contact, she doesn't pull away. "Winnie, do you know how fucking crazy I've been?"

Her smile turns down. Just one side, like she's holding the expression back in a losing battle.

"I'm really sorry."

"No. I wasn't trying to make you feel bad, I was—" This is coming out wrong. I'm supposed to be comforting her, reassuring her about *us*, but instead she's just feeling guilty for running. I kiss her knuckles. "I know why you left. I get it."

"I didn't mean to scare you. I never wanted *anyone* to fuss over me."

"I know, and I'm not blaming you. I'm blaming me. I'm just relieved as hell you're okay." When she doesn't flinch, I brush her hair back and trail a knuckle over her cheek.

She turns her eyes to me.

When I lean in for a kiss, she puts the arm with the IV around my neck and pulls me down.

I swear, if she wasn't here recuperating in a hospital bed, I'd shut the door and show her just how relieved I am she's okay. For now, I check my instincts, very damn reluctantly.

"I didn't think you'd come," she whispers again.

"I always will, even if all you want is to punch me in the face." I shake my head, a lump hardening in my throat. This woman makes me too emotional. "I'm sorry I made you feel abandoned."

She looks down at our joined hands on the pale-blue sheets.

"I don't remember what was real and what was just a dream. You found me and carried me out. But you said so much." The redness in her cheeks deepens.

"No dream," I say. "I meant every word, Sugarbee."

Her breath catches. I know she's about to ask me to repeat what I said then.

I steel myself to tell her again since she's fully aware—but a knock at the door interrupts us.

"Come in," Winnie calls.

"Oh, Winnie, you're awake!" A small, faded woman who looks like she's been dipped in beige walks in. Linda Emberly, Winnie's mother, I'm guessing.

She rushes to her side, leaving me alone to face the tallest pile of misery I've ever met. Carroll Emberly.

We might've spoken for ten or fifteen minutes at the command center before the wild hunt for her began. We reached a truce. After I brought her back, he agreed to drop the charges, but that doesn't mean I like him after the enormous shit he stirred.

I don't bother playing nice.

Winnie gasps when she sees her father and squeezes my hand so tight it almost hurts. Her mom throws her arms around her neck.

She just looks between her parents stiffly.

"I regret the recent unpleasantry," Carroll says flatly, clearing his throat after a heavy moment where I'm not sure if he'll ever speak.

Hell, I don't know if he's talking to Winnie or me, but it doesn't matter. This stuffy turkey fuck has a mountain of apologies to make.

Winnie says nothing, lying there more guarded than ever.

She tolerates her mother's presence while the older

woman blubbers all over her, hanging on and wailing, but she's still just glaring at her dad.

Waiting.

"Honey." He clears his throat and steps forward, but when her expression hardens, he stops. "I mean it. You can't fathom how truly, deeply sorry I am for how we've treated you. If I'd known it would lead to this..."

He swallows and shrugs.

"What? You would have treated me like a human being?" she asks coldly.

Silence.

My fist shakes at my side, hungry to grab this prick and push him right out of the room. I don't care if it gets me handcuffed for assaulting a state official or whatever the fuck.

"I should have considered my choices more carefully, Wynne. I wish to God I had, but... I was proud. Too focused on doing what was best for the family, for—"

"For you," Winnie spits.

Goddamn, that's my girl.

I have to bite my cheek to avoid grinning at the way Carroll's head drops.

"Almost losing you was the revelation I shouldn't have needed," he growls, swallowing thickly. "When you were lost out there, when everyone was looking, I had a lot of time to reflect. My anger, my pride, my arrogance, it almost got you killed. Regrettably, I never knew how foolish I could possibly be until my actions nearly cost me my own daughter."

Guilt is pure sorcery, transforming the biggest assholes into weeping kittens.

I know it well.

Later, when they're gone, I'll show her how sorry I still am for making her feel like she doesn't belong in my life.

"Holden told me what he did. He broke the law and our

trust. I warned him there will be criminal charges if he ever comes near you again. I won't be on speaking terms with Senator Corban for the foreseeable future," Carroll continues after another long pause where there's nothing but Winnie's rough breathing and Linda's awful sobs.

They may be bad people, yes, but they're sincere.

Winnie never told me much about her parents' marriage and I had to read between the lines, but now I've seen enough to understand.

I see why she couldn't marry Holden, even before he came stomping around, clinging to her like a fucking comfort blanket.

"I don't care about Holden. What about him?" Winnie whispers, nodding in my direction. "I care about what you're going to do to the man who saved my life."

"Yes, Archer Rory." Carroll looks me full in the face for the first time.

He's an egomaniac to the core, but I can see the toll this has taken. He looks old and shrunken, all the lofty authority he normally wields like a sword has turned into a giant limp noodle.

To think I ever felt threatened by this goon and his stupid damn antitrust probe.

"No man will ever be more worthy," he says.

Huh?

I stare at him in shock.

"I see it now, Mr. Rory. You did your utmost to save Wynne's life. Since I can never repay you, rest assured that I won't be standing in your way."

"You can repay him by ending the probe," Winnie snaps. "And then stay the hell out of our life."

Our life.

Fucking chills.

Nothing has ever sounded so divine on her lips.

"Yes, well, I'm withdrawing all open inquiries into Higher Ends' business practices immediately," he says, glancing back at her. This time, he walks closer and stops by her side, almost reaching out to take her hand before changing his mind. His eyes flick around the room, almost panicked. "As noted, I'm severing ties with Senator Corban as well. He knew what his son was capable of, and as far as I'm concerned, he was complicit in Holden's cruelty."

That doesn't surprise me. Senators don't wind up where they are with great moral compasses. I doubt Holden or his father could find true north much faster than the tortured monster in front of me.

What surprises me is the way Winnie's eyes fill with tears.

"Really?" she whispers.

He nods decisively and turns to me.

"If you'd like, Mr. Rory, I'm prepared to go public with property damage claims on Higher Ends' behalf. Holden told me the truth, so the proof is ironclad. I'll ensure he repays every penny owed."

Winnie waves her sobbing mother off to one side so she can look at her dad with a clear view. He glances down at our linked fingers but says nothing.

"I'll discuss it with my brothers and let you know later. Right now, all that matters is she's safe, and she needs rest. So if you'll kindly wrap this up..."

Linda bursts out sobbing again as her husband takes the hint.

With halting steps, he marches his wife out of the room, and the air becomes easier to breathe again.

* * *

Colt's waiting at home when I get back around ten o'clock in the morning.

Last night, I called Mom to sleep over and watch him, but she had to leave this morning for her art group. I find my boy alone, staring at his phone. He drops it in his lap the instant I walk into the room.

"How's Winnie?" he asks eagerly.

For a second, he looks so grown-up it makes my throat tighten.

Only thirteen and the kid's a damn mini-me with twice my maturity at his age.

"She's good, Son. She rested up and she was looking much better when I left."

I texted him brief messages about her progress last night, but I guess he needed to hear me say it to be certain.

I can't blame him. Typing lies is easy enough, but your face tells things you can't hide.

"Holy crap… thank God!" He fist pumps the air. "I was watching TikToks about people who went missing, all the bad stuff that can happen…"

I can't help smiling when I rush over.

I drag him up in a bear hug and hold him so tight my shoulders ache.

I need to hold my kindhearted, nervous boy.

I need to banish his fear.

Hell, maybe we should be hugging like this more often, even if I know how much teenagers become allergic to it. I'm sure he needs it as much as I do.

I feel the way he exhales slowly, the fear draining out of him.

"She'll be okay, Colt," I say. "She was dehydrated and delirious, but she's awake now. She's getting plenty of fluids. Do you want to visit later? I'm sure she'll love it."

"Sure," he says, his voice muffled. He doesn't let go, and neither do I. "Is it true you found her in the woods?"

"Yeah. She was hanging out by some bees. I picked her up and carried her back to the rescue team."

He laughs loudly.

"Bees? Damn, that's Winnie, all right. Cool, Dad."

"Yeah?"

"Yeah." He pulls back and looks up at me with the biggest smile I've seen him wearing in ages.

He doesn't have to look too far to meet my eyes anymore.

He's been growing like a thistle all summer, and though he's awkward and gangly, I know he'll grow into his own tall body soon enough.

I couldn't be happier he's my flesh and blood.

Later, we're on our way out to the hospital when I notice another vehicle following us. I'm scowling before Colt says a word, annoyed how I know it'll cut in front of us.

By the time we're in the parking lot, Rina's standing next to her Jeep, waiting.

The way she's standing makes me wary. She's all tucked in, looking at us with both her hands clasped in front of her.

"Wait in the car a sec," I tell Colt before striding over.

We haven't spoken since our meeting at that little coffee shop where she told me all about her reasons for coming back, and how she was almost angry enough to destroy the bees before Holden beat her to it.

I don't know what else she has to say.

This certainly isn't the time or place.

"Not a good time, Ri," I tell her as I approach.

A strand of chestnut hair falls over her face and she brushes it back. I think I spy a new tattoo on her wrist, an intricate mesh of fine lines I can't decipher.

"Colt told me about Winnie," she says. "I'm so sorry."

"She'll be fine. Nothing to worry about," I clip.

"Oh, I'm glad. I know Colt was pretty scared."

I glance back at our son, who's still strapped in the

passenger seat, staring at his phone and pretending he's not watching us every chance he gets.

Another reason to try to keep this civil.

"What did he tell you?"

"Not much. He didn't know a ton when he called last night."

Damn, that's a first, calling his mom because he was worried?

I know I was too busy to take his calls or help his anxiety much beyond sending the occasional update, but shame still creeps through me.

He's my son. I should've done better.

"Why are you here?" I ask.

She sighs. "Look, I know I'm hardly your favorite person right now, but I'll only be a second. I emailed you those photos I took of Holden Corban attacking those bee box things. I don't know if you're going after him legally, but if you are, it's proof. And, you know, a gesture of goodwill."

I wait for more, near certain that's not why she's here.

"And?" I prompt.

"...and there's one more thing, yeah," she says. *No shit.* "I was just offered a new art job in Chicago."

The fuck? The blood drains from my head as I stare at her.

"You're leaving," I growl, anger flicking through my veins.

"I mean, I know it sounds bad, but—"

"Goddamn you, Ri. Colt just started getting used to having you around and you're pulling up stakes again? I should've known." I snort, struggling to keep my voice down.

She's so predictable it's ridiculous. Yet I still let myself get pulled into the possibility that she could do something new.

That this time would be different.

The definition of insanity, doing the same thing repeatedly and expecting different results.

Rina will never fucking change.

"I've heard enough," I say coldly, already sick of this.

She grabs my arm as I turn, ready to storm back to the vehicle and be done with this whole conversation.

"Archer, wait."

"No. I don't have time for your bullshit excuses right now," I grind out. "Let go, Rina."

"Just listen!" She plants her small body firmly in my way. "I know you're pissed. I get it, but this isn't like last time. I want to see him. Often. I want Colt to visit me."

I stare at her.

Rina, the ex-wife I once thought I loved, the mother of my child.

Age really is catching up with her, and in the evening sun, she looks a little like she could blow away in the breeze.

"I've discussed it with him." She swallows. "I was thinking we'd take a trip together this fall, maybe he could fly in for winter break... but you were so worried about Winnie, I didn't know how to bring it up. And that's when I realized this isn't the right place for me after all, even aside from the job."

"What do you mean?"

"I mean, you were so caught up with her, you couldn't think about anything else. That's not your fault, it's honestly kind of sweet. Colt loves her too. You guys made a life here, and I'm not part of it. That's my fault, no one else's."

I don't understand.

I also don't recognize the woman she's become.

She might look the same, but this isn't the Rina I know, who resented me for having near total custody every time she came back to ruin Colt's life.

It's like something getting washed away from my eyes so I can see clearly again.

Are we finally being adults?

Goddamn, it's taken long enough.

"We're both committed to burying the past, right?" she says gently. "You've been trying and so have I. But Archer, that's easier if I live elsewhere."

"Like Chicago," I say numbly.

"Chicago, yes. Not too far, but far enough. A comfortable distance and a quick plane ride away." She smiles and pats my arm. "Go get her, Arch. We can talk more later, after she's back home."

Home.

No matter how weird it sounds coming from her, it still feels right.

It's almost felt like Winnie always belonged with us. Not that there's any guarantee she'll just move back in with me like nothing ever happened.

"Later," I agree, raising a hand and jogging back to the car.

It's only when I'm walking in with Colt that I notice I don't feel the same lingering melancholy frustration I usually do over Rina's antics.

Once stung, twice shy, they say.

Winnie Emberly has broken the cycle, and I can't wait to bring her home for good.

XXVII: BEE MINE (WINNIE)

*E*ven a couple weeks after my discharge, I'm still bursting with gratitude to be free.

I spent way too long cooped up in that hospital bed. My parents visited every day, which was definitely *something*, and Archer rarely left my side to shower, which was sweet but unnecessary.

The not showering part, I mean. Keeping me company and bringing Colt around every day was a nice bonus. A gesture that told me he really, really meant everything he said on that delirious walk back to civilization.

If he was going to tell me he loved me, he could have done it with roses and a tasty dinner like most guys. Or at least when I was fully awake and able to process words drenched in emotion.

I hate that I have blurry half-assed shards of a core memory I wasn't totally present for. But I love that his confession kept me alive more.

He did it again, too, which was even better.

Several times, actually.

Once when we were still in the hospital, when he kissed

me and told me he loved me and never could've forgiven himself if something awful happened to me.

That was adorable.

So was the moment he brought me home and I stood on his threshold. He asked to carry me in, and I told him absolutely not.

They haven't let me do much standing over the last few days. Walking still feels like a newfound luxury and my legs still hurt plenty from my time in hell.

But Archer gently swept me up, carrying me into his house like a total gentleman while I laughed and demanded to be put down.

I'm glad he didn't listen.

He told me I didn't have to stay, but he wanted me to.

What girl could say no?

So yes, I stayed.

We didn't even bother pretending I had the guest room this time, not after we set up my stuff in Archer's bedroom. Colt was amazingly cool with it, turning down his chance to crack a hundred cheesy jokes.

"I know you're with my dad now, Winnie," he said, rolling his eyes. "You guys make each other happy and all. It's cute, but just don't get all kissy in front of me."

This kid is going to grow up *just* like his father, and I couldn't be happier.

Because I'm more madly in love with Archer Rory by the day.

Not a little bit in love.

No, this is full-on obsessed in a slightly unhealthy way.

The kind of smitten where I like to watch him sleep if I wake up before him and wonder how someone who's a certified mess ever wound up with a man as wonderful and gentle and sweet and strong and *perfect* as him.

I mean, he's not always perfect.

When he's tired, he can be the king of grouchy, but his heart never wavers. It's always in the right place, and I can tell he's working on being less snarly.

He rolls over sleepily, catching me in the act of creeping on him.

His eyelids flutter open and he squints at me through the darkness. I don't know what time it is, but fall has come, and there's a lot less natural light seeping through the blinds than summer mornings.

"Are you watching me?" he mutters.

"Edward watched Bella sleep in *Twilight* and that was totally normal," I assure him. "I rest my case."

"Normal, huh? I promise I don't sparkle, woman."

"Hey, look at you! So you *do* get my references, old man!" I snuggle back against his chest. Today, we're going back to Solitude for the first time since my little escapade, and I'm buzzing with excitement.

If you thought the bee puns would ever stop, you're wrong.

"Do I *feel* old?" His arm curls around me, tucking me more firmly into him.

"Nah. You're aged like a good whisky," I tease, and he bites my ear. It's playful, but it makes me gasp.

Heat floods through me.

Archer has been extremely gentle with me since I got back and settled into recovery mode, but what I really want is for him to rip away my panties with his teeth.

To my disappointment, he presses a kiss against my hair and shifts his body away so his cock doesn't press against my hip. "We should get up soon."

"Can't you go back to sleeping first?" I protest.

"So you can go back to ogling me? No thanks. For all I know, you'll catch me drooling next."

"You don't drool in your sleep. But you do snore

sometimes."

"See? No secret's safe with Sugarbee around."

"But you love me anyway." It's still weird saying it, like this big secret that shouldn't be spoken just yet. But he turns me around and kisses me on the mouth, hard and deep, like my words trigger something deep inside him.

That's my cue.

I wrap my arms around him and kiss him with everything I have, hoping he'll delay whatever he has planned today. But he disentangles from me with a laugh and swats my ass.

"Get moving or we'll be late."

"For what?"

In answer, he rolls out of bed. The bulge in his boxers makes it very clear that him not taking full advantage of me this morning has nothing to do with his attraction.

"We seriously don't have time for a quickie?"

"Don't you want to see your bees?" he counters. "Colt also needs a ride. He's got a lab today and I'm not risking some college punk inviting him to a drunken party or some shit."

I sigh because he's right—I *do* want to see how my bees are doing and Archer is understandably protective of his genius son who skips his normal school a few days a week for college classes.

"Fiiine," I whine, forcing myself up to get dressed quickly.

Once we've dropped Colt off at the science building on campus, Archer drives us to Solitude. It's framed with vibrant red leaves from the forest behind it beginning to change over. It's a dry, warm autumn day, and I hunch my shoulders in my sweater.

His hand finds mine and we take a minute, just standing and staring at the little cottage and the garden beyond. Late blooms of summer flowers still give the place a lovely streak of color with other plants going dormant.

This is my favorite time, before the cold weather rolls in

and everything shrivels up. Change is in the air, so thick you can smell it.

Long hikes won't be on my menu for a while, but I don't have PTSD over camping or anything.

Even though I almost died there, the thick trees still look beautiful from a distance, especially with gold leaves showering the ground.

"How does it feel to be back without freaky stalkers and endless stress?" Archer asks softly beside me.

I blink back tears. "So good. You have no idea."

"I think I do," he says gruffly, hiding a smile.

Together, hand in hand, we walk around the back of the house to the gardens next to the woods.

Everything feels so still, like the whole world is holding its breath. For the first time in a long while, I'm at peace.

My hand tightens on Archer's fingers. I'm so grateful to be here, to be with him, I could practically fall over.

"What is it?" he whispers.

"Being here, with you... I'm happy."

"Always what I love to hear."

"It's making me think... maybe I've never been happy before. Not like this."

Archer pulls me closer until I'm in his arms, looking up at him, this bear of a man I've given my heart to, wholly and completely.

The feels are overwhelming.

I need to get them out so I can breathe again.

"I love you, Archer Rory," I start, but my phone vibrates in my pocket, and I hesitate, the moment interrupted.

"I know you do. You should answer that, Winnie." His blue eyes shine, impossibly soft and smiling as he looks down at me.

I shake my head, but when I flip the screen over to see who's calling, my heart leaps into my throat. I actually *squeak*.

It's the lab from the University of Missouri calling me back.

A few weeks ago, we sent them a sample of the honey and all the info I had about the bees. I thought maybe they could analyze it and see if there's anything special, beyond the neon violet color.

"Oh my God, if that's who I think it is…"

"Go on, pick up." Archer chuckles when he sees the panicked look on my face.

I don't need more encouragement.

As he wanders along the path where the bee boxes used to be, I swipe the screen and hold my phone against my ear.

"Hello?"

"Is this Miss Winnie Emberly?"

"Speaking."

"I hope you're well, Miss Emberly. This is Tyler In-ho, an assistant to Dr. Mackay. We're calling about the lab results of the honey you sent us a few weeks back." The male voice pauses like he's checking data. "The results came back yesterday and I wanted to follow up."

"Okay, great. And?" I can hardly breathe.

"It turns out, the honey has remarkable anti-inflammatory properties, stronger than ordinary kinds by several orders of magnitude. I cross referenced the results with a few other researchers, and they say they've only seen this a couple times in samples from overseas. Never here in the United States," he says cheerfully. "It's early, of course, but it's possible more bee colonies like this could serve the medical community very well."

"For medicine?" I'm gobsmacked. This is like my greatest dream come true.

"Well, if the results hold up under more rigorous testing, yes. This could have significant impacts on treatments and therapies designed for mitigating severe inflammation."

My breath stalls.

Am I dreaming?

Did I ever really make it out of the woods?

"Wow. So, um... what are the next steps?" I ask. "Can I see the data?"

"In its raw form?"

"Yes, whatever you have."

"Certainly. I can have that emailed to you along with the report we promised, provided you sign an NDA. With your permission, Miss Emberly, we'd love to do further studies. Where did you say these hives were based again?"

For a second, I hesitate.

"Only if the bees won't be disturbed too much. Assuming the honey comes back just as strong next year, I mean."

We talk a little more about logistics while Archer waits patiently in the morning sun, looking back fondly every few minutes.

I love how he's content to just be here while I have my moment.

And suddenly, the excitement hits full blast. I'm pumped about the bees and the honey and the unexpected miracle.

The details the researcher rattles off start to wash over me. I agree that the bees need to be studied, as long as they can be protected, and clear my throat.

"I'm sorry, but I have to go. Can you send over the data today?"

"Absolutely."

"Thanks for calling. I appreciate it." I walk over to where Archer waits and beam up at him.

"No problem. Have a good day."

I'm still smiling at Archer as I say, "I will."

"Good news?" Archer takes the phone from my hand as I end the call. He tucks it into his pocket.

"Yes." I cock an eyebrow. "Is there a reason you just took my phone?"

"Because I'm done with distractions, Sugarbee. Just you and me now."

I smile. "Did you know the lab would call today?"

His fingers slide through mine as we walk toward the brand-new wall Archer had built around the property, roughly where the forest begins. His very own bee-protecting privacy wall with small nooks for hidden cameras.

I feel a lot better already.

"I figured it was coming," he says. "I called them last week to see how things were progressing. They told me they expected results back soon. Yesterday, they told my receptionist you'd hear something by afternoon."

"And you wanted me here when I got the call…"

"I know this place means a lot to you. I wanted to celebrate somewhere that makes you happy."

God, this beautiful man.

I'm about to wrap my arms around his neck and tell him I could've gotten the news anywhere, as long as he's with me—when I notice something else.

Four new bee boxes, glistening in the sun, tucked in a smaller enclosure not far from the wall's metal gate.

"You've been busy," I say.

With his hand in mine, he pulls me toward him. "The wall wasn't the only renovation. I made plenty of room for the bees next season so you won't have to go chasing them through the woods."

I was lying when I said I was happy before.

This is happy. Freaking giddy.

Everything keeps falling into place. I still don't understand how I'm actually sharing it with an incredible man who does little things like this for the bees.

For me.

As we move closer to the new boxes, I see each one has a small note painted across the side, unmistakably written in Archer's blocky handwriting.

"Bee Brave?" I read it out loud as we approach, smiling. "Arch, was that you?"

He shrugs, though he obviously did.

There's a grin breaking through his broody face. No matter how hard he tries to hold back, the smile slips through, transforming his face like the sun.

He gives me this reckless, heady joy that makes me want to laugh along with him.

And when I see what's on the next few boxes, I fall more in love.

Bee Happy, the next box says.

Bee True. I keep reading down the line.

And finally, as we get closer to the final box, *Bee Mine?*

This one has a question mark.

Hmmm.

I look at it several times just to make sure I'm not misreading anything—I'm still a little afraid that nasty fever caused brain damage—before I look up at him, confused.

"Be yours? Archer, I already am."

So much more than he can ever know.

I can't imagine belonging to anyone else. Like it or not, he's stuck with me now.

Archer's smile fades into a blank, paper-thin mask, and something else, too.

Uncertainty? But why?

"This one's special, Winnie," he tells me. "Go ahead and open it."

A strange feeling washes over me, this tingly excitement flicking through my nerves.

I feel like a kid on Christmas morning with a present bigger than me. I go to open it, reaching out.

The lid pulls up on a hinge like a regular wooden trunk, and inside—

Holy hell.

It's amazing that I keep standing.

Inside, there's a blue-lined velvet box, already open and holding the most gorgeous silver and gold ring. Small bees are engraved into it with wings of sparkling diamonds.

When I turn around, stunned, Archer waits on one knee.

"When I was young, I rushed into a bad marriage for all the wrong reasons," he whispers, his eyes on mine, lit with emotion. "Now, I want to rush into marriage again. This time, though, for all the right reasons. You gave me back my courage, Winnie. You woke me up. You set me free from the past. Now, I need to know… will you bee mine forever?"

Oh my God.

Archer Rory is asking me to marry him and he's using bee puns.

Ohhh my gawd, I'm crying until he looks like a blurry, smiling mess.

Probably the worst response to any proposal ever, but for once, it doesn't feel inappropriate or annoying or wrong.

He doesn't judge my feelings when they're out of place. He's not like my parents.

Mostly, I'm overwhelmed with the feeling that this is meant to be.

Sorry, meant to bee.

"You… you punned me," I say, half laughing and half crying as I tug him up so I can kiss him. "Of course, I'll be yours! I told you, I already am. I was from the start."

"You'll marry me?"

"Yes, yes, a thousand times yes!" I throw myself into his arms.

My next kiss is sloppy and wet, but he doesn't seem to mind, folding both arms around me and pressing me against him until we both need to come up for air. He takes the ring from the box—from both boxes—and I hold out my hand.

It slides on my finger perfectly.

"It's beautiful," I whisper. The ring Holden gave me was just this soulless giant diamond some woman at a jewelry store probably told him was the height of fashion. But this ring is me—all me.

"I love you, Winnie Emberly. Keep making me crazy forever," he growls.

Laughing, I wiggle my fingers so the ring sparkles in the light.

"Let's get married soon so I can take your name. I'd rather start over as Wynne Rory."

He grins. "Just say the word, woman. We'll be married however you like." He smooths a thumb across my cheek. "We could elope and get hitched in New Zealand for all I care."

"While skydiving?"

He snorts.

"Not sure you'd hear my vows, but if that's what you want, so be it."

I grin wickedly. "Springfield. All the media should be there. I can see the headlines now. *Business Mogul Marries Attorney General's Daughter.*"

"*Will She Make it Down the Aisle?*" he quips, and I laugh.

"You're right, I can't imagine anything worse."

"If it was between that and not marrying you, I'd still do it in a heartbeat."

"Oh, Romeo," I say, slapping his arm and crushing myself against him again.

We're alone and we're still wearing too many clothes for this.

"If I didn't know better, I might think you want to sweep me off my feet," I tease.

Without hesitation, he scoops me up and starts to carry me back toward the cabin. "How's this?"

"Very hot. Where are we going?"

"Your next surprise. I rented out Solitude for the weekend. So you do the math." He pretends to think. "First, I'm taking my fiancée inside to fuck her brains out. Then, after we order whatever food you like, we'll do it again in the shower."

Heaven.

My insides go liquid just thinking about it. "So this is why you waited this morning..."

He places his lips to my ear.

"Now you know. Next time I fucked you, I had to see that ring."

Insanely hot.

I don't know what I did in a past life to deserve a man like Archer, but in this one, I'll do everything in my power to keep him.

The ring on my finger suggests I have a good shot.

Then again, didn't I know that?

He came for me.

When I was lost and alone and dying in the woods, my prince came. Dad flew in and helped organize rescue efforts, sure. He threw tons of money at it and leveraged his connections.

But Archer went into the woods for me.

No one made him.

No one promised him anything but grief if he couldn't find me in the dark, dense maze of trees, yet he did it anyway.

Because he could.

Because he couldn't bear losing me the same way I know losing him would shred my soul.

So I wrap my arms around his neck and find his lips with mine.

He gives back a rough groan, kicking the door open and striding inside, letting it swing shut behind us.

Not so long ago, I fled here to escape an arranged marriage.

Who knew I'd find a husband?

I break the kiss. "How do you feel about more kids?"

His eyes widen.

"No, not now. But later. After we're married, when we're settled." It's a conversation we probably should've had before, but with Colt almost grown, I get it if he needs time.

Yes, I want my own baby or three.

Something small and sweet to hold and cradle and nurture the same way Archer raised his son. I need it with an intensity that makes my chest ache.

"How many babies you want, woman?" Archer asks, walking into the bedroom and laying me down on the bed.

He falls on top of me, and I wrap my legs around him, holding him close.

"One," I whisper, blushing. "Maybe two."

I hold back so I don't scare him away.

"Two?"

"I know with Colt that makes three... is that too much for an old man?" I smooth the dark hair back from his brow.

He chuckles.

"Two, three, what the fuck ever," he rumbles. "As long as it's us, Winnie, I'm open."

Us.

The best word in the universe.

"Then it's settled," I say happily. "Two girls, then we'll see. Colt will be the best big brother."

"Girls, huh?" Archer presses his hips against me, rubbing his erection against my belly in a way that makes me squirm.

"I want a little girl I can spoil, all the ways my parents never spoiled me," I say, although it's more of a gasp when Archer shifts again. It's getting harder to keep my mind on the conversation I started. "But do you think we should ask Colt what he'd think?"

Archer kisses me fiercely, cradling my head in his hands. "I love that you think of him. I'm sure he'll be down for whatever makes us happy."

"He feels like my son sometimes. I know he's not and he'll never be, but—"

"He is," Archer insists hoarsely. "He has another mother, yes, but you'll always be around more. He already sees you as part of our family."

My heart swells.

My eyes fill with tears.

So unexpected, the sweet sting of it.

Never once did I think I'd fall for a single dad. To my younger self, that was too much baggage, too much difference in life experience. Honestly, I wasn't sure I'd ever be ready for kids.

But with Archer, it's so different.

Colt isn't like anything I imagined, kind and gentle and ridiculously smart.

Best of all, marrying Archer doesn't mean I'm being tossed into motherhood.

Not when it's something I *want* to take on, and they make it so easy.

I want to be an older, loving woman in Colt's life—a mom he can trust when his real mother is still a whole lot of 'wait and see.'

I want to be there to tease him about the girls he has crushes on.

I want to see him off to prom.

I want him to come home to cakes and coffee and good conversation if he blows a science test or doesn't nail down his first dream job—though with how bright he is, it's not likely—and to celebrate his wins.

I'm honored Archer loves me that much, enough to give me the privilege of helping Colt grow up.

And with our own kids, I have zero doubts it'll be smooth sailing.

Colt will always have Rina, of course, and I'm hopeful in time we'll all get along.

She sent me flowers, which was unexpectedly nice. It makes me think maybe in the future we can get over—well, the fact that we're sharing a family.

But daughters of my own…

"I hope they have your eyes," I whisper, threading my hands through his thick dark hair. "And I hope they'll be just as clever as you."

"As long as they're as kind and intelligent as their mother," he says, nuzzling his nose against mine.

We're still lying on the bed.

Although my body hums with need, and I can feel him throbbing against me, there's this lovely stillness.

"I'm so pumped to share a life with you," I whisper.

"I hope they have your hair."

"Archer!" I laugh, and he kisses me.

He's greedier this time, though, his tongue sweeping into my mouth, stealing my many questions about the future.

There are so many things to think about.

Will we keep the same house? Where will we get married? Does he want an official engagement announcement?

None of that matters now.

Today, there's just us, together and whole.

He slides his hands down my waist, finding the hem of my pants and toying with slipping his fingers under.

"I love you," I say, "but if you draw this out, I will lose my patience."

"What will you do, Sugarbee?"

I pretend to think, tightening my legs around him, rolling him over until his back is on the bed and I'm straddling him. Even through the material separating us, I can feel how big and hot he is, how much he needs this just as bad as I do.

"How about this?" I whisper.

His hands settle on my hips, squeezing until it hurts so deliciously.

"Can't say I mind."

I push his shirt up and reach for his jeans, ripping open the button, the zipper, and tugging them off.

He helps me, kicking away his pants and boxers and quickly stripping off his shirt until he's gloriously mine.

Then, it's my turn.

Passion erupts in this frantic movement as he yanks off my shirt. It gets tangled in my hair, and we laugh as I fight to free it while he unhooks my bra.

My pants and panties come down easier, and soon we're fully bared, panting with anticipation.

We've done this countless times, but he still leaves me soaked.

I know his body better than my own after I've mapped it with my tongue.

I know the chiseled lines of his muscle, the dips and valleys, the dark ink mingling with chest hair.

I know exactly how sharp the arrow pointing to his groin is, and where the tiny scar on his abdomen came from.

I know so much about this man, but I'm still awestruck when we're caught in the moment, almost trembling with the raw urge to have him in me.

And now there's this beautiful ring on my finger.

That's new and it gives this a special edge.

I don't want to ever take it off.

His hands make me gasp when he touches me.

"Winnie, fuck," he growls out my name, just the way I love. "You're too perfect."

"Archer—"

"No. Let me touch you." His voice is raw, so I stay where I am, kneeling before him as he traces his fingers down my stomach, around my thighs, and finally to my pulsing center.

I gasp.

Holy hell.

Why does it feel so *different*?

I don't know if it's the ring or the promise of marriage hanging over us like this wild aphrodisiac, or even the emotional sugar rush that makes my skin tingle. But it's like my body comes alive with new nerves when he touches me.

It sings.

"You're so wet for me, good girl. Do you really need this cock so bad?" he mutters, sliding one finger inside me.

I go tight and loose at once, the electric pleasure intensifying.

The noise I make sounds obscene.

Oh, I love it.

"I'm yours," I whisper, watching the way his face changes when I tell him.

His eyes widen and his nostrils flare.

His blue gaze sharpens, all midnight stars, ready to devour me like the night.

His cock jerks, but I stay where I am.

It feels so good to surrender and let this man lead.

"You're mine. Tell me." He slides another finger in my pussy.

"Yours, yours," I whisper.

I roll my hips, helping his strokes.

His eyes are dark on me, watching as I moan and writhe on his fingers, just like I'll do on his dick soon.

I know it turns him on to see me like this, and knowing that makes the fever in my blood absolutely crazy.

I'm dangerously close to coming.

I should be used to it now, being so hilariously quick to finish when it's Archer freaking Rory, but it doesn't stop me from loving it.

The O barrels closer.

I don't need to tell him.

He can sense it from my heaving breaths, the way my nipples pucker, my pussy clenching his hand so tight.

"That's fucking right," he urges, increasing the tempo of his thrusts and trailing his free hand along my breast—a light touch, a tease to keep me wanting.

Yes, it's working.

But it's also just nudging me closer to the brink without pushing me over, torturing me in the most exquisite way possible.

Then Archer meets my eyes, baring his teeth. "Let me feel that pussy come, sweetheart. Don't you dare hold back."

"Yes! Archer!"

I obey, slurring his name like a desperate prayer as pleasure cuts through me, swelling and cascading and drowning my senses.

He holds me as I slump against him, until he finally removes his hand, slick from my pussy.

I watch him in stunned silence as he takes his sweet time licking each finger.

This time, he doesn't give me time to recover, or even ask.

He just pushes me back with a feral glint in his eye until I'm lying against the pillow.

His face hovers just over mine as he slams himself in balls deep.

It's not gentle when he's so huge, filling me so completely.

It's sudden and sharp and it almost makes me come again.

Totally unheard of before this man.

But now, Archer could practically tell me to come without touching me and my body would listen.

It's like he has me conditioned, trained to obey his commands.

And he links his strong fingers with mine as he moves.

All I can see are his eyes, wide and intense, inviting me to lose myself.

All I know is Archer, my almost-husband—and he dominates my senses the same way he rules my heart. Soon, he'll take over every part of my life.

God, I welcome him.

Sighing, I cup his face in my hands, smoothing his cheeks, and he kisses my palm. It's this tenderness that takes our sex from great to mind-blowing.

He doesn't just make love to my body, he fucks my mind, too.

Another delight I never imagined before Archer.

Another act of worship I'll always adore—even if we have the most rough, inhuman sex sometimes, it'll always have love.

That's what it means, I suppose, to love a man this deeply.

"I can't wait to marry you," I strangle out, my breath caught in my throat.

"And I can't wait to breed this little pussy." He reaches between my legs and squeezes possessively.

I. Am. Dead.

Especially when he kisses me again, and I press my body against his, holding on to every movement and meeting his thrusts with my own trembling hips.

Archer is mine with every grunt, every pump, every guttural curse leaving his lips.

I might be his, but he's mine, and I'm half-crazed when I say, "Do it, do it, I'll love you forever."

It's not really possible, no. I'm not even off birth control yet.

But just imagining it, the way I could let him erupt and let his molten seed find its mark…

My teeth catch my bottom lip.

I bite down, smiling like mad as his rhythm quickens.

He's *pounding* me now, bringing me closer with every thrust, lifting me off the bed with punishing strokes.

I'm on the edge of a cliff.

When he grabs my chin, tilting my face up so I meet his gaze, I'm so gone.

"I love you, Winnie Rory," he says.

Destroyed.

I don't have a prayer of holding back another second, not after that.

I just hold on, throwing my head back in the best orgasm of my entire life.

All-consuming, soul-ripping, eye-rolling ecstasy.

And I know he's just as tormented as he thrusts straight through my convulsions, reaching that fever pitch that only halts when he pushes so deep.

His cock swells.

He turns to stone.

Archer groans like an avalanche, biting my lips as he comes.

He floods me with so much heat.

It's too divine, the way we go spiraling down together in perfect rhythm.

When my vision isn't white anymore and I can catch my breath, I smile into his strong, bearded face.

"Winnie Rory might be the best thing I've heard you say all day."

"Yeah? Better than 'will you marry me'?"

I hold him tighter, tracing his brow.

"Better. Because I can't wait to make it official. I can't wait to start the rest of our lives."

XXVIII: WE BEE-LONG (ARCHER)

Months Later

Planning a wedding is stressful as hell, so we decided against it.

Winnie woke up the next morning, wanting to get married right there in Solitude with an officiant sent out to us, but I convinced her my mom and brothers should get to see us off.

Probably a good thing.

Mom would curse me until her dying day if her eldest son got hitched without notice.

Even Rina's okay with the whole affair after hearing about it from Colt.

I thought she'd be bitter when I called to tell her Winnie and I were engaged, but she just sounded amused.

"I knew it was coming," she'd told me. "Just don't fuck it up this time, Archer."

This time.

I resented that because it almost implied I was at fault last time, but hell, why argue?

A man can learn from his mistakes. He can bury his darkest days. He can seize a second chance and make it thrive.

Colt aside, everything with Rina was a mistake.

Winnie is not.

I don't think I'll ever get used to the way she loves me.

I don't think I ever want to—not if it means losing my sense of awe that I could ever win a woman like this.

It's a beautiful spring morning when our wedding day arrives.

We adhered to tradition and slept in separate rooms, even if I hated how weird it felt waking up without her by my side.

I've gotten used to having her morning bed head in my face.

Still, it's just one day and I can't be mad.

My phone pings with a text and even without looking, I know it's her.

Winnie: *I'm excited. Are you freaking out yet?*

Me: *Only because I have to wait at least twelve more hours to fuck you boneless.*

I smile at her emoji-speak of laughing faces and hearts before I set my phone aside.

The only two parts of this wedding I had much say in is the officiant—goddamned Patton, who got himself licensed specifically so he could marry us—and the rings.

Oh, and the food, stacks of gourmet pizzas and snacks because we didn't want white-glove fancy.

We've both lived enough of that.

I only wish I'd been able to talk my way out of getting stuffed into this monkey suit, but she wasn't having anything less than her groom dressed like a prince. According to my brothers, that's the best part.

"All the girls go on about the dude's face forever," Patton told me, "but watch hers when she sees you for the first time. Odds are, she's never seen you look so good."

I grin like the sappy, lovesick fool I am today and roll over, ready to get up.

Good timing too because someone's banging on my door.

"Hey, Sleeping Beauty!" Patton calls. "You up yet? We have less than an hour to get there and settle in."

"Fuck off. Don't rush me."

He opens the door and sticks his head in, his hair sticking up all over the place.

Mom has Winnie and her friends over for a 'bridal brunch' before the ceremony. They'll probably do their hair and makeup with plenty of time to spare.

"Not too late for a stag party," he tells me. "Let me know and I'll call the strippers."

"And I'll call your wife," I growl back.

He winces. "Hey, I only offered for your sake. Last chance to be a dirty old man since you decided to tie the knot and *try* to be normal. Blah."

"Like hell. Don't tell me you wouldn't rather see your wife, twerking her ass off."

"Not for your eyes, I don't." He clucks his tongue. "But her and Junie are with Winnie now, so who knows what debauchery they'll get into. Women are twice as crazy."

"Oh, yeah. Mom will give them a workout flipping through her artbooks. I swear every one of those things weighs thirty pounds." I smile.

"So are you nervous yet?" He gives me a once-over.

"No. Are you?"

He snorts.

"Hell no. I memorized all my lines just for you, Bro." He

beams at me like this is something to be proud of and not just a stunt he signed up for purely to screw with me.

Groaning, I flop back on the bed.

"I knew I shouldn't have agreed to this," I mutter.

He walks in and starts tossing my clothes at me, belting me in the stomach with my shoes.

"Tough luck, buttercup. It's all about to go down and I'm gonna make you a married man. Have you heard from Winnie? How's she holding up?"

"She's alive. Reaching critical mass from the excitement right now, I'm sure," I say dryly.

"As long as she doesn't bolt."

"Shut up. She won't," I snap, shaking my head. "Jesus. Are you always this good at wedding shit?"

"What do you mean? Dex had it worse. I spilled the beans to *Mom* about his fake engagement. I figured the poor girl would bail the next day." He shrugs. "Still might be true."

"You're so full of shit."

"I mean, I hope not. I'm pretty fond of those eclairs she's been bringing over lately." He grins.

Perfect timing.

Dexter appears in the doorway, already showered and dressed. "And I warned you about office romances. You didn't listen."

"Bastard. Glad I didn't, we see how it worked out."

"Only because you knocked her up before she ever called you boss. Without little Arlo around to give you an in, you would've been boned, my man."

"Well, *someone* had to give Mom another grandkid, since you guys are being so slow with the babymaking."

Dex's face darkens.

I laugh, mostly to myself.

There's one little piece of big news we haven't shared

with the world just yet. We only found out a week or two ago.

Winnie's not far enough along to mess with the fit of the wedding dress, thankfully, so that's good. Turns out, all that dirty talk about knocking her up wasn't just heat-of-the-moment bedroom play.

We didn't plan this, but it happened anyway.

We thought we'd announce it this afternoon at the reception my mother keeps calling a 'little party.'

Family and close friends only and that's fine by me. We're going to mingle and eat deep dish pizza at Solitude before I grab my bride and blast off for the Pacific.

That was my idea.

Tropical islands are a nice break from the winter chill, plus there'll be loads of exotic bees for her to freak out over. Makuna and Hawaiian honey colonies are all over the place.

Dexter swings his attention back to me. "Get dressed already. We need to be there by nine."

I check the clock. "It's half past seven."

"So? You know what Mom's like, and she's coming over here as soon as she's got Winnie in her wedding dress."

I roll my eyes. "I thought the plan was for her to stay with the bridal party?"

"Like Mom was going to do that," Patton says with a snort. "You're her baby, the firstborn, and the last to get married."

"Slacker," Dexter adds, flashing a grin.

"Get ready. She's going to be weeping all over you. When you guys got engaged, she told me she knew it was going to happen. But you know what else she said?"

I don't think I *want* to know.

"About fucking time?" I suggest.

"How did you know?" Patton looks genuinely surprised. "But it's Mom, so obviously she didn't swear."

"Obviously," I spit.

"Anyway, if you're not dressed when she shows up, she's going to hit you," Patton says.

"You're not dressed yet either," I point out.

"Yeah, but I'm just marrying you today, not *getting* married."

I convince them to let me have breakfast first to quiet my gut rumbling, and from there we start the wedding prep.

Dexter wakes up Colt.

As a growing boy, he's hit his 'sleep in forever' stage. It takes effort.

Once he's alive again, though, we all get ready together.

"What do you think, Dad?" Colt asks, tightening his tie and turning to face me.

All four of us—my brothers, Colt, and me—are wearing matching suits. Now that he's starting to fill out just a little, it looks good on him.

He also looks way too old to be my son.

"Looking sharp, Son."

Dexter pats Colt's pockets as he grins. "You have the rings, safe and secure?"

Colt rolls his eyes. "Yes, Uncle Dex. Trust me."

"Don't give me lip, kiddo. It never hurts to double-check." Dexter pats Colt's cheek affectionately. "Did I tell you about the time your uncle Pat was best man for—"

Patton looks up in alarm. "You do *not* need to tell that story."

"Don't I?"

To Patton's visible relief, Mom chooses that moment to arrive, sweeping in and wearing a flamingo-pink floral dress and a wide-brimmed hat.

"Archer," she says warmly, hugging me like she's drowning. "Oh, you look so dapper today!"

"What about me, Mom?" Patton asks with a grin.

"You're always lovely, but today isn't about you, Patton." She frowns.

"I can still look handsome," he grumbles.

Mom sighs and kisses them both on the cheek, then turns to gush over Colt.

I'm not surprised my son steals the show until she says, "You boys all look amazing, but Archer is the star of the show."

"Thanks, Mom. How's Winnie?"

"Glowing. She's more radiant than ever," Mom says cheerfully. "Try to keep it together when you see her. But remember, there's no shame in crying."

I shake my head.

"If she doesn't bail," Patton whispers.

"No way. If Salem didn't, it's not happening," Dexter mutters right back.

"Boys!" Mom snaps her fingers. "Stop it. You're grown men and you should know I won't have your bickering today."

Patton nudges Dexter, who nudges him back pointedly.

Mom ignores them both.

"Are we ready?" I ask.

"Almost. Don't you want a photo or two first?"

I really don't. We're going to be bombarded with at least a hundred more soon, but for Mom's sake, fine.

Colt groans, but Dex grabs him by the shoulder and raps him across the head with his knuckles. "Come on, horsey. Less attitude, more smiling. If we have to put up with it, so do you. Consider it a Rory rite of manhood."

"You'll love the memories when you're older," Mom reminds us and pulls out her phone. "Okay, guys. Line up and show some teeth."

We assemble into what almost passes for a line.

Colt grins at the camera. Mom hums a little in appreciation and snaps her shots before getting Colt to take some with her and my brothers.

Then just the three brothers.

Then Colt and me.

Winnie and I opted to have a real photographer focus on our candid moments. No formal sit-down pics to make the wedding photography less burdensome.

Phones are good enough for most things these days, and we didn't want a zoo. When Winnie said she wanted a low-key wedding, I was quick to agree.

"There," Mom says, flicking through the photos with a misty-eyed smile. She reaches up to pat my cheek. "I'm so proud of you, Archer. You've achieved so much and helped your brothers find happiness. You deserve your turn."

"Thanks, Mom."

"You deserve Winnie, too. I couldn't have picked a better girl."

Damn it all.

My throat tightens with the emotion I've suppressed all morning whenever I think about her and what's happening today.

Winnie Emberly.

My soon-to-be-wife.

"We'll see about that," I say after a heavy second. "I'm glad I have her and she wants me. I know I'm a lucky man."

"Archer, please. She'd have to be blind and deaf not to want you."

Either way, I have no doubts.

Soon, she'll be mine in every sense of the word, and it just feels *right*.

Mom pauses, looking up into my face with a tiny, sad smile.

"You know, your father would've loved to see you today. He would have adored your wife."

That fucking lump in my throat.

I was barely grown and out in the world when he died in that plane crash, really.

It was such a long time ago.

Sometimes, I almost forget about him, which is the worst part. Pain has a way of scabbing over memories, and you have to fight through the scar tissue to sort the good from the bad.

I'm grateful as hell she reminded me.

Today, it's not so bad. When I woke up, I heard a small plane humming overhead, just like the kind he used to love.

I think that's Dad, wherever he is, giving me his best wishes.

"Thanks, Mom. I know you're right. I love you."

"Love you too, honey." Her voice trembles as she kisses my cheek.

* * *

I ARRIVE at Solitude with time to spare, which helps us make sure everything's in order.

Not that there was much setup involved.

A few rows of chairs, a wooden arch Mom insisted on having because it 'makes everything look so special.' She attached a pair of painted cardinals Colt carved to the top, a bright-red male and a soft-brown female.

And, of course, a bee-inspired backdrop.

Could anything be more fitting?

It's too early in the season for real bees.

I just arranged the bee boxes so they'd show the messages I painted on them when I proposed and moved them closer to the middle of the garden where the ceremony will take place.

Colt also carved up a bunch of small wooden bees painted

gold and hid them in the flowerbeds around the property. I can see them glimmering in the sun, drenching the entire property in specks of glitter.

Later, I'll ask Winnie to find them if she doesn't notice.

It's just the sort of thing she'll love. Plus, a friendly mental break from the wedding spotlight.

Soon, we're ready.

Colt stands beside me as my best man—did you really think I'd give my dumb brothers the honor?—the rings tucked safely in his pocket.

Patton stands at his podium with an oversized Bible in front of him, grinning like he's about to swear in the president. He doesn't even *need* the Bible to do his job, he just said it seemed more 'official.'

Whatever.

I don't care if he grows ears like the jackass donkey he is during our ceremony, just as long as we're married by the end of it.

As long as I get to call Winnie my wife by sunset.

The minutes creep by so slowly.

I'm not an impatient man, but I'm counting every second.

"Dad, are you nervous?" Colt whispers.

"Not quite. More excited, I'd say."

"Is that why you can't stay still?"

Behind him, in the front row, Mom dabs at her eyes again. The waterworks have started early.

It's an interesting contrast.

My last marriage was drab and small, set at a courthouse in Kansas City after Rina insisted on saving money, with about as many people but less than half the joy. Mom objected until she was blue in the face, but with a kid on the way, I settled.

This time, it's different.

Everything about it, especially the way I feel standing up there, like I'm waiting for my whole life to start.

"How about you, bud? How you feeling?" I whisper back.

Colt grins at me. "Good! Unless she gets cold feet…"

I snort. "C'mon, you're almost as bad as your uncles."

He's about to protest when the music swells, and I turn to see pure sunshine in human form standing at the end of the Rory red carpet.

Holy fuck.

My bride materializes in a sleek white dress, off the shoulder and A-lined, with a modest skirt that fits her like a cloud. There's something different about it, though, and as she gets closer, I see why.

Bees.

Of fucking course.

Hundreds of tiny bees are embroidered into the skirt and bodice.

If it were anybody else, I'd throw back my head and laugh. But because it's my Sugarbee, my breath stalls in my lungs.

Most of her auburn hair is piled high on her head in an elegant updo, but a few curls hang down, brushing her bare shoulders. She wears the tiara like a princess, the big silver bee in the middle catching the light and throwing it back, making her glow.

Fuck me.

She's wearing minimal makeup, but somehow, whatever she has on makes her eyes pop.

Stunning isn't good enough.

I can't even find a word that does her justice.

I love this woman with my whole soul and I don't know how to stop.

I don't want to.

She's everything wrapped up in one neat honey-sweet

package, and it's like time grinds to a halt as we take each other in.

We lock eyes in silence and I watch her bashful smile.

There's no one beside her.

A high definition camera livestreams the wedding to her parents back in Springfield, but she's opted to walk down the aisle by herself. It's the most she'd agree to at this stage of mending their relationship.

Her father isn't handing her off to me today. She's presenting herself like the smart, lovely, independent woman she is.

Her wide-eyed gaze travels from my suit to my face, her red mouth parting slightly, and although I can't hear her, I can imagine the way she gasps.

It does terrible things to my cock.

She beams, too, so bright it's almost blinding. I can practically taste her happiness every time she breathes.

I remember what Patton said about watching her face.

And I'm already grinning back at her like I'm deranged, my face split with joy, my stupid smile spurring hers on.

As she reaches me, I lean in. "I love your dress. Almost wish I could leave it on you."

"Well, yeah. It's bees," she whispers back.

She's gilded in the morning light, a patchwork of sun and soft shadows.

If our family—*my family*—wasn't watching, I'd have kissed her until she gasped and melted by now.

Patton clears his throat, as if the smarmy prick can read my thoughts.

I take Winnie's hand and face him.

Save it for later, you idiot, his eyes warn.

Winnie looks at him with a grin and his face softens.

There's no denying he's taken a real shine to her, just like the entire family. I think if we got into a fight, they'd take her side, no questions asked.

Can't say I mind.

"Dearly beloved, we are gathered here to celebrate the union of Archer Rory and Wynne Emberly in legal matrimony," he starts, holding out his arms, no doubt loving the attention. "Friends and family, please bear witness to this union."

Winnie glances at me. I roll my eyes.

Show-off, I mouth at her.

Let him have his moment, she mouths back.

He's already married.

Patton glares at us and clears his throat loudly.

Snorting, I squeeze Winnie's hand as we look at him again and try to keep our faces straight.

We haven't written long vows, thank God, so the ceremony finishes relatively fast. You know how it goes.

I promise to love her for the rest of my life, to have and to hold to my very last breath, and she promises I'll always be her first and last, in sickness and in health, till death do us part.

Even then, I'll find her again.

Come heaven, come hell, or a hundred more lives in the Great Beyond, I will *always* claim this woman.

"I choose you," she says, her voice shaking. Mom lets out an audible sob behind her. "I choose you today and tomorrow, next week and next month, next year and all the years to come. Every day I wake up, every moment, I choose you, Archer. I choose you forever."

Damn, she's good.

There's not a dry eye in the house by the end.

Finally, Colt steps up and presents the rings to Patton, who directs us to put them on.

First, I slide mine on Winnie's finger. It's white gold and it matches the ring that sits beside it.

She doesn't know it yet, but I had them engrave a small bee inside our rings.

I don't give a crap how eccentric or overdone it seems. I'll lean into my wife's life obsession because I know I'll always be manic about loving her.

Then it's my turn.

She slides her ring on my finger, and there's this heady feeling of release, of relief, of finally being able to breathe again.

I don't wait for Patton to tell me I can kiss the bride.

I wrap my arms around her and crush my mouth down on hers. And yeah, maybe I'm a little emotional and watery-eyed, but no one can tell besides Winnie.

She pulls away and wraps her arms around my neck. "I hope calling you husband never gets old. Because I already love it, hubby."

"How do you feel about wifey?"

"Hate it!" She wrinkles her nose and kisses me again.

We're both laughing, though.

Only our second kiss as husband and wife.

Only our first morning on the edge of eternity.

It shouldn't feel different, but it does.

That quiet inner voice whispers she's mine now in every conceivable way. I can feel the ring on my finger, a promise written in gold.

In time, I know I'll get used to it, but right now, I'm hyper-aware it's there. Another physical reminder I have a wife.

I have a new life and she's fucking it.

Cheers erupt around us.

Patton wraps his arms around us both. "I hope you guys are happy," he says over the sound of loud whooping. That's Colt. "Be gentle with him, Win, okay? He's old."

"Bastard," I snarl.

Winnie grins at us.

"I'll be careful," she promises. "I used to help my grandpa with his walker so I have plenty of practice."

"That's it."

And I grab my wife around the waist and haul her over my shoulder as she screams before I stride down the aisle through the happy crowd.

Someone's taking photos and people shower us in flower petals. Her best friend Lyssie dumps a huge handful over Winnie's head.

And Winnie laughs her sweet ass off, wiggling uncontrollably against my back.

This is heaven.

The moment I want to remember.

Somehow, I know that when I look back on this day, this will always be etched in my mind.

And even if I live long enough for a damn walker, I know it'll still make me smile.

* * *

The pizza is amazing.

We hired caterers from the top pie shops in town to serve up a feast.

Mom thought it was a shame we settled for a fancy pizza party on our wedding day, but Winnie tells me she wouldn't stand for anything else.

We spend the rest of the long, lazy afternoon dancing and laughing and playing party games.

Winnie squeals every time she finds Colt's hidden bees.

It's silly and carefree and every kind of awesome.

Then comes the last big moment of the day.

"Okay, people," I say, coming to the front. "Can everyone pipe down a second?"

"Speech!" Patton calls from the back, clinking his glass. Arlo stands up in his lap and claps his hands, joining his old man in yelling, "Speech! Speech!" over and over.

Sigh.

"You heard my vows. That's all the speech you're getting today."

Winnie holds up a champagne glass of her nonalcoholic cider and comes over to stand beside me.

"It's not a speech," she tells them. "We have news."

I look at her, but it's her announcement, and I know she wants to be the one to break it.

It's only fair when she'll be carrying the baby for the next eight months.

She smiles at everyone like they already know.

Letting her deliver the news was the right call. I slip my arm around her waist and look down at her, this tiny, beautiful, wild little honeybee I get to call my wife.

"So," she says. "It's really early yet, but I wanted to let you all know I'm pregnant."

I think Mom screams first. Are my eardrums still intact?

Juniper grins and Salem whoops, bolting up and doing a little dance.

"Knew it," Dexter calls. "It wouldn't be Arch if he didn't upstage me."

"Get moving then," I call back.

Teary, arms open wide for a hug, Mom comes racing toward us.

"Oh, my boy. Oh, I'm so happy for you," she says in a choked voice. "For both of you, really. Congratulations! I'm the luckiest grandma in the world."

After Mom's done, Winnie and I both look at Colt.

We told him a few days ago, when we decided we'd announce it to the family, but we'd discussed the idea of siblings with him months ago. He told us it was fine, just as long as he wasn't expected to 'change diapers all the time or clean up gross barf.'

He's not wrong.

But Winnie promised he'd get to do the fun big brother stuff like story time and building castles and spaceships. His eyes lit up and he clammed up fast.

He sees us looking and rolls his eyes, but when I hold out my arm, he comes and joins in the hug.

I think Winnie might be crying the hardest as we fall into this big family group hug.

One big Rory tribe.

"Hey, Winnie," I say after a second. "I think there's a bee in your hair."

"Bee still," Colt snickers. "That's the worst one yet. But I promise it's real, not one of mine."

Looks like it's not too early in the spring for them after all.

I watch as the fuzzy brown bee wanders lazily across her glittering silver and diamond headpiece, its antenna waving.

I swear the little creepy-crawly looks right at me with its ten eyes or whatever the fuck. It looks so at home on her I should be jealous.

Only, Winnie looks up at me, her eyes dewy and glowing with happiness as the bee takes off.

"I think it's a sign," she whispers.

Against my better judgment, I smile and caress her cheek. "You know what? I think you're right."

FLASH FORWARD: LET IT BEE (WINNIE)

Years Later

Camping.

Never thought I'd be doing this again, but life serves up endless surprises. There are a lot of things you *think* you'll never do twice until they creep up on you.

Back when I was young and under my father's thumb, I never thought my husband would be a billionaire—an actual good one—and if I'd thought too hard about what billionaires were like, I figured he'd be old and gross and mean. Or so full of himself he's basically Lucifer incarnate.

Archer Rory is none of those things.

Lucky me.

Also, for the record, I never thought I'd be a mother to a wonderful young man whose genius knows no limit. The colleges are practically in a bidding war over Colt's future, throwing generous scholarships and special opportunities at him left and right.

My eyes flick to him now in the rearview mirror, smiling at the big decisions he'll have to make soon.

Archer pulls up in the parking lot and kills the engine.

"Who's ready?" he asks, twisting to look at the kids in the back. Colt, still reading on his phone, and the girls.

Twins.

Icing on the cake of awesome things I never thought I'd have.

They don't run in my family, to my knowledge, and they don't run in Archer's either. So, yes, this was a mammoth surprise.

A good one, but holy insta-fam.

Colt looks up at Archer and says, "Hey, did you know a bee's brain is the size of a sesame seed?"

I point at him. "He's been married to me for almost five years. Of course he knows."

"Okay, okay!" Colt laughs. "Here's another one—it will take over a thousand bee stings to kill the average person."

"Old news." I give back a mock yawn.

"According to Greek mythology, Apollo was the first beekeeper."

That stops me.

Huh.

I might be armed with bee facts, but I don't know a ton about bees in mythology.

Colt's blue eyes flash when he sees my face and he whistles triumphantly. "Gotcha, Winnie."

It's a friendly competition.

Usually bees, but it can be about any bug, really.

Colt is even set on studying insects at a higher level (actually, it's just advanced biochemistry, but I like to tease him a little). So far, he's leaning toward the University of California, Los Angeles, in the fall and we could not be prouder.

Archer rolls his eyes at us both. "Can we pause today's edition of bee trivia?"

Luna, my eldest daughter by fifteen minutes, is already fidgeting with her kiddie seat, ready to be unleashed.

"Mommy," she whines. "I'm *bored*."

"Can't we go?" Adelaide, my youngest, asks, pawing at the car door like an anxious puppy.

Two easily excitable little munchkins, almost four years old.

Who, in their right mind, would sign up for this?

Totally kidding, of course. I would murder for them ten times over and not even blink.

"Colt, help Delly with her belt," I say. That name still makes me smile. The elder Delly was absolutely thrilled when she heard the news. "I've got Luna."

Colt, the best big brother in the world, reaches over and helps his little sister out of her car seat. Everyone tumbles out and I lift my face into the breeze.

It's a warm spring day in the Ozarks and we're primed for a family outing.

I'm pretty sure it doesn't get better than this.

Certain, in fact.

"Hey, Bumblebee, wait up. You have to wait for Mommy and Daddy!" Archer calls after Luna, who's already sprinting into the campsite as fast as her stubby legs will carry her.

Colt flies ahead of his dad after her, long legs catching up faster than we ever could.

When he reaches her, he scoops her up into his arms while she shrieks with laughter.

I lean against Archer, who's standing behind me, looking dumbfounded.

Little Delly holds my hand.

"Luna naughty," she announces.

"Luna's having fun giving us grey hair," I tell her. "Do you want to be the nice one today?"

She hesitates, her little face scrunching adorably. "But will Colt pick *me* up and spin?"

"If you ask him nicely. What do you say?"

"Please! Please!" She claps her hands.

I bite my lip to keep myself from laughing.

At a glance, Luna's the trickier child, always full of mischief and plenty hyperactive. But when she gets going, Delly's the girl you really have to watch out for.

Like Archer says, it's always the quiet ones.

"Go on, then. Stay close to Colt," Archer tells his daughter. "We'll be with you as soon as we've gotten our stuff."

Delly doesn't even answer. She just rips her hand from mine and sprints across the parking lot like a rocket.

"Slow and careful!" Archer yells after her, then sighs. "If she falls over, it'll be her third skinned knee in a month. Hope she learns."

"Like you wouldn't run right after her with a Band-Aid."

"I would. I'll always get my kids patched up even when I'm all out of sympathy."

I laugh harshly, twisting around in his arms so I can look up at him. At this distance, Delly shrieks as Colt swings her around.

"You are a dirty, dirty liar, Archer Rory. You'd baby her all evening and we both know it," I tell him. "But I love you."

"I hope so." He snorts.

I giggle again because I can't help myself, and tear myself away so we can get our stuff from the trunk. Even though we have our hands full, I'm grateful we still get couple time.

Once a week, Delly takes the girls for an evening so Archer and I have time to unwind together.

Plus, Elder Delly gets girl-time. She's already throwing

them the most lavish tea parties any little girl ever had and getting them hooked on Inky the Penguin stories.

The perfect compromise.

Today, though, we're taking a long family weekend to go camping.

I already know I'm going to be woken up at the butt-crack of dawn by at least one small girl jumping on my belly, and then it's going to be a long happy day of stop and go, walking, complaining, eating and bad camping food.

I can't wait.

Archer and I promptly work on unpacking our stuff from the car. Thankfully, I've learned my lesson. This camping equipment hasn't been bought from any secondhand marketplace—it's state of the art, because there's no way Archer would let his two princesses sleep in anything but the best.

Colt's face is red with exertion, fighting to hold on to two wildly squirming little girls, when we reach him.

I pity my poor son.

"Delly-girl, Luna," I say, holding out my hands. "Come on, let's go find a nice spot to rest."

"How do we know, Mama?"

I show Luna the online ticket I bought which gives us our options on the campground. "It says on here."

Luna looks at it with wide eyes, trying to decipher words that are too big for her until she gives up.

The other tents are nicely spaced out. People are cooking dinner on stoves or playing with children and dogs. A few steps away from the campsite, there's a shimmering lake where a few people are fishing, and a few more kayaking on the water.

I can smell relaxation in the air.

"Here we are," I say as we reach our pitch. There's a small *21* at the back and the grass is smooth. Archer dumps the tent and grins at everyone—specifically Colt. "Who wants to help me put this up?"

I hold up my hands. "Not me."

"C'mon, Sugarbee. We all know how good you are at putting tents up," he teases.

We're at that stage now—it was traumatic when it happened, but like all things, time has dimmed it, and we've even been hiking since, together and with Colt.

Slowly, I've grown to love the woods again. Now that I'm not scared of dying from dehydration or exposure or bear attacks, camping is back to being a pleasant experience.

And Archer likes to camp 'properly.' Not the kind of camping I was used to before.

Who'd have thought a rich man could love sleeping on the ground so much?

"Who wants to fetch some water with me?" I ask.

As predicted, Delly volunteers and Luna decides she's going to help with the tent. Archer hands her the bag of pegs while Colt stands by to help. A bold move.

He tells her she has the most important job of all, because without the pegs, the tent won't be able to stand.

But I know the boys and little Luna will figure it out.

Delly slips her hand in mine as we walk to a small water well with a pump. It's a decent walk uphill, and I'm glad the water carrier we've got for the jugs has wheels.

"Mommy?"

"Yes, sweetie?"

"Are we gonna stay here all night?"

I try not to laugh. "Yes, honey. We're too far from home to go back tonight."

"But it'll be dark…"

"And we'll be right there with you, telling stories around the fire and melting marshmallows. You always sleep when it's dark."

She considers that for a moment, the worry on her face easing. "Only when I close my eyes."

"You'll just have to close your eyes tonight, won't ya?" I squeeze her small hand and lean in. "You know, outside there's light, too."

"I know," she informs me. "The moon."

"And stars."

"But they're sooo far away. Colt told me all about it. Bajillions of miles away."

I smile.

Honestly, I'm not strictly sure how far away the stars are, but it sounds right. "But they still give us a little light, don't they? It's never really dark unless it's really cloudy."

Unless you're trapped in a forest with no escape, I mean.

But that's long behind me.

Delly purses her lips as she thinks.

We reach the tap and slowly start filling up our water drums. From a distance, it looks like Colt and Archer are having no trouble with the tents.

Archer and I will sleep in one with the girls and Colt has his own tent.

I'm going to be sad when he leaves.

Soon, he'll be all the way across the country and I'm going to miss him so damn much. He's too good with the girls. But Rina has plans to visit us come Christmas with her new boyfriend, and it'll be like a big family reunion.

I hope.

Maybe one day I'll even invite my parents. Dad stepped down from politics after his term ended. Our relationship is cordial, but still surface deep.

I'm not sure it'll ever be anything more, but I want the girls to know their grandparents, if they prove themselves.

I want them to know everything, one day. How I met their dad and all the wonderful things he's done for me since.

The way we got married.

But for now, I just finish filling the water and let Delly help me drag it back to camp.

When we arrive, I kiss Archer on the cheek. Colt's back on his phone, resting from getting the tents up.

"He's on bear and cougar duty," Archer jokes in a whisper so the girls don't hear.

The last thing we need is hysteria.

I elbow him playfully. "Oh, hush. We can't risk scaring them."

As I learned after I got home from my little adventure years ago from pulling up a national bear map, black bears wander the Ozarks, but they're easy enough to avoid and chase off with a little common sense.

I nudge Archer. "If they come looking for a sacrifice, you can go first."

"See, Sugarbee?" He nudges me right back. "And who says romance is dead?"

I smile up at my husband.

Even now, almost half a decade later, it still feels like a miracle that I get to say that. This gorgeous man is mine—and he's given me three wonderful children.

Colt jumps in, phone out and grinning. "Did you know that when black bears hibernate, their heart rate drops to around eight to ten beats per minute? And if you wake them up, they'll kill you?"

"Relatable," I deadpan. "But did you know that eighteen year old punks who hand out bear facts nobody asked for might suffer an early death?"

His grin widens. "I could take you, Winnie."

He's right, so I just stick my tongue out at him.

"Mature," Archer says.

We point at each other.

"He started it," I say at the same time as he says, "She

started it."

Archer rolls his eyes, muttering gruffly under his breath.

But there's no hiding his smile as we lock eyes.

Then to Colt's horror, he walks over, pulls me into his arms, and kisses me for a whole minute that leaves my soul spinning.

"I love you," he whispers.

"But I love you more."

While our son makes loud gagging sounds, we trade those three little reckless words a few more times until we're laughing too hard to speak.

ABOUT NICOLE SNOW

Nicole Snow is a *Wall Street Journal* and *USA Today* bestselling author. She found her love of writing by hashing out love scenes on lunch breaks and plotting her great escape from boardrooms. Her work roared onto the indie romance scene in 2014 with her Grizzlies MC series.

Since then Snow aims for the very best in growly, heart-of-gold alpha heroes, unbelievable suspense, and swoon storms aplenty.

Already hooked on her stuff? Visit nicolesnowbooks.com to sign up for her newsletter and connect on social media.

Got a question or comment on her work? Reach her anytime at nicole@nicolesnowbooks.com

Thanks for reading. And please remember to leave an honest review! Nothing helps an author more.

MORE BOOKS BY NICOLE

The Rory Brothers

Two Truths And A Marriage
One Big Little Secret
Three Reckless Words

Bossy Seattle Suits

One Bossy Proposal
One Bossy Dare
One Bossy Date
One Bossy Offer
One Bossy Disaster

Bad Chicago Bosses

Office Grump
Bossy Grump
Perfect Grump
Damaged Grump

Dark Hearts of Redhaven

The Broken Protector
The Sweetest Obsession
The Darkest Chase

Knights of Dallas Books

The Romeo Arrangement

The Best Friend Zone

The Hero I Need

The Worst Best Friend

Accidental Knight (Companion book)*

Heroes of Heart's Edge Books

No Perfect Hero

No Good Doctor

No Broken Beast

No Damaged Goods

No Fair Lady

No White Knight

No Gentle Giant

Marriage Mistake Standalone Books

Accidental Hero

Accidental Protector

Accidental Romeo

Accidental Knight

Accidental Rebel

Accidental Shield

Stand Alone Novels

Almost Pretend

The Perfect Wrong

Cinderella Undone

Man Enough

Surprise Daddy

Prince With Benefits
Marry Me Again
Love Scars
Recklessly His

Enguard Protectors Books

Still Not Over You
Still Not Into You
Still Not Yours
Still Not Love

Baby Fever Books

Baby Fever Bride
Baby Fever Promise
Baby Fever Secrets

Only Pretend Books

Fiance on Paper
One Night Bride

Grizzlies MC Books

Outlaw's Kiss
Outlaw's Obsession
Outlaw's Bride
Outlaw's Vow

Deadly Pistols MC Books

Never Love an Outlaw

Never Kiss an Outlaw
Never Have an Outlaw's Baby
Never Wed an Outlaw

Prairie Devils MC Books

Outlaw Kind of Love
Nomad Kind of Love
Savage Kind of Love
Wicked Kind of Love
Bitter Kind of Love